asl
5/19

the
Orchid
Girls

the Orchid Girls

LESLEY SANDERSON

bookouture

Published by Bookouture in 2018

An imprint of StoryFire Ltd.

Carmelite House
50 Victoria Embankment
London EC4Y 0DZ

www.bookouture.com

ISBN: 978-1-78681-580-4
eBook ISBN: 978-1-78681-579-8

To Mum and Dad, with love

PROLOGUE

On days when panic cuts me down, when her features fade and I can't quite picture the face I knew better than my own, I take my mind back to that day on the cliff, opening my eyes to the grey Dorset sky, my throat coated with fear. Sweat pools on my back as I grab a fistful of grass and hoist myself up, hearing the crashing sound of the sea below. The wind whispers 'Charlotte, Charlotte', and I remember.

Everything is changed forever.

She's running towards me, hair blowing out and wild like seaweed. Her blue eyes hold mine as she pulls me to my knees so that we are facing one another.

'But...'

'Shhhh,' she says, 'don't say it.' I look away from her so that she can't read my eyes. The fear pumping in my chest adds to the roar of the sea.

Her hands are shaking as she takes the penknife from her pocket, unfolds the blade and takes my hands. She slices once across her palm, and then does the same to mine. She presses our hands together, the warmth of the blood and the cold of our skin mingling into one.

'Now we are bound forever,' she says, her eyes determined. 'I will never tell anyone, I swear. This is between you and me. Now you swear too.'

And now, it's happened. I knew the time would come, no matter how many years it took – she's back in my head. I'll keep her there for as long as it takes. I will find her. I will. I'll never rest until she's out of my mind and back in my arms where she belongs.

Forever.

MONDAY 15TH AUGUST 2002

A frantic search is under way for a missing fourteen-year-old girl who disappeared over the weekend after leaving her friends in town.

Charlotte Greene was last seen walking along Church Street in Lyme Regis at around 1 p.m. on Sunday, after spending the morning on the cliffs with two friends. Yesterday police searched through the night for any trace of the missing girl.

Charlotte is described as white and roughly 5ft 3in tall, with a slim build. She has green eyes and blonde hair, which was tied back in a ponytail. She was dressed in light blue jeans and a pink hoodie with white Nike trainers, and she was wearing a turquoise backpack.

Her mother Tracey Greene told *BBC News*, 'This is so out of character for Charlotte. She'd made some new friends who she was hanging out with on the beach – she had no reason to run away. We love her and want her to come home.' Caroline Conway, whose daughter was with Tracey before she went missing, said, 'Everyone has been out searching for her. We're all desperate for her to get in touch.'

Hundreds of local people were said to have met at a church early this morning to distribute flyers. Dorothy Mutton, who works at the RNLI charity shop in Lyme Regis, commented, 'It's worrying – being a coastal town there are so many hazards in the area. People are looking everywhere they can think of.'

With strong winds forecast in the next few days, police are widening the search and deploying the use of local coastguards, determined to find the missing teenager before unseasonal weather renders the search even more difficult.

CHAPTER ONE

Present day

GRACE

Lights flash green in the half-light. Something rattles. My mobile vibrates on the coffee table. Shadows fall through the large glass window and dance on the pale floorboards, while outside a black expanse of nothingness hangs over the canal. The sofa creaks as I sit up and rub my eyes, confused to have fallen asleep as the afternoon crept away. Then I remember the photo shoot, my exhaustion, the excitement of creating my first book cover, how it isn't a dream.

'Hello?' My voice croaks. A clicking noise, followed by a woman's voice.

'Gracie?' Only one word and I'm wide awake, my body taut. I dig my fingernails into my hand. 'Hello, Gracie, is that you?'

My hand wobbles as I put the phone up close to my mouth.

'Wrong number,' I say, and end the call.

The tick of the clock is loud, as if it's beating in my head. I switch on the lamp, stare at the glow it casts on the floor and hug my arms around myself in a vain attempt to get warm. I make myself a hot drink, take it out onto the balcony, my fingertips white against the red of the china mug I am clutching to my chest.

Boats huddled along the banks make sinister shapes at this hour and the dark canal is still. Lights from the office block opposite gleam on the water, and I tell myself the voice on the Phone could belong to anyone. *But only one person ever called me Gracie.*

Scratching sounds of a key in the door alert me to Richard's arrival and I take a deep breath, attempting to push her voice to the back of my mind before I go to tell him about the rest of my day. Everything apart from the phone call, that is. He can't know about that.

The following morning, Richard helps himself to a large portion of the granola I made yesterday, and I'm pleased with the way the creaminess of the oat and yogurt matches the colour of our new Smeg fridge. He eats while he stands, checking his phone at the same time.

'This is good.'

'My followers thought so too.' I grin as I remember the explosion of little hearts on Instagram.

'Are you baking today?'

'Later. I'm being interviewed this morning, remember, the journalist I told you about? We're meeting in Highbury. I'll wait for the rush hour to finish, catch the later train.'

'Wish I had that option. But my car is due any minute,' Richard glances back at his phone, 'in exactly ten minutes' time – traffic is going to be hell. Can't wait, sorry. I've got a meeting in Finchley this afternoon, I'll ring you later when I know what time I'll be home.' He kisses my cheek and then he's gone.

The fridge buzzes into the silence of the kitchen and I wipe up the little trail of coffee he's left on the marble work surface. I wash the china mug in the sink, wishing he wasn't working late again – we don't get enough time together these days, and I'm missing him. The cupboard door is open and I close it, restoring order to the kitchen ready for my baking session this afternoon. Everything needs to be perfect.

*

It's a short walk to Camden Station to catch the ten o'clock train. Enclosed in the apartment lift, I remember the phone call and wonder if it was her. *What if she's following me?* The walk feels different now she is back in my head – a glimpse of red is her coat disappearing around the corner, heels clipping the pavement behind me are her footsteps, but when I turn around, of course she isn't there. I wouldn't expect to recognise her voice after all this time, but I do. *Why would she call?* The thought propels my feet to move even faster, and I don't see the man stepping out from a cafe until I've crashed into his cup, causing coffee to slop in milky drops which land with precision on his black woollen coat. His face twists in surprise and my hand clenches around the pack of tissues I carry in my pocket, offering it to him.

'Shit! I'm so sorry. Can I get you another?'

He dabs at his coat. 'No, it's fine.' He inclines his head towards my pale designer jacket. 'It could have ruined yours, which looks a lot better quality.' Then he's gone and I take a moment to breathe hard, as I have taught myself to do, before I follow the other commuters into the station.

There's a *Metro* newspaper on the seat next to me and I snatch it up, determined not to speculate any longer on what was probably a wrong number. As I unfold the front page, I wish I hadn't, because the headline *MISSING TEENAGER* jumps off the page at me. Again I attempt a moment of mindfulness but all it does is heighten the noise of slamming doors and loud announcements telling me the train is about to depart, and when I go back to the paper I'm compelled to read about a thirteen-year-old who has gone missing after an outing with her friends. Charlotte is in my thoughts once again – she's there hiding at the back of my mind as I read about the weather and the traffic, trying to distract myself from the image of the Dorset cliffs which lurks in my mind. The man opposite me has an irritating cough and I press up against the window and close my eyes, not wanting to breathe in his germs or read any more about missing girls.

Lily, the journalist, is smart in her designer suit, her high heels tapping along the pavement as we walk. I'm glad I chose to wear my fitted dress and heels; my long blonde hair is neatly swept up.

'There's a new gluten-free bakery down the road, I thought that would suit you,' she says, waving her hand in the direction of Upper Street.

'Perfect. I'm trying out a new recipe for banana bread this afternoon, so it will be good to check out the competition.' I add a laugh, but it's a little forced; memories of the phone call and the missing girl are not entirely erased from my mind.

'Their cakes are amazing.'

'I'll be interested to know how they sweeten them, whether they use all-natural ingredients like I do.'

Lily chats about her own attempts to go gluten-free as we take the short walk along the busy street. I relax as an unexpected ray of autumn sunshine warms my hair.

'So how does it feel to be such a successful food blogger?' she says, as we carry our herbal teas over to a table at the back of the bakery, where the smells of freshly baked bread and cinnamon are reassuringly familiar.

'How do you quantify success? Having hit a certain number of followers? Yes, that's happened, but I've been so busy I haven't really had time to stop and think about it. I love doing what I do, it means so much to me to make a success of my life, and getting to indulge my passion, I know I'm lucky to be able to do

that. Not everyone gets that opportunity.' I break off a piece of
my date loaf, crumbling it onto the plate. I look at her studying
me and I wonder if she thinks my success is all down to Richard.
'It's taken a long time and a lot of hard work to get where I am
today. It's not as glamorous as it looks.' I laugh, and Lily smiles
back. I talk her through today's post, which will take up the rest
of my day – the shopping, the testing, the photographs. 'I spend
a lot of time selecting ingredients,' I tell her, 'and standing in a
hot kitchen, repeating a recipe over and over until it's perfect.'
Her red fingernails tap at the keypad and I answer her questions
until our cups are empty. It's only when I think we're done that
she catches me unawares.

'Can you tell me a little about your background?'

I push my plate away, the crumbs no longer acceptable, like
a blemish on smooth skin, but she's unaware. Words spill from
her glossy pink lips.

'What's the story behind your success? Did you learn to cook
at home, with your mother? Where is home – originally, I mean?'

Lily's eyes are wide, eager to find out something new about
me. A part of me admires her approach, unlike the majority of
interviewers, who are more interested in what it's like being married
to a handsome politician. I shake my head, wrapping my silk scarf
around my neck to indicate our time is up, dismissing her question.

'That's not how it happened for me.' I force a smile, knowing
it's important she believes me. 'I trained in nutrition, before setting
up my own business. When we first got married, we used to eat
out all the time, but when people started recognising Richard it
became less enjoyable for him. He loves the public, but there's a
limit when the interest intrudes into your personal life. I'd forgotten
how much I love creating my own recipes, so I started cooking
more at home, and somehow I became the face of clean eating.'

'It must be hard, having such a perfect image to live up to.' We
both smile, but I don't let her see the frisson of anxiety her words

bring up. 'You say "somehow", but how much of your success do you attribute to being the wife of Richard Sutherland? So many food bloggers jostle for attention, but very few hit the big time.'

My shoulders tense at the inevitable question, but I look her in the eyes as I speak. 'There's no doubt that Richard being who he is works to my advantage, but I'm sure I'd have got here regardless. I've worked like crazy. It might have taken a little longer, that's all.'

'Of course,' she says as she switches her iPad off. 'I'm sure the book will speak for itself. You mentioned Richard and how he deals with being recognised. How do you handle it?'

For a moment I experience a stab of alarm, before realising what she means.

'It's not a problem for me.' I flash her a smile and stand up.

'Yet,' she says, and we kiss goodbye as if we are old friends.

She's about to go when I place my hand gently on her arm. 'I want you to know I'm not all hard work and no play. Cooking is my passion, it's fun. I'm living the dream – my dream – and this success has exceeded my expectations. I'm so happy.'

'Any plans for the weekend?' she says as we make our way to the cafe door.

'Holiday research. I'm planning a surprise minibreak for Richard – this is strictly off the record, but I know I can trust you.' I laugh and she nods, giving an exaggerated wink. 'A few days away as soon as the election's over and we can breathe again. I'm thinking Rome, or Florence. He's been looking for a new piece of art for our lounge. I know some lovely little galleries.'

'Keep me posted,' she says with a smile. 'The article will be up sometime this month.'

I'm thoughtful as I watch her disappear into the crowds, wondering why her last words make me nervous, hoping I can trust her. As I move through the street, exasperated by the slow pace at which people walk, I wonder for the first time since I moved over from France whether I've made a mistake coming back here.

But I wasn't to know how successful Richard would become, how high his expectations would be. My shoes clatter on the tiles as I enter the station and lose myself amongst the commuters. If only I could lose my thoughts so readily.

It's only later, when my first batch of bread is in the oven, that I check my mobile. There's a missed call from the same number as the night before, but no message. I'm not sure how long I sit and stare at the phone, wondering why she's got in touch now, after so many years, when the smell of burning jolts me from the sofa. But it's too late, the banana bread is ruined.

By the time I've created a bread I'm happy with, the light is fading outside and I decide to postpone the photo shoot until the morning. Pacing around the flat isn't enough to release my energy so I get changed into my sports gear. Our apartment's canal-side location – making it perfect for running – is one of the many things that attracted us to it. I work out I can manage fifteen minutes each way and I'll be home before it's fully dark.

Black water glistens as I hurry down the steps to the canal-side. Fewer people are down here in the evening and I glance around to see whether I am alone. A man disappears into the gloom ahead, and a woman is unlocking a bicycle further back. I transfer my keys to my pocket and set off at a steady pace.

The cyclist overtakes me, red curls blowing in the wind, and I slow my pace, reminded of the girl with red hair from my past watching me, in that silent way she had. I've only been running for five minutes when a drop of rain lands on my forehead, sliding into my eye. I wipe the water from my face; I hadn't thought to check the weather before I came out and the thin T-shirt I pulled on offers little protection against the elements. By the time I reach the point where I'm turning around, the shirt is sticking to my shoulders and the wind is picking up.

I increase my pace and follow the canal as it flows alongside the park. Not far to go now. The flats are visible, their balconies with 'desirable views' stacked one on top of the other, the matching window boxes resplendent with pink blooms. Not a hint of originality. Most of them are in darkness, cold and unwelcoming. The dark cloud hovering overhead bursts and rain pelts down on me. The wind picks up, gathering leaves and twigs as it hurtles past, and I wish it could carry me along too, and drop me at home, warm and safe.

There's a tunnel ahead and as I enter it a bicycle bell sounds behind me. A female cyclist is approaching too fast, and I move aside to make space for her. There's a whoosh of air as she cycles past, so close, her arm brushing my shoulder. As she turns to look at me I recognise the woman I saw earlier. I stumble against the wall, feel the cold brick through my top. Darkness presses in on me and I sprint back to my flat, collapsing against the flat door, panting hard, sweat clammy on my back.

It takes a few moments to get my key in the lock. A white square glows on the doormat, an unaddressed envelope. It isn't sealed and I slide the contents out. There's a picture postcard inside, the seafront at Lyme Regis. My legs feel unsteady and my pulse races like a stopwatch. No stamp, nothing written on the back.

The intercom buzzes three times, which is Richard's signal he's home. I shove the postcard into my pocket and dash upstairs.

Sounds filter up as Richard bashes around in the kitchen, and I look once again at the postcard – the jaunty angle of the boat with the red sail on the beach, the perfect blue of the sky. But it's the cliffs in the background which draw my attention, make me hold onto the dressing table to steady myself. Our beautiful bedroom is reflected back in the mirror, the pure white furnishings, the splash of crimson from the designer fabrics in the wardrobe, shoes piled up in boxes, a hint of expensive perfume in the air. Everything I have worked so hard for. *I can't afford to lose it, I can't.* I push the postcard to the back of my underwear drawer, closing it with a thud.

'Stop being dramatic, Grace,' I tell my reflection, before walking to the mezzanine stairs. I pause to look down at the vast open-plan space, full-length windows spanning the far wall. But the satisfaction I normally get from looking at this gorgeous apartment eludes me.

Richard sprawls on the sofa, two glasses of wine in front of him, and he pulls me into a hug.

'Let's watch the news,' he says, 'something's going on in Ash Fenton.'

'I can't believe that.' Nothing ever happens in the sleepy village where Richard's parents live. I press the remote and the breaking news story slides across the screen:

POLICE SEARCH FOR MISSING GIRL, 13, IN BUCKINGHAMSHIRE VILLAGE

I squeeze my eyes shut. *Not this again.*

'I read about this earlier, but I didn't notice where she was from.'

'I can't believe this is happening in my constituency. The whole village is out looking for her. Wouldn't be surprised if Mum and Dad don't go and help. You know what they're like.'

A reporter is speaking to camera, the village green behind him marred by clusters of people milling around, news vans and equipment ugly against the pretty green. Richard continues speaking but I no longer hear his words. The rest of the news plays out in front of me: refugees from war-ravaged countries, equally distressing. The weather follows: a woman presenter with a maroon dress and matching lipstick moving her mouth and pointing at a complicated map. But I don't see any of it, still too shocked by the reminder of the upheaval of a missing person in a small town.

Richard falls asleep, his head snug against my shoulder, so I mute the sound on the television and log on to my laptop, checking out my latest post on Instagram. Thousands of likes cover the page, and tears spring into my eyes as it hits me. I am making a success of this; all my late nights and determination are beginning to pay off. Richard grunts, and I put my hand on his arm, drawing comfort from his presence. My eyelids prickle and words wiggle on the screen as my eyes close and images muddle together in my head. The red sail of a boat; the journalist and her questions; Richard's trusting eyes. I'm about to log off when a name jumps out at me and I gasp, waking Richard.

'What's the matter?'

'Nothing.' I turn the screen away from him as he rubs his hands over his eyes, stretching out his legs. Richard switches the sound up on the television where the missing girl is back on. A photograph appears on the screen, the usual school shot, a white Alice band in her long blonde hair, a toothy grin for the photographer, school tie knotted in place. A chill rushes through my body as I note the likeness to Charlotte for the first time. Richard sits up, alert, giving me a shocked look.

'It's her, Christ, I don't believe it.'

I freeze. 'Who?' What does he mean? How can he know her?

'Emily Shaw, remember? The girl who interviewed me for work experience a couple of months ago. Mum knows her from Girl Guides – she set it up. She must be worried. I'll give her a ring in the morning.' Lines crease his forehead as he switches the TV off. 'I'm going to bed. Are you coming?'

'Soon.' I pull him towards me for a kiss.

The image of the girl fades from the screen but not from my mind. I'm wide awake now, and as soon as Richard's gone I go back to the comment left by OrchidGirl: it's nothing to do with the recipe for blueberry and chia mousse I posted yesterday.

Gracie, it's me: 07775435555

It's the number from last night, and I'm glad Richard has gone upstairs because although I thought I was prepared for this moment, I've been caught out. The walls of the flat crowd in on me and I push the balcony doors open, needing to be close to the canal, the poor substitute for the sea of my childhood, which I can never go back to. Silver slivers of water ripple in the artificial lights watching over the canal. I focus my gaze on a black silhouette, which for a moment I fancy is her. As I stare out, I realise that no matter how much I've managed to convince myself that the past would stay buried, the threat that lives deep inside me has resurfaced. She's back, like I knew she would be. And my whole life could fall apart unless I stop her.

CHAPTER TWO

MOLLY

If I lie still maybe my heart will stop jumping and last night's dance music will quit thumping in my head. In a sitting position, I count to five, opening my eyes. My throat feels raw, as if I've been yelling. It's possible.

Through sticky eyelashes I make out two empty wine bottles sprawling on the floor, and a large red stain decorating the carpet. My dress is hanging over the back of a chair and the contents of my bag are a mess on the carpet. A sheet of paper lies next to the ashtray on the glass table. Breathing makes me feel like throwing up.

Gingerly I place my feet on the floor, switching on the bedside lamp. I am wearing one sock and my vest is inside out. Now my eyes are focusing, I see that the piece of paper is a note and I pick it up. The slight movement makes my head swirl.

SEE YOU IN THE CROWN AT 8. J

So Jodie was here, with her raven-black hair and blue eyes which make my insides dance. The red numbers on the digital clock tell me it's 7 p.m. I've been asleep all day. Something important taps at the edge of my mind, and I massage my forehead, trying to tease it out.

Did we argue? Is that what's making me feel sick? I see the dance floor at Highlights: I'm spinning, my arms wild and loose, people watching and laughing. A blonde girl, her hand on Jodie's arm, fingers tracing Jodie's snake tattoo, which slithers from her wrist to her shoulder. I wanted to thump her. *Maybe I did?* Then I remember, me hunched in the corner, a mess. The look of exasperation in Jodie's eyes, the look I've seen so many times before. I bolt to the bathroom and throw up.

It's already time to go out, but I can't leave looking a state. Dry shampoo is the answer, and I brush my red curls out so my hair looks less like a bird's nest. I slap some foundation onto my face and paint my eyes black. Dark jeans and jacket. A quick shot of vodka, and I'm out of the flat.

The smell of beer and grease hits me as I walk into the pub. It's Jodie's favourite, and if she's here, I'm good with that. A group of rowdy youths surround the pool table, and a boy flashes his tattooed arms as he chalks up the pool cue. Two men argue, voices raised, in one of the dark corners. It's the same old scene and the music is loud, pulsing inside me. A lazy smile crosses Jodie's face as she clocks me walking towards her, and I slow my pace, shift my hips a little, before leaning forward. Then we're kissing each other hard. I get a hit of whisky from her lips.

'I'm late, sorry,' I murmur into her hair.

'You're always late. The usual for Molly,' she calls to the barman. We sit by the window, looking out over Camden High Street, where the pavement is crowded with characters. A group of teenagers, all zips, piercings and black clothes, are looking at Amy Winehouse T-shirts for sale; the stall owner is openly watching them, his tired green Mohican drooping to one side.

'I feel rubbish, I need some paracetamol.' I scrabble around in my bag, but all I find is half a packet of throat sweets and some chewing gum.

'Get that down you,' Jodie says, 'you know it always makes you feel better.' Ice is piled high in the glass of neat vodka Jodie places in front of me.

She picks up her lighter and taps it on the table. The sound is like a woodpecker on the side of my head.

'I was meant to be taking it easy last night. Two drinks, max.'

'Shut up, Molly. You're a laugh when you drink. Well, mostly. You got into a right state at the end of the evening. Do you remember?'

Heat burns my cheeks and I drink some vodka, holding the glass to my face, but the cold doesn't take away my embarrassment. 'Yes, but forget it, you know what I'm like when I've had too many. I'm sorry.'

She narrows her eyes. 'You're seeing the shrink, right?'

'She's not a shrink, she's a counsellor.'

'Whatever,' Jodie leans forward. 'Because last night you were going on about being desperate, not being able to confide in her, in anyone, about time not making it easier... but you can talk to me, babe, you know you can, whatever's wrong.'

My eyes won't meet hers. Different eyes flash into my mind. I drain the rest of my glass, get to my feet. 'Forget it, seriously.' I lean forward and kiss her, hoping to convince her. 'Ready for another?'

Jodie lines up some coke as soon as we get back to my flat, and I open a bottle of wine. My hand is unsteady and a ruby droplet falls onto the counter. It looks like blood. A girl's face flashes into my mind. I frantically sweep my hand across the work surface and the drop vanishes.

I put some music on, snort some coke and at last I feel in control. I'm hoping Jodie will forget my earlier mood, so I lean my body along hers and press myself against her, smiling as I look into her eyes.

'That's better,' she says, 'I hate it when you're miserable.'

*

It's only later, when Jodie has gone back to her real girlfriend who we don't discuss, that I think about what she's said. I blow out a trail of smoke, watch it coil up towards the ceiling, wishing I could blow my fear out of me and watch it float away. Yes, I've got my weekly appointments with Janet, my counsellor, but I won't be able to tell her anything. My brother Darren's cheeky grin flashes into my head followed by a pang of sadness. We used to spend hours chatting, despite him only being little back then – at least he gets why I'm like this. But even he won't want me to ring, not after last time. No, there's only one person I can talk to, and lately the need to speak to her is bursting inside me.

My head feels as though it's thick with wool when I'm woken by the sun sneaking through a tear in the blind, and I lie still until I've worked out what day it is. It's my day off, and all I have to do is see Janet, my therapist, in the afternoon. My foot lands on an empty wine bottle as I climb out of bed and it spins across the floor, out of control. It clinks as it hits the metal bin, a clanging sound which hurts my head. I make a snap decision to spring-clean today; it doesn't matter that it's autumn. It'll make me feel better and I've got to get my shit together. I open all the windows to let fresh air in, stick the TV on and drink a cup of strong black coffee while I try and wake up.

For once I've surfaced early enough to catch the news, and I doze through a segment on a royal visit to a local academy school where pupils wriggle in excitement in front of a princess. I bet they're disappointed she isn't wearing a sparkly crown. The coffee starts to work its magic and I stretch my legs out, resolving not to drink today. The man on the screen looks familiar, and I remember the pamphlet shoved through my door: Richard Sutherland wants me to vote him in as London Mayor. I imagine his looks will get women voting but they are wasted on me, his super-white teeth and hair combed back into a slick style. I can't even remember the last time I bothered to vote. But the news item isn't about him. The woman on his arm has model looks. In the first shot her face is turned towards her husband, but as she turns to camera the newsreader announces that Grace Sutherland's first book is about to be published, and then she's on the screen being interviewed and I forget I'm holding a cup until cold liquid hits my foot. I swipe it away, not taking my eyes off the TV. It's her. A blade slices through my stomach and I reach for a cigarette. I watch those familiar lips speaking in an unfamiliar accent, but she can't hide from me so easily – I'd know her anywhere. I knew I'd find her eventually. Adrenaline lights me up inside.

The flat looks different when I've finished. Under a pile of clothes I find a ten-pound note, which adds to the high I've been running on ever since I saw her. I decide to nip across the road to Abdul's shop and treat myself. I only drink a tiny swig of vodka before I start my internet search, but this time it's different. This time I know her name.

At first I don't believe it. After wondering for years where Grace is, knowing I shouldn't look but feeling unable to stop myself – bam – she's on TV. Online, she writes a blog. She's all over the internet. You couldn't make it up. She tells the world where to find her. How could I have missed her? And how could she, after everything? Her Instagram feed reveals that just this week she had an interview with a journalist for *Eat Clean*, whatever that is, visited her publisher to discuss book covers and the rest of the week she's going to be at home, cooking and posting details and photos for anyone who wants to look. *Well, I certainly do.* Can you believe it? It's a pinch-myself moment: Grace is cooking in her kitchen and I can watch her doing it. There are even YouTube videos. There's no way I'm going to the counsellor now. I switch my phone to silent, engrossed in my findings.

Once I've got over the excitement and poured myself a large vodka, I wipe my sweaty palms on my jeans, scroll right back to the beginning of her blog and read right up to this month, when she's got a book out. A fancy recipe book called *Graceful Cooking*. It's been ages since I've looked at a book. Grace used to read to me; she was always better with words than I was. She was better than me at most things. I remember the first time we met at primary school. Me scowling in the corner of the playground while boys and girls ran and yelled around me. This girl with a straight back and a long golden plait walked purposefully over. 'Come and play with me,' she said in a confident voice. It was an instruction. We used to do everything together after that. Just the two of us was how I liked it. Thinking about it makes me feel hot. Washing my hands and face in cold water helps, and I snuggle up with my laptop, learning about Grace's world.

Watching her on video is weird. It makes my skin feel as if ants are creeping all over me. She hasn't changed, not really. Of course she's plastered with make-up, primed to perfection, as are most people on television these days. She always liked to look after herself, flicking through magazines, looking at clothes and sometimes at the boys, which used to piss me off. But I wouldn't have changed anything else about her.

A quick email to my mate Ed who works magic with computers, and it doesn't take long before he gets back to me with her phone number and I do a little dance in front of the window. After all this time, I can't believe it's so easy. I gaze at the tiny tattoo on my wrist, the perfect purple flower, wondering if she still has hers.

She's seriously into her food, is Grace. 'Clean' food seems to be something to do with avocados. 'Fancy food', as Mum would call it, but Grace's mum always had snobbish ways – must be where Grace gets it from. *Aunty Deborah*, I used to call her, although she wasn't a real aunty.

I fetch the vodka from the kitchen and top up my glass, already knowing I'm going to get through the bottle by the time I'm done here. Janet has left a message asking where I am. But I'm more interested in Grace. On Grace's Instagram her face can be seen from every angle and I flick through the images, my leg juddering up and down on the floor, drinking the whole time. Then I have another little dance when I work out from her photographs that she lives in one of those swanky new flats overlooking the canal. I'm shocked at how easy it is – she should really be more careful. But this is great for me. I know if I can speak to her, say the right thing, I'll reach the old Grace, my Gracie.

Registering to post comments doesn't take a moment, but choosing the right name is important. It has to be something she'll recognise. She has to know it's me. Of course there's only one possibility; I think back to that awful time and the large-print headlines in the *Daily Tribune*. 'The Orchid Girls', they called us, and it stuck. OrchidGirl logs in and posts a comment. My eyes flicker to the tattoo on my wrist, see the flowers on the cliff, wish I hadn't.

After half an hour the type is swimming on the screen in front of my heavy eyes. One more cigarette, I'm sure she'll have answered by then. But she doesn't. My hands are jittery and my back feels cold with sweat. I can't wait any more – I need to make contact. I swill the vodka around in the glass, staring at Grace's phone number. Images I've refused to face for years dance around in my head. The beautiful girl with long blonde hair and marble blue eyes. For a moment I see her rushing at me on the cliff, with fierceness in those eyes. And now I know where she lives.

The room blurs as I pick up my phone and punch in the numbers, hitting the wrong keys, willing my fingers to work properly. It takes a few tries before I get the right number. Pressing the phone against my ear, the ringing sounds distant and I imagine a smart glass flat by the canal in darkness, a light going on. A voice breaks through my thoughts.

'Hello?'

That voice. I feel my heart splinter. 'Gracie?' The silence is loud. 'Hello, Gracie, is that you?'

The dialling tone buzzes like a bee stuck in my ear, and I drop the phone on the floor.

When I wake up a few hours later, my back is stiff from lying on the floorboards, my muscles cramped. I sit for a while with my head in my hands, waiting for my stomach to settle. I swallow half a pint of water and some painkillers before heading down to the canal – it's quite a walk and my legs ache. White mist hangs over the water and I shiver despite the thick jumper I'm wearing; the early-morning sun hasn't thawed the morning frost yet. My breath bursts out in white puffs. There's no way of knowing exactly which flat is hers, so I just stand and watch. The sky goes from dark to light and I have to pace about to stop my legs from going stiff, trying to avoid looking at the water in case it sets the memories off. Water has done that to me ever since.

A man wearing a checked cap steps out from one of the barges moored up at the side of the canal. He's holding out a steaming mug of tea.

'You look frozen, love. Have this.'

I force my cold lips into a smile.

'That's better.' He taps the roof of the boat. 'Leave the cup here, when you've finished.'

The tea is strong and warms me a little. Only a few moments after I've left the cup on the boat, a woman emerges from the swanky flats. I stand up, my nerves stretched taut, my heart pumping. *It's her.* It really is. She straightens the collar on her expensive trench coat before her high heels clip-clop past me. I keep my head down as a man passes by before tucking myself in behind him, making sure to keep her in sight.

A few people are around now and I keep to the right as runners and cyclists whizz past. Most people are in a hurry, as is Grace, who is walking fast. My chest is tight and I regret not bringing my bike.

After about ten minutes she climbs the steps leading into Kentish Town and walks along towards Camden Station. As she slaps her pass onto the barrier and slides through the gate, I scrabble around in my pockets. A two-pound coin is caught up in the lining, but it's not enough for a ticket. The bus stop on the other side of the road is empty and I sit inside it and light a cigarette. Rumblings from underground make me wonder where the train is taking her. Next time I'll be more prepared. I know I can't sit here any longer, but I want to get a reaction. I don't want to have come all this way for nothing, and I've thought of a little memento I can drop off at the block she lives in. If I address it to Grace it will find its way to the right flat. Because she's a celebrity now, which makes everything so much easier.

CHAPTER THREE

GRACE

The next day is an ordinary weekday, an ordinary morning. Richard drinks his coffee in large gulps, glancing at the clock.

'I've got a busy day today, won't be back until late. I'll probably eat while I'm out.'

Ordinarily I don't mind, but today the thought of an evening in alone makes me feel cold. The postcard might be hidden away in the drawer, but that doesn't keep it from my mind and an image of the seafront flashes into my head. Richard gives me a look.

'You don't mind me working late, do you?'

'Of course not.'

'It's just that you were restless last night, is something bothering you?'

'No, I'm fine. You worry too much.' I open the fridge and pretend to study the contents. 'You go, I've got heaps to do this morning.' He looks concerned and I can't resist pulling him to me, inhaling his lovely Richard smell, a mixture of aftershave and him. 'But I love you for caring.'

He kisses my forehead, pushing my hair away from my eyes before he pulls away.

'OK. Mum phoned about our visit this weekend. She's pretty shaken up by Emily's disappearance. People are out looking for her. I can't believe this is happening in Ash Fenton. It's the last place you'd expect.'

'Maybe we should cancel. It's been ages since we've had a day to ourselves.' I tilt my head to one side and he grins.

'No, they still want us to visit. And hopefully they'll have found her by then. You know what teenagers are like, she's probably run off with her boyfriend or someone she's met on the internet.' He takes a last look at his hair in the mirror. 'Right, must go. I'll see you later.'

As soon as the door closes behind him I put my arms around myself, rubbing warmth into my bare arms. A lemony fish smell lingers from last night's meal and I push the balcony doors wide, but I am reluctant to go outside. My eyes are drawn to the tall buildings across the murky water. They remind me of the menacing cliffs in my dreams, which loom over me like the shadow of the past. Details from last night's phone call tumble into my mind, making me shiver. I push my thoughts aside, head into the kitchen, arrange my bread and set to work.

The early light is perfect, and by mid-morning I've edited the shots and added them to my site. My followers never let me down but today there's only one I'm looking out for, and I chew on my nail as I search through the messages. She hasn't posted anything since last night. I delete her comment, switching the radio on for some background noise. The news presenter is talking about the girl from Ash Fenton, who is still missing. I switch it off.

I hope she turns up soon; I won't be able to stand it if it drags on. And I don't want Richard getting drawn into it. He's always one for a cause and he'll be all over it – as if he isn't busy enough already.

Cold air blows in from the balcony and I close the door, but the flat feels small and stifling. Cleaning uses some of my pent-up energy, but even though I make the kitchen surfaces gleam and everything is in place, I'm a mess. I need to get out. It's a bit early for my lunch date with Julia, my publicist, so I decide to walk, adding a few steps to my Fitbit total.

Autumn colours decorate the trees and I walk fast, aware that footsteps behind me sound too close. But when I turn around the man coming up towards me peels off in a different direction. Something compels me to constantly look back, and I can't shake the feeling I'm being followed. No posing for selfies on the route like I usually do, adding to my #londonlife series, where I add to my story as a city girl. I'll make up for it later, hoping Richard won't notice any slump in my online activity. After all, he was the one pushing me on to social media and encouraging me to go for it.

Julia is already seated in the restaurant, raising her glass to me as she talks on her phone. I check behind me one last time, seeing a woman sitting on a brick wall opposite the cafe, kicking her boots against the ground, a bike resting beside her. A memory flashes into my head, the woman overtaking me on the canal. I push hard against the cafe door, almost falling inside.

Julia finishes her conversation as I place my order.

'Got to go darling, speak soon. Grace, hi.' We air-kiss. 'Congratulations on the TV appearance. How did you find it?'

'Good, I enjoyed it. Thanks to Richard, I knew what to expect.'

'Well, it's done wonders for the book, pre-orders are in their thousands.'

I can't help a massive smile at the news, excitement fizzing inside.

'Great. My Instagram followers are up, too. How are plans for the launch?'

'Everything is ready, the venue has been reserved and I've invited everyone who needs to be there. All you need to do is check over the guest list. Richard is coming, isn't he?'

I hesitate before answering.

'Of course, he'll be lurking in the background somewhere.' *But this is about me, not him.*

'And are we finally going to meet any of your family?'

I flick my hair over my shoulder, avoiding looking at her. 'Richard's parents will be there.'

'And your dad?'

My salad arrives and I pour some San Pellegrino, my favourite sparkling water.

'It's too difficult. He'd need a carer and I haven't made any provision. There's no point even telling him about it.'

Thinking about my father unsettles me. *Michael*, as I think of him now. I hadn't planned on ever seeing him again once I returned to the UK, but his poor health changed all that. And Mum is long gone. The thought catches me unawares and I sip my water to stop a lump from blocking my throat. How she would have loved my book launch. She would have been so proud, I'm sure of it. *Enough, Grace. Focus.*

Julia breezes on. Time with her is always a bit of a whirlwind. How she manages to fit everything in I don't know. Half an hour later she's on her way, her ample proportions weaving a path out of the cafe, with me close behind, my salad barely touched. I notice that the woman is no longer sitting on the wall and as Julia disappears into a cab, I make sure there's nobody else in the station before I pass through the underground barrier.

The cleaner has left me a note when I arrive home, telling me she's going to be away for the next few weeks. My skin feels cold from the autumn wind outside. I check the flat over to ensure everything has been done properly, before I give in to my growing obsession and search for Molly on the internet. But there's no sign of her. She must have married and changed her name. *What does she want? Why does she want to talk to me? Why now?*

I place an Ocado order and sort through my emails for the next hour or so, making sure everyone I want to be at the launch has been invited. Carrie, a close friend, texts me about going for a drink sometime next week and I accept, thinking it will be just what I need to take my mind off Molly. Richard messages to remind me he won't be back until late; it's dark outside and I'm hungry. On cue the shopping arrives, the usual delivery guy who doesn't speak much English, which suits me fine. Too many unwelcome thoughts mean I'm not in the mood for conversation. After unpacking I cook up some wholewheat noodles and I'm about to eat when there's a bang on the door. It must be the delivery man again, although everything I ordered is here. I'm about to open the door when I hesitate – a gut feeling that something isn't right stops me. I know I've been paranoid over the past couple of days, but I check the spyhole and step back, my hand over my mouth. I see a flash of red hair. It's her. My breath catches, and I hold myself still.

The figure outside is distorted, but she's so close my legs feel wobbly, as if I'm about to fall. I press my palm against the door to steady myself. How does she know where I live? Even as I'm asking myself the question, everything falls into place. The way I talked myself into believing being in the public eye wouldn't matter, convincing myself that it all took place so long ago. I press my eye to the spyhole again to make sure, holding myself still for fear that she can hear me. Does she know only a strip of wood separates us? Is her heart racing like mine? She bangs once more, her metal rings knocking against the wood; the noise is a drill in my head. I sink down to the floor. When I take my hands away from my ears, complete silence unnerves me. I am scared to breathe, lest she stands outside, waiting for me to make a move. Five minutes pass by, ten. My legs are cramped and it's hard to stand so I lean my weight against the door, looking through the spyhole at an empty corridor. Relief floods me. The noodles are cold and glutinous and I throw the whole lot into the bin and pour myself a glass of wine. Only when the wine is drunk do my hands stop shaking.

Richard is talking on his phone when he gets in, looking exhausted, mouthing to me that he's off to have a bath. I check around the living room, making sure everything is exactly how he likes it. I linger a while downstairs, take my glass of water over to the sofa and switch the television on, keeping the sound low. My eyes are heavy and when I close them I can no longer fight the memories. Molly is in front of me, not the stringy adult with auburn hair whose features I can only guess at, but as she looked all those years ago. Molly. The Molly I used to know. The girl who used to be my best friend.

Although the last time I saw Molly was in the courtroom, I don't want to remember her as she was in that horrible week, staring with vacant eyes at one of the many adults whose opinions were listened to with rapt attention by all the people in the room. The Molly I remember has soft curls and freckly skin; strong, muscular limbs from pulling herself up cliff faces and clambering over rocks. Arms darting like arrows as she swam through the surging sea while I watched her from the water's edge, shivering. Her fierce expression when we made that promise to one another...

Richard is moving around upstairs and I snap myself out of my ridiculous daydream. I can't believe I've allowed myself to go there. Aunt Jenny's words are loud in my head, the concern in her voice when I told her I was coming back to England. 'You'll regret it, Grace, you are so much safer here in France.'

The news is on when I open my eyes and the face of Emily Shaw stares out at me. For a moment she is Charlotte, her eyes looking deep into mine, before she spotted someone more interesting over my shoulder. My heart thuds and instantly I'm wide awake. Richard appears in the doorway.

She presses her lips to my forehead and places her hand on the small of my back as she follows me upstairs. As I lead the way into the flat, her arm slides around my waist, pulling me towards her for a kiss. A proper one. She pushes me onto the sofa but for a split second it isn't Jodie that I'm holding, but a softer, paler body is pressing into mine, different lips are sharing secrets with me. I blink the image away, focusing on Jodie, whose mouth tastes of whisky and cigarettes. I try but the moment is gone and I push her off me, hoisting myself back up and pulling my knees to my chest.

Jodie helps herself to a couple of beers from the fridge and takes a swig, her dark eyes narrow.

'What's up?'

She hands me a can and I take a mouthful. Tomorrow, I won't drink. Tomorrow. 'Nothing. Tired, that's all.'

'Something's bothering you, I can tell. I know you, Molly.'

No you don't.

She takes her tobacco tin out of her pocket and rolls a joint. The beer relaxes me, and Jodie blurs a little at the edges. Maybe she'll understand. Maybe I can open up to her after all. The need to talk roars inside me and smoke curls up towards the ceiling.

'Had a shock, yesterday. I saw an old friend of mine on TV.'

'*Crimewatch*? Armed robber, is she now?' She chuckles to herself.

'Hardly. She's a food blogger. Married to an MP.'

'So why was it a shock?'

I wish I'd never said anything now; I want to keep Grace to myself and the past in the past. But it's too late now. 'I was gutted when we lost touch. Our parents made friends when we were at primary school together, then she moved away, but she used to stay with us in the holidays when her mum was ill. She had breast cancer, although they didn't tell us what it was at the time. We did everything together. We were close, more like sisters. I wrote when she moved away but she never replied.'

I light a cigarette, inhaling enough smoke to control the nerves that thinking about those unanswered letters set off.

'Sisters, eh?' Jodie blows smoke towards the ceiling. I watch it rise. 'So. Unfinished business.' She grinds the joint end harshly into the ashtray. I press my back against the sofa, wishing I could take the words back. 'You fancy her, don't you?' she says, a brittleness to her voice.

'Shut up.'

The real reason I want to see Grace is like poison running through my veins. Even Jodie would run a mile if she knew what I'd done. How everything that happened back then is my fault.

Jodie looks at me for what seems like ages, nodding her head, then holds her hand out. 'Come here.' She pulls me to her and I snuggle into her, feeling her cold hands on my back. 'Forget her.' I stop her smile with my mouth, trying to focus on the moment. But Grace is in my head now and everything is different.

Jodie's left after telling me she won't be around this weekend. She doesn't tell me where she's going and I don't ask. On my phone I'm watching Grace, who is baking some sort of custard in her fancy kitchen – sugar-free, dairy-free, some crap like that. Custard takes me back to school dinners and the Grace I used to know telling the cook it looked like cat sick and getting detention. The new Grace is different. Her kitchen is all chrome like in posh magazines, with one of those island things in the middle. I look around my studio, where the kitchen is at the end of my bed, tiles chipped and loose, with a tap that wobbles. Grace wouldn't be seen dead in this place. She always did like nice things. Her snobby ways used to make Mum laugh – until she stopped laughing because of what I'd done. Because of us. It's been months since I called Mum, and shame curls inside me. I haven't seen her since Dad's funeral.

I left home when I was sixteen, sick of being stuck in my poky bedroom, where I wrote letters to Grace in my round, bubbly teenage writing. Nobody would tell me where she'd gone, or if she'd ever come back. Agonised, I waited for answers which never came. Mum's normally rosy face had lost its spark. She slammed drawers in the kitchen and made the pots and pans shake whenever I mentioned Grace. Dad just kept out of the way, busied himself with his gardening – he was passionate about wild flowers. He hated raised voices, and I hated seeing the disappointment I put in his eyes. With Mum, I soon learned to shut up. She didn't want to hear about Grace, and I wondered what she knew about us. My cheeks flushed whenever I thought about it. Living by the sea soon became impossible. The cliffs closed in on me and the sea air choked me. I was glad to get away, taking one long, last look at the ocean and leaving, no longer able to stand the guilt.

Birmingham was the longest place I stayed, two years in total, trying so hard to forget. I kept away from London because I thought Grace would go there. But I knew I'd end up here one day, no longer able to fight the urge.

As I walk downstairs I notice the lace on my boot is tangled and I yank it so hard it breaks. Another thing I need to replace. Rain threatens so I wear my hoodie, managing to secure my boot. Mrs Bird from downstairs is gathering letters from the hallway mat, one hand on her back as she stoops over.

'Let me do it,' I say, bending down to help. There's a lot of post today, fingers crossed no bills for me, I've already got a drawerful upstairs. There's a postcard for the bloke upstairs, a sunny Majorca beach on the front, and it's enough to conjure up the seafront at Lyme Regis. I wonder if Grace got the postcard, whether she showed it to her husband. I should have guessed she'd be married – that could be a problem. Mrs Bird has one letter, and there's nothing for me, thank God. She takes the envelope from me, both of our hands trembling. She has age as an excuse. Feeling ashamed, I shove my hands in my pockets, and set off for the canal, wondering how Grace could choose to live by water after everything that happened.

At the canal, the water is a gloomy green and beer cans float in the scum. I look straight ahead. Underneath Grace's flats there's a Costa coffee shop and I work out I've got enough points on my loyalty card for a free hot chocolate. I stand on the canal-side looking up at the shiny glass windows, trying to imagine what Grace is thinking about the postcard. I bet she knows it's me. She won't know what to do. Why didn't she answer my call? Is she avoiding me? Perhaps she's scared her husband will find out and she's waiting for him to go out. That must be it. I'll keep trying.

My hot chocolate doesn't last long and I stamp my feet to warm myself up. An elderly woman stops outside the flats and I watch as the door opens and she speaks to the man who is exiting the building. He's tall and wearing a suit. Good-looking. *It's him. I flatten* myself back against a wall and stare down into the chocolate slime in the bottom of my cup. There's a whoosh of air as he passes, close enough to touch, and I want to run after him and tell him who I am. He goes into the cafe and I watch as a woman at the table in front of the door whispers to her friend and points to him. The man behind the counter seems to know him and they exchange a few words. He's wearing a blue suit, carrying an expensive-looking case. He comes back out and I have the urge to chase after him. I've got nothing better to do, so I follow him.

Trailing him is kind of fun. It's easy to slip in behind him, with my music on and the sun peeking behind the clouds. He walks at a steady pace, not too fast as he holds his coffee in front of him, stopping every now and then to take a sip. It's funny watching people pass him by. The ones who recognise him turn around, foreheads creased as they try to work out where they know him from, or nudge their partner, trying to be discreet. Until last week, I'd never even heard of him. But the mayoral election has put him right smack in the public eye. On the high street he stops outside Waterstones, so I stop too, lighting a cigarette, my eye on him. He takes a photograph of the window, turns and he's off again. He sticks his arm out and disappears into a black cab. In a matter of seconds he's gone, so I wander over to the bookshop to find out what grabbed his attention. It's a poster for Grace's book, prominently displayed in the window, with a large photo of Grace wearing an apron and holding a wooden spoon. I'm rooted to the spot. It's the lettering on the poster that draws my eye, advertising her book launch, in the main store in Piccadilly, this week. Tickets available.

Inside the shop an assistant is sorting out piles of books, another is serving a customer. It's years since I've been in a bookshop. When I try to read, words wriggle about like black ants trying to escape the page. The stationery section catches my eye, pretty notebooks and diaries. My mind strays back to the past. We kept diaries as teenagers, and it hurts me, deep in the gut, when I remember the words I wrote – I don't want the memory. Everything went into my diary, and I drew little pictures when I couldn't find the words, kept it locked away in a drawer so nobody could laugh at the thoughts that harassed me. Eventually I destroyed it, although I tried to remove the orchid pressed into the back pages, but it crumbled into purple dust, my emotion crumpling with it. I thought if I burnt my diary to cinders it would take my feelings with it, cleansing me, but it didn't work. Guilt gnaws at my gut, always has done, knowing what I'm responsible for. After destroying my diary, not being able to relive what we went through was worse, and I started to forget. Not her, never her, but the details, the little things I'd written down so that I would remember them.

All around the bookshop there are posters of the face I've been hunting for years. Suddenly my head feels light. I notice that the bookshop assistant has left her stool and I sink down onto it, my head in a spin.

'Are you alright?' The shop assistant is back, with a concerned look on her face and a pile of books resting effortlessly in the crook of her left arm.

'Yeah, dizzy spell. Can you tell me how I book a ticket for this talk?' I nod towards the poster, keeping my eyes on the ground. I daren't look at that face any more, those blue eyes with so much to tell me.

'Sure, you stay put and I'll sort it out for you.'

'The name's Charlotte Greene.'

The name pops out of nowhere and I instantly regret saying it. The shop assistant adds me to a list, handing me a ticket which I tuck into my pocket. Ever so simple. She has no idea of the emotions running wild in me, the guilt that grips me and won't let go.

Charlotte's Diary

TUESDAY 23RD JULY 2002

This is going to be such a cool summer!! I've met this guy, Jason. He's older, must be at least eighteen. He works at the kiosk on the beach so I'm buying a LOT of ice cream and Pepsis. A one-month break from gymnastics is heaven and I'm making the most of it. Me and Belinda have found our own sunbathing spot on the beach – right opposite Jason's kiosk – and we're making sure he notices us. Jason is tall and tanned and really fit. He knows our names already. Bel knows I fancy him and she's cool with it cos she's going steady with Harry. Today we were hanging out there and Belinda nearly choked on her ice cream. Bloody Molly Conway was coming out of the sea. Her hair was wet and straggly and she was wearing a black swimsuit. I feel bad whenever I see Molly. It was so much easier when she moved schools. If Belinda hadn't been forced to sit next to Molly that day in Geography none of it would have happened. Bel's face – I nearly died laughing. Me and Belinda hated being in Year Seven – the rest of the class were all like little kids with bows in their hair and swapping sweets at break – they even still called it playtime. We used to put our hair up and wear make-up, we looked so much older. And we'd make Molly do things for us, it was just a bit of fun. Molly had tight curly red hair and freckles and enjoyed PE lessons – enough said!! She even dressed like a boy.

I saw Molly's mum once – a larger version of her – imagine knowing you're going to grow up to look like that. I'd kill myself.

Anyway, on the beach today Molly saw us looking at her and stopped dead, staring right at us. The sun must have gone in at the same time cos I couldn't stop shivering. I wish Belinda wasn't going to Spain tomorrow. The beach on my own won't be much fun. I hope I don't see Molly again, we didn't mean it really. It was just a bit of fun.

CHAPTER FIVE

GRACE

Richard snaps my necklace into place and spins me around to face him.

'It reminds me of last summer when you wear this.' For a moment we're back on our honeymoon in Greece, the simple stall in front of a cave, exquisite silver and turquoise jewellery laid out on the rocks. 'You look gorgeous.' He smells of citrus from the shower and I breathe him in, pressing myself against his chest. His hands are firm on my soft skin as he looks into my eyes. 'What is it? You're not nervous, are you? On TV the other day you were so composed. But you seem unsettled lately. Are you OK?'

Our faces look back at us from the mirror. Richard's dark eyes never fail to move me and I put my arm around him, admiring how good we look together. The shiny blue of my dress shimmers as I reach for my Chanel N° 5, a present from Richard – 'to reward my success', he said. Fifty thousand followers. The light spray feels cool on my skin and my mind races ahead to this evening. The guests, the speech, the reading I've planned from the book. Sometimes I wish his expectations of me weren't so high, but tonight adrenaline fires me, and I can't wait.

'Nothing's the matter. And I'm not nervous, I'm excited.' I rest my hand on his arm. The buzzer downstairs breaks into the conversation. 'Come on, that'll be the cab.'

*

The launch is at a central London bookshop, and the upper bar area is decked out for the occasion. It's already dark and lights from the rooftops form a backdrop outside, as though all of London is twinkling and listening in. My face is everywhere on the strategically placed posters, and copies of the book are stacked up on a long table, where people are milling around. Julia spots us the moment we step out of the lift and sashays through the crowd, her ample figure clad in her trademark black with a silky shawl draped over the top half of her body. Richard puts his hand on my back as we hand our coats into the cloakroom and I catch sight of the evening's guest list. Excitement fizzes inside me as I recognise high-profile celebrities along with friends and Richard's family. But then my stomach drops as I read the name *Charlotte Greene* and I grab at a stone pillar for support.

'Whoops, steady,' Richard laughs. 'You haven't had any champagne yet.'

I force a smile back and watch the crowd part as Julia walks us through the room. I feel Richard's light touch on my shoulder as he whispers, 'Do us proud,' in my ear.

I will my pounding heart to settle, my mind to focus, and push the murky fear away, telling myself it's a common name. Julia stops at the drinks area where a waiter immaculately dressed in black and white holds a tray of champagne. She takes two glasses and leads me to my publishing team, who hover around the book table, their casual office jeans and jumpers swapped for slinky dresses and heels. I spot Richard's parents in the corner and wave to them. Jean's face is radiant as she nudges Des, who is pointing at something outside, no doubt acquainting her with London landmarks. Knowledgeable about everything, just like his son. They will have already checked into the hotel and Jean will be loving this special occasion and spotting the odd familiar face, grabbing Des's arm and whispering as she recognises a model or an MP. Des, on the other hand, is unimpressed by celebrity culture. Richard joins them and Jean's face lights up once more. The champagne fizzes straight to my head, quelling my fears and I smile at Julia, feeling a pang of affection for Richard. He's right about putting a baby on hold. We both need to concentrate on our careers for a few years before we start thinking about raising a family. 'Build a brand,' as he says. Richard's always right. A twinge of anxiety takes me by surprise, and I swallow some champagne.

'Happy?'

'It's wonderful.'

'It's a great turnout.'

We both look around the room; the bar is packed. Lots of strangers, but also many people I recognise. Several wide-eyed, unfamiliar individuals clutch copies of my book and I guess these are the real fans. *One of whom happens to be called Charlotte Greene.* The thought leaves a lump in my throat. Different pockets of conversation buzz into a background hum and Julia has to tap a spoon against her glass to get the attention of the crowd.

'It's fantastic so many people are here. Can you hear me at the back?'

Shouts and laughter affirm 'yes', so Julia introduces my book and I, gesturing to two chairs placed to the side of the table on which copies of my books are piled high. The talk is to comprise a question-and-answer session with a *Guardian* journalist, before further questions will be taken from the floor. Julia's shown me the questions in advance, and I'm not feeling nervous. My hands are steady as I shake the journalist's hand, take my seat and blank out everything except my interviewer and her confident voice. The conversation flows naturally and time flies by before questions are invited.

'Given that your book is about food, and women often have complicated relationships with what they eat, do you feel a pressure to look a certain way?'

The very thin woman who asks this is holding a copy of my book up and looking at the cover as she asks the question. A conversation I had earlier with my editor flashes through my mind, her comment about my 'model looks' and her insistence on putting me on the cover. Now isn't the moment for being indignant.

'My looks are irrelevant. What's important for me is to feel healthy – I haven't always. I care about how nutrition impacts on my health. So many women have a self-destructive relationship with food, and if my recipes and attitude can help change this then my book is making a difference, and that makes me feel good.'

As Julia selects the next question from the audience, my attention is drawn to the door opening and a latecomer rushes in. Something about the woman's deep red hair and angular body makes my breath catch in my throat. As she turns towards me, I see that it's Molly. My head goes into a whirl. Julia coughs and I've no idea what the audience member has asked.

'Could you repeat that please?' While I'm answering the question I watch Molly edge to the back of the crowd out of the corner of my eye. I clasp my hands in my lap to stop them from visibly shaking and force myself to smile as I speak, keeping the fear from my face.

After my talk a book signing has been set up, and a queue forms at the desk. Richard's mother Jean is first in line, and as she throws her arms around me, the corner of the book she holds digs into my spine, so eager is she that she forgets she's holding it. Her warmth always makes me emotional, reminding me of my own mum before cancer got to her, changing her beyond recognition. *If only she could see me now*. Richard takes after his dad in that respect – showing affection in public is not the done thing. Over Jean's shoulder I see Molly watching me, but I don't meet her eye. Instead I hug Jean harder, turning my eyes away.

'You were marvellous, darling. We're both so proud of you.'

My signature, which I've perfected over the years, looks dramatic. The signing takes ages as I chat to those I know in the queue, taking my time. As I work through the line, I sip from my champagne glass, which is regularly topped up by the waiter who hovers nearby. Molly stares throughout. Every time I look up, she's there.

Carrie's next, with a wide grin on her face. Ordinarily I'd be thrilled, but Molly's presence makes my mouth wobble as I attempt to smile back.

'You didn't need to queue, you know I owe you a copy for putting up with me stressing over this book.'

'Don't be daft, it's all part of the occasion. You know how proud I am. Shall we have that drink later this week? Cocktails on me.' Carrie's normally infectious grin is lost on me as Molly lurks in the background.

'Yes, lovely,' I say, 'text me.' My gaze flickers to her shoulder, where I catch sight of Molly's dark, staring eyes. I grip Carrie's hand. 'Thanks for being there.'

She squeezes my hand, gives me an enquiring look.

'You OK? Your hand is shaking.'

'Of course.' I sit up straight. 'It's excitement. Let's catch up over that drink.'

The hum of conversation fades as the evening wears on and I pause and flex my fingers to ease my growing cramp. A discreet glance at my Fitbit tells me we're into the last half hour. Richard is chatting with his parents in the corner and I wish I could join them. I'm dreading having to deal with Molly. There are two women and one man left in the queue and Molly walks slowly across the room and joins them. As the lady in front of me rummages around in her bag for her book, I take a moment to control my breathing.

'Sorry, sorry to keep you waiting,' she says, after clearing her throat. 'You must be exhausted.'

I attempt to smile and will my hand not to shake as I sign. My heart pounds against my ribs. There's no escape. She's getting closer. My panic is growing and sweat gathers on my back.

The final woman in the queue towers over me in a red floral dress; Lycra poppies stretch across her body, petals cling to her curves. She breathes heavily, like she has run here and a faint smell of sweat lingers in the air. As I'm about to start writing, she grabs my hand.

'You don't know how thrilled I am to be here,' she says. Her hand is warm and clammy, and I hope she doesn't notice the tremor in mine. 'The bus arrived late and I thought I wasn't going to arrive in time. Your cake recipes are to die for.'

She tells me her name is Clarissa, and I keep her talking, adding my own name to hers with a wobble of the pen, trying to stretch out the moment, but inevitably she turns and leaves. When she finally moves away I fix a smile on my face but it freezes as I look up and see Molly. The girl from the past, the girl I used to know so well, is in there somewhere, buried deep in a narrow face with tired-looking eyes masked in heavy make-up.

A smell of alcohol hangs over her and I want to look around the room in case anyone is watching, but I am unable to move. Julia's belly laugh rises over the crowd and Richard has his back to me. Molly picks up the display copy of my book from the table, strokes her fingers over my face on the cover. It feels like a punch to the gut.

'What are you doing here?' I lean forward so she can hear my voice, deliberately pitched low. Sweat creeps down my back.

'You won't answer my calls. Tell me we can meet, and I'll go.' She sways.

She's drunk. Over her shoulder I see Richard looking in my direction; he's noticed the queue has gone.

She taps a pen against the table. Her sleeve rides up and the purple orchid tattoo flashes into sight. I gasp. Richard is crossing the room.

I compose myself and nod.

'The Camden Angel pub,' she says, 'tomorrow, two o'clock.'

'OK.' I stand as Richard appears behind Molly. 'Richard,' I say, trying to make my voice sound light and breezy. 'I'm pretty much finished here.'

Molly looks from Richard to me, and sticks the display book in front of me with a defiant look in her eyes. She flicks her wrist and I almost drop the pen. The orchid catches me unawares again. The pen shakes as I sign and she doesn't take her eyes off me the whole time, before shoving the book into the pocket of her grubby parka. She knows I've seen it.

'Cheers. So good to see you again.'

I move closer to Richard, and he puts his arm around my shoulder. I try not to shudder, willing Molly to leave. I'll cover the cost of the book. I just need to get rid of her.

'Do you know her?' We watch as she walks to the door, grabbing at a bookshelf to steady herself.

'She went to my primary school. I never liked her much,' I lie.

Molly turns when she reaches the exit and our eyes meet.

'Tomorrow,' she mouths.

Back home, I'm relieved when Richard mentions an early start and goes straight to bed. I'm always up early but there's no point in me trying to sleep. I can't get Molly's face out of my head. Despite my fear, I can never forget the closeness we once had. During all my years abroad I managed to stop myself searching the internet, but tonight I can't resist. I want to see a picture of Molly, how she was back then, the girl with the cheeky face and freckles who has lived in my head all this time. The Molly who climbed back up the rocky cliff without protest because I'd dropped my cap, who washed the sand out of my hair after a day at the beach. The Molly who wouldn't hurt me. The little circle spins round on the screen as it searches and I will it to go faster, but the connection is taunting me tonight.

Finally the page loads and there are hundreds of thousands of possible avenues to follow The Orchid Girls down. But it's not the stories I'm interested in. I click on the images, and there she is. Wide grin, red springy hair, wearing her favourite green T-shirt. The look in her eyes catches me out and I remember when that photo was taken – the first time she let me use her precious camera and capture the smile that got me into so much trouble.

Richard calls my name, making me jump, and I wipe the search history and log out before I make my way upstairs.

He's surprised but doesn't object when I reach for his shoulders, kissing him with a hunger I haven't felt in a while. I lower myself on top of him in an attempt to rid those images from my mind.

I'm with Richard now, and nothing will change that.

CHAPTER SIX

MOLLY

On the way back from the bookshop I pass a McDonald's, seeing friends and families through the glass windows, laughing, eating, joking around. I go inside, buy myself a meal and sit next to a woman and her three noisy kids, listening in on their conversation. The Coke tastes better with a nifty shot of vodka. Halfway through my meal I picture Grace behind the desk, her lips as she says to her husband, 'I'm pretty much finished here'. My stomach twists. The burger looks greasy and I push the tray away, pick up my drink and stumble against a table as I leave, feeling the glare of the mother on my back.

Back home my flat looks small and unloved compared to my image of Grace's sleek canal-side apartment. I imagine her curled up with her husband on a pristine cream leather sofa. How much does he know about her past?

The news is on; there's a piece related to a kid who has gone missing and I'm compelled to watch. Her parents are on TV, raising their teary faces to the camera and holding hands, pleading for whoever has taken their girl to please get in touch, and telling their daughter they aren't cross with her. I can't help remembering my shock at seeing Mr and Mrs Greene doing an appeal for Charlotte; it made it all real. It meant Grace was wrong, that what we had done had consequences. I go to switch the TV off when the girl's face flashes onto the screen and I grab at the sofa to stop myself keeling over. Straight blonde hair, the same grey school tunic they made us wear. The likeness makes me gasp out loud.

I go to my bedside drawer, take out the only photo I have of Grace and I, two girls sitting on a wall, squinting at the sun. I wish I could go back to that time. But I can't. Before I switch the light off I flick through Grace's book, look at all the pictures, tracing my finger over her immaculate skin, the perfect angles of her face. I place the book by my pillow when I go to sleep.

The following day I don't get up until it's time to go and meet Grace. Energy ricochets inside me at the thought of seeing her. Camden High Street is rammed full of people. They spill out of the tube in a line of chatter, noise, excitement. Teenagers emerge into the market, buzzing, reminding me of the first time I came here, aged sixteen. I remember the rush to the head as I first saw the mysterious shops with their fronts adorned with signs advertising tattoos and piercings, rock star posters and huge platform boots, with more secrets and surprises inside, and vintage stalls bursting with alternative fashion, shades of black everywhere. Long nights drinking cider and dancing at the Electric Ballroom. So different to Dorset. I can't imagine Grace here, in her neat suit and high-heeled shoes. Excitement lights me up inside.

The pub isn't one I normally visit and it's pricey, but it's important to get it right for Grace; it has to be fancy enough for her. I'm the only person in jeans and sturdy boots. I arrive early and order a tonic, slipping in a little vodka from the bottle in my pocket and knocking it back before she joins me. The liquid slides down my throat, soothing my nerves. She's taking her time and I sit with my back to the counter, avoiding the looks of the witch at the bar. It's hot in here and I loosen my collar, clenching my fists in my pockets. Ten minutes in and a dull ache appears behind my eyes, anger rising. After fifteen minutes I know she isn't coming, but I sit it out for thirty. When I finally leave I don't look back, letting the door crash behind me.

She'll pay for this. I'll make sure of it.

On the way home I pick up some cans for Jodie, who's texted that she's coming over. At least my flat isn't such a tip this time. While the kettle boils I stand in a cold shower, flinching at the icy drops of water on my face, waking myself up. Two paracetamol should help. I stick Grace's book under my bed, out of sight.

Jodie is over an hour late. She doesn't reply to my texts, which pisses me off – she mustn't be able to get away from her girlfriend. The girlfriend she never talks about, but who I know everything about. She's small and mousy and looks like Jodie would eat her up for breakfast. Mouse Face, I call her. I've no idea what Jodie sees in her. I try to imagine the two of them together. The idea of Mouse Face at a club – Jodie's usual scene – doesn't make sense. I can't visualise it in my mind, which is how I try and imagine things. At home doing a jigsaw puzzle, that's how I see her. Thinking makes my headache worse and I switch the kettle off and grab myself a beer.

I'm halfway through it when I hear the roar of Jodie's motorcycle coming down the street. I stand by the window and watch her take off her helmet, parking her bike up at the rack outside. Abdul is standing outside his shop. He waves, but she turns her head. I think about not drinking but it's too hard and I'm already one beer in. I'll try again tomorrow.

Jodie opens some cans, passes me one. Her deep brown eyes narrow.

'Still thinking about that old friend of yours?' The way she emphasises the word 'friend' winds me up. I tighten my hands around the can, remembering Grace not turning up, how stupid I felt. I hate that she still has this power over me.

'No, why would I?'

Jodie shrugs. 'I dunno, the way you were talking about her, made me think she was on your mind.'

I know I shouldn't tell Jodie any more details, but I can't resist.

'Do you want to know who she is? You'll never guess who she's married to…'

Jodie shifts to an upright position when I tell her.

'I've heard of her,' she says, tapping into her phone. She shows me a picture and I hope she can't tell the way my pulse quickens when I see Grace. 'She's a looker.'

'If you like that sort of thing.' I add a laugh and hope it's convincing. Sudden panic rises inside me; I wish I hadn't shared Grace with Jodie. She watches me with fierce eyes and I'm suddenly aware of cool air blowing in through the window.

'She's a celebrity now – you must be tempted to see her.'

'No.' I stand up and head towards the window, looking down at the street as I light a cigarette. 'Not at all.' *If only you knew.*

Jodie goes into the kitchen, gets another can and I wonder how long she's staying. She pats the sofa next to her when she sits down again, treating me like some kind of dog, and I ignore her. I still want her, but it has to stop. The way she treats me isn't right. Seeing Grace again has helped me see Jodie for what she is. What me and Grace had was way more special.

'Tell me what you talk to your counsellor about.' Jodie leans forward, her shoulders rigid.

Why won't she let this drop? If that's how she's going to play it, then I know how to make her change the subject.

'I talk about you. How you're with someone, how I've never even spent the night with you. How much it would mean if you would stay.'

She purses her mouth and blows out air, her mouth tight. 'You knew my situation when we first met. I've always been honest with you.'

'So why do you get funny when I mention other women? If I got involved with someone else, then you'd be free of me.'

'I don't want to be free of you.'

'Maybe I do. This isn't working for me, Jodie, my head's too messed up.'

The can is empty and I crumple it into my palm, the cold metal digging through my skin.

'Tell me what's messing you up.'

'I can't talk about it, Jodie.'

'You never confide in me. We're supposed to be close, in a relationship, yet you don't tell me anything. Don't you trust me?'

'But it's not a proper relationship, is it? You go home to wifey, she gets to be with you every day, every night. And it's not like you talk about important stuff either.'

'That's because I haven't got anything to confide. You're the one with all the fucking secrets. I've said it before, Molly, you need to get yourself together. Makes me think seeing you isn't worth the hassle.'

'Well, that's what I've been thinking.' I clench my fists together, gathering my courage. She won't like this, but I've got to do it. 'I don't want to see you any more.'

'Where's this coming from?' Her mouth is open, as if she can't believe I'd dare.

'Haven't you been listening to me? Being your bit on the side isn't what I want.'

Jodie stretches her legs out and pulls herself up. 'The timing feels off to me. It's her, isn't it, your *sister*?'

My stomach curls at the poison she pours into the word.

'She's your first love, isn't she?'

I bite hard into my lip.

'I knew it.' She laughs. 'Get real, she wouldn't look twice at you now. But if that's what you want.'

She shrugs her leather jacket on and crosses to the door.

'You know where I am. Bet you'll call me before the end of the week.'

The door slams and she's gone. I tell myself it was the right thing to do. Now that Grace is back, there's no time for anyone else. Shame she doesn't show me the same respect. But I'll prove Jodie wrong. The can is still crumpled in my hand and there's a nasty mark, the colour of a rotting apple, where I've been squeezing it so tight that my skin's cut and my blood has smeared. All of a sudden Charlotte's face is back in my head, her eyes taunting me. She made me do it. But it's still my fault, everything that happened.

I run my arm under the cold tap and think about Grace not turning up. I haven't decided how to make her pay yet. But I will.

The phone rings and rings and rings. Stops. Starts again. It's eleven when I wake up to four missed calls. For a second I think it might be Grace, then I remember I was supposed to work this morning. *Shit*.

Sitting up makes me retch. Breakfast is probably a good idea, but when I open the fridge all that's on the shelf is a carton of yellow milk and an ancient tub of margarine. A glass of water will have to do.

I write a list for the day: BUY FOOD and DON'T DRINK are my two items. The first is possible, the second doubtful.

Tom from work has left a message and I call him back. He doesn't waste time on small talk.

'What happened to you this morning?'

'Usual. I overslept.'

'Out on the town again?'

I wish. 'Something like that.'

'Gavin's not impressed. You're on a warning already.'

'Put in a good word for me, will you?'

He says he will but we both know Gavin is waiting for an excuse to get rid of me.

'I'll call you later. And Molly, try and sort yourself out.'

A pile of leaflets catches my eye. AA, the local counselling centre, freebies from the doctor. I've had them for ages, but something is different now. I've got to get a grip on myself, otherwise I'll end up back with Jodie. And Grace will like me better if I'm more in control of myself, like I used to be.

A memory hits me, Grace in the sea, swimming in a lazy circle while I watch her, hot sun on my shoulders, sky so blue it dazzles, happy in that moment, just me and Grace with her hair flashing gold in the sun. She challenges me to a race to the rocks and I set off at a disadvantage, just behind her all the way, pumping my arms so hard my chest feels as if it will burst. Concentrating only on the rocks in the distance. Last time I beat her, but she's determined today, half a width ahead now, water splashing and there's no catching her. Suddenly she cries out and disappears under the water. 'Cramp, help me, Molly.'

Panic spurs me through the waves towards Grace. I grip my arms around her chest, pulling her towards me, feeling her heart beating fast against mine, realising just how much she meant to me.

'I knew you'd save me, Molly,' she says later.

I knew then I'd always be there for her.

There's half a can of beer left over from last night and I hesitate before knocking it back, hoping it will ease the dancing feet in my stomach. It gives me the courage to make the call. I speak to the counsellor, words falling out of my mouth about last night, about my life, about the mess I'm in. More words than I've said in ages, all to a woman on the phone, a stranger who has a soft northern voice and sounds like she cares. She tells me her name is Ellis. She's based in the local counselling centre round the corner. And she's coming round.

I get a black plastic bin bag and clear the table, sweeping the beer cans into it, tipping the contents of the ashtray into the mix and taking the lot downstairs. Afterwards I run across the road to Abdul's shop to buy milk and a jar of coffee, in case Ellis wants some. Abdul doesn't say anything as he's on the phone but his eyebrows twitch when I don't buy the usual quarter of vodka, or beer on special. Mrs Bird is sitting by the window with a cup of tea, aching to know what's going on, but it makes me feel like I'm being spied on. She waves and I force a smile before letting the front door close behind me, flinching as it slams.

Mrs Bird isn't the only one looking out of the window when Ellis arrives. I've been pacing up and down, watching the street, ever since I got back from the shop. A tall woman with cropped blonde hair and a large leather bag slung over her shoulder slows and checks door numbers as she walks down the road. The next thing I know she lopes down the path greyhound-style and the bell is ringing in my flat.

Ellis is northern and smiley and would love a coffee, but somehow she's making it herself.

'You're not expecting guests for dinner tonight then,' she says in her broad Manchester accent, putting the milk back into the empty fridge, but she's grinning.

'You're lucky to get coffee. Milk is a bonus, trust me.'

I collapse onto the sofa, suddenly exhausted. I've never opened up to anyone before in the way I spoke to Ellis on the phone, and now she's here in front of me I feel hot and my hair sticks to my face. But I mustn't say too much. Some things I must keep to myself. Once she's found the mugs, which isn't hard as there's nothing much in my cupboards, she's sitting across from me, perched on the edge of my armchair right on the red wine stain from the time I threw a glass at Jodie.

I clutch my mug of coffee close to me and listen as Ellis tells me her story; a rehab clinic four times, then a couple of detoxes.

Her face tightens when she talks about how she left home.

'Dad caught me searching through Mum's purse. She'd just been to the bank and drawn a large amount of cash out, to pay for my brother's school trip. I went mad when he tried to stop me, desperate for drugs, I was.' She shakes her head at the memory. 'Out of control. Mum tried to stop Dad kicking me out, but he wasn't having any of it. Said he couldn't bear to look at me any more. I spent a few nights on the streets before I managed to get a hostel place. It was rough, Molly, believe me, the crowd I ended up with. I've spent more nights in police cells than I can remember.'

But Ellis doesn't resemble the person she is telling me about. She holds herself like someone who matters, and her voice is clear, confident and caring. Straight away I feel like I get her. It doesn't happen to me often, when you first meet another person and you click. Just like that. Like me and Grace. I try to push thoughts of Grace aside.

'You're not what I expected. I don't want to waste your time.'

'Was it my stripy *Dr Who* scarf that put you off? I made it myself, you know.' Her wide grin almost makes me smile. 'Something compelled you to call. That's as good a reason as any.'

I stand up and wander over to the window. A dog has been tied to the tree outside Abdul's shop and it's straining against its lead. *Why did I make that phone call?* Memories crowd my head and I recall the shame, the row with Jodie, missing another shift, turning up drunk at Grace's do. Grace.

Before Ellis leaves she puts her phone number into my mobile and makes me promise to stay in touch. I watch her pull up her collar against the wind as she sets off down the street, waiting until she turns the corner. The ring pull clicks as I crack the can open.

CHARLOTTE'S DIARY

FRIDAY 26TH JULY 2002

Belinda's gone but she's promised she'll ring me as soon as she gets to Torremolinos. She wants me to keep an eye on Harry cos Melanie's been hanging around him a lot. Today I went down to the beach on my own and I was reading a magazine and keeping an eye on Jason when he started talking to this blonde girl. I went straight over cos she was blonde and gorgeous and I didn't like the way Jason was looking at her. She doesn't go to my school – she must be from the posh school on the hill. He introduced me and I swear she looked me up and down. I don't care cos I know I look good in my leopard-print bikini. She was wearing a long T-shirt over shorts, hair loose and shiny. I bought a Pepsi and sipped it at the counter until she got the hint. I asked Jason who she was and I couldn't believe it when he said she's a mate of Molly Conway's. Grace, her name is. Stupid religious name. He said his mum knows Molly's mum and Grace often stays with them in the holidays. Sure enough I watched Grace as she laid out on a stripy towel and a bit later Molly came to join her too. Molly had shorts on and she's so pale the red scar on her arm stands out. Oh my God, when I saw that it made me wonder if that was there because of us and I wish I hadn't seen it. Remembering what we used to do to her makes me feel bad all over again.

MONDAY 29TH JULY 2002

No word from Belinda. This summer is turning out to be shit. Yesterday I bumped into Jason in the burger bar. I was so excited until he asked me to come and join 'us' and when I saw who he was with it was too late to say no – Molly and Grace. It's so awkward with Molly. I wonder if she's told Grace about me. Molly was eating an ice cream and it dripped on her leg and she saw me looking at her. Back at school her neck would have gone red like it did every time she saw me and Belinda coming towards her. But today she just stared at me again and it proper freaked me out.

It was Belinda's idea to have a bit of fun with her back then. That's all it was. Don't know why I keep going on about it. So we were in the cafe and I ignored psycho Molly and chatted to Grace and she's actually not bad. She was telling us about her dad who's a vicar and spends his life trying to make her be a good Christian. And I was right, she goes to the church school, which is why I've never seen her hanging around town. I've been so fed up without Belinda and I was laughing for the first time in ages. And if we made friends and she knew how I felt about Jason then maybe she could help get us together. So I chatted back and Molly scowled. I told her my mate was away and she said I should come to the beach with them!! Turns out she can swim but she doesn't like getting her hair wet – another thing we have in common! It takes me ages to get ready for the beach, no way I'm getting into that dirty water. Grace said she gets bored cos Molly's always in the sea. Molly can't have told her about me. Shame she has to be there, but we can get to know each other while Molly is swimming. Molly will hate that, though. Oh well.

CHAPTER SEVEN

GRACE

My fingers run along the red silk of the dress, spilled out on the bed like a bloodstain. The first present Richard bought me for Valentine's. It fit perfectly, showed off my curves, seemed to generate electricity between us. I want to glow at Richard's side tonight as his team celebrate his campaign so far. Polls have picked up, and it's a real possibility that he could become the Mayor of London. Red is the colour I choose when I'm at my most confident, but today cold fingers pluck at my nerves and I can't settle. My eyes flicker along with the minute hand of the clock which counts down the remaining two hours until I am due to step into the car which will be collecting me.

Sounds emanate from the bathroom; Richard's voice is loud and off-key as he sings. This would usually make me smile but today it puts me on edge. Not meeting Molly seemed like a good idea at the time but now I'm not sure. It's made me feel even more anxious.

The whoosh of the water subsides and silence envelops me, making my thoughts sound louder. I pull my bath wrap tight around my waist and go in search of a glass of water. Back in the bedroom Richard is pulling his boxers on, a fresh lemon smell from his shower lingering in the air.

'Great outfit,' he says, as I slip into the red dress. 'Are you looking forward to this evening?'

'Do you need to ask?' I love that Richard is doing so well. He deserves it. 'Are you nervous?'

'Me? Never.' He sits down on the bed beside me, doing up the buttons of his crisp shirt and runs his fingers through his half-damp hair. 'It means a lot to me, you being there, Grace. You know how important tonight is.'

How could I not – he's been going on about nothing else for weeks. Apparently this speech is the most important of the campaign. All I have to do is be there.

'It's not going to take long. Once the speech is out of the way we'll be able to relax over dinner, apart from the odd bit of networking, of course. Lucky we're both so good at it.'

The word 'network' jolts in my head and I feel responsibility pressing down on me. My reputation must remain untarnished. We both want this so much. What am I thinking of, letting Molly get to me? It was no lie that I'm looking forward to this evening, and Molly doesn't belong in our world. The best thing to do is tell Richard, make light of it, laugh it off with him. Once this is over maybe he'll decide the time is right for a baby… I almost convince myself. Richard snaps his cufflinks into place.

'Take your time getting ready. I'm going ahead to go over my speech, but you don't need to be there until eight, that's when the presentation is. We'll go in together. I'll pour you a drink, then you can chill for a bit.' I imagine the scene in my head, the two of us hand in hand, posing for the camera. If only Mum were there to see this version of me, the successful daughter she never got to meet. Sadness stings my eyes. My arm itches, as it often does, and I rub the raised skin where the tattoo once was. Thank God I got rid of it.

When I'm ready, I join Richard downstairs where the television is on, loudly documenting the story of the missing girl. It's still dominating the headlines, and it's the last thing I want to hear about. It's bad enough Molly reminding me of the past, without this too.

'Wouldn't you rather have music on?' I ask, sipping the white wine spritzer Richard has poured for me.

He jumps and I realise he hasn't heard me come down the stairs. The remote is in his hand but he makes no move to quieten the sound. 'I want to hear what they say about this evening.'

He'll be lucky. The only story on the news is Emily. Everywhere I look there is something to remind me. I shake the liquid in the glass, not wanting to drink it, unable to settle. Richard has never seen my anxious side. The facade I normally have in place is cracking. I wish I could confide in someone – I can talk to Carrie about the baby stuff, about Richard, but with this I'm on my own.

Richard's phone pings. 'My driver is here,' he says. 'You're in a funny mood, Grace. Better not drink any more, OK? We want to create the best impression.'

I'm annoyed he's picked up that something is wrong. This evening is so important. I can be better than this.

Once he's gone I step outside, longing for a cigarette. I haven't smoked in years but the craving has been growing in me ever since Molly returned. Outside, the water is dark and the banks are still; boats are cloaked in darkness as if everyone is out tonight, waiting for Richard's speech. The shrill sound of the landline ringing brings me back inside but by the time I reach the handset the caller has rung off. Only Richard's parents ever use the landline – it's probably his mum wanting to wish him luck, or his dad reminding him where he stands in the polls. I press to play the message back. The line crackles and then Molly's voice fills the room. I freeze.

'You didn't turn up. Big mistake, Grace. But I've got something you won't want your husband to see. So unless you want me to show him, you'd better talk to me.'

My knees buckle. Fear rattles through me and a trickle of sweat runs down my back because I know exactly what she means. My dress clings and I rush upstairs and cool myself down with cold water, holding my arms around myself, trying to keep calm.

How did she get this number? Downstairs the phone trills again injecting another shot of panic into me. This can't be happening, not now. Why did I think not turning up was going to keep her away? How could I be so stupid?

There is an hour to go until the car comes. I pace up and down the bedroom, trying to work out what to do. I've got to stop Molly contacting me. One phone call, a few firm words, that should do it.

My fingers feel clumsy and I misdial, making three attempts before I hit the right buttons. I drink some of my spritzer to steady my nerves as the phone rings and rings. What's taking her so long? I've almost given up and I've downed half the glass. But then I hear Molly. Her voice is loud, her words slurred. I hold the phone away from my ear.

'You've got to stop ringing me. I want to leave the past behind, Molly, and I'm sorry if that hurts you, but that's the way it has to be.'

'Too important now, are you?'

She lashes out in such a familiar way: it's like stepping back in time. But I won't let her hurt me now. I'm not that version of Grace any more. I have to make her stay away. I have to.

My heart starts to thud and I drop onto the sofa, closing my eyes. 'Molly, please, let's not do this.'

'I'm coming over.'

I hear a clatter and then the phone buzzes like a mosquito in my ear.

The stainless-steel clock indicates there are forty-five minutes to wait until the car arrives. Powerlessness sweeps over me; the cars are always booked through Richard's campaign office and there is nothing I can do about it, apart from make sure I'm ready and pray that the car will arrive before Molly does – if indeed she's coming. She's obviously been drinking again, doesn't know what she's doing. Hopefully she's forgotten already. But the thought doesn't reassure me. Outside it's dark and a light drizzle falls on the pavement; a plastic bag darts along the bank as if searching for a means of escape.

The face in the mirror doesn't look like me. My make-up is immaculate, every accessory is coordinated, from my bag to my tights. But my face is all wrong. My mood plays havoc with my body language, making my shoulders stiff and tense. I sit down on the sofa with another half-glass of wine. I don't want to overdo it before I get to the function, but my mind is whirling and the alcohol might ease it a little. No matter how hard I try to control my breathing or push thoughts of Molly away, images dance in front of my eyes, pictures flashing back at me, as I try to deny knowledge of them even to myself.

The doorbell cuts into my daydream and I know it's her. The driver who comes with the car always texts to let me know he's here. I jump to my feet and pace up and down, unsure what to do. There's no way I can get out without going past Molly. The bell rings again now, and again, and again. She's got her finger on it like a drill boring into my head and I put my hands over my ears like a cartoon character. My mobile is on the table and I snatch it up in panic. I could call the driver and tell him there's a stranger at the door harassing me, but who knows what state Molly is in, and what she would say. I can't risk it.

The noise is unbearable and I lean back against the wall, sweat gathering on my forehead. I put my eye to the spyhole, but all I can see is black and I realise she is leaning against the door.

Eventually I give in, unable to bear the relentless ringing any more. Molly stumbles forward as I release the door, but I leave the chain on as the sweet smell of alcohol announces her arrival. Her eyes are wild, with black make-up smudged at the corners, and her face is white, making her loom like a ghost in the dark. The car is due in fifteen minutes, so I need to be swift and sharp, deal with her.

'Tell me what you want, Molly, and then you need to go. I've got to be somewhere. I'm being picked up in five minutes.' The less time I give her the better.

She steps back, wavering slightly on her feet. Her smile is a weird slash that bites into her ghostly pallor.

'What do you want?' I repeat.

'You know what I want. Us back again, friends, like before.'

'That's not going to happen. Look, I've got to go out, you said it was important.'

'You didn't turn up,' she says, her voice rising into a wail. She rubs at her hand as she talks and it looks red and sore. Surely she can't be a self-harmer too?

I keep my voice low and level; I need to get through to her. 'This is pointless, Molly. We lead different lives now.'

'Stop saying that!' Her eyes are bloodshot. In her black clothes she looks like she's stepped out of a horror movie. The minute hand on the large clock moves in a relentless march and I expect my phone to go off any minute, announcing that the driver is here. I can picture him pacing around by the car, whistling puffs of breath into the cool evening air, ready to tip his hat at me as he holds the car door open, ever polite, attending to every detail like the true professional he is. But these thoughts are distractions from the matter in hand. I need to get Molly away from the flat. If I can persuade her to accompany me outside, I can probably reach the car park without the driver seeing her. It's better if I go downstairs before he arrives, wait there. Yes, that's a good idea.

'Let me in, Grace, for fuck's sake!' As she speaks, she crumples down to the floor, head in her hands.

Please don't let her be sick over the floor. I move fast, grab my bag and wrap, unlock the chain, slip out into the corridor and slam the door behind me.

'I'm leaving now, Molly, we can talk as we go down. Tell me what you want and I'll see if I can help.'

The beep from an incoming text alerts me to the driver's arrival. 'My car is here.'

'Why did you never answer my letters?'

'What letters?'

'The letters I wrote to you after we moved, every week. I never gave up…'

'I didn't get any letters.'

'So if you had received them, you would have replied?' Hope flashes across her face.

'This is pointless, Molly. I didn't get your letters, OK? You should have left it alone. You need to leave it alone now.'

As I look at her, it hits me how thin she is, her collarbones visible, jutting out of the top of her faded T-shirt. She's so different from the muscular, strong, teenage Molly, who was ready to take on the world. The girl who swam the length of the bay when cramp seized my leg and I panicked, helping me back to the beach.

My phone beeps again and I picture the driver, getting impatient, engine running downstairs. I should leave right now, but something stops me. I have to know.

'You mentioned something you had on me.'

A sly look crosses her face. 'Remember what Charlotte had, in her bag?'

My feet move of their own accord and I cross the space between us, grabbing her shirt with both hands. '*Said* she had, you mean. Never, ever mention that to me again. She was winding us up and you know it.'

'What if she wasn't?'

Spittle hits me and I drop Molly's shirt as if she's burnt me. I step back, our faces so close I can feel her breath on my cheek.

'What if I know something you don't?'

Before I can stop her she leans forward and kisses me hard on the lips. Then she steps back and smooths her hair away from her eyes.

'I can destroy you, Grace. You run off to your posh dinner with your precious husband, and while you're eating have a think about what Charlotte said. Why would she make it up?'

My whole body is shaking and I run the back of my hands over my burning lips, trying to rub the memory of her kiss away. My phone rings. The lift is at the top of the building and I run down the stairs, desperate to escape. But when I reach the car park, I see the tail lights of a car disappearing into the distance. Another text arrives on my phone.

Unable to complete pick-up as nobody at home

One more flicker and the lights vanish, leaving me alone in a deserted car park.

CHAPTER EIGHT

MOLLY

It's late when I wake. My knuckles hurt and I'm trying to remember why when it hits me. Bashing on the door of her flat, Grace talking to me through the chain, keeping me out. Me kissing her. Sweat pours down my body as I hold my arms around myself and try to stop the shakes.

I think about Ellis, her words, the sense of calm that surrounded her, her wide grin. I wish I could be like her. I need a drink.

I feel better once my hands are wrapped around the glass. Sorting my head out will have to wait another day. *Just for today,* Ellis said. More like *Just for tomorrow*. Concentrate on the present, she meant. I can try, at least. I won't drink tomorrow.

There's a missed call from Ellis on my phone. She's left me a voicemail. Her voice is confident and calming. She tells me not to beat myself up if I'm struggling. I'm not sure how to manage that; beating myself up is my default. I look at her name on the screen: Ellis. Unusual name for a girl. I think about Jodie as I rub my palm. I don't need her any more. Then I think about Grace. As if on cue my phone rings, but it's neither of them. It's Ellis. I watch her name flash on and off. Ellis. It's a good name. But I don't answer, I'm too ashamed.

Out in the street the wind blows my hair into my eyes and makes them smart. My bike isn't tied to the railing where I usually leave it, and for a moment I try and work out where I left it when I was last in a drunken stupor. I decide it's been stolen and kick the wall, before I recall having seen it in the hallway at home. The bottle in my pocket is empty and I stick it in the recycling bin, enjoying the crash as it drops. I go to ring Jodie but then I remember ending it. It's not lust I want, but someone to put her arms around me and hold me tight. Jodie's not enough any more. I want to call Grace, but I stop myself. I don't know what to do and I don't want to go home. I'm standing in front of a Starbucks and I have a fiver in my pocket, so I go inside, order a tea and head for an armchair tucked away in the corner, turning it so that I'm facing the wall. I let myself fall asleep.

A loud cough wakes me up and it takes me a moment to work out where I am. I stop off in the ladies' and drench my face in cold water, feeling better. It's nearly six o'clock and my shift doesn't start until nine. Gavin has left me a voicemail, which I don't want to listen to. I sit on the stairs outside the loo and finish the contents of my hip flask before playing the message. His nasally voice gets my nerves screaming.

'Gavin here, Molly. You didn't turn up to work on Tuesday and you were on a final warning. I'm sorry to have to do this but I can't keep you on the staff any more. You don't need to come in today, you'll receive any wages we owe you at the end of the week.'

He doesn't bother to say goodbye. Bile rises in my throat and I swallow hard. Stuff him and his stupid job.

Grace's husband's picture is plastered on the front of the *Evening Standard*, a copy of which I pick up on the way home. My face flushes hot when I give in and dial her number. The disconnected tone sounds in my ear.

Why won't she talk to me? How can she forget everything so easily?

Back in my flat, my thoughts won't stop. I throw my duvet onto the floor, kicking a cushion after it which sends a can clattering over the lino. She didn't receive my letters. *How dare he? How dare he hide them from her?* Grace's dad, Michael, it had to be him who kept them from her; Grace's mum wasn't well enough to do anything as devious as that. *Did he read them? Did he laugh at them?* I used to hate being around him, with his cold, judging eyes, his disapproving expression. The lectures he used to give us, as if he was in church where he got to preach as much as he liked. Me and Grace would sit so close together in the pews that I could feel her shaking. She was always scared he'd hit her again. He always terrified me. I was relieved I wasn't the daughter of a vicar. Nobody could ever live up to his expectations. No wonder Grace rebelled. My heart pounds with embarrassment as I try not to remember the words I wrote to her, the hurt and rage. I can't believe she never even got them. All those years of waiting, for nothing.

There's a drop of Jodie's whisky in a bottle in the kitchen and I add some to my coffee, sitting on my bed with my back against the wall. I've done it this time; actually lost my job, messed up big.

I read about Richard Sutherland in the newspaper and his connection with Ash Fenton. The village the missing girl is from. He's quoted, explaining it's the place he grew up in and that his parents still live there, as well as his father-in-law who is in sheltered housing nearby. That gets me up, wandering round and round the flat, thinking. Grace's dad, Michael. If he opened my letters then he owes me an explanation. I'm not scared of him. Not any more. This fires me up again and I stick some music on and settle down on the floor. I wish the whisky hadn't all gone. I keep my mobile close, in case Grace calls. I don't believe she's angry, not really. She can't be. Not at me. When she has a proper think about us she'll be in touch, I know she will.

In my old battered coffee tin I have one hundred pounds, plus another twenty and some cash in my purse. I go through all my pockets and find another fifty pence, plus a few pennies. I do a few sums in my head to work out how much I can get by on in a day. Abdul let me run up a tab last time I lost my job. Maybe I can get Tom to write me a reference. I give him a ring and he picks up straight away.

'Gavin's fired you, hasn't he? He rang me earlier. I'm sorry, I tried to cover for you, but he saw through it. I warned you, Moll, after last time.'

'Yeah. Thanks for trying, Tom, you've been a good mate.' I ask him about a reference.

'Sure thing. Stay in touch, Molly, and listen, maybe try and sort out the drinking, now that it's starting to mess with your life.'

If only he knew. The messing started way back before I ever moved to London, once the trial got underway, before Mum and Dad gave up on me. Drink seemed the answer back then, after Grace and I were separated and I blamed myself for everything. It was the only thing I could rely on.

My phone rings. It's Ellis, but I don't pick up. Canned laughter mocks me from the television. Later when the walls are blurred and I'm promising myself that I won't drink tomorrow, I listen to her message.

Ellis's voicemail explains how she reached 'rock-bottom' and I realise something. Slumped here on the bathroom floor, jobless and hung-over, rejected by Grace, staring at a blob of crusty toothpaste stuck to the side of the bath, this is what rock-bottom looks like.

The tone rings into my ear, each sound a shriek in my head escalating the fear that she may not answer. But then I hear her voice and I can't get my words out, something sharp is lodged in my throat. I don't know what to say. But somehow she understands and I manage to tell her that I am at home and she tells me to sit tight as she's coming over. 'Sit tight' reminds me of 'sleep tight', which Mum used to say to me at night, and then the tears start. I hate myself for crying, hate myself for no longer being in control of my feelings.

Splashing cold water on my face helps me feel a little better and I try to make the bathroom look respectable. I stash the whisky bottle in the overflowing bin; I haven't got the energy to empty it. By the time Ellis arrives I'm wearing a clean pair of jogging bottoms and my favourite T-shirt, which I've had forever and gives me the kind of comfort my toy rabbit used to until his ear fell off. Ellis fusses around the kitchen and I cringe at the thought that she might realise I've been crying.

God, I'm a mess.

She makes herself a coffee.

'I lost my job.'

'Do you want to talk about it?'

'Not much to tell. I overslept.'

'Had you been drinking?'

Memories flash at me. Jodie's twisted face, the bathroom floor. Bashing at Grace's door like a madwoman; sleeping it off in Starbucks.

'Yes. Pretty much all day. It's crap living like this.' Shame tears through me.

'I'll help you. Have you eaten this morning?'

I shake my head. 'I can't.'

'How about I make you some tea and you can try one of these?' She produces a packet of Rich Tea biscuits from her bag. 'They used to be the only thing I could keep down. I hate to see you in so much pain. It's not much of a way to live, is it?'

'Why are you being so nice? You don't even know me.'

She shrugs. 'I need someone to laugh at my jokes. And I'd like to get to know you.'

The tea warms me up and the biscuit stays down. 'Do you think there's any chance you can get your job back?'

'No. I need to work, though. I'll have to get out there, see if there's anything around. Pubs always want staff.'

'Maybe not the best job for someone who's trying not drink?' She grins as she speaks.

'I don't have a choice.'

'Is there anything else you'd like to do?'

'Take photographs.' My response surprises me. I haven't touched a camera in years. Not since what happened.

'That's interesting. Do you have a camera?'

I'm thrown for a second; I don't want to think about what happened to my favourite camera.

'Only my phone. My uncle will lend me one, though – he's a professional photographer. But that would mean going back to Dorset, seeing my mum.'

'Well, no rush. Use your phone for now. Get snapping! It would be great, even as a hobby, if it's what you like doing. Making clothes for a living really helps me. It's so important to have something to do when you first stop drinking, to keep yourself busy. Go and borrow your uncle's camera if you manage to get back into it.'

'I haven't seen my mum for ages. I'll think about it.'

'Why don't you sign on for a while? Take a bit of time to look after yourself. Take the pressure off. Getting sober takes energy. I wasn't knocking up my own creations straight away, you know.'

She waves her scarf at me and I can't help smiling. Her eyes dance with life and I wish some of her vitality would rub off on me.

'That would be worse. Having nothing to do all day. Although if I was taking photos…' Plus it would give me more time to spend with Grace, wouldn't it? Perhaps I could get her to open up to me. That's exactly what I need. Ellis makes me another cup of tea.

'Today is a fresh start in another way. I've finished with my girlfriend.'

An expression I can't read flickers across Ellis's face.

'Are you OK with that?'

'She lives with someone else, so it wasn't going anywhere.'

'You deserve better than that. It sounds like you've lost your self-respect, drinking does that. I was the same, believe me. Try giving it up for a while, look after yourself, that will be a start. I'll help you. How about we get out of here, go for a walk, maybe get something to eat later, on me?'

We walk around the park and Ellis asks me where I grew up. I tell her about Lyme and how we never used to go on holiday but it didn't matter to me because the sea was where I wanted to be. Just thinking about the deep water makes me shudder now.

'How come you left? It sounds like you were happy there.'

'I was.' I pull my jacket around me, suddenly cold. 'Usual teenage stuff, I fell out with my parents and left home when I was sixteen.' It's not a total lie.

'And are they both still around?'

'There's only my mum and my brother left now, Dad died five years ago. Mum would probably forgive me, but I'm too ashamed to go back.'

'I'm sorry.' She squeezes my arm, taking me by surprise. Strangely, I don't mind.

I shrug. 'I hadn't seen him since I left home.' I screw up my eyes, blink away tears that I didn't expect. I remember holding his hand in the queue at Boots, hopping from one foot to the other at the excitement of getting my first photos developed. We'd look at them together, laughing at the shot where I'd chopped his head off, our heads so close that the smell of tobacco on his hair made me sneeze. He was a quiet, kind man. He'd do anything for me and Mum. Happiest outdoors, hunting orchids, or fussing around the garden. My favourite times were when it was just me and him, out on the cliffs, hunting the wild flowers in my flower book, him kneeling down to point them out to me.

'I went back for the funeral. I was so pleased to see Mum but I couldn't show it, eaten up by guilt at what I'd put them through. I drank so much that day I don't know what I did or said. It was one of the last times I saw my brother, too. He was too embarrassed to tell me what I'd done. Like I said, it's difficult.'

Ellis's expression is filled with sympathy. 'How old's your brother?'

'He's eight years younger than me. Darren. He lives in Manchester – well, he did five years ago. I've only seen him once since then.' Just thinking about it makes me cringe. 'We speak occasionally.'

'Go and see your mum. Get the camera you were talking about. Do it while you've got time between jobs. And think about calling your brother. I'm sure he'd like to hear from you.'

Back at home, I keep thinking about my camera.

Is it where I left it? Darkness pressing in, hands scrabbling at the earth.

I know Mum would love to see me. She's always there for me, no matter how much I push her away. And she's on her own now. Guilt slams into me for leaving her alone all this time. I wonder if she's still working as a nurse. Now I've allowed myself to think about Mum, after so long pushing her to the back of my mind, I realise I'd love to see her, make it up to her. We were close, before.

I watch crap television and drink lots of tea, trying to switch my head off. I can't resist looking at my phone to see what Grace is doing. I register surprise again that I called myself OrchidGirl, after trying to escape that nickname for so long, but it got a response. I wonder how it made Grace feel.

I wish she'd reply, but she's still keeping me waiting.

Under my bravado it niggles me. I didn't always hate that name, but nobody remembers that. It was the first summer Grace came to stay with us and Dad's orchid was entered into the 'Best in Show' category in the local flower show. We were posing for Dad and the photographer from the local gazette came over and asked if he could take a proper photo, for his newspaper. We made the front page on that occasion, too. That was the first time we became known as 'The Orchid Girls', the headline above the photo of us standing either side of this big purple flower. Dad explained to Grace that orchids came in different shapes and sizes, and next time we went up to the cliff I showed her the wild ones Dad had noted in my book. We each picked one and put it in our diaries. That's what made us get the tattoos done. We liked being The Orchid Girls until I went and spoilt it all.

The craving for drink gnaws at my stomach and I'm in bed by nine. But I can't sleep because my thoughts keep returning to my camera. Grace thinks I destroyed it, but that was a promise I didn't keep. She doesn't need to know about it, not yet. Under my thin duvet I hug the secret to my chest, try to get warm as I go over Grace's words in my head, each one a precious stone I've been waiting so long to hear. She might be telling me to leave but I know what she's really thinking. She doesn't mean it. All we need is a proper conversation and we could be mates again. Best mates. Just like we used to be.

CHARLOTTE'S DIARY

I haven't had time to write cos I've been having such a laugh with Grace. Belinda sent me a postcard and said she's met a Spanish waiter. Slapper! Grace and I hang out on the beach every day and Grace knows I like Jason. He hasn't asked me out but I reckon he's about to. He said he's going to teach me how to swim. I can't wait, I've been on at Mum to get me a new bikini for it. She doesn't understand why one isn't enough. Grace has three. Anyway it's a good job I've met Grace cos there's a party on the beach tonight and Mum would never have let me go on my own. Grace knows me and Molly don't get on great but she persuaded her to let me stop over. I'm not telling Belinda that!!

This afternoon we did the coolest thing. If Mum knew she'd kill me, but I reckon I can hide it from her. The weather wasn't great and Jason suggested we go see his mate Dean, who works at a tattoo parlour. On the walk up Molly and Grace went ahead and I got talking to Jason who said he's got a tattoo on his back and he'd show me some time!! I actually pinched myself to make sure he really said it. He did!! I said I'd love to have one too and he didn't say anything moronic like you're too young (I've told him already I'm sixteen – well, it's almost true) but that Dean was sound and he could organise it if he was on his own in the shop. I was really excited and when we got there I took Grace aside and told her I was going to get a tattoo. She only went and told Molly, and next thing I know we're all gonna have them done. The shop was all black with designs everywhere and I decided on a rose cos it looks cool in black. Grace was looking at the flowers and then she looked at Molly and pointed at this weird-looking flower and they both said 'an orchid' aloud at the same time and giggled. Apparently Molly's dad's really into flowers and he once found a really rare orchid. We all decided on the inside of our wrists as we can hide it with a sleeve, or a bracelet in summer. Grace went first and then Molly and they held hands like stupid kids while they had it done. I went last. It hurt like hell but I bit my lip hard so that Jason wouldn't see. I don't know how it happened but Dean only went and gave me a bloody orchid instead of a rose. Obviously I couldn't see what he was doing, and it was only when we were all done and he said, 'There you go, Orchid Girls,' that I realised what he'd done. Molly was furious, her face got all red and puffy and I actually thought she was going to cry. God, she's such a baby. And she's mad – she was gabbling on about wild orchids on the cliff or some shit. As if I cared about fucking flowers. I'm so pissed off because I'm stuck with this ugly flower on my wrist. I'm gonna get the rose done somewhere else but I'll take Belinda, not them.

We had to all promise NEVER to tell where we got it done and Grace suggested if anyone asks we can say it was at the fair in the next town cos we're going there at the weekend. Mine is covered with a plaster now and Dean said it will be scabby for a bit but I don't care. Belinda is going to be so jealous. I won't tell her Molly got one too, just me and Grace. I'd never live it down if she knew that.

Anyway it's the beach party tonight and you never know, I might end up sitting on the beach all night with Jason, chatting and watching the sun rise and who knows what else. He might even show me his tattoo!! I'm so excited.

SATURDAY 10TH AUGUST 2002

The shit hit the fan after the party last night. My head feels like it's going to burst. I'm NEVER, EVER drinking cider again. I want to die. I ended up going back to Molly's, we got back really late and I threw up over Molly's carpet and Molly and Grace have been grounded. Some nosy neighbour saw us heading down to the beach with 'much older' boys and told on us. Grace's dad came round to visit her and he went mad, terrifying us. He's so scary. I wish I was in Spain with Belinda. Her mum lets us do what we like.

The worst thing ever, ever, ever happened at the party. Molly said she was going swimming in the dark and Grace stripped off in front of Jason – her white bikini glowed in the night and he couldn't stop staring. I was wearing cut-off jeans and my off-the-shoulder sparkly top but it felt all wrong. I got Jason a cold beer to distract him and we were chatting but the whole time he was watching Grace who was just paddling – showing off – she must have been freezing. How could she do that? Next she came over and sat next to Jason and this other boy started chatting me up but I wasn't interested. Molly came back and one of the boys started strumming a guitar and we all listened. Next thing I know I turned round and Jason and Grace were kissing. Proper snogging. My stomach turned over and I thought I was going to be sick. How could he? And I thought she was my friend. But the weirdest thing was that Molly was watching them. She was proper staring and her hands were clenching the sand, fury all over her face. She looked how I felt. But why?

CHAPTER NINE
GRACE

Richard is in the middle of his speech when I arrive. There's a hush in the room and I cringe when the silk of my dress swishes as I make my way to my seat, so obviously late as I zigzag in and out of chairs. It sounds like the speech is going well, there are outbursts of laughter which should make me laugh too, but all I can think about is how my face glows as red as the scarlet of my dress and how disappointed Richard will be. Drinking the large glass of water in front of me cools me down and for the rest of his speech I sit with my hands in my lap and try and look interested, a smile painted on my face.

When Richard has finished speaking, there's rapturous applause and I am disconcerted, my mind still back in the flat, stuck on Molly. Glasses clink and conversation fills the room as plates of neatly arranged poached fish and steamed asparagus are served to the tables. Richard's face is set to his public mask, polite and interested, poised to smile. He's always confident when he has an audience. Just like Michael. An image of Michael preaching in church flashes into my head; the hush as he speaks; sitting on my hands to keep myself still, not wanting to draw his attention to me. Molly sitting on her hands, red cheeks looking down at her knees, trying not to laugh. *Where did that thought come from?*

Once Richard is finished, he walks over. But when my arm winds round his waist his muscles are tense and I know the only reason he isn't shaking me off is because we are in public and all eyes are on us. I sense them boring into me and I am shaken to the core, feeling incredibly self-conscious, just like I did when I first came to London and left my old self behind. My transformation into the Grace I am today didn't happen overnight.

But tonight, Richard needs me, even if I have let him down, and I pull myself together. I switch on the charm as I turn to the man at my left with my winning smile. Heads turn towards me as I laugh and nod and slip back into my public persona. I control the urge to tell Richard what happened; it will have to be dealt with later. But he can't know the whole truth. No one can.

Everyone wants to speak to us and we don't get any time together, so it's impossible for me to explain. As time passes the urge to talk about what happened, or at least some of it, surges inside me and the last place I want to be is stuck amongst all these people. There's a moment when we're together and I open my mouth to start but Richard turns away coldly. I grit my teeth and fix my smile back in place.

Time drags, and I'm watching Richard talk to an attractive brunette who drops her head back and laughs at whatever he's said. I have to speak to him. Waiting is killing me. I take a glass of champagne from a passing waiter before I tap Richard on the arm.

'Darling.'

He switches his attention from the brunette for a second and smiles with his mouth. It doesn't reach his eyes.

'Grace, perfect timing, we were just talking about you. This is Sophie, she's a food blogger like you.'

'Hi Sophie,' I say. 'Richard can I—'

He waves to someone across the room, not paying me any attention.

'Excuse me, ladies…'

He cuts me off and I compose my face, trying not to show my frustration to this familiar-looking woman.

'Richard was telling me you're developing a range of products. That's so exciting.'

Her words remind me that I've forgotten to confirm the branding meeting tomorrow. *Shit*. Another thing to worry about.

She holds her hand out. 'I'm Sophie Ingram. We messaged each other on Instagram the other day.'

'I remember, you've got a book out too, haven't you? I'm so happy to meet you.'

Sophie is easy to talk to and I spend the rest of the evening chatting to her. We exchange phone numbers before I leave, but all I can think about is apologising to Richard. I can't stand it when he's angry at me. The champagne should take the edge off my nerves, but I can't forget my dramatic evening. Tomorrow I'll think of a way to deal with Molly, stop her impacting on me and Richard. Stop her from ruining everything.

The car is filled with unspoken words. The driver appears oblivious, but I know better than to speak in front of him. Richard slams the car door, and I thank the driver before I get out. Rain assaults me and I pull the hood of my jacket over my head. Memories from the car park flash through my mind and I run the short distance back to the flat, wanting to put them behind me.

I shake the drops off my raincoat before I hang it in the hall, slipping out of my heels. Richard has poured himself a glass of whisky by the time I get in.

'What happened? Do you know how embarrassing that was? You know what the press are like, expecting us to make a public entrance, and then I turn up on my own. It was humiliating.'

'Darling, I'm so sorry.'

His muscles twitch and he moves his arm as I automatically go to reach for him. It's just a small movement, but visible enough.

'A call came through from my editor and we were talking. I must have missed the text saying that the car was outside.'

'But how? You'd have seen it on your phone.'

'I had it on speaker, I was fixing my make-up. You know how it is.'

He opens the balcony door for some fresh air and a shout filters in from outside. He paces as he talks.

'The slightest little thing can be turned into a big drama. Did you see the way people were watching you when you came in?'

'Oh come on, everybody was listening to you. No one even noticed me. And I tried to explain, but it was impossible to get you alone.'

'You know how important tonight was.'

'I know, and I'm sorry, I really am. Your speech went down well, why can't you just be happy about that? It was a lovely evening, and I made a good contact in Sophie. I liked her.'

Richard runs his hands through his hair, shrugs, his shoulders slumping with fatigue.

'It's done now. I'm going to bed.'

Once he's gone upstairs, the evening plays back in my mind. I hate the fact that it's ended with Richard in a mood. I feel guilty for letting him down, but I can't help thinking that he's being harsh. Not for the first time in recent weeks, I notice how different he is from the man I first met. But I remind myself that he doesn't know what it cost me to move back to England. And he must never find out.

Richard is asleep when I climb into bed, which frustrates me as I lie still and listen to his regular breathing. Only now do I allow the cinematic reel of scenarios to play in my head. The nightmare of Molly turning up this evening could have been a lot worse. She might have forced her way in, or kept me prisoner. She was so out of it she may not even have known what she was doing, and my whole body feels cold at the thought of what she might do next. I can't believe how much she's changed. Young Molly was always laughing, full of energy she couldn't contain. I barely recognise her now. My mind spirals into various fanciful scenarios, each worse than the last, but one thing is clear: Molly is not going to go away.

Richard sleeps on, and I can't stand it any longer. As I get up, my bare feet make no sound on the wooden slats of the staircase, no creaks give me away. Insomnia used to be a regular friend all those years ago, my eyes snapping open at my memories every time I tried to sleep. I spent many nights staring at the ceiling, eyelids heavy with exhaustion. Wishing I had Molly to talk to. The kettle is quiet when it boils and I take my camomile tea and laptop over to the sofa.

For years I resisted the urge to look up the actual case – our case, but tonight, just like the other night, the lure is too strong, and when the search engine opens my heart starts to beat rapidly when it lands on a recent link. It's a story by someone called Alex Foster. My heart thumps as the search loads, horrified as the page opens with the latest news on the disappearance of Emily Shaw. What has that got to do with it? I skim over the article, which blurs as I reach the words I'm looking for, unable to imagine why this page has loaded. This Alex person is writing a series on his blog covering past cases where girls have gone missing in similar circumstances. My eyes skim over cases in Bradford, Gloucester, Manchester, London, dating from the 1930s to the present day. A crime series, a different case each day, starting from the oldest and moving forward. There it is in black and white, big, bold type to make sure that nobody misses it: *The Orchid Girls*. The words pierce my skin. It's only then that I realise my hands are covering my mouth in shock. A warm hand lands on my shoulder and I jump, knocking my mug, causing tea to slop over the floor. I get up to find a cloth to wipe the mess away.

'What are you doing?' Richard is looking at the page I've left open on screen.

I breathe slowly in and out, pull down my top which is riding up my back, cold air chilling my skin.

'I couldn't sleep.'

Richard looks at Emily's photo. 'It's her, it's upset you, hasn't it? But you've never even met her, Grace.'

He mustn't have seen the Orchid Girls headline, and I breathe out slowly, relieved. I stroke my finger over my wrist, where the little purple flower used to be.

'No, but you did. I remember you talking about her. She's only a kid, so vulnerable. I can't bear to think of her out there alone, or even worse.'

'They'll find her,' he says, but he doesn't sound convinced. 'She's feisty, resourceful. She seemed a lot older than she was. We have to believe she'll be OK. It's late, come on, let's go back to bed.'

Back in bed Richard stretches out on his side, his mouth set.

'Talk to me, Grace, something's wrong, I know it is. You're so jumpy. A random missing girl can't be upsetting you like this. What is it? I've never seen you like this before.'

'It's being in the public eye. I'm finding it a strain.' The lie tastes bitter on my tongue.

'How can you say that? You're doing what you always wanted, aren't you? It's a bit late to change your mind.'

'That woman from my childhood turning up the other night unsettled me. She was a bully at school. Got me thinking about internet trolls.'

'You can't let stuff like that bother you. They're cowards with nothing better to do. Your business is doing so well it won't be long before you can hire someone to take over your social media accounts. Work hard, don't do anything to upset people and you can't go wrong.'

'People might start telling stories about me, you never know what they could make up.'

'Now you're being ridiculous. We've talked about this before and you've got nothing to hide, so don't worry.'

An image flashes into my head, a skeleton emerging from a cupboard, pointing his bony finger at me.

'Unless there's something you haven't told me?'

'No, don't be silly.' I turn a nervy giggle into a cough, easing myself out from under his arms. He rolls over onto his back.

'You know I trust you, Grace. I've never pushed you to talk about your childhood, have I? Everyone has things they want to forget. I get that. But you've always seemed so in control. If something is bothering you, maybe it's time to talk about it. You can't let your emotions affect your work. Not now, when everything's coming together.'

'That's all you care about, isn't it? How I look, how I reflect on you.'

Richard props himself up on one elbow and looks down at me. His eyes glint in the darkness, his breath so close, in and out. Seconds tick by. I've gone too far.

'You're beginning to annoy me. Everything is going well. When I saw you on TV, I was so proud of you. I thought you wanted success as much as I do.'

'Oh I do, Richard.' Thoughts reel through my head. Get to the top in my career, then children. That's my plan. I want this even more than he does.

'I hope you're not regretting falling in love with me and having to uproot to the UK.'

His voice sounds cold and tears spring into my eyes.

'Don't get emotional. You know it annoys me.'

'I don't regret it, it was my decision to come back.'

He moves so that his arms pin him above me. 'Show me how much you want me, Grace.' His voice sounds harsh.

I hug him to me, needing to feel secure, but he pushes me back against the pillow, pulling my top over my head. I can't let Richard see the vulnerable side of me. I can't show him what I'm feeling inside. I kiss him hard, sliding my hand under his waistband. I will not let Molly jeopardise what we have. I have to fight for us. I scratch my fingernails over his thigh.

'That's more like it,' he mutters into my neck, biting into my skin. 'I love you.'

I love you, too, I want to say, but he's hurting me and it takes all my energy not to cry out. What would he do to me if he knew the truth? Would he still love me? My dreams are under threat. Everything I've worked so hard to build. Everything I've tried so hard to escape. Tomorrow I'll look into booking the trip to Rome, he'll like that. But the journalist's words run on a loop through my head, unlocking a place I thought I'd secured away forever. *The Orchid Girls…* Before that, I need to deal with Molly. How can I get through to her? Making her angry is only stoking her fire. It's better to work with her, rather than against her, even if I have to fake it. I'm good at faking. My whole life is based on my ability to play a role. *The new Grace*. My heartbeat thuds along with the loud tick of the clock outside and I turn away so that Richard can't hear it.

CHAPTER TEN

MOLLY

On the way over to Janet's I call in at the chemist, who puts a dressing on my hand. It's the first thing Janet notices as I take my usual seat on the cream sofa. Everything in this room is cream, plain and bland. There's just a coffee table and box of tissues between us. No pictures on the wall, no knick-knacks to distract me.

'What's happened to your hand?'

'Accident.'

'How did it happen?'

I look behind her through the large window, watching a pigeon peck at something on the windowsill, jabbing his beak, over and over.

'I finished with Jodie. She wasn't too pleased.'

'She did that to you?' Janet stiffens, horrified. Things like this don't happen in her nice life.

'No, it was me. An accident, like I said.' I drop my head into my hands. 'I lost my job.'

Janet waits, head tilted to one side. She prefers me to talk. It winds me up. Worst is when she sits there without saying anything, eyes focused on me, as if she can drill my thoughts out. But there are some things only one person can access.

'I overslept. One time too many,' I say with a shrug. 'It's OK. Ellis said I shouldn't work in pubs.'

'Ellis?'

'The woman from the counselling centre, the one you told me to ring. I finally got in touch with them. It's taken me what, a year?'

Her mouth twitches, almost a smile. It's a game I play, trying to make Janet smile.

'I'm pleased you've reached out for help. Do you think that's it with Jodie, that you won't see her again? Apart from anything else, she's in a relationship already.'

'She's not very supportive about me stopping drinking either. But I've got to. I've done some stupid things this week.'

Janet waits for me to say more but I can't talk about going round to Grace's, all that. My cheeks feel hot and I fiddle with the tape on the dressing, deciding to stick to safe ground.

'Ellis said I shouldn't look for a new job straight away, that I should take some time to sort myself out, get in touch with my mum.'

'That's a big step. Do you think you're ready?'

My throat is dry and a wave of tiredness hits me. 'There are things that happened back home that I need to look into. If I want to sort myself out, then I don't have a choice.'

'Can you tell me about those things?'

I think of the darkness, the black mist that descends, like a leech, sucking everything out of me. The thought makes me shudder. Janet is leaning forward, elbows on her knees, watching me.

'I can help you, that's what I'm here for,' she says.

An image from a recurring dream I have floats into my mind. I am standing on the edge of the cliff, searching, hunting desperately to see if she is there. My head snaps up.

'I can't talk about it, not yet. There are some things I need to find out first.'

After leaving Janet's, I can't stand the constant chatter in my head. I try to force myself to think positive. Ellis's idea to get back into photography makes sense – I've got to distract myself. An idea is lurking at the back of my mind but I can't squeeze it out. Something to do with photographs. My phone camera will have to do.

What shall I shoot? Grace uses Instagram a lot, so I set up a new account, using a fake name – I don't want her to know it's me this time. For now she's the only person I need to follow. The urge to peep at what she is doing bites me but I control it and look up a couple of photographers whose work I like. There's a street-art account that gives me an idea. I'll go down to the canal and take some shots of the recent graffiti. Once I've made that decision I click on to Grace's blog, and the idea that wouldn't surface hits me when I'm looking at her blue eyes and flawless skin. The idea that's been lurking in my mind ever since Ellis suggested taking pictures again. Grace's blog is full of photographs that I'm sure she's taken herself with her phone. She's added a post about some cakes she's made, disgusting sugar-free cakes for skinny celebrities. The photos are OK, mostly close-ups, different angles, filters, basic stuff. Nothing original. What she needs is someone to take decent shots for her.

The idea fires me up. I pull on my hoodie and as I'm walking down to the canal, my thoughts are spinning. *Me and Grace, together all the time, just like before.* She'll be more comfortable with someone she knows, not some random man sent in to do the job. Us, together, busy in her flat, like when we used to make coconut ice in Mum's kitchen, scoffing the lot as soon as we'd made it. Pastel-pink sugar. Poking at trays with dusty white fingers. Chunks of sticky toffee in a boiling-hot kitchen. Us, together. My memories make me feel warm and glowing. And for the first time in forever, I've not thought about having a drink.

Of course, as soon as the thought about drink hits me, it's back in my head, churning. Why am I kidding myself about being Grace's photographer – she won't even talk to me. I chew some gum, bite down on the tension. No harm in taking some photos, anyway. I'll have a coffee near Grace's once I've got a few shots. I'll be near her flat, but this is different, I've got a purpose. That's what I need, a purpose.

Down by the canal the light is clear and the graffiti shines out luminous green, orange and black. Grace would hate this, but it's practice; I need to get used to taking some good shots again. While I'm leaning into different angles to get the picture I want, I work out where I can take some shots of food, something I can show her to impress her. The market is the answer, the fruit-and-veg stall, which is piled high with bright colours and different shapes. I love the smell, too; shame that can't be captured with my lens.

When I've taken enough photos of the graffiti I stop at the cafe. I jump every time the door opens in case she comes in, or even the husband, who I could follow again. A woman at the next table wearing dark red lipstick catches my eye. I play out a little fantasy in my head where I follow him and catch him stealing kisses from a different woman with red lips and Grace is grateful to me for sussing him out, realising she doesn't need him any more. I sit there for ages with my coffee going cold, making up stories in my head.

The woman beside me leaves her *Metro* newspaper on the table and I snatch it up, knocking my bandaged hand in the process. The pain brings tears to my eyes. *Fuck, it stings.* The story about the missing girl fascinates me. It's like picking a scab. Her bag has been found by a member of the public. I wonder what's in it. Could be important, I know that well enough. What Charlotte had in *her* bag started all this. Or what she *said* she had. Charlotte's bag fell with her in a flash of orange against the green grass of the cliff, and Grace said the photograph wasn't in it, but I didn't know if she was telling the truth. If she didn't have the photo then the fight needn't have happened, and I had to know if it was all for nothing. That's one of the things I wrote to Grace about, before she disappeared.

When Grace didn't reply, the not knowing was driving me mad, like bees in my brain, buzzing and bothering me, so I went round to Charlotte's house. We'd been acquitted by then. Her mum was all drugged up, held me so close her heartbeat sounded hard and fast in my ear like a drum and I had to pull away, I couldn't bear her pain. While she made orange squash that had way too much cordial in it, I nipped to the loo but on the way went into Charlotte's room. It was exactly as it was when I was last there, while Grace and Jason went next door doing things to each other I didn't want to think about and I dug my fingernails into my thighs. Remembering makes me feel sick. Charlotte's bag was folded on the floor like she'd only popped out, as if deliberately left there by Mrs Greene, who wanted to forget the bag had been dusted and tested and God knows what else the police did to it after it was found on the beach. Obviously the photograph wasn't there but I knew Charlotte's hiding place. She'd shown me it herself. A different photo, the one she'd sneaked of Mr Owen, our chemistry teacher and her major forbidden crush, was slid into the frame behind the picture of her nan and grandad on the dressing table in her bedroom. I moved her CK One perfume aside and slid the photo out of the frame, hands shaking so much that I cut my finger on the sharp edge and blood beaded onto it. One-handed, I pulled out the photo while I sucked the blood from my finger. I was right. There it was. But it wasn't a photo of Mr Owen any more. It was of me and Grace. The one Charlotte threatened us with. Seeing it made my breath disappear, made me stand still for so long that Mrs Greene called up the stairs. I shoved the photo in my pocket before I bolted back down as if Grace's dad was running after me.

*

It's cold outside and the wind beats against my top – I wish I'd put my parka on. But the food market is only on today and if I want to get some good pictures I have to head down there now.

My mate Danny's on the fruit stall.

'Hey, Molly. What are you doing here? Not after fruit, are you?'

'Nah. You know me, Dan. More of a burger girl. Do you mind if I take some photos of your stall, though?'

'Go ahead. I didn't know you were into photography.'

'Yeah, I used to be. Thought I might take it up again. Do something different.'

The veg is a happy splash of greens and reds, deep purple aubergines and bright orange carrots. I forget about everything while I'm snapping away and I get some good shots. Danny gives me a paper bag full of ripe bananas and sweet-smelling apples and I kiss his bristly cheek, making him blush.

Back home I upload the photos onto my laptop and it's not until I've finished and my stomach is rumbling that my mind strays to having a drink. An ice-cold lager to soothe my throat. Jodie would bring some round, but we're finished and I have to be strong. I pace around the flat, remembering Ellis's advice.

No. No Jodie and no drink. Ellis doesn't answer her phone, so I recall what she said earlier: keep busy. I know she wouldn't approve of the amount of time I spend thinking about Grace. She suggested I take up running and from her Instagram I know that Grace runs. It will give me more in common with her. Never mind that I don't have any fancy gear like she does, shiny white trainers from Lululemon, Lycra clothes that glow in the dark and fancy water bottles. My old Converse will have to do, and I dig out a faded Adidas sweatshirt – designer labels Molly-style.

Street lights cast a glow on the pavement, showing me where to put my feet. I start small, aim for the corner of the road but I only make it as far as the lamp post before I'm doubled over, unable to stop coughing, lungs on fire. I can't remember the last time I tried to run. Not since the muddy field at school, our butch PE teacher shouting at girls who lagged behind, but not me. Not back then. Bitchy girls mocking others, making jokes to a student about her girlfriend, making me feel uncomfortable and not understanding why. A stitch digs in my side but I won't give up. I run for a few steps, walk a few more and it's not long before I'm at the path that leads to the canal. I tell myself it doesn't matter that it's the second time today I've been here.

I look up. There's a light on on Grace's balcony. A figure steps out of the shadows. It's her. I stand behind some trees and pull my phone out of my pocket. The phone camera isn't great in the dark, but these aren't for show, they're for me. A flash and Grace's face appears as she lights a cigarette. Why is Grace smoking? I bet the husband doesn't know about that. Blowing dirty clouds into the air. Polluting her body. Smoking was one of our special things we did together. Sneaking out into the garden after dinner, lighting up behind the shed, taking it in turns to keep watch. Maybe all this clean living is down to him and she can't wait to break free.

She leans forward and looks down into the water. My stomach lurches. What can she see? A woman's body was pulled from the canal only a week ago, her secrets submerged under the water. That was before that girl Emily went missing, otherwise they might have thought it was her. Maybe Emily is still submerged deep under the pool of black, waiting to appear and shatter the dreams of her loved ones. They said it was the sea that took Charlotte in the end. Overnight the tide came in, picked her broken body up in the wild waves then threw it back again. Imagining the rough sea makes me shiver – I haven't been in since that day, and I used to love swimming. How can Grace bear to live here? Why doesn't it freak her out like it does me? Time to get over it, and fast, if I want to be near her.

But I'm beginning to doubt everything. More than ever the need to talk to Grace, to find out the truth, burns inside me. Only she can tell me what really happened. As if Grace can read my thoughts, she lifts her arm and hurls the cigarette butt over the canal, a tiny glow in the dark flitting through the air. I blink and it's gone, swallowed by the water.

'*I'll make you talk,*' I whisper.

On the way home I receive a text from an unknown number.

So why do they call you OrchidGirl?

The words steal my breath from me. I look around as if the sender is behind me, but the black water of the canal gives nothing away. Could it be Grace, trying to play me at my own game? But no, Grace is afraid of history catching up with her, exploding her life apart, exposing who she really is. She's made that clear. Someone else wants me to talk, and I wonder what I've set in motion. Footsteps break into the silence and a man approaches. I glare at him as he passes, standing still and listening until his steps fade into nothing. Then I run, feet flying, chest bursting. Running like I ran home from school, away from Charlotte and Belinda, thinking that if I ran fast enough I could escape their threats, make them stop. But they were stuck in my head like a noisy clock, ticking down the seconds until they found me again.

I need to do more. I'm not getting Grace's attention. I've had another idea for using my photos, let her see how I won't stop until she responds. Because we're meant to be together – she just hasn't realised it yet.

CHARLOTTE'S DIARY

Grace has been all apologetic and swears she'd had too much cider and she isn't interested in Jason, but I don't trust her. I don't want to hang around with her any more but it's the only way I can keep an eye on her. If I find out she's been tricking me, there'll be trouble. And there's something weird going on with her and Molly. Ever since the beach party I've been watching them.

Belinda rang this evening THANK GOD, and I rang her back so we could talk and talk. Mum will go mad when the phone bill comes, but so what. I told her about everything and she said Grace sounds like a right bitch and not to trust her. She couldn't believe it about Molly. I told her how she's different now, confident, like she doesn't care. Besides, we're never gonna be bessie mates, and it's only for a couple of weeks. After I got off the phone I felt bad again about what we did to Molly. Bel goes mad if I bring it up – she's totally over it, says it was an accident. She's right, it wasn't as if we'd meant it to happen. And Molly started it. We'd arranged to meet her in the park after school so she could give us the make-up we'd made her promise to get us. She said she hadn't got any money so Belinda told her to nick it from Woolworths – everyone was doing it back then. So when she turned up and emptied her pockets, we couldn't believe it. Talk about a stash. Belinda nudged me with her bony elbow and I know she was thinking we were on to something and could place orders. But Molly wouldn't hand it over, said we had to promise to leave her alone first. Belinda said 'yeah, ok' but the minute she took it off Molly she told her she wanted more and reminded her of the time Molly refused to give her the fiver she'd asked for, so she pushed her head down the toilet. Belinda was drinking Pepsi through a straw and made a loud sucking noise. Molly's neck and face were flaming red like her nasty hair and she suddenly lunged forward to grab the stuff back off Belinda. Bel screamed and they did a tug of war with the bag and Molly fell onto Belinda, the Pepsi bottle smashed on the floor and Molly fell on top of it. Her arm started bleeding. It was an accident. But she never told on us and we left her alone after that. A month later, she moved schools. I didn't expect to ever see her again.

CHAPTER ELEVEN
GRACE

'You seemed a bit overwhelmed at the book launch, which isn't like you. I thought it went well. Was everything OK?' Carrie sips at her cocktail, a pale pink concoction of vodka and raspberries. Her long nails match the colour of her drink, shining under the light as she takes a selfie, pouting.

My cocktail is green and tastes of apples. The tang of gin is an unusual treat; I've been persuaded by Carrie that this is a celebration. But my nerves are too taut to feel like celebrating. Everywhere I look I see red hair, staring eyes.

She leans back in the comfy chair, smooths her suit skirt over her knees, stirring the pink crystals of ice in her glass. 'Is it the baby thing again?'

I seize on her words as the excuse I need, nodding. Richard won't mention it unless I bring it up, and I remember how reluctant he was to talk about it on the last occasion.

'He isn't going to change his mind, you know what's he's like. His life is planned out for the next five years at least, and so is mine. A baby doesn't fit into that scenario. Maybe if he loses the election he'll have a rethink, but I don't want that.' I suck some ice into my mouth, welcoming the chill in my throat. 'And I should be grateful to him for driving my career; the launch the other night was proof of how well I'm doing.' I remember my excitement at the recent photo shoot, how that enthusiasm evades me now. 'He's so busy, I've got no right to pressurise him. It's what we agreed, after all.' I crunch the ice between my teeth, feeling emotional. I want more than anything to have a baby, but usually I manage to suppress these thoughts; maybe Molly's appearance is playing with my emotions.

'Jean was talking to me about that missing girl at the launch, how they all know her. I didn't realise she had done work experience with Richard. That can't help – it must be tough for him. I wondered if that was upsetting you too.'

I hide my expression in my glass, letting the drink go down slowly, shrugging my shoulders.

'It is upsetting, and having Richard's parents involved makes it even more real.' An image of the girl's face flashes into my mind, her disconcerting likeness to Charlotte, and a wave of anxiety hits me again. *Why are we talking about this?*

Carrie looks concerned and I feel a pang of gratefulness towards her. Getting close to another woman hasn't been easy for me since I severed ties with Molly, and keeping things from Carrie is the way it has to be. The thought doesn't help assuage the guilt, and I try to swallow down my anxiety with a long sip of my cocktail.

'Enough of me. Tell me about your new man,' I say, changing the subject. Carrie's face lights up with a wicked grin and I can't help smiling back; her excitement is infectious.

'Second date this weekend. He's taking me to that new French restaurant in Mayfair. I'm booked in at the salon on Saturday for the full works.' She sips through her straw, tapping her nails on the glass. 'You're so lucky, Grace, married and settled. Dating is so traumatic.'

She's right. I've got Richard, the most important person in my life, and I have no intention of losing him. Last night flashes into my head, the sex that was rougher than usual, Richard's rigid jaw as he held me down. Passion, that's what it was. I push my doubts, Molly's reappearance and babies to the back of my mind. So far

I've dealt with every obstacle in my path. There's no reason this should be any different.

Molly sends me a photograph early the next morning, when I am restless and unable to sleep. It makes my heart drum loud in my chest, and affirms my resolve to meet with her, put a stop to this. My nerves can't stand it. It's a murky shot, light from the flat illuminating me from behind against the purple night sky. I hold my phone low down over the floor, so that the light doesn't wake Richard, who sleeps sprawled on his back, snoring occasionally.

Sleep must have claimed me eventually, a deep, dreamless sleep, because Richard has left when I next wake. The face staring back at me from the bathroom mirror looks different and it scares me. Despite my attempts to forget my past with Carrie last night, the features of the girl I thought I'd left buried in Paris are returning. I put thicker foundation on and attempt to cake over her fierce expression, but her eyes blaze back at me. *I won't have those feelings again. I won't let myself.*

I slide a pod into the coffee machine, watch the dark drips fall into the cup, drink it black. Bitter. Espresso became her drink of choice in Paris, the new Grace. *Me*, I remind myself. Molly would never have found me in France. There I was in control, confident.

Richard has changed since we returned from Paris. It began when I moved to live with him in England. Roles were reversed; in France I was on my home territory, I was the tour guide, the one who knew which restaurants to eat at, which cocktail bars to drink at, where to party. He was the one who needed help with the language and sharing my knowledge was fun. I felt in control. But that version of me is no longer required. Now he has a team around him catering to his needs, responding to his whims, at his beck and call. So different to the first time I met him in my favourite cafe, looking out on the wide Parisian boulevard, the smell of tobacco in the air, eating a flaky croissant, my attention caught by the man sitting outside with a copy of *Le Parisien* newspaper. His thick, dark hair fell over his face as he read, and every now and then he'd put the paper down and look around. He caught me watching him and I held his gaze for a moment, felt a flutter in my pulse. He sent the waiter to invite me to join him for a coffee and when he asked me out for dinner the following night I accepted, despite my resolution not to give into my emotions ever again. I told myself that he was a man this time and he was special.

Sometimes I wish it could be different, the two of us back together in France. But it can't be.

The caffeine does its job and I fire off a text to Molly asking her to meet. The sooner I get it over with, the sooner I can get back to my real life. I'm hoping to see her later this afternoon, when I should be at a meeting that I only remembered last night and for which I'm not ready. I'm letting things slip.

Richard would go mad if he knew – he arranged the meeting and I can't mess it up. Simon Farrer is the best designer around; I know what a huge deal this is. I can't believe I've let Molly get to me so much I'd forgotten about it. A few hours' work should be enough to finalise my first product: 'Grace's Cereals, Exclusive to Harrods'. I can visualise the subtle wheat-coloured boxes with sophisticated, striking yellow-and-gold lettering. but I need to get the details down. I need more time. A phone call will make a better impression than an email.

Simon sounds as if he's on the move when he picks up my call, blowing sharp breaths into the phone. It's the first time I've spoken to him. I explain, feeling ashamed, that I'd like to postpone the meeting.

He sucks his breath in.

'My schedule is pretty tight, let's see. I can squeeze you in tomorrow afternoon. After that I'm in New York until the end of the month.'

'Tomorrow is perfect, thanks so much. And I look forward to meeting you.'

I take a deep, calming breath when I put the phone down, tension eased. Richard doesn't need to know I've postponed it. Unprofessional, that's what he'd think. But Simon didn't mind and I'll be ready tomorrow. Imagining my product range in shops usually fires me up, but today my thoughts won't focus. I could look at the prices of Rome flights for our surprise getaway, but I daren't book anything while this is hanging over me. Every few seconds I pick my phone up, check for messages. Nothing from Molly yet. I expected her to reply immediately. My head throbs. *Is this all a game to her?* After feeling like I've been waiting forever, my phone beeps. It's her. Of course she wants to meet, what was I thinking? For a moment I allow myself to think back, to remember the turmoil I felt when we saw each other for the last time, not knowing we wouldn't see one another again. Until now. The phone buzzes and I snap out of my reverie, furious that I'm indulging myself. That's the old Grace. That isn't who I am any more.

I make sure to get there first. I tap my foot against the table leg as I wait, planning it all out – I want to get this right. Molly brings a gust of wind in with her which ruffles my hair, and I pat it back into place. Her face is flushed, as if she's been hurrying. The adult version of Molly is becoming familiar to me, the lines drawn on her thin face, the freckles forming clumps over her nose. She looks down at me, hands in the pockets of a creased-up parka, fiddling with something. She used to collect stones to photograph from the beach, loading up her pockets and hiding them from her mum who went mad if she found them in the house. Her dad didn't mind, he let her stash them in his shed. One of hundreds of memories I have of Molly. The memories I've tried so hard to forget.

Molly hunches over a mug of tea and warms her fingers on the outside, still wearing her parka over a scruffy pair of jeans. She blows down onto the steaming tea. She hasn't looked at me yet. Her red hair no longer looks natural; the scarlet dye is harsh and cheap.

'Hello, Gracie,' she says.

'Don't call me that.' That name doesn't belong to me any more.

'I shouldn't have come to your place,' she says, dragging her hair away from her face. '*Grace*.'

'You scared me, Molly.'

'Do you know how hard it was to find you?'

'That was the idea.'

'It drove me mad, wondering where you were.' Her tired eyes look like those of a hurt animal. 'I'm just trying to get through to you. I'm sorry for following you about, but I had to make you talk to me.'

'Why? Let's leave the past alone. I've made a new life for myself. Why can't you do the same, move on?'

Something is different about Molly this time. She's calmer. Sober, I realise.

Her hurt eyes fix on mine and I look away.

'How comes you're so normal?'

'I don't know what you mean.'

'This is so weird. Seeing you, after all this time. After what happened. Look at you, with your smart clothes, your fancy job and husband. That wasn't what you used to want. Even your accent sounds different.'

'It was a long time ago, Molly. People change.'

'I haven't. That's why I had to see you. I'm pushing thirty, and it's time I sorted my life out. The only way out is to talk to someone.'

My breath catches. 'Don't you remember the promise we made?'

'Don't worry, I've kept my promise. But I'm not sure I can keep it for much longer. I need to talk.'

My throat tightens, but I keep my face composed. 'Is it money you want?'

She looks upset. 'I don't want your money. How could you ask that? I just want to get my shit together.'

'I don't understand why you can't.'

'I felt responsible, I wanted to know what happened to Charlotte…'

'Christ, Molly, you know what happened.' The woman at the next table looks over and I lower my voice, leaning towards her so that Molly alone can hear my words. 'You have to stop this.'

'How can you be so cold? Don't you have feelings any more?'

My tense shoulders feel as if a steel rod is holding them up.

'Of course I do. But bad things happen all the time, that's life.'

Molly sighs. 'Until I sort this out in my head then I can't move on.'

I lean forward, lower my voice.

'Look, you couldn't find me because I was sent away. Michael sent me away.'

She raises an eyebrow. 'Michael?'

'He doesn't deserve to be called Dad after what he did to me. He wouldn't let me contact you. I was sent to live with my aunt in France. I didn't want to go. But I took her name, started my life again. There's no reason you can't do the same.'

'So that's why you didn't get my letters?'

'I suppose it must be, yes.'

'You were everything to me, Grace.'

'We were young. Stop being melodramatic.'

Molly doesn't like that, purses her mouth up, glares at me. This isn't going to work. I'm itching to leave, but I need to ask her before I go. I need to ask the question that's been on my mind. My pulse speeds up just thinking about it.

'You said you had something on me, you mentioned Charlotte's bag.'

'Didn't like that, did you?'

'Are you talking about what I think you are?'

'Might be.'

'This isn't a game, Molly. Why are you doing this?'

'You know why.'

She looks into my eyes and for a moment we are swept back to before, when no one else existed. When it was just the two of us. It takes me by surprise and I look away.

'I've got nothing to lose.' She takes a sip of her tea.

'But I have. If you still cared about me you wouldn't do this. Apart from anything else Richard's reputation is so crucial right now. His public image is everything to him.'

'Who cares about him? I don't get it, anyway. Why have you chosen such a public life? After everything that happened?'

'I can do whatever I choose with my life, and so can you. I'm proud of my business and rightly so. I'm not the same person any more, Molly, you have to understand that.'

My hands are clenched tightly in my lap. Aunt Jenny warned me at the time, said I was taking a huge risk, coming back to England and leading such a public life. But I'd been so relieved to have fallen in love, and with such an ideal man, I'd have done anything for him.

'If it wasn't for Richard, I would never have come back to England. Sometimes life takes you by surprise. I asked you to destroy the camera. You did, didn't you?'

She nods.

I want to believe her, I have to.

'But somebody else is on to us.'

'What do you mean?'

'I got this text last night.' Molly's fingertips dart over her phone. They're chewed down, look sore. She gives me the phone, and when I see what's written, I thrust it back at her as if it's scalding my fingers.

'Who sent you this?'

'I thought you might have.'

'Don't be stupid. Show me the number.'

The number is unfamiliar, as I guessed it would be. I put my hands out of sight so that she doesn't see they are trembling. I need space to think, and I can't while Molly is with me, unsettling me, clouding my thoughts, reminding me of too much I'd rather forget. The message fades from the screen and my photo appears. She's got me as her backdrop. My trembling increases. *What is going on here? Has she made the text up to mess with my head?*

For a moment we stare at one another, then the cafe door opens and a group of women come in, noisy, laughing. I stand up.

'You're a mess, Molly. Don't you dare drag me into it. You're making this up to get me rattled and it isn't working. How you live your life has nothing to do with me. You might not care about my husband but he cares about what happens to me. We know a lot of people, so I'd have a good think before you do anything stupid.' I take a twenty-pound note from my leather handbag, put it down on the table in front of me, snapping the clasp shut.

'Buy yourself another drink. This should cover it. But leave me alone, I mean it.' I don't look back as I walk out.

Later that evening Richard dozes beside me and I'm scrolling through my emails, unable to concentrate. He'd been buoyant when he came home, buzzing with more ideas for me. He'd even cooked, despite the shadows forming under his eyes. When he took me in his arms and kissed me passionately, his pride for me was evident.

I open Molly's message again, enlarging the photo she sent of me on the balcony. Was I right to threaten her? How will I know she's stopped pursuing me? The thought that she could be out there now, watching me, makes me shiver. She said she'd destroyed the camera, but what about the photos we took together? I should have made her be more specific.

Richard opens his eyes and there's no time to close the screen. He looks at the photograph.

'Is that you?'

I go to fob him off, then stop. Maybe involving him will help. It could help to talk about it.

'It was sent to me this morning. Remember that woman, the one from school who turned up at the book launch? Molly, her name is.'

'Why did she send it to you?' He pulls the laptop onto his lap, enlarges the photo. 'It's creepy. It was obviously taken in the evening. What's she doing, hanging around out there? Should we be worried about this?'

'I don't think so. She's seen who I am, who you are, and she wants to know me now I'm a celebrity. I'm hoping if I ignore her, she'll soon get bored.'

He narrows his eyes. 'Let's hope she does.'

I nod, willing him to believe me. His moods can change so quickly.

He stretches. 'How was your meeting? I can't believe I forgot.'

'What meeting?'

Richard looks at me as if I'm a complete idiot.

'The branding meeting with Simon?'

I concentrate on my nails, hoping the look I flick him is convincing. 'It's tomorrow.'

'I could have sworn it was today.'

'He postponed it. More time for me to work on my designs.'

'But you're ready, aren't you?'

'Of course, I can't wait to get my products out there. Having my own range is what I've been working towards. Shall I make some tea?'

As I fuss about, filling the kettle, I hope I've done the right thing telling him. Maybe I shouldn't have lost it with Molly, but now I can say that Richard knows about her and she'll have to leave me alone. As I'm pouring water over the loose tea leaves, I remember the anonymous text Molly mentioned and my hand jolts. *What if it's genuine?* If it is, it's more imperative than ever that I stay away from her. I can't stop thinking about Aunt Jenny's response when I told her I was moving back.

'You'll regret it,' she said. For the first time since my return I'm wondering whether she might have been right.

CHAPTER TWELVE

MOLLY

Grace didn't get my letters. She's telling the truth. She went to France, that's why the letters never reached her and why it was impossible to find her. It did my head in, looking and wondering and worrying. It's her dad's fault, sending her away, no surprises there. But there's still so much we haven't talked about, so much I want to know. She threatened me as she left the other day, but she didn't mean it, not if she thinks about it. She said it in the heat of the moment, that's all. Otherwise she's making a big mistake. Because I kept it for a reason. Let her believe I destroyed it – for now. The time will come to hit her with it. Despite what Grace said, she might call, so I daren't turn my phone off and I switch it to silent instead.

The curtain flutters as I walk up my front path and I know Mrs Bird is snooping. Her door creaks and her face is hidden by a huge bunch of flowers, a mass of bright orange roses. They must have come while I was out signing on. I hate roses; Charlotte's front garden was full of them the last time Mum made me go round there.

'These came for you, dear.' The surprise on her face is mirrored in mine. 'A woman delivered them, a friend of yours.'

My pulse quickens, but they can't be from Grace. She doesn't know where I live.

'The one with the motorbike?' She comes out into the tiny hall.

Jodie. My heart drops. Mrs Bird's voice lilts upwards in a question and I know she wants me to talk about this friend. I've seen her watching Jodie, wondering. But I won't.

'Cheers.' I'm about to go upstairs when I notice the peeling wallpaper, yellow patches and grime where time has left its mark – I don't want Grace here in her smart clothes and fancy attitude. I can be better for her. I have to be. Then the doorbell stops me. Mrs Bird shuffles back along the carpet, voices follow and Jodie appears. This time she's not coming in. The flowers are still in my arms as I push past Mrs Bird and close the door behind me.

'Your favourite colour.'

Jodie sits on the garden wall; I stay standing. Water drips from the stems of the flowers over my arm and onto the floor.

'Why aren't you listening to me? I told you we're finished.'

A truck trundles by, filling the street with a rattling noise and Jodie looms across the path of the sun casting darkness over me.

'I've been doing some research on Grace Sutherland.'

'Leave it, Jodie.' I try to swallow, but my throat is too dry.

'Or what? Look, I've met this guy who's interested in talking to you.'

'What guy?'

'He's a journalist, writes for the *Sun*. I got chatting to him in the pub and he gave me his card.'

I stand up so she can't see the alarm on my face and I move away from her. 'I'm not interested.' The downstairs curtain twitches. 'Leave me alone, Jodie, I mean it. If you don't, I'll tell Frances all about us.'

Her face darkens and we stare at each other before she turns and jumps on her bike. The tyres screech as she disappears off down the road.

A thorn in the stem of one of the flowers digs into my hand as I throw them into the street bin. Blood beads on my palm. I smudge it away but it reappears a second later.

*

Cold water washes the blood away but I stand and stare at the plughole for ages, waiting for my pulse to return to normal. I'm trying to ignore the voice telling me that a drink would make me feel better, help me to forget Jodie and all her shit. Ellis has told me to ring her any day, any time, so I dial her number, rapping my fingers against the wall, willing her to answer, telling myself she won't pick up. I'll be getting on her nerves, big time. But she doesn't show it when she answers. Instead, she suggests I meet her in the park.

Ellis is sitting on a bench in Finsbury Park, watching a man struggling to control his dog. She's just finished a run, and she tells me she comes here most mornings before she goes back home to work. Freelance, she is. That would suit me, and I wonder again if it would be possible to be a photographer without a boss, setting my own rules.

'Hey Molly, what's up?' she greets me.

'You know I finished with Jodie the other night? She just turned up at my flat. Flowers and everything.'

Ellis is giving me her full attention, unlike Jodie, who is always looking over my shoulder to see what else is going on.

'Does she want to get back with you?'

'It's not that. Do you know Grace Sutherland? The food blogger?'

'Not the Queen of Clean?'

'What?'

'That's what she's known as.'

That fits. I didn't used to recognise my bedroom when she was sharing it, folded clothes, smoothed-down bed covers, make-up lined up on the dressing table.

'I love her recipes,' Ellis says, 'but I don't believe her image. People like that are always too good to be true. She'll be indulging her secret passion for cream cakes at home.' She laughs, a glorious chuckle.

I picture Grace cutting food in her precise way. 'I doubt it. She's a friend from a long time ago. I reconnected with her.'

'Facebook?'

I nod, it's less hassle to lie.

'What's she got to do with Jodie?'

'We went through a lot together, me and Grace. Stuff I still need to sort out, that she might be able to help with. It was an intense time. You know how teenagers are. What you were saying about getting rid of all the baggage – well, Grace is one bloody huge suitcase. I'm such an idiot, I told Jodie about knowing Grace. I knew I shouldn't have. She's been talking to this journalist, reckons he thinks I have a story to tell. I bet I know what kind of story he wants.'

'Like?'

'Some made-up sleaze, no doubt – you know, how she bullied me at school, that kind of shit, which she didn't, by the way. I'm sorry to dump all this on you. You said to ring any time and I didn't know what else to do. Stuff like this makes me want to drink.' I place my head in my hands.

'I said any time, and I meant it. I'd much rather you call me than have a drink. But are you sure there's nothing more to it? Are you in some kind of trouble?'

'No, nothing like that.'

'Were you and Grace together? Is that what she means? Some kind of lesbian kiss-and-tell? Or is there something else?'

I shake my head, my cheeks hot. 'Don't look at me like that. I know what you're thinking, a scruff bag like me. How does that fit with Miss Super Healthy? She's married, moved on.' I look away, letting her work it out.

'I don't see you like that, Molly. And Jodie can't make you do anything, you've finished with her now. Ignore her, she'll go away.'

I'm not so sure.

'Do you know what kind of journalist she's spoken to, who they work for? Are you sure there isn't something you've told her to make her think there's a story?'

'No, nothing.'

'Then leave it in the past, Molly. But if there is anything, you can trust me, you know.'

'I know.' *But I don't know if I can.* 'You must think I'm a nightmare.'

'I've seen worse, believe me. The last woman I was helping had a relapse and ended up in Amsterdam. Had no idea how she'd got there.'

'Seriously?'

'Sure. She went into blackout. You must know about those?'

'Don't. Story of my life.'

Shame colours my cheeks. So many missed evenings. Banned from the local club for being abusive to a woman I don't even remember meeting. Jodie reckons I hit her once, but she must be messing with my memory, surely that can't be true. I tell myself that's not me any more. I don't want it to be.

The man yanks at his stubborn dog, who leaves whatever he's sniffing and follows him out of the park. Ellis grins as she watches.

'That would have made a good photo, don't you think? Try and keep yourself busy, get your camera out, maybe think about a project. Come round to my flat tomorrow evening, I'll make you something to eat.'

I don't know what to say.

'You OK?'

I swallow hard.

'I'm not used to nice people asking me to do things.'

'Only because you don't give them the chance. I'm persistent. If you're serious about photography, I can help you set up a website to display your work.'

'Really? That would be great. But what about your own work?'

'It's fine, I haven't got much on at the moment.' Ellis gets to her feet. 'Come on. I'll buy you an ice cream. Photography will give you a focus. Keep you away from Jodie and old friends with baggage. You're not drinking, and that's the most important thing. You just need to focus on that.'

Despite Ellis's reassurances, Jodie's words about the journalist whirl round and round in my mind. I go online but Grace hasn't posted anything yet today. Annoying. A link flickers to the right with today's news headlines. The missing girl is still one of the top stories and I can't help myself from clicking on it.

The search continues in Ash Fenton today, home to missing teenager Emily Shaw. The last known sighting of Emily was on Wednesday at Drake's Common with two school friends, who left her in town at around one o'clock. Anyone who may have seen her is asked to come forward and speak to the police. MP for Fenton North constituency, Richard Sutherland, today appealed for witnesses to come forward.

I wasn't expecting that. There's a link to a clip of him talking to a news reporter and I click on it. I zoom in on his face, trying to see what it is that attracts Grace. Handsome face, good teeth, and he's fit-looking – with his money I bet he's got a personal trainer – but his eyes lack warmth and the photograph makes him look arrogant in his designer suit. I zoom out, not liking the twisting jealousy he awakens in me. Takes me back to when Grace was with Jason.

That time at the Burger Palace when he couldn't take his eyes off Grace, and she leant in closer to him and made him laugh. Even though I knew she was only doing it to wind Charlotte up, it made me want to scream, to slap his ugly face away from her. Charlotte was watching me and the look of recognition on her face made me realise I had to be more careful. I smirked at her and she turned to Jason, her mouth set in a pout.

I try to push those thoughts aside. I can't believe that this Emily girl comes from the same place where Richard works. I bet Grace feels uncomfortable about that. Just reading about the case brings back memories that loom like tombstones in my mind.

The next morning I'm awake early, but my head's clear. I believe Grace when she said she never received my letters. It makes sense. But would Michael still have them? I don't want to see him again, but if he's got them I want them back. I tell myself I'm not scared of him any more. There's nothing he can do to me. It takes me twenty minutes to locate the only sheltered housing in Ash Fenton. I wonder when he relocated from Dorset. I'm struck by an image of him in a deckchair on the beach, fully clothed, with only his ankles exposed. I never saw him relax.

When I arrive, it's not bad-looking, not what I expected sheltered housing to be like. A row of identical bungalows. It's in better nick than where I live; the crumbling old Victorian house that looks as if it's going to fall down every time the fat bloke from upstairs leans against the wall for a smoke.

I ring the doorbell. The woman who answers the door tells me her name is Angela and that she's Michael's full-time carer.

'How is he?' I ask, wondering what's wrong with him. 'I haven't seen him for a while.'

Angela talks as we make our way to his room. 'His emphysema has been worse lately. He's been admitted to hospital twice this year already, it makes him very weak.' She knocks on the door. 'Michael, you've got a visitor.'

I'm led into a room lined with books, and there's a framed photo of a crucifix on the wall. I look down at the frail old man in front of me. It's the first time I've seen him without his collar. Watery eyes look out from a lined, parchment face, wary.

'Charlotte?'

His words hit me like shock. I'm unable to move. He can't think I'm Charlotte.

'No, it's your niece, Molly,' Angela says.

Michael looks away, staring at the view of the back garden. Angela fusses around the table beside the bed, straightening a photograph of him wearing his robes with his ever-serious expression.

'You haven't seen her for a while.' She touches my shoulder and I move to the side. 'I'll leave you to it,' she says. 'I'm next door if you need me. And you should know his memory isn't what it was, he gets a bit confused.' She bustles out of the room.

For a moment I'm unable to move. I can't get over how different he looks. He seems to have shrunk. To think he used to frighten me.

Michael is looking at me, unsure.

'It's me, Molly.' I shuffle the armchair over towards him as I sit down. 'Grace's friend from Lyme Regis.' He doesn't react so I scrabble around in the front pocket of my bag, pulling out an old photograph of us sitting on the wall – Grace and I squinting into the sun. The spots on Michael's hands are like inkblots, dark and irregular, but his hands are steady as he peers at the photograph. 'Do you remember? This was taken outside your house, we'd been at the beach.' He brings the photo closer to his face.

'I know who you are. You shouldn't have come. What are you doing here?'

'I wrote to Grace back then. I wrote hundreds of times. She says she didn't get my letters. What happened to them?'

'You weren't supposed to get in touch. We told you not to. We stopped her from reading them. Didn't even open them. I know what you were up to.' He sneers over his glasses.

Anger ripples through me. 'What did you do with them?'

'Why wouldn't you leave it alone? Do you know how upset her mother was? Do you know how much she suffered?'

'What did you do with my letters?' *Answer me.*

'Under my guidance Grace was able to move on. Letters from you would have kept her stuck in the past. We prayed together and she soon saw the error in her ways. God sees everything. I sent her away to rebuild her life.'

'We weren't doing anything wrong.'

'You sinned in the eyes of the Church, no matter what they tell you these days. Leading my daughter astray. All this modern liberal claptrap. Anything goes, it's wrong. Why have you come here? Grace is married now. Stay away from her.'

Michael spits the words out, saliva spraying at me. I move backward, shocked by the hateful look in his eyes. The old fear I used to feel in his presence returns. I had no idea that he knew. *The bastard.* But I remind myself he's ill, that he can't hurt me now.

'Shocked you, haven't I? Want to know how I knew what you were up to? She told me. Big mistake. I warned her what would happen if she wouldn't keep quiet.'

My mouth falls open at his revelation. *Why would Grace tell him about us? Is that why he sent her away?* The look on his face scares me, and I'm twelve all over again and he's shouting at me for losing my temper and I'm clenching my fists behind my back. It's time to get out of here. I reach my hand out to take the photo but his claw-like fingers are gripping it with a strength that surprises me.

'They've found her, you know, her picture is in the paper.' His voice is louder and his breathing becomes erratic. 'I told her not to say anything but she refused to shut up.'

What is he talking about?

Angela appears in the doorway.

'Is everything alright?' She leans over Michael, loosens his shirt. The photograph flutters to the floor and I snatch it up. Angela's face and neck are pink and patchy. 'What's that?'

'Nothing.' I cover the photograph with my hand and slide it into my back pocket. Michael's breath comes out in gasps, but he is quieter.

'I think you'd better go,' Angela says. 'I'll get you some tea, Michael,' her voice is loud and she touches his shoulder. 'Would you mind waiting outside a moment while I get him settled?'

The soft carpet swallows my footsteps and within less than a minute I'm outside, walking as fast as I can away from the bungalow, my feet pounding in frustration. So it's true he sent her away. Grace wasn't lying. But he didn't say whether he'd kept the letters, and I can't go back now. His comments about Grace and I circle round in my head. He knew about us? She told him? My boots feel heavy as I stomp through the park, kicking at piles of muddy leaves. Why didn't she warn me? Or did it happen after she'd moved? She used to share everything with me. Even after all these years, it hurts that we aren't close.

I think back to what just happened. When he got all confused, talking about a photo in the paper. What photo? And what did he mean about Charlotte?

How can I get Grace back on my side? She's got to help me understand.

CHARLOTTE'S DIARY

I knew Molly and Grace were up to something and today I found out what. Belinda will die when I tell her. Since the party I've been going to the beach on my own. Jason still flirts with me so he can't be that into Grace really. He was probably drunk. When I tell him what I found out today, he'll see what a slag she is. This afternoon the sun went in and when Grace and Molly left the beach I followed them to Molly's uncle's cottage. I waited a while and then went round the back. Through the windows I could see photographs laid out on the table, with cameras and equipment and a tripod thing in the corner. The curtains were drawn across the next room and I could hear giggling. I peered through a gap and nearly fell over when I saw what they were doing. Grace was lying on the sofa, stretching her tanned legs across the seat. Molly came in with two glasses of what looked like lemonade and I moved back fast, but she was totally focused on Grace, not seeing me. She put the drinks down on the table and Grace pulled Molly down on top of her. She slid Molly's vest strap down and I couldn't look any more. Now I know for sure. What I need next is proof. Jason will be so grateful to me.

On the way back the sun came out and I was walking so fast to get away, it made me feel sick. Grace's dad needs to know about this. He's already made clear what he thinks about that kind of thing, she'd be in so much trouble. That would pay her back. All I need is to wait for the right moment.

CHAPTER THIRTEEN

GRACE

Running water wakes me. Richard's in the shower and I stretch my arms out, groaning when I see how early it is. Since his decision to stand as London Mayor, lie-ins are a distant memory. As soon as my eyes flick open, thoughts crowd in. *Molly, Charlotte, the photo.* But at least Richard knows – it's dealt with. For now.

'What time are you back tonight, honey?' I ask as he steps out from the en suite, a pale blue towel slung around his defined waist. My gorgeous husband stands in front of me, yet it's Molly who's on my mind. Thoughts of her don't belong in my life now, and I try to ignore them, noticing that the tan he picked up in Croatia four months ago has completely faded. Holidays have also been put on hold.

'Around eight, I reckon. What are you thinking?'

I sit up, tucking the sheet under my arms. It's been weeks since he's tugged the covers away from me and risked being late for work. The other night doesn't count. He's made his views on starting a family perfectly clear, and I've given up pestering him. '*Not while you're establishing your brand, Grace.*' Now I have to push my yearning for a child back where it won't catch me unawares. I try to convince myself there's plenty of time yet. For now it's our relationship that matters. Our relationship and my career.

'I'll cook us a nice dinner. Something special. Let's get dressed up and have a date night.' It's exactly what we need, a cosy night in with just the two of us, to help me reinforce the message that everything is under control. But why does it feel as if it's not just Richard I have to convince?

'Have you been reading one of those magazine articles that tell you how to keep your marriage alive? Got some sexy lingerie stashed in the drawer?' Richard's mouth twitches. He's mocking me, making me wish I wasn't so transparent.

'Shut up!' I toss the towel he's left on the bed at him, smiling. 'And put that in the bathroom, where it belongs.'

My meeting with Simon Farrer is short but efficient. He's excited about my ideas for the project range, and I come away feeling relieved that I had the extra time to get ready. I can't believe I almost jeopardised that. One more day and I'd have missed the meeting and Richard would have found out. I mustn't let anything get in the way of my work again. Especially not Molly.

Afterwards I go to the supermarket and stock up for the next few days. Today I'm making what is supposed to be a simple butternut squash, barley and feta bake, but I spend hours poring over ingredients and trying out different combinations. A memory flashes: me perching on a high stool in the kitchen, Mum with rosy cheeks flushed from the oven. A stab of pain. Lunchtime passes but I work through, thoughts of the anonymous text niggling at me. *What if Molly is telling the truth? What if someone has found out what happened?*

It's late afternoon by the time I make the final preparations for my bake. I won't let my fears ruin our evening, and I take a shower, shivering despite making the water as hot as I can bear. Dark grey clouds cover the sky and my mood plummets along with the temperature as I wrap myself in a thick towel. My thoughts drift to Richard, trying to recapture my enthusiasm for this evening. We used to arrange date nights more often, a different restaurant each time and cocktail bars after, but these days people recognise us and it's hard to relax. It's easier to do them at home. But everything has to be right.

I choose from my range of little black dresses, adding a simple gold necklace and sweeping my hair up into a French pleat, which looks effortless but takes me ages. I'll add a final spritz of perfume once I've completed the meal. Selfie snapped, posted online and instantly liked.

Half an hour later the table is set, a salad is in the fridge and a hearty smell wafts out from the oven. I light candles, dim the lights and put some music on, Greek *bouzouki* music which evokes the ambience of the hot evenings of our honeymoon. The balcony windows are pushed open and candles flicker on the table outside but I stay inside and sip my wine, mindful of the shadowy photo taken from the canal. The alcohol rushes to my head and I try and relax. My mobile is silent and, if I persist with my strategy, Molly has to give up. I'll tell her what she wants to hear, but keep her distant. She'll soon get bored and move on. She hasn't mentioned a partner, and I doubt she has someone in her life when she's obsessing about me. If only she could move on from the past, as I have. How could she not be over it?

Richard is only five minutes late. He leans into me for a lingering kiss and runs his hands over my shoulders. I hope this means he's forgotten my wobble the other day.

'Something smells delicious.'

We kiss again and my stomach feels warm as I watch the way the light falls on his face, highlighting his stubble and the set of his jaw. *So different from Molly.* God, why do I keep thinking about her? I push the thought aside.

'Shall we venture outside?' He takes the bottle and I join him on the balcony. There's no need to be anxious now he's with me. But each time a burst of conversation filters up from the canal, or feet run past, I try not to jump.

He sits opposite me and drinks some wine.

'This is good,' he says, inspecting the label on the bottle. 'Grace's organic choice, of course.' He loosens his tie, rolls up his sleeves. 'I can't be bothered to get changed, I'm knackered. You don't mind, do you?'

I wipe a speck of dust off the table, feeling disappointed. He always used to make an effort.

'Have you heard any more from that woman?'

'No, and I don't think I will. How was your day?'

'Meetings and more meetings. The dinner the other night was a success, publicity-wise. Marianne's polling slightly less than me at the moment.'

'Not bad, considering you don't have a huge party backing you like she does. But slightly less isn't good enough, I want you to beat her by a landslide,' I say with a laugh.

He grins. 'How was Simon?'

'Great, he loved my packaging ideas. He's full on, isn't he? Talks as if he's trying to catch himself up. You can see he's the kind of person that gets things done. He's going to do the designs for the cereals first, then move on to the drinks later. The colour scheme is to die for. I can't wait to see what he comes up with. And we talked about developing a range of boxed meals to cook – they're the latest thing, especially among young people.'

'That sounds like a great idea. Try one out next time I'm away.'

Richard's phone trills and he stops to take the call. I sip from my wine glass, welcoming the slight fuzziness that descends. He rolls his eyes and I can tell it's his mum who's talking.

'Of course, I'll tell her.' He listens some more, waves his glass at me for a refill. This time my hands are steady.

'OK, Mum, see you soon. And try not to worry, OK?' He hangs up.

'Mum says to thank you for booking the hotel. They loved it. Especially the breakfast – even Dad was impressed, and you know how hard that is. Not that he would say as much, but Mum can tell… They're still helping with the search for Emily. The police have been interviewing her friends, trying to work out what happened before she went off.'

Molly's mother, Aunt Caroline, led the search in Dorset. As soon as Mrs Greene rang to say Charlotte hadn't come home, she sprang into action. She was in her element, out organising everybody, taking charge. Spending all her free time with Mrs Greene, trying to keep the hope alive. Providing cups of tea at the community centre for all the volunteers. I hate remembering.

'I wish you wouldn't keep reminding me.'

He looks intently at me.

'Mum knows her, it's not just some random schoolgirl. Why does it bother you?'

I've said the wrong thing again. I wipe a drop of wine from the side of the bottle, stopping it inching its way down to stain the table. Richard is so careless.

'There was an incident when I was at school, one of our friends went missing.'

Concern flickers across his eyes. 'What happened?'

'I don't like talking about it.'

'You always do that.'

'Do what?'

'Change the subject when I ask you anything about your past. We've been married for over a year. Surely you trust me by now?'

A hint of a burning smell catches my attention and I jump to my feet, making a dive for the oven. But even before I pull the door open and retrieve my bake I can see the black spikes of burnt cheese. In my haste to get the dish out my arm grazes the side of the oven and I bite down a cry as my skin burns. Cold water does nothing to soothe the pain. Being so anxious must have made me forget to set the timer and I swear under my breath. Richard drinks outside, oblivious.

'Richard! Couldn't you smell burning? The food is ruined.'

'It'll taste great, I'm sure.' He plonks his glass of wine on the table and large red drops splatter the tablecloth.

'Oh, why don't you mess up the table as well! I'm supposed to be taking photographs of this. It's ruined now.' Alcohol gives me courage to stand up to him.

'Chill out, will you?' He swipes at the wine with a serviette, his movements exaggerated, making a messy red-coloured stain.

I serve the food onto plates, biting down on my tongue to stop myself from saying something I'll regret.

'Bring another bottle over, will you?' His voice is loose and I force myself not to slam the bottle down in front of him, a less fancy one this time. No point wasting it on him. He'll crash out later. How romantic.

Richard takes a small mouthful of food, and I sip my wine, trying to gauge his mood.

'You realise you shouldn't be drinking that.'

'Why not?' Maybe he's changed his mind and wants me to get pregnant after all. But after a second he dashes my hopes.

'The *Daily Tribune* are calling you the "Queen of Clean".'

'You're joking.'

'I'm not. Do your fans know you drink alcohol?'

'Of course. I'm all about quality, moderation. Obviously I wouldn't go out getting drunk, falling out of nightclubs, that would be stupid.'

'I should hope not.'

He pours more wine, takes another mouthful of dinner, picks at the salad.

'You don't like it, do you?'

'It's good, I had a big lunch, that's all.' His fork clatters as he drops it onto the plate.

'I told you I was cooking.'

'You know how work meetings go, I was hardly in a position to say no.' He covers his mouth as he yawns, pokes at his plate some more.

I want to scream in frustration. 'So I've completely wasted this afternoon. Why didn't you let me know? I'll have to do the whole thing again tomorrow.'

The fridge buzzes into the uncomfortable silence now the music has finished. My hope of recapturing the ice-blue sea and pale golden sand of our honeymoon, when we couldn't keep our hands off each other, no longer seems appropriate, so I zap the music player off. By the time I return to the table Richard's chin is slumped on his chest. Rage grips me and I imagine dropping the uneaten food onto his head, clumps of soggy cheese messing up his perfect hair. I wouldn't dare, but fantasising is good. Doesn't he realise people clamour for my food and my book is flying off the shelves? My editor emailed me earlier this week to tell me it went straight into the top ten of the non-fiction charts.

Richard pushes me to do well and then he doesn't take me seriously. I work fast to clear the table around him until the dishwasher is stacked and all traces of the meal are removed. I'm about to go upstairs when my phone rings. I freeze: what if it's Molly?

But it's Angela.

'I'm sorry to bother you, Grace, it's about your father.'

Her voice is loud and I hold the phone away from my ear. I sit down at the bottom of the stairs.

'What's happened?'

'I'm not sure. It was something his niece said.'

A car alarm goes off in the distance. 'He doesn't have a niece.'

For a moment all I hear is Angela's breath down the line as she takes this in.

'Well, she said she was his niece. Said her name was Molly.'

I lean back against the bannister, feel the hard wood press into my side.

'Do you know what she said to him?'

'No, I was in the other room.'

My fingers go white as I grip the phone. I can't believe Molly's done this; I thought I'd got through to her.

'Do you know who she is?'

'I've got an idea.' A stab of pain reminds me how much there is at stake here, and I swallow down my fury. Would Michael have recognised her? 'What is he upset about?'

'No idea. He keeps talking about sin. You know how he gets. But he's quiet now, reading his Bible. I'm so sorry, Grace. I asked her to wait but by the time I'd finished settling Michael she had gone. Maybe you could come over?'

I mentally scan my diary. Tomorrow morning I'm supposed to be working on the ideas from the meeting while they're fresh in my head. I can't get behind with my work again. Added pressure from the *Daily Tribune* headlines, and now this. A headache threatens.

'I've got a busy week. I'll be over as soon as I can.'

I hang up, glaring at the phone, then look up. Richard's eyes are wide open now.

'Who was that?'

'Angela.'

'Is Michael OK?'

'He's getting muddled again. She wants me to go over.' I stretch my arms out, making out I'm tired. 'I'm going to bed.' I escape to the bathroom and lock the door. My legs feel wobbly and I collapse on the side of the bath, my head in my hands. I can't bear to think about Molly and Michael. What would they have talked about? Surely she wouldn't have said anything about us? My stomach heaves and I throw up the wine, a deep pink stream of liquid, and a memory surfaces: Molly leaning back against a tree, sipping a bottle of strawberry milkshake. I'd taken the bottle from her hand and sipped some of the thick pink drink. Then I put the bottle down and pressed my lips onto hers. We both tasted of strawberries. Gently I pressed my tongue against her top lip and then the bottom one, then parted her lips with mine. I breathed into her and she breathed back. Her tongue met mine and I pushed her hard back against the tree.

'Strawberry kiss,' I said.

'Don't stop.'

I feel sick at the unwelcome memory, sick that she won't leave me alone, sick that she's digging everything up. My stomach cramps. I haven't got time to chase around after Molly; I need to follow up from the meeting today. My electric toothbrush whirrs in tandem with my mind, but unlike my thoughts, the toothbrush can at least be turned off. I get into bed, knowing another restless night awaits me.

CHAPTER FOURTEEN

MOLLY

No word from Jodie, which is a relief. But it's still bugging me that she mentioned the journalist. I'll kill her if she's given him my number. This is my story, and I want to deal with it in my way. Not because some lowlife journalist wants to cash in with a racy title and use my secrets for a scoop.

Unusually, Grace wasn't online yesterday, but there's activity on her Instagram now.

She's making an appearance at an organic cafe in a department store today, giving a live cookery demonstration. That's exactly what I need. Beans on toast for breakfast is the best meal I've made myself for ages, not quite Grace's style but it's progress. Mum often made us beans on toast on a Saturday and Grace'd cut the toast into neat squares and eat the beans separately. That was before she got all snobby about food. It's probably being in France that's done that: frogs' legs and snails, God knows what else they eat over there. I've never even been abroad.

The demonstration is in one of those posh stores, where you can spend more money than I've ever earned in a week on a watch or a designer bag. Those things never mattered to me. It's people that count. People like Grace.

I've got a plan today; I've brought my phone and I'm going to take some cracking shots that she'll wish she could use on her fancy website. But when I get there I see there's a bearded man with a camera hanging around his neck – he's not part of my plan. He's wearing skinny jeans and a bright yellow jumper. One of those hipsters. Struts about arrogantly.

I find my way to the homewares section. The shop assistant who's clearly in charge is holding a clipboard and ordering members of the public around. People are crowding around the desk and I spot Grace in the midst of them all wearing a grey leather jacket. She's perched on a high stool, patting at her hair. She always did that when she was nervous and it makes me happy that I can still recognise how she feels. Not many people know her like I do.

I don't want her to see me yet, so I loiter behind some shelving, looking for a good vantage point to take photos from. Set to one side and slightly behind Grace seems perfect. I've got a good view of her but she can't see me. The photos will be my surprise, and hopefully she'll reward me with that lovely smile and maybe more. Just the thought excites me. I keep looking around for her husband but there's no sign of him. I bet he's too busy and they hardly ever spend time together. She's neglected and unhappy, I can tell just by looking at her. I would never treat her like that. She's too precious.

The man with a camera leaves his bag on one of the chairs at the front and sets up a tripod. All I've got is my phone, but it's the best I can do. I don't like taking static images, I prefer to roam around my subject, circle in and catch the right mood. He doesn't see me but I can spy him through the shelves. His face looks familiar, and I imagine he's one of Grace's celebrity friends. People like him are fake and shallow; she needs real people like me in her life. She'll soon realise that I'm a breath of fresh air. That I'm exactly what she needs.

The man sits down and the woman with the clipboard fusses around Grace, checking through the equipment and the ingredients, which are set out on the shiny chrome counter. Grace realigns everything, with tiny movements. She's discreet but I notice everything she does. She used to do that with her dressing table, arrange bottles and lotions in neat rows. I won't make my move until she's begun her talk, catching her at the right moment. I want perfection.

About thirty people make up the audience, shop staff mill around and a security guard hovers in the background, muttering into his radio. He looks at me and I nod. A woman who can't stop smiling introduces Grace. She's making a selection of flapjacks and bars which can be eaten on the go, cooked up in large batches and frozen for the week. No sugar in sight. A KitKat is a lot less hassle. Once the demonstration has started, I move around behind the chairs and start snapping.

Grace doesn't notice me straight away, which bugs me, because my connection to her is so strong I reckon I'd know if she was in a room with me without even seeing her. Her hair is twisted behind her head into a chic knot and covered with a blue mesh net for the demonstration. Gracie even manages to look good in that, she's so beautiful. *Grace*, I mean. A memory flashes into my head: Grace, age thirteen, dressed as a vampire for Halloween. A glamorous vampire, of course. It was the first time I'd noticed how boys followed her around, tongues hanging out, but it was the way Grace lapped up their attention that made me scrunch my fists up in my pockets. The photographer guy steps away from his camera for a moment and watches me. I smile at him and he repositions his tripod.

'The beauty of this recipe is that when all the ingredients are ready, you can pop everything you need in the processor and in a couple of seconds they're finely chopped.'

If I were making these I'd have to bash them with a wooden spoon in a plastic bowl. Grace whizzes the blender around, stops it then unscrews the top part and holds it up. Our eyes meet. A flash of recognition crosses her face. I raise my phone and capture her looking at me but she doesn't lose her composure. She's good, I'll give her that. It's a satisfying moment. She's pressing the mixture into a tray now and putting it in the oven, asking the audience if there are any questions. Pictures stored, I slip away.

On my way home I stop off at the internet cafe in town where my mate Steph works. She's staring at the laptop screen in front of her. Her cropped pink hair sticks up in tufts.

'Shit, Molly, you distracted me. I'd just got to level four. What's up?'

'Remember that favour you owe me?'

'You remind me every time I see you. How am I supposed to forget? What do you want?'

'Can I print some photos?'

'Sure. Log on to that PC in the window. It's free until three o'clock.'

Ellis calls as I let myself back into the flat, throwing the windows open to welcome fresh air in. It sounds like she's at home, I can tell from the television chatter in the background.

'You don't really do any work, do you? Just sit around and watch TV all day,' I say, jokingly. I'm in a good mood after earlier.

'You can talk! What have you been up to today?'

'Taking some photos.' Ellis doesn't need to know what of. 'I'm going to work on them this afternoon. You were right, having something to do takes my mind off wanting a drink.'

'Well done, Molly. Only a few days ago I couldn't imagine you spending time with yourself like this.' She pauses. 'I wondered whether you'd like to come to an AA meeting?'

I squirm around on my seat. I tried one once, a musty church hall full of strangers who were nothing like me until they started talking. Sharing things with them would be like opening myself up for an operation.

'No thanks, I'll stick to calling you if that's OK. I'm doing alright, I haven't had a drink today. Not planning on going down the pub either. Quiet night in, just me and the telly.'

'Oh, Christ,' Ellis says and I wonder what I've said. 'I've got the news on. That poor girl who's gone missing. They're still out searching for her. It's been a few days, though, not a good sign. That's what they always say, isn't it, the first few hours are so important? Oh look, it's him, your mate Grace's husband.'

'Hang on, I'll switch the TV on.' I scrabble around for the remote. It's on the floor under a pair of jeans which should be in the washing basket, and find the channel. Richard Sutherland is standing on a village green, a circle of residents gathered behind him.

Local residents are assisting the police in searching the area. The MP for Fenton North, Richard Sutherland, has been talking to residents in town today. The husband is seen chatting to an elderly couple while a helpline number scrolls across the screen. An uneasy feeling settles in my stomach. I remember when Dad went into work on the evening of Charlotte's disappearance to make posters to put around town, but she was found the next morning. I look for Grace whenever the husband is in shot. Maybe she's in the background, waiting, kept out of the way so as not to steal the limelight. I'm disappointed when I can't spot her. It's just him, Mr Smarmy. He always looks so pleased with himself, with his posh accent which grates on my nerves.

'I hope they find her soon,' Ellis is saying as the girl's picture fills the screen and I breathe in sharply. The dainty face and blonde hair, it could almost be Charlotte. That bloody school photo that haunted me for years. I zap the screen off and tune back into Ellis.

'Don't you think it's strange, that he's there?'

'Not at all. It's his constituency. It would be weird if he wasn't. He's trying to get as much interest in the case as possible. It's a good thing. Why would you think otherwise?'

'No reason.'

'Hmm,' Ellis says. She can see right through me.

'You're right, I'm just trying to find fault with him.'

'I like the fact that he's not attached to any party. He might even get my vote.'

'See, the publicity isn't hurting him, is it?'

Ellis laughs. 'No, but I get what you mean.'

After the phone call I forget the girl's face and put some music on, spreading the photos out on the table, dancing around as I check them out. My mood is so much better, seeing Grace's face all over the table. So close, yet so far. I'm convinced she's not in love with her husband. She looks too uptight, not relaxed and free and blossoming like she used to be. He's the weak link in this, the husband. If I could find something on him, make her see that she's chosen the wrong path in life. Then I remember what Ellis said. I'm kidding myself again, I know, but at least it keeps my mind occupied.

I rip the takeaway menus off the cork noticeboard on the wall to make space for a Grace collage. The dark images from outside her flat and the light ones from the brightly lit department store. There's room for plenty more.

I wonder what she'll think of my photos. But my collection isn't ready yet. I want to win her over first before I surprise her with my work and she sees how good it is. I thought she might be in touch after seeing me this morning, but my phone stays silent. I'll give her a bit more time, and if I don't hear from her I'll send another photo to stop her forgetting me. The photo board looks good on the wall, makes the flat feel more like home. Grace's eyes follow me around the room, warming me inside. The adult Grace has taken over from the teenager who used to live in my head, whose face I was afraid of forgetting. My favourite photo is the one where she looked up and saw me this morning. When our eyes met across the room. I've captured the haunted look that flitted across her face.

I won't stop haunting her until she gives me what I want.

GRACE'S DIARY

MONDAY 15TH DECEMBER 2003

Aunt Caroline, Molly's mum, came to visit me today. I didn't expect to see her after the trial ended last week. At first I was relieved – Dad had said we wouldn't be seeing them any more – I love it when he's wrong, but oh my goodness was he right.

She was alright at first, asked how I was, but I could tell something was wrong. She didn't give me a hug and wouldn't have tea and cake, and she even kept her coat on, as if she couldn't wait to get away. I asked how Molly was and it was as if I'd lit a bonfire. She exploded. She was always firm but I've never known her lose it before. That's Dad's speciality. Said she'd been watching me during the trial and she knew what was going on between me and Molly. I pointed out that I had a boyfriend, but she told me to be quiet and listen. She said Molly had always confided in her and was a different person now, wouldn't talk, wouldn't eat, keeps asking when she can see me again. Caroline – because she's not my 'aunt' any more, never was, really – stood up at this point and hovered over me, trying to frighten me, but I wasn't scared. She said I was to leave Molly alone, never contact any of them again. Caroline said she was glad Michael was sending me away, which made me panic but I didn't let her see it. I made sure to look serious and nodded at everything she said, but all the time I was stroking the scar on my hand. Me and Molly made a promise and nobody can break us apart. I know Molly – it's only a matter of time before she contacts me. Whatever it takes.

CHAPTER FIFTEEN

GRACE

A moth flutters onto the bedside table and I squash it with my thumb. If only Molly could be dealt with so easily. The little sleep I managed was broken with bursts of worry. Richard stirs and I shift onto my side and look down at him. His eyes are barely open, and I place a kiss on his forehead.

'What day is it?'

'Saturday. We're visiting your parents this afternoon, remember.'

Ordinarily it's my favourite day of the week when Richard is free. No alarms, no deadlines, just the two of us having some much-needed time together. But Angela's call has unsettled me. I'll have to see Michael before I do anything else, find out what Molly said. If he's making any sense, that is. It's only recently that his carer has had to call us to go over more often, concerned about his fading memory. It's hard to believe he used to stand up in church, giving sermons which took him no time at all to learn, his memory almost photographic. He gave a service the weekend after the body was found, when everyone was reeling from the news. He stood in the pulpit, a tall figure, formidable in black, and his eyes appeared to be focused on me, addressing every single word for my individual attention, his thin arms waving in the air making him look like a crow. Molly's leg was pressed against mine, trembling, as he talked about the power of forgiveness and how Charlotte was in a different place, taken for a reason. Molly rocked to and fro when he said that, and I held onto her arm, stroked inside her elbow. I had to stop her making a dash for the exit and giving herself away.

'You were restless again,' Richard says, as I snuggle into the crook of his arm.

'I was thinking about what Angela said. I might have to go over to check on Michael this morning.'

'Do you want me to come?'

'No, it's fine. It's easier if I go on my own.'

Richard looks surprised. He finds Michael easier to deal with than I do; they slip into football banter, and it makes it less stressful for me to be in his company. But I can't have him there today. I pull him towards me, kissing him. 'Thank you, though.'

I choose a pale blue skirt and a matching jacket. I put my hair up, along with a full face of make-up, ready to deal with whatever Angela has to tell me.

Downstairs, Richard is tying the laces on his trainers.

'Thought I'd squeeze in a quick run, it's the only chance I'm going to get this week.'

'Are you still planning on running the marathon?'

He pulls a face. 'I think I'm going to have to defer my place. There just aren't enough hours in the day. I won't run if I'm not properly trained, I can't make a show of myself.'

'I guess you'll have to decide which you want more – London Mayor, or...'

He grins and kisses me. 'No contest. And there are plenty of years ahead to run the marathon in.'

'Good,' I say. 'I can't wait to be the Mayor's wife.'

Michael's house is the last in a row of bungalows, all with tiny front gardens and colourful front doors. Angela's Mini Cooper is parked on the street outside. The door swings opens before I reach it and Angela twists a tea towel between her hands as she ushers me in.

Michael is in the living room, sitting in his usual chair. It still shocks me how diminished he seems. Always so tall and towering, but now he's lost height, no longer the commanding presence he used to be. He can't hurt me physically any more, but I still hesitate. I fuss about with my hair, making sure it's in place.

The kitchen is barely big enough for the two of us, so different from the grand vicarage kitchen we grew up in, open to a constant flow of parishioners wanting Michael's advice. It's so lonely here by comparison. Angela sets out cups and saucers on a tray, adds a blue-and-white jug of milk and empties a packet of jam tarts onto a plate.

'His favourite,' she says. 'Not ideal for his teeth, but…' She shrugs and we both know it's not worth putting him in a bad mood.

'I'm sorry to drag you down here on a Saturday, but he's been so unsettled this week. He accused me of hiding his things, and I want you to know that I would never do that. I'm fond of him. He's always been difficult, but lately…' Angela's movements are fast, nervy. 'And then that woman who said she was his niece, I feel awful about that.'

'Don't. She's a bit of a crazed fan, someone I used to know. Did you hear any of their conversation?'

'No, but she showed him a photograph, that's what may have upset him.'

I draw in a sharp breath.

'Does he remember anything about it?'

'It's hard to tell. You must have seen the missing girl story in the news, it's been upsetting him. It's one of the things I wanted to talk to you about. Do you have any idea why?'

The milk that I am passing to Angela almost slips from my hands.

'No.'

'It's strange. He gets agitated every time it's on. I tried to switch channels but he made such a fuss.'

The photograph. He's seen the likeness too.

'Well, you know how he is with me, but I'll do my best.'

She puts everything on a tray, an embarrassed smile on her face.

'Angela's made us some tea,' I say, too brightly, as we go into the living room.

'Where's Richard?'

'He's out running this morning. Training for the marathon.'

'I don't know where he finds the energy,' Angela says.

'He's always wanted to run a sub-three-hour marathon, but I'm not sure he'll manage it this year. He won't do it if he can't get a good time.'

The copy of my recipe book I sent to Michael sits on the table.

'Did you like my book?'

'I don't see the point in you giving it to me when I don't cook.'

I feel the sting of rejection, so familiar with my father. Mum used to cook when I was little, before illness took her away. I'd stand on a chair and she'd guide my hand to stir the gooey mixture, sharing my excitement at the resulting tray of cupcakes. *Baking magic*, she called it. I almost made that the title of my book, but the memory wasn't entirely a happy one. I don't have many that are.

Cups clatter as Angela pours the tea into small china cups with matching saucers. She takes the tray back to the kitchen. As soon as she's gone Michael picks up the remote and switches the television off.

'I don't remember everything, but I'm not stupid.' He jabs his finger in the direction of the kitchen. 'She hides my things, I know she does.' The last words are a splutter as he coughs a deep, rumbling cough.

'She's only trying to help you by tidying up.' I move closer to him. 'I need to talk to you. Do you remember the visitor you had the other day?'

'Of course I do, I told you, I'm not an idiot. She showed me a photo to remind me. As if I'd forget her after what she did.'

Fear grips me. 'What photo?'

'Of you and her.' His mouth curls into a sneer. 'You're not supposed to see her any more. Why don't you ever do what you're told? Stupid girl.' I clench my fists in my pockets, familiar rage bubbling.

'I'm not a child any more. And I can't stop her coming here.'

'Why couldn't you stay away? I was trying to help you by sending you to France. She would never have found you there.'

'Look, let's forget she ever came here. Angela knows about her now, and she won't let her in again.'

'She tried to surprise me but I'm no fool. Everybody treats me as if I'm losing my faculties. But I remember everything that happened.' He jabs at his head with a bent finger. 'It's all in here. You thought I didn't see what was going on but I know exactly what you were up to.'

I'm suddenly aware that Angela is at my side, holding out a glass of water, and I'm not sure how much she's heard.

'Are you alright, Michael?'

He drinks some water, swallows hard, stabs at a photograph in the newspaper with his pencil. 'And this is wrong,' he says. 'Charlotte's school uniform was blue.'

The cup I'm holding rattles in the saucer and I put it down on the table.

Angela slides the newspaper away from him, sighing. 'It's Emily, Michael. This is what I meant, Grace. For some reason it's upsetting him. You need to watch programmes that will cheer you up, not all this depressing news. *Coronation Street* is on later, Michael.' Her voice is louder when she speaks to him.

He picks at a piece of fraying wool on the sleeve of his blue cardigan.

'I can't watch that any more. No morals, men together as if it's normal, the world isn't like it used to be.' Spittle flies out with the words.

I take the newspaper from Michael's lap and fold it, putting it out of his reach.

'Angela's right, Michael. What about watching an old film? You used to like those.'

'You don't know anything about what I used to like.'

The look he gives me is so cold I can't contain my anger any longer.

'Only because you pushed me away. But you always had time for the church, didn't you? "Such a good man", they all used to say. Your reputation was all that interested you. Never mind the fact that you had a daughter who needed you. Do you know what it was like when Mum was sick after her treatment and you were always at work, helping other people? That's why I couldn't wait to go and stay with Aunty Caroline. She looked after me properly. It's no wonder I was close to Molly – you pushed us together.' I bite down on my lip. Angela looks astonished at my outburst. I hope she can't see that my whole body is shaking.

Angela recovers her composure and picks up Michael's cup. 'Drink your tea,' she says and he grabs her wrist. Tea spills onto the table.

'Where have you hidden those letters?' Michael's voice is a hiss and his fingers are white where they're gripping Angela's wrist.

'Michael! Let her go. You've got to stop this. Angela isn't hiding anything. You're not making any sense.'

But he is, and we both know it. He's kept them. The letters. Fear stabs at me.

'Richard doesn't know, does he? But I know. She told me.'

I count to five and take in a lungful of air. I'm not sure what he means.

'Maybe he ought to see the doctor, have another memory test.' I take Angela's elbow, leading her out of the room. 'And it might be best to keep him away from the news.' I lower my voice so that he doesn't hear. 'He's talking nonsense, you understand, so please try not to let him upset you. Something he's seen on television will be preying on his mind.'

Angela rubs at her wrist.

'Are you OK?' Her rosy cheeks have lost their usual glow.

'Michael's never been like that before. He's always seemed so gentle until recently.'

I see his arm raised in the air, his mouth twisted. Bile rises in my throat as I think how wrong she is. But it's important that she's happy. We can't afford to lose her, not now when there's so much pressure on.

'Has he hurt you?' My legs feel unsteady at the thought.

'No, I'm fine,' she says, but she can't hide the concern in her eyes. 'What about you?'

'I shouldn't have let him get to me. I shouldn't have lost my temper like that, but he knows how to wind me up. Please don't take any notice of what he's saying. You do such a great job here. We honestly couldn't manage without you. Work is stressful for us both at the moment. I don't want to bother Richard with this if I can help it. He's got enough to worry about. I'd appreciate it if you didn't say anything.'

'Of course.'

'I must go, we're visiting his parents this afternoon. Thank you for looking after him, Angela, and call me any time you need anything.'

I don't bother saying goodbye to my father.

Richard picks me up from home and we drive over to Ash Fenton. He's listening to the radio and I'm grateful for the time to think. Current events are obviously confusing Michael, but there's still a lot he remembers. His comment about the letters is bothering me. Has he kept hold of them? I need to find out what was in them. And what he said about Charlotte. My thoughts spin round, making my head pound.

When we arrive Jean and Des are out in the front garden. Across the street TV crews and journalists amass in front of a policeman. He addresses the group, moving them back, a roll of tape in his hand. One of the group breaks away, talks urgently into his phone; others shake their heads, exchange words, scribbling frantic notes.

'I'll see what's going on,' Richard says. He crosses the road and speaks to the policeman, and everything is captured on camera. His face is set when he comes back, taking my hand in his.

'They've found Emily's jacket,' he says, and his words carry over to Jean, who gasps and claps her hand over her mouth.

My muscles stiffen and I drop Richard's hand, not wanting him to notice the effect this has on me. Seeing Jean's reaction makes my throat contract. Charlotte's denim jacket flashes into my mind. It was finding the jacket that did for Aunty Caroline. She'd been so positive up until then, jollying everyone along, her hope contagious. But when she took the phone call about the jacket she dropped down onto the hall chair as if her legs had given way, her fingers white against the green telephone cord. I knew it was only a matter of time before worse news came.

The mood is sombre and a presenter broadcasts the news. People stop talking, the journalists are moved further back and quiet descends, save for the sound of a dog whining, as if in sympathy for Emily. But the presenter reminds us that it doesn't necessarily mean she won't be found alive, and offers a message of hope to the family and the nation, who wait with baited breath. This is one of those cases that captures the public imagination – a newsworthy white, pretty, middle-class girl from the countryside, not a washed-up refugee trying to enter the country in the back of a van. Charlotte was one of those pretty girls, too. One of those missing girls who grab the nation's attention. I gag, turning it into a cough, and Jean leads me inside for a glass of water. As we're going in, a reporter breaks away from the crowd and approaches Richard. He nods and follows the journalist.

'I'll be back in a minute.'

'Finding her jacket doesn't mean she's not alive,' Jean tells me as she leads me inside, her arm around my shoulder. Although we all know that it is likely Emily's broken body will be the next thing to be discovered. The thought makes me want to throw up.

'I wish Richard didn't have to get involved.'

'It's understandable, though. He knows her, after all.'

I sip at a glass of water and will my heart to stop thudding. Through the window I watch the journalists move across the common, microphones and cameras poised to capture any detail that comes their way. Richard comes in and puts his arm around my shoulders.

'Horrible, isn't it?'

'What did they want?'

'A quote from me. And once the journalist knew I'd met her he had lots of questions.'

My mood sinks even lower, imagining us being dragged into the story.

Richard's phone beeps and he moves away to take the call.

'I've got to go into work,' he says. 'I'll drop you home first.'

'Now? You promised you weren't going to work today.'

I push the irritation down inside me. I don't want to be left alone in the flat again. Left to think about Molly. It feels important for Richard and I to be together, but I don't want him to see me as needy.

'You could do some work, too. I noticed you didn't post anything yesterday.'

'Are you checking up on me?'

'I look forward to your daily posts. I missed it yesterday, that's all. You don't want to miss days, Grace. You need to keep on top of your brand. If I've noticed others will too.'

'I know. Don't worry, I'm on it.' I keep my hands hidden so that he doesn't see them shaking.

Back home, my intention to edit my last write-up evaporates as soon as I log online. First I go to the news channel, watch the clip from this morning, and once again wish Richard wasn't involved with this story. We don't need this kind of attention. After that I'm compelled to read a résumé of the case when I see a link to 'new developments'. I read how Emily Shaw was last seen by the village green in Ash Fenton when she left her two friends. The friends were seen arguing and a physical altercation was caught on CCTV, which the girls lied about to the police. A sick feeling rises to my throat. A memory ambushes me: the three of us in the town park, Molly kicking her legs on a swing, me and Charlotte in the shelter. Charlotte smoking a cigarette, smoothing her hair, telling me how Jason said it was weird that I was always with Molly. She wanted him for herself, that's why. When I told Molly, the wind blew our laughter up into the sky as we pushed our swings as high as they would go. Charlotte watched us, lips pinched, grinding her heel hard into her cigarette butt. I should have realised then she was on to us.

Next I go straight to Alex Foster's blog. He's starting his series of crime stories on Monday and I click on the link to check the cases he's covering, hoping I misread it last time. He's written a paragraph about each one that will feature. My palms sweat as I scroll through, praying that it won't be there, even though I know I'm kidding myself. And sure enough, there it is: *The Orchid Girls*.

He doesn't say when he's going to write about it. But the link he's making as to what these cases have in common is that the culprit was never found.

The aftermath of the trial is a blur to me, as I was whisked away to France where I was determined to forget the whole thing, almost convincing myself it never happened. But Molly wasn't so easy to forget. I prowl around the flat for a while, trying to persuade myself that there is no reason to connect me with this in any way. But one factor stops me believing this: Molly.

A text on my phone makes me jump. *Is it her?* My heart races. It's Richard.

Don't forget to post today.

I throw the phone back down on the sofa. I hate it when he checks up on me – I don't interfere with his work. But the memory of the burnt meal and how irritated I was is stuck in my head. I rarely make mistakes like that, and I hate it when we're not getting on, when I'm not perfect. He's right. It's easiest if I get on with the post. He wants what's best for me, that's all. Missing one day won't hurt if I get straight back on it.

But there's no way I can concentrate until I've made a plan about Molly. How can I make her see sense? I'll have to meet her again. To boost my morale, I log on to Instagram and check on my feedback. My jacket has attracted attention today, noticed by the designer. Richard will like that. My mood lifts. After that it takes no time at all to edit the article I've written and post it online. This is the Grace I'm meant to be; the perfect version who gets everything right. But the threat of Molly looms in the background, a dark shadow eclipsing the sun. And there's nothing I can do to stop her.

GRACE'S DIARY

Back to my diary. It's so much better to write things down, I find, rather than talk to people. People can't be trusted. Everybody tells lies to me, even *her*. So much for staying in touch.

Molly's phone number doesn't work any more, either. She must have moved or changed her number because of all those calls we were getting. Irritating little men from the newspapers crowding at the end of our front garden and yelling questions. So uncouth. The last straw was when Mum tried to go to the bakery for some pastries and she couldn't get out of the drive because of all the men with cameras following her. She broke down and cried and I hate them. She hasn't really stopped since. Charlotte's family moved to Scotland, and the local paper did a big story on her before they went, talking about setting up a charity to remember her. The girl in the story was unrecognisable. So what if she could do the splits and win gold medals, was Gymnast of the bloody Year. They forget to mention how she bullied people and said nasty things. They don't know what she was capable of. Newspapers tell lies, I know that now.

I've stopped wondering when it will all be over. When I look at Mum I know the answer is never. She doesn't have Molly's mum Caroline to talk to any more, and it's all my fault. Caroline was her rock. She was like a mum to me too when Mum had cancer, but nobody thinks about that.

I knew everything would change once the trial finished. I can't stand it here, but I don't want to leave. There are too many memories. Not until I've spoken to her again. I don't understand why she hasn't been in touch. Could it be because of Jason? I never meant for her to know I slept with him, she wasn't meant to find out. I only did it to make Charlotte jealous – I might have known she couldn't keep her bloody mouth shut. The last thing I wanted was for Molly to get hurt. We made a promise, and I have to know she's keeping it. It's easy for me to keep it because there's no one to tell. I won't even write it down.

Once upon a time I could talk to Mum, but she isn't well now. Dad says everything I've put her through hasn't helped. He's got worse lately, preaching all the time. Going on at me. He says if I had faith then I'd understand why I need to repent. But I haven't done anything wrong. He doesn't know about Molly. He can't. It's impossible.

Last time I saw Molly she tried to tell me something about Dad. She was frightened of him, more frightened than usual, and she said it was to do with Charlotte. I worry he must know something because he watches me with his cold eyes and nods to himself. I hate him.

At dinner he takes so long to say grace the food gets cold. Then he gets mad because I'm not eating, says I'm ungrateful and goes on about starving children in countries I don't care about. Mum never did eat much, and I'm getting the same way now. My throat has closed up and I can't swallow. It makes him even angrier. He doesn't realise I can't eat because I can't stop thinking about her and what we did. I'd give anything to be with her now. Sometimes I think I've imagined those special times we had. We loved each other. Because that's what it was, love, I don't care what anyone else says. Lying together in sin, that's what he would call it. The thought of him knowing terrifies me. He's kinder to her but he calls me wicked, a wicked, ungrateful brat. How can my own dad call me that? That's when I started calling him Michael.

Last night I overheard them talking. Sleeping's another thing I can't do. Usually I lie awake, tossing and turning, thinking about her and going over the lines of her face so that I don't forget her. I couldn't bear to forget, but if she's forgotten me… His voice was a deep rumble through the thin wall and when it went quiet I knew she must be talking. She doesn't get a chance to say much, but I like to think she's sticking up for me. He raised his voice and I swear he only did it so I would hear. When the words went from muffled jumbles to making sense I sat up and cold sweat stuck to my back. He wants to send me away, somewhere far, where I'm no longer a blot on his reputation. He didn't say that last bit, those are my words. But it's what he means. I know it. He's made me feel it often enough.

He didn't say anything the next day, waited until the weekend when he's not got a service until late morning. He sat opposite me while I tried to eat my Weetabix, which stuck like straw in my throat. He chose that moment to tell me he's sending me away, says too many people around here know about '*that business*'. He always calls it '*that business*'. What on earth does that mean? Sometimes he looks at me with such disgust it's as if he knows about us, but I can't bear that to be true. It's meant to be our secret, no one else's. So I play along, talk about the obvious.

He's got it all arranged. Mum's sister Jenny lives in Paris and he wants me to go and live with her. Go to a foreign school, change my name and everything. Learn to speak French, he says children learn quickly. But I'm not a bloody child. He goes mad when I say that. Never mind that him and Mum don't speak French, he couldn't have made it clearer that he wants to get rid of me forever and never to come back.

I met Aunt Jenny once. She looks like Mum but a shinier version. She wears designer clothes and writes for French *Vogue* magazine. She was a model once. Best thing is, she thinks religion is nonsense. A free spirit, she calls herself. Maybe living with her won't be so bad. Even so, I can't tell her about being in love with another girl. I can't tell her the truth.

If he does send me away and I lose Molly because of it, I'll make him pay. I'll send him off to his precious God but it won't be heaven he goes to. Not that I believe in all that shit.

CHAPTER SIXTEEN

MOLLY

Ellis asks me to phone her every day. She's doing it so that she can check up on me, make sure I'm not drinking. It seemed like a stupid idea at first, not something I want to bother with, but today when I get up and don't know how my day is going to pan out, I begin it by calling her. And it feels good. It's been so long since I made a friend.

She's working from home again this morning. It must be fun, making clothes. That's why we get on. Mum and school were always telling me how creative I was. At the time I thought it was their way of being kind. Why not come outright and admit I was thick? But now being creative feels like a good thing to be. Grace is creative.

Ellis tells me she's free this afternoon and invites me over earlier than planned. Gives me something to focus on. I spend the morning in my pyjamas watching daytime TV. When that gets boring I switch to the news channel, and *he's* on the screen again, the husband. Ellis says things happen for a reason and I decide that if he keeps being put in my path then I should take notice. It must be a sign.

Grace's on screen now, hanging on his arm at some posh do, wearing a silky red dress which clings to her curves and does things to my insides. He's confident, clasping the hand of the interviewer to make his point, gently rocking backwards and forwards, his warm eyes welcoming me in. His charm almost works on me. I'm reminded of another boy, back in Lyme Regis. *Jason*. I couldn't understand why I curled my fingers around the stones in my pockets when she told me how handsome she thought he was, and cried myself to sleep because she didn't have time for me any more. When Gracie got dressed up for the town's youth disco, the sight of her looking all grown up in a black dress that slid down her suntanned shoulders felt like a punch in the stomach – because it was all for him. Not a good way to hurt. That's when I understood what these feelings meant. That it was only ever going to be girls for me.

Then the missing girl is on screen, her school photo, which I bet she hates. Charlotte's school shot was splashed all over the papers, which she would have been so mad about – she never liked photos being taken of her. I didn't realise then that she would never see a photo again, and it was all my fault. Emily's likeness to Charlotte hits me again; I can't get over how similar they are. Now he's on screen, Grace's husband. It's weird, him cropping up constantly. What if he had something to do with it? Grace might need protecting from him. Maybe I could follow him, get some evidence, catch him out. It's a ridiculous thought. I'm more likely to catch him playing away.

Emily's mum and dad are on screen now, and they're both crying. I can't watch it any more; my mood is changing like a light switch flipping on and off and I'm grateful to have something to do this afternoon to stop me moping around the flat looking at my photo gallery. It doesn't look as good on the grubby wall with the blinds pulled up and the light streaming in.

I run the shower hot, dress in clean clothes, stick everything else in a bag and head down to the launderette. While my clothes spin like a roulette wheel in the machine I wander the streets nearby and take pictures of people in the market. I focus on different hair colours – pastel pinks, lilac and blue. Every time I see a blonde head my heart jolts, but it's never her. I've been seeing her in shadows everywhere I go for years, but it's different now I know it could actually be her. I can't really see Grace in Camden Market; she'd be more at home in Kensington.

While the washing dries on a plastic rack in my flat, I set off for Ellis's. The afternoon used to be my favourite time for going to the pub and for a second I wonder if Jodie's there, but I've lost track of her shift pattern. And that's good. *Forget Jodie.* Ellis's directions are easy to follow and I'm early when I get to her flat but I know she won't mind.

She leads me into her tiny one-bedroomed flat, where everything fits into its place. How my flat was meant to be. It's the end building in a row of mews houses, a quiet backstreet away from bustling Camden High Street. The air in the white-walled flat is calm; brightly coloured prints add a splash of colour. The corner where Ellis does her crafts has shelves full of baskets of wool and fabric. A sewing machine sits on the table. The large sash window behind the desk looks over towards the park in the distance. A yoga mat is rolled up in the corner.

'What exactly do you do again?'

'I run a freelance craft business. Make clothes, bags, my own knitted range. Sell a few pieces. I'm hoping to earn enough to open a shop one day. That's the dream, anyway.'

'Is that one of yours?' I point at her scarf; it's a deep turquoise colour with a pretty pattern. Looks soft, like cashmere.

She nods. 'One of my early creations.'

'It's lovely.'

We sit on a low leather couch. Ellis makes us coffee in a cafetière and I enjoy watching her go about her business. I can't imagine her twitchy and thin, a raving junkie, but I know she's telling the truth because she's that kind of person. She's got a cork noticeboard covered in photos of her with different people. The same guy appears in quite a few of them: hiking; on a beach; his arm around Ellis, squinting in the sun.

I sit at the kitchen table and Ellis tells me about her job and her family. It's good to be with someone who isn't complicating my life. I relax and inhale the buttery smell of shortbread which she's baked specially. She seems to like me and I believe she's genuine, which is refreshing for me. I'm so used to people using me or disappointing me. Whenever I was with Jodie I felt like an elastic band, stretched out and about to ping back into place. It was exhausting. I feel better not hearing from her. Maybe she's finally got the message.

The white walls in this quiet flat help me feel calm. Where I live it's impossible to escape the noise of the traffic, the bustle from the shops across the road, Mrs Bird's TV turned up loud and buzzing through the ceiling. On the spot I make up my mind to decorate my flat, get rid of all the stains and fingerprints from my messy life. Try and start a new one. I want it to look decent in case Grace ever comes round. Because she might.

After she's made a second pot of coffee, we move to the table and Ellis gets her laptop out. She uploads my photos from the market and the graffiti from the canal and we spend the next couple of hours designing a website. She suggests keeping it private until I've got a proper camera and can take more professional shots. Ellis says more than once that anything she advises me to do is just a suggestion, that I have a choice. So different to Jodie. Pushing me and shoving me in every direction she wanted me to go.

Ellis is talking about how she made amends to her family, made up for all she'd put them through, apologised, worked hard to earn their trust.

'We get on well now. I never thought it would happen. My sister even lets me babysit her kids. That would never have happened while I was using. What about your family? Tell me about your mum.'

Thinking about Mum makes my stomach squirm and I wriggle around on the chair, trying to get comfortable.

'I haven't seen her since I left home. Not even when Dad died. She didn't tell me, said she didn't know where I was. It was Darren who let me know about the funeral.' *Bet he regrets that now.* 'I wasn't in a good place. Me and Dad were close.'

A sympathetic expression crosses her face. 'What made you leave home?'

The answer is too big for the question and I can feel it eating away at me inside. 'Something happened that affected the whole family. Serious stuff.' I scramble around in my pocket for a cigarette, pulling out a crumpled-up packet. Then I put it away again. She won't want me to smoke in here, messing up her clean room. I wonder what I'm doing here. Why I'm kidding myself.

'You don't have to talk about it,' she says.

'I was a teenage brat, usual stuff. My parents were good to me, tried to help me and I threw it all back at them. I feel ashamed just thinking about it.' That, at least, is the truth.

'Does she live on her own?'

I nod. 'But her brother Bill lives nearby. The photographer I told you about. He's the one who taught me how to use a camera.'

'And I bet she'd like to see you. Why don't you go and visit her? It would give you some space from Jodie. Geographical, at least. Take a bit of time to think about what you want to do.'

She's right. Book my ticket to Lyme Regis to get away from Jodie, that's what I need to do.

'That means I'll have to ring her. I'm not sure I'm ready for that yet.'

'No rush,' Ellis says, shrugging her shoulders. 'It's just a suggestion.'

'Tell me about you,' I say, needing to move the conversation on. Too much navel-gazing gets me into trouble. 'Who's the guy in the photos?'

Her face gets a little flushed and for the first time I catch a glimpse of a different Ellis, one who's not so in control.

'You mean Steve. My ex-boyfriend. We met at college, were together since then. He wanted us to get married, babies, the works.' She looks sad as her sentence trails off.

'Not what you wanted?'

She pulls a face. 'For a long while I thought I did. Expected to follow my older sister. She lives in a big house with lots of kids and animals, up in Yorkshire. Proper housewife, she is. But when Steve asked me to marry him for the second time I realised I wanted something different. I'm not sure what, mind. He was gutted. Still is, apparently. We had a big group of friends and they couldn't understand it. Makes it difficult. I've had to distance myself from them all. Most of my energy has gone into getting my business off the ground. But just talking about it now makes me realise you're doing me a favour, too.'

'How?'

She shrugs. 'Chatting like this, getting to know someone. It's fun. I've been far too isolated lately.'

I know exactly how she feels. 'Are you still in touch with Steve?'

'No. He'd like to be, but it makes everything much harder. To be honest, I'd find it easier if he got himself a girlfriend.'

'Or you might meet someone, then maybe he'd get the message,' I joke.

She laughs, looking away. 'I can't imagine being with anyone other than Steve.' Her face is flushed and it seems odd for her to be flustered.

Maybe she's not so good at talking about herself, although she did open up to me the other day. I guess addiction is easier to talk about for her – it's what we have in common after all. But the underlying problems aren't so easy to reveal. Christ, out of everyone I should know that, and the thought makes me smile.

'What's funny?

'Nothing, just crazy thoughts.' She must think I'm mental. But it's good, sitting here, talking. And for a couple of hours I haven't thought about drinking. Or Grace.

That changes as soon as I get home. Being back in my flat, switching the light on – which illuminates the dirty marks on the walls – makes me wish I was back in Ellis's cosy home again. Not on my own with nothing to stop old thoughts coming back and not being able to blot it out with drink. Just like that, I'm back to wondering what Grace is doing with her husband and what I can do for her to forget him and look at me. Like I did with Jason all those years ago. I think about the time we were lying on my bed and Grace told me my hair was gorgeous and that loads of boys would want to go out with me. I thought she was just being nice. She ran her fingers through my curls and asked me if I wanted to know what kissing a boy was like. She was so close I could smell peppermint on her breath and I said yes, even though I already knew I wasn't interested in boys. But I couldn't get over how perfect her mouth was. We pressed our lips together and after what seemed like ages she pushed herself up onto her hands, one each side of my head.

'Don't stop,' I said, her hair feather-like on my cheek.

Her eyes were blue like a summer sky as she stared into mine. 'I'm not planning to,' she replied.

In the end I upload a photo, one from the canal that I didn't show Ellis. The second shot of Grace on her balcony. A different angle this time. She'll know I've visited Michael by now, but it obviously wasn't enough because she hasn't been in touch. *Why can't I get through to her?* His words are still a puzzle in my head, which only Grace can solve. I click send on the photograph. She can't ignore me, she must realise that.

It doesn't take long before she replies. She wants to meet me, tells me to choose somewhere discreet. I've got exactly the place in mind. And I don't think she's going to like it.

MOLLY'S DIARY

TUESDAY 9TH DECEMBER 2003

Today was the worst day in court. I can't stand the stuffy atmosphere. Each minute dragged by. Going over and over the same questions was doing my head in, it was so hard to stay awake, and the slug I'd taken of Dad's vodka didn't help. This morning the 'expert' was up, hours and hours of tedious detail about head injuries. When I asked my barrister – Mr Foxglove, 'call me Edward' – what it was all about, he said the bottom line was there was no conclusive evidence on Charlotte's head injury – it could have been caused by a fall. I could have told them that, I was there, but me and Grace have got our stories sorted, we know what we're going to say, it's easier that way. We made a pact, haven't said a word about what really happened to anyone since the first interview, before I knew better. Grace will do whatever it takes to protect me.

The witness woman was up this afternoon. Mary Fish. Mr Foxglove did a lot of paper-straightening and adjusting his wig, and I could tell he was nervous. She was wearing a raincoat and clutching her bag as if someone was gonna try and snatch it from her. Her voice was like a mouse and the judge asked her to speak up and she clutched her bag harder. You could tell she didn't want to be there. She said her piece about going for a walk with her dog and seeing three girls over on the cliff, standing in a triangle, like they were talking. She said she thinks one had reddish hair and they could have been arguing. I'm surprised he didn't ask her if she was close enough to see our tattoos, the way the papers have been going on about them. That would have made Grace laugh, but I hate the way they've taken our special name, The Orchid Girls, and made it into something horrible, all because Charlotte got the same tattoo. But when my barrister jumped up for his turn he made Mary think the sun might have been in her eyes and she couldn't be sure the hair was red. She looked like she wanted to cry. I could have told him I don't remember any sun that day. See, it's much better if I don't say anything. At the end of the session Mr Foxglove was smiling when he talked to Mum and Dad about the lack of evidence and credible witnesses and I had a feeling we were going to be OK. If I could just catch Grace's eye, I'd feel better, but her Dad won't let me anywhere near her.

WEDNESDAY 10TH DECEMBER 2003
IT'S ALL OVER. NOT GUILTY!!!
I can't wait to see Grace.

THURSDAY 1ST JANUARY 2004
Grace hasn't written back. I posted the letter five days ago so she should have got it by now. I thought we'd get a chance to talk after the trial, and I couldn't believe it when Mum bundled me off home without letting me speak to her. I cried for two whole days. I keep picking at the cut she made on my hand so it stays fresh. A scar will keep her with me until we meet again. We made a promise, so she'll stick by it. Won't she?

I still can't believe all this has happened. That summer was supposed to be Grace coming to stay, like every summer since I can remember, just me and her, like it always is. Why did we have to meet Charlotte on the beach, her of all people? I'd just moved schools to escape her and her bullying friends.

I hate Charlotte for starting all this. Why did she have to introduce Grace to Jason? First I was scared Grace would like Charlotte more than me – she was girly and pretty in a way I'll never be with my red hair and freckles everywhere. Always the odd one out. Plus she was such a bitch to me in school, and then being all nice that summer when Grace was around. So two-faced. Drove me fucking mad. Not to mention she got in the way of me and Grace.

Grace asked me what was up once. How could I tell her my gut ached because of how much I liked her? The day it all kicked off she was wearing a white vest which showed off her body, and those sexy denim shorts. She looked like a woman. Her legs were tanned and made mine look like twiglets. That's when I started taking photos of her. Photos she made me burn. Wish I hadn't now. That same day she got me to plait her hair and when she flicked it back it tickled my arm, like an electric shock. She stuck her legs out and her hair shone like gold, soft to touch. I massaged her head like I'd seen the hairdresser do to Mum, felt her warm body against mine. That made me go all tingly and I thought she liked it because she sighed out loud, and the knot in my stomach unravelled. Was it then that she started to like me too? She was the only person I could talk to, but how could I tell her I didn't understand the way she made me feel? It's called irony – we learned it in English the other day. And now she's not writing back to me, I'm left not knowing.

Before I lock my diary at night I look at the wild orchids she gave me, picked up on the cliff and placed in my hair. I've pressed them into the back of this diary, pretty purple smudges that I look at every night and imagine her smile.

FRIDAY 2ND APRIL 2004

Still no letter. Mum and I had a massive row last night because she won't give me Grace's phone number. Said she's not at home anyway, but won't say what she meant. Is Grace getting my letters? I just don't know. I can't sleep or eat, all I can think about is us. When my hand throbs I feel closer to her. Mum took me to the doctor and he said I'm depressed but I'm not, I just wanna be with Grace. But I couldn't tell them that, they wouldn't understand.

Does she still love me? She won't change her mind about us being together, will she? People say teenage love isn't real but they don't know anything, they've just forgotten. Or maybe she did prefer Jason after all. After the barbecue, when I caught her kissing him, she hated how upset I was, told me it was all an act to wind Charlotte up. Was I wrong to believe her? Every day I don't hear from her makes me less sure. I go up to the cliffs a lot when I want to get away from everyone and think. What with everything that happened there I thought it might not feel the same, but it does. Our initials are still carved into that tree. I keep trying to work out what happened that day, but it's like my head is full of air. Nothing. I so wish we could talk. Sort it all through. I'll keep writing until she writes back. I won't give up.

CHAPTER SEVENTEEN
MOLLY

Chez Elle is dark inside, with crystal lights hanging low over plush leather sofas, while a mirror reflects the light behind the bar and coloured liquids glow inside the bottles. A couple are draped over one another on one of the sofas, a woman sits on a bar stool, talking quietly into her mobile, and the beat of the music travels up from the floor through my feet and pulses into my body. I feel alive. My phone buzzes in my pocket and when I see who's calling, I stare at the screen as his name flashes over and over. *Darren*. What the fuck does he want? I shove my phone in my pocket; I can't deal with this now. Nothing is going to spoil this.

I place my order at the bar and take my coffee over to one of the booths facing the entrance, feeling proud that I've resisted a drink. I'm buzzing with the anticipation of seeing Grace. It takes me back to Dorset, the first day she came to stay that summer; she was late and I jumped up to the window at the sound of every car that turned into the street. I remember Mum giving me a funny look when she asked me why I was so impatient to see her.

We went down to the beach on that first evening. Grace's dad wasn't keen for us to go alone at that time of day, but Mum talked him round. I think she was glad to have a break from me – my energy used to wear her out. And I was lit up when Grace was around. Months of longing had driven me crazy. The sun was low in the sky and the water was warm and everything was glorious. Grace kissed me when we had swum out far enough to make sure nobody could see. On the mouth, like we had kissed at Christmas, and I wondered, for the millionth time, if she felt the same as I did. But that was before she met Jason.

A familiar scent makes me look up and Grace is walking towards me with a serious expression. Her sleek hair glides as she walks. She slips her pale pink leather jacket off, sits opposite me and orders a glass of wine. It must take ages for Grace to put her make-up on in the morning; she looks perfect. Her rosebud lips have a touch of gloss and I could sit and watch them dance in conversation for hours. I still can't believe she's here in front of me. I imagine framing her face through a camera lens and posing her to capture the best shot.

'Stop staring at me,' she says, and I turn my attention to the red neon *WOMEN* sign flashing above the door of the ladies. There are large red spots everywhere I look now, the sign flashing in my head.

Grace reaches for her glass and I glimpse her wrist. Instinctively I reach for it.

'Your tattoo's gone.'

'Don't.' She snatches her hand from mine. The betrayal hurts as if she's hit me. 'Of course it's gone. I told you to stay away.'

'Not after what Michael said to me.'

She grips the stem of her glass. 'I can't believe you went to see him. It was such a risky thing to do. Why?'

'I wanted to ask him about the letters. To check if you were telling the truth.'

'Of course I was telling the truth. What did he say?'

'Is he alright in the head? The woman there said he has emphysema, but he was confused. Didn't recognise me until I showed him the photograph.'

'What photograph?'

So she thinks I showed him *that* photo. I wouldn't. I'm not that messed up. 'Relax, one of us when we were kids. Mum took it.'

She shrugs. 'I don't remember. What else did he say?'

'He was confused. He was talking about that missing girl as if she was Charlotte. Have you seen that picture in the papers?'

Grace looks at me and I know she's spotted it too. The uncanny resemblance. 'He told me that he knew about us, that you'd told him.'

She looks shocked. 'That's a lie. He said the same about you to me.'

I study her face, trying to figure out if she's telling the truth. 'Why would he say that?'

'I told you, he's not well, he doesn't know what he's saying. Have you forgotten what he was like? Do you really think I wouldn't have told you at the time? We told each other everything.'

'So you remember?'

She bites her lip. 'This has to stop, Molly.'

'Promise me you're telling the truth. Look at me.'

She raises her eyes and holds my gaze. I know Grace, I know her better than anyone. She's telling the truth. So what was Michael talking about?

She looks away first and I wish I could read her mind. I'm about to speak when a woman walks past in a smart trouser suit. She pauses and her glance lingers on Grace.

'Grace, isn't it?' she comes closer and my shoulders droop. My time with Grace is precious and I don't want to share her with anyone.

'Love your sourdough bread basket,' she says.

'Thanks.'

'Any chance of a selfie?'

'Sure! No problem.' The woman crouches down beside her, her hand over Grace's silver-grey nails, and together they hold the phone up high. I might as well not be here. I stir sugar into my coffee, the spoon clinking against the side of the cup, waiting for them to finish.

'Cheers!' she says, touches Grace's arm and goes back to the bar and sips her drink. She watches us. I look back at Grace.

'That would drive me insane,' I say.

The bar is filling up now, a group of older women sliding into the booths behind us, but Grace seems unaware of her surroundings. I wonder if she's realised yet. Maybe she wouldn't have been so welcoming to that lapdog of a woman if she had. She continues watching us from the bar and I give her a look. She picks up her lager and moves away. The music's still pulsing and I sip my coffee, wishing it was a glass of vodka that would send a stronger burst to my head. *Don't, Molly.* It's being here with Grace that makes me nervous. Needing something to take the edge off.

'How do you deal with it?'

'Being recognised?'

'No. What happened back then with—'

'Shhh!' Grace leans forward. 'You have to find a way to deal with it. I went on this mindfulness course recently, "unwelcome thoughts", they call them. You put them on a little bus in your mind and they trundle away. Just like that. If they come back, you put them back on the bus. I boxed it up and threw away the key. You should try it.'

Shock reverberates through me. *Was it really that easy for her?* After everything we went through? 'It was alright for you, moving away. I was stuck in Lyme, where it all happened, on my own. Me and my crazy thoughts. The cliffs forever haunting me. It might have been different if you'd stayed in touch. That's why I wrote the letters.'

'Don't start on about that again, you know it was out of my hands. You need to take a leaf out of my book.'

'Grace, really? A fucking bus! Like all my problems will zoom off, just like that? How can you live in the public eye? Aren't you worried?'

'Why should I be worried, Molly?' She's lowered her voice and leans forward to make sure I hear. 'The courts were on our side, there's nothing to be ashamed about.' Grace puts her hands on the table, leans forward. 'You can't keep pursuing me like this. We need to sort this once and for all. What is it you want?'

'You know what I want. I need to know what happened that day.'

She flicks her hair back over her shoulder. I wonder if it's still as soft to touch.

'You didn't answer me properly last time. What happened after the fight? We thought she'd gone home, and then… don't you want to know?'

'Stop it, Molly. Why are you dwelling on it? At least she made it into town, which wasn't inevitable given what you'd done to her. We'll never know why she went back to the beach. Nobody was ever charged with the crime. You have to forget it.' She reaches out and takes my hand. Her touch is electric, it's so unexpected. 'I have, and you can too.'

Grace gazes into my eyes and my stomach turns to liquid. Her lips are slightly parted and I look back into her eyes to see if she feels it too, but she avoids my gaze. I don't want to let go, but she drops my hands and the moment is gone. Did I imagine it?

People are dancing. A couple slow-dance behind Grace and she notices me looking and turns to watch. When the women kiss, long and slow and deep, she turns to me, her eyes flashing.

'This is a gay bar.' Her voice is filled with venom.

'So?'

'You've done this deliberately, haven't you?'

She purses her lips together and takes a sip of her drink.

I shrug. 'You said to find somewhere that you didn't normally go. So I got that right, didn't I? I come here a lot, I feel relaxed. We can move to a straight city pub if you prefer.'

'I'm not staying.' She picks her bag up, then pauses. 'What about the anonymous text? Who could have sent it?'

'I'm not sure, but you ought to know my ex has been talking to a journalist. I guess it could be her.'

'Christ Molly.' Grace takes a long sip of her drink. If she hadn't realised before, she has now. It looks like it's only just sinking in.

'Have you always had girlfriends?'

I nod. 'Men have never interested me. How about you?'

She looks annoyed. 'Why ask me that? I'm straight, obviously.'

'How long have you been with Richard?'

She pushes her glass away. 'I'm not doing this, Molly. This isn't a normal catch-up with an old friend. All that secrecy, hiding away, it's not what I want any more. I love Richard and I'm proud to be seen with him, OK? The anonymous text changes everything. Surely you understand? We can't be seen together. Please, Molly.'

The couple behind Grace continue to slow-dance, hips locked together. It takes me back to the town disco, watching Grace with her arms wrapped around Jason's neck, sat on my fists to stop myself from dashing across the room and pulling her away from him. Charlotte was glaring at me, her over-painted lips moving rapidly, telling me to stop staring. She said I was acting as if I'd never seen anyone kiss before. That had made me look round and my stomach had clenched into a knot as I watched Grace snog the face off him. I had to bite at the inside of my cheek to stop myself from crying. She'd only known him two weeks. Charlotte didn't look happy either, and we both watched as Jason put his hand on her lower back. Any lower and he'd be grabbing her ass – it made me furious. I stood up and the bottle of Coke crashed onto the table, sending a stream of brown liquid right into Charlotte's lap. She screamed at me for ruining her top. But it was all her fault we ended up hanging around with him.

That's when I decided I was going to get her back. Big time.

In front of me, Grace is pulling on her jacket, standing, wine left unfinished. It tugs at my insides that she's leaving, but I force myself to stay seated. I try and understand how she feels. She's explained about her reputation, why she can't be seen with me. I watch her cross the bar, like a model on a catwalk, heads turning in her direction. But she's stopped now. It's the woman who bothered her for a selfie earlier, and now she's touching her on the shoulder, just a tap, but I don't miss anything where Grace is concerned. They speak for a few seconds and Grace disappears through the exit. A second later there's a flash of red as the woman picks up her jacket and slings it over her shoulder, following her out. Grace's undrunk wine tempts me to drink it. I decide I'll count to fifty, see if I still want it.

'Molly!'

Ellis is standing in front of me holding a pool cue. I push Grace's glass away, her pink lipstick decorating the edge. Instead I pick up my cup. I can't help wondering what Ellis is doing here.

'I noticed you a while ago, but didn't want to interrupt. Fancy a game?'

I nod. It'll give me something to take my mind off Grace, stop me from running after her.

'That was her, wasn't it? What was she doing here?'

'We had things to talk about.'

'It's a good choice of venue. Women will respect her privacy here.'

I hope she's right. 'Are you ready for me to thrash you?' I reply.

I want to win. I switch my mind off, focus on the game. Ellis is good, but I won't let her beat me. Halfway through, the woman in the red jacket returns and I wonder where she's been. Then I remember the call from my brother. Why is he calling me now? Has something happened to Mum? I wonder if he's forgiven me. My cue slams so hard into the ball it jumps off the table. Ellis wins easily after that.

Away from the music and voices, walking home in the silent street, Grace is back in my head, crunching thoughts that won't let up. It hurts when I scrape my knuckles against the wall. I concentrate on the stinging sensation as I count the minutes down. I'm furious with myself for ever mentioning Jodie and her threats – I should have known it would frighten Grace away. I chew at my knuckles, the metallic taste of blood flooding my mouth.

GRACE'S DIARY

Tuesday 1st June 2004

It's been six months since I heard from Molly. Six months in a new country, new language, new me. I hate her now. How dare she forget me? After everything we went through?

Aunt Jenny's told me this is a fresh start, and she's right. She wants me to change my name to hers. GRACE MARTIN. No more Grace Cavendish. It looks good.

Dad's rung once a week since I've been here but I won't speak to him. I'm so pleased to be away from the bastard. He's no dad to me.

Today I've made some decisions:

1. Change my surname to Martin.
2. Dad's now called Michael, and I won't answer his calls until he gets the message.
3. Date guys. No more girls.
4. Invent a new past for myself.

Number 3 is because I will never let a girl get close to me again.

Number 4 is because all that shit is over.

PS: Number 3 is also because I've been thinking about Jason a lot lately. I was attracted to him until Molly got in the way. It was like she cast a spell on me and I couldn't break free. Next time a hot guy comes along nothing is going to stand in my way. I'm not a gullible teenager any more.

CHAPTER EIGHTEEN

GRACE

A black cab speeds past as I leave the warmth of Chez Elle and I pull my scarf around my neck. The door bangs and the sourdough woman emerges, her perfume so strong I feel dizzy. She slips a pack of cigarettes from her clutch bag, lights one. She sees me watching.

'Do you want one?' Her blonde fringe falls over her eyes.

It's cold and the cab has long gone. My nerves are twisted up; I have to calm down before I go home. I don't want to be recognised standing outside. I feel a flutter of anger – is this a set-up? Was it Molly's intention all along? But the woman seems friendly enough.

'Please,' I say, needing the comfort of the ritual, lighting up and breathing smoke deep into my lungs. It stops me fiddling with my hands and revealing how agitated I am.

'You won't have long to wait for another cab, they come round pretty regularly. Which way are you heading?'

'Camden.'

'Shame, I'm going south. We could have shared.'

She looks at me, blinks her long eyelashes and I look away. Another black cab is pulling up outside and I raise my arm, calling it over.

'Ladies first,' she says. Her nails are painted bright purple and she places them on my arm. 'I've not seen you here before.'

'No, you wouldn't have.' I wave at the cab driver again, wanting to get away from her now. He's pulled into the kerb and is waiting for me. 'Thanks for the cigarette.'

'No sweat. Take my card, in case you fancy a drink sometime.' Her purple nails release my arm and she slides her business card into my pocket, her fingers lingering on my thigh.

'Sweet dreams, honey.'

The cab pulls away and I don't look back, not wanting her pretty face to see the reaction her touch has set off. The bar has unsettled me. Seeing women together so naturally. All over each other. Not a care in the world. It's the first time I've ever been in a place like that. Despite coming close in Paris, I've deliberately kept away. Buried it deep. Those feelings I had when I was younger weren't real; they had nothing like the strength of my feelings for Richard.

But later, when he reaches for me in bed and rolls on top of me, I flinch and find myself picturing the pale blonde hair of the woman, painted nails pressing into my thigh.

It's silent when I wake and I rub my eyes, checking the time. It takes me a moment to realise that I've overslept. My plan was to get up early and start cooking. The brand designer wants the names and details of the products to be included in the range, and I've not done the required recipe-testing. I'm supposed to be taking printouts of the recipes to a meeting with my editor for her to sign off on them later, but I'm not ready. I need more time. I need structure. I've let things slip yet again. I sit cross-legged and do some yoga breathing, trying to calm my breath, which feels like it's trapped in my throat. If I work out a timetable for myself, I'll be able to negotiate a new deadline. But what I can't factor in is the emotional ups and downs that are stopping me from doing my work, getting in the way of everything.

Richard has left his ironed shirts out and I can't settle down to my baking while his pristine white cotton garments hang like a blot on the landscape. They spoil the clean lines of the flat and have to be put away. That cuts half an hour out of my day. Today I'm making an apple and poppyseed cake, and the kitchen is soon flooded with the smell of sweet apples and cinnamon.

Julia calls when the cake is in the oven. Despite the heat pumping out, I'm shivering. I put another jumper on but it does nothing to keep out the cold. I take the call on the sofa, wrapping a cashmere shawl around myself.

'You haven't sent me the proposal for your next book.' There's an edge to her voice and I feel a prick of guilt.

'It's not ready. Something came up. I'm really sorry, but I'm going to need more time.'

'Can you send it to me by the end of the week?'

I calculate the week in my head. 'Yes.' I have no choice.

'By the way, Grace, what's happening on social media? Have you seen the photos of you?'

Fear creeps over me. 'No, what photos?'

'There's a photo of you smoking.'

Christ. My heart gallops. 'Give me ten minutes, I'll have a look and ring you back.'

I can't believe I haven't seen the photos yet. I've been so stressed I've barely been online. It's not like me. There are two images. Outside in a doorway, a close-up of me sucking a cigarette like I'm desperate for oxygen. But the second photo disturbs me more: it's a shot inside the bar last night of me with Molly. *When was that taken?* I look drunk, there's no denying it, glass raised to my lips and caught at an angle where it's tilting, so it looks like the wine is about to miss my mouth. I clench my fists as I stare at the screen; the reality is so innocent, but who will believe me? As I scroll through the comments my fingernails dig deeper into my palms and I catch sight of the name Alex Foster. His comment reads,

'*Who is Grace's mystery friend?*' There's a shot of Molly, sideways on, leaning in to catch what I'm saying. *Fuck, fuck, fuck.* What am I going to do?

'I can explain,' I say when I call Julia back, excuses pouring out. *Old school friend, yes, I had a glass of wine but I'm no saint, contrary to media perception…*

'Grace, calm down, this is me you're talking to. I'm on your side, remember.'

I slump in the chair, out of breath. 'Of course. I've got myself in such a state. Richard will be furious.'

'He'll be supportive, I'm sure.'

I doubt that.

'He's paranoid about our brand, drums into me how important our media profile is. He acts as if we're the Beckhams.'

'It's understandable. He's just trying to be supportive.'

'How should I respond?' *So what if I drink? I don't hide the fact, I'm just careful what I choose to put into my body. Most of the time.*

'It's unfortunate, it isn't the image we want to present. But for now, let's deal with damage limitation. Have any journalists been in touch?'

'No.' But Alex Foster lurks in the background. Cold air blows through the flat. He can't have been in a women-only bar, which means someone else is following me. *Who?* Purple nails flash into my mind and shame makes my face hot.

'Grace, I'm on your side. I know you don't smoke.'

A twinge of guilt pricks my conscience, but there was only one other time, on the privacy of my balcony.

'Who is the woman you're with?'

The chilly sensation intensifies. Despite my determination, Molly is encroaching into my life. And there are some serious consequences.

'She went to my primary school. I wouldn't call her a friend, even.' I sigh. 'She showed up at my book launch and asked to meet. It seemed like a good idea at the time.' *How wrong I was.*

'Is she likely to talk if she's asked about it? Maybe you need to have a conversation with her – these journalists can be so devious. Ask her not to talk to the press. I'll send you a couple of lines as a quote to put out – that will be our only response to this. Don't get drawn into a dialogue with anyone. Try not to worry, Grace. But it is unlike you to miss a deadline, plus you haven't posted much this week. Your daily features are important for building a brand. You have a huge following, and you want to keep them loyal. Is something wrong?'

I reassure Julia that I'll get straight back on it, but when the phone call ends working is far from my mind. Richard is still at the office and I'm dreading seeing him later. If he knew about Julia's concerns he'd be furious. Like picking a scab, I delve further and further into the comments on my page, endlessly studying the photographs, getting more and more worked up.

The photos are all over the internet. Shared, reposted, retweeted. Hashtag Queen of Clean. How the hell did I miss this earlier? So many people with so many opinions. A picture can tell so many stories, but the one the public picks on is the one that does me most damage. Typical. Richard has warned me about this: if our image is good, then people want to knock that, take us down to their level. It's only now that it's happening I fully understand. I curse the journalist who named me 'Queen of Clean'; I never wanted that title. It's going to be my undoing. Part of me wants to curl into a ball and hide away, like an animal hibernating in winter, coming back up for air when everything is back to normal again. But that isn't an option. I'm in the public eye and I have to deal with it. Deep inside I hate to acknowledge that part of me that resents Richard for forcing me into the limelight. For a moment I even wish I was back in France.

Unable to focus on work, I look up Alex Foster, delving into his background. Television and radio appearances have made him well known in his field, and he's often the 'go to' journalist when a talking head is required. I click on images, but his face is unfamiliar. Now based in London, he has a huge following online. I can't help feeling threatened by it.

On his blog today the featured case is the murder of a hairdresser in Southend, whose stepfather was jailed for the crime but released on appeal, thanks to a huge campaign for his release. Opinion is divided on his innocence. Alex's countdown is getting closer to 2002. Dread fills me. Reading the details makes my stomach churn and I snap the laptop shut, no longer wanting to read about unsolved cases. There must be something wrong with someone who chooses to focus on this stuff. How does he sleep at night?

The door slams, announcing Richard's return. Although I've eaten nothing all day I want to be sick. He throws his bag onto the sofa and pulls his tie off so aggressively I think it's going to rip.

'I take it you've seen this,' he says, holding out his phone. 'What on earth were you thinking?'

'It's not what it seems.'

'Promoter of clean living, Grace Sutherland, is caught drinking and smoking. Which bit of that statement have I got wrong?'

'Yes, I had a glass of wine and I can't excuse the cigarette. But you know I don't smoke. You know what these photographers are like. And no way was I drunk, it's just an unfortunate angle. Christ, Richard, you know me.' Tears prickle my eyes and I will them away, not wanting to look weak.

'I didn't say anything when you were so late back last night, but I should have done. Staying out late and drinking isn't an option for us. And you overslept this morning. You're usually up before me, but I thought it best to let you sleep it off. You can't afford late nights like this. It's impacting on your work. And the timing is terrible – you can't go off the rails when I'm fighting an important election.'

'I'm not going off the rails. I just fancied a drink. I'm only human. I had one.'

He sinks down on the sofa. 'I know, I know. But I've looked at the other photos online and I recognise the woman you were with. It's her from the other night, isn't it? Your old school friend. You didn't tell me you'd seen her. I thought you said you were out with Carrie.'

I can't believe he's been studying the photos and made that connection. I have to be more careful.

'I bumped into her, that's all.' The lie slips out so easily.

'After she sent you that photo? You should be avoiding her.'

'It was a difficult situation. She was there and I was on my own. It would have been awkward to make a fuss. She's alright. It's not a big deal.'

'It is when people are asking who she is. You don't know what she might say. She doesn't sound all that stable to me.'

'I spoke to Julia and she's told me how to handle the situation. Suggested I have a word with her.'

'And have you?'

'Not yet, but I will. Look, I'm sorry it happened, I really am, but can we put it behind us? I feel bad enough as it is, without you making me feel worse.'

Richard shakes his head. 'What a day. I need a shower.' His face is set and I know he hasn't forgiven me. It's so hard at times to read what he's thinking, unlike Molly, who has her emotions written all over her. I curse myself for comparing them.

'I'll get some food on.'

I gather ingredients together but my thoughts couldn't be further from eating. Red Camargue rice will cook quickly and is Richard's favourite. I'll make it specially for him, to help him forget his bad day. He's my priority. I chop aubergines and red peppers and wish my life could go back to how it was a few weeks ago, before Molly got catapulted back into it. But she's here now, seeping her way into my thoughts. As I'm washing basil I puzzle again over the photographs. I don't remember anyone taking them. I stir diced shallots, the heat too high, the oil sizzling and spitting at me. One of Molly's friends, that must be it. How can I believe anything she's telling me? I should know better by now than to trust her. I stir the vegetables, the fragrant smell of basil soothes me and the wooden spoon jerks against the pan as my nerves get the better of me. It's not the first time the *Daily Tribune* has given me an unwanted title, sending journalists snooping into my life. I was able to run away last time. *But this time?* I don't realise Richard is behind me until his arms go round my waist and I almost knock the pan onto the floor.

'I'm sorry,' Richard says, nuzzling his chin into my hair, and I let myself sink into his arms. I love him so much. 'We're a team, always have been. We'll get through this.'

This time I'm not running anywhere.

CHAPTER NINETEEN

MOLLY

I'm up early the next morning, unable to sleep, last night's conversation with Grace buzzing in my head. She draws me to her and I walk as fast as I can, force myself back to the canal. I shudder at the sight of the murky water, but it's worth it to be near her. I can't help looking up at Grace's flat, wondering whether she's up there. Is she going over and over last night too? Seeing women together, I wanted her to know that it doesn't have to be a secret, that attitudes are different now – that not everyone thinks like her dad. I keep on walking – fast, determined steps – trying to drive my anxiety away. By the time I get to Victoria Park I'm feeling light-headed, so I cut across the grass where a van is selling food and drink, and I buy myself a flaky Danish pastry and a warm cup of tea. A little boy runs past, chasing a squirrel, an older girl following him, exasperation on her face and I think about Darren. He looked up to me once, until I let him down. Over and over. He'll call again if it's important. Heat hits my cheeks when I remember the last time I saw him. No way I can face calling him.

I take a slower pace on the way back, the pastry sticking heavily in my stomach and I realise I'm not used to eating so much. Without drink in me I'm hungrier, which can't be a bad thing. By the time I get back to Grace's flat I can't resist sitting outside for a bit, smoking a cigarette on the bench. Niggling inside me is Grace's voice telling me not to pursue what happened to Charlotte.

Maybe she's right and we'll never know. But if that's the case, how will I ever forgive myself? I know what I did. An image appears in my mind, the courtroom, harsh lights making my head pound, a man in a ridiculous wig firing questions at me. Not daring to look at Grace for reassurance, losing it when the man wouldn't stop with the questions, yelling at him to stop. Men scribbling furiously until the judge ordered everyone out. What else was I supposed to tell them?

The canal is busy with commuters now and I'm about to head home when a man exits the flats, walking with purpose, briefcase in one hand, head to one side as he talks into his phone. It's *him*. I slide my mobile out and take a series of shots, zooming in on his face. I'll get these printed, add them to my collection. Work out what he's up to.

On the way home I pick up some bread to make toast, resolving to eat more. My phone pings as I'm unlocking my flat and I catch my breath when I see that it's Darren.

I picture his boyish face with a cheeky grin, so like Dad, and just thinking about him sends a pang of loss through me. Dad would know what to do. And he would want me to answer.

I pick up.

'Molly, is that you?' His voice is also like Dad's and my throat seizes up.

'Hey, Darren.'

'You OK?'

'Yeah, I'm OK, better than last time anyway.'

'That's not difficult.' He's silent for a moment and then we both laugh. 'Seeing as last time I saw you was when the police called me from the hospital.'

I rake my hand through my hair. It needs a wash. Dad's funeral. I was so gutted when he died, I couldn't believe I'd not spoken to him since I left home, and then it was too late. Drunk until I could face the funeral, so blotto it was all a blur. Shame heats my body.

'Molly?'

I'd come to in hospital, covered in bruises and on a drip, with Darren at my side, his face drained of all colour.

'No, I haven't forgotten.'

'Are you still seeing that woman?'

'Jodie? No, thank God.'

Jodie had turned up when Darren was there, still a bit out of it. That was in the early days when I thought she'd leave her girlfriend. All I could think about was whether she'd told her yet. My life was like that, a series of events with gaping holes in between where I had no idea what happened. The thought scares me now.

'How are you, Darren? Is everything OK?'

'I'm fine, still in Manchester, same job. But it's Mum I'm ringing about, I'm worried about her.'

'Is she ill?'

'No, well, she's not been herself since Dad died, but she's not looking after herself properly. The house is a mess.'

'You're joking.'

'I wish.'

'She's still working, but... she misses you, Molly. You sound a lot better—'

'I am – just about. I'm sorting myself out. I was wondering about going to see her, but I'm scared, I'm not sure it's a good idea, you know, to be in Dorset.'

There's a silence on the end of the line. Darren was too young to understand at the time and Mum tried to keep him from finding out what happened, but it was impossible. The legacy of The Orchid Girls.

'She'd be made up,' he says, 'she misses you. We speak most weeks and she always mentions you.'

'Does she?'

'Get in touch with her, Molly, she's having a tough time. It would do her good.'

We chat some more and my mood is better than it's been for ages. After our call ends, I'm ready for some toast. As I reach for the bread my phone pings again.

Jodie. I thought she'd got the message. What's she contacting me about? She's sent me a link to a website so I log on to my laptop; the loaf of bread lies unopened on the counter.

The link takes me to a blog page of a journalist who's been inspired by the recent case of the missing girl, Emily Shaw, and is looking at old cases linked to missing teenagers. I slam the laptop shut, feeling sick. A drink would help me blot all this out. But one drink would lead on to the next, and who knows what else, so I make myself a cup of tea, forcing myself back to my laptop. Great – he's going to be looking into The Orchid Girls. I wonder if Grace knows about this. It's funny that I've been thinking about it all so much, and now this is happening. The thought stresses me and I chew my thumbnail, unable to leave it alone.

Steph from the internet cafe rings when I'm eating cheese on toast, interrupting me reflecting on last night's conversation with Grace for the hundredth time.

'Have you been online this morning?'

'No, why?'

'Come to the cafe, I want to show you something. Now's a good time, not many people are in.'

Ten minutes later I'm sitting behind the counter with Steph. She prints my photos while she shows me what she's seen. A photograph of me and Grace at the bar last night. A picture of Grace smoking has gone viral.

'It is you, isn't it?'

I nod. 'Yeah. Me and Grace were at school together.' I drag my fingers through my hair. 'All this fuss about a cigarette is like being back at school.'

'She won't be happy. It's not the best publicity for her healthy eating, is it?'

Steph tightens her lime-green scarf around her neck. It clashes with her pink hair. 'I don't know if this is a coincidence, but a woman was in here asking after you the other day.'

'Jodie? You know we're finished.'

'About time! I couldn't stand her. I can say it now you've seen sense. But no, it wasn't Jodie. I'd never seen this woman before.'

Heat rises in my body and my armpits feel sweaty.

'What did she look like?' *If it's not Jodie, then who could it be? Not Ellis, surely?*

'She had a black woolly hat on covering her hair, but I didn't get a good look at her. It was busy at the time.'

'Did you say anything to her?'

'Shut up! What kind of a friend do you think I am? I told her to get lost.'

'Cheers.'

On the way home Ellis texts me, inviting me to dinner. Last night obviously didn't put her off. I say yes because it gets me out of the house and I'm still intrigued by her being at the bar. Was it a coincidence? Ellis has to be genuine, she has to be – I'd be gutted if she wasn't. But the person who went to the cafe is playing on my mind, making me paranoid. Is this how Grace feels, living in fear of the past, always expecting her identity to be found out?

Back at my flat, I chew on Haribo sweets to keep the jitters at bay – Abdul's been selling them at bargain-basement prices. I hate the feeling that I'm being watched, it's making me nervous as hell. I eat one pack after the other while I pluck up the guts to ring

Mum. I pick up the phone, tapping in the only number drilled into my memory. Then I put it down again, desperate for a coffee.

The coffee tastes bitter. *Stop putting it off.* My hand trembles as I dial the numbers, listening to the sound as it rings out into the room. It's easy to picture the scene even though it's years since I left, swearing never to go back. Dad was around then, his slippers by his chair, my pebble photos framed on the wall. I wonder if they're still there; what they did with my room. I hated leaving him, but even he'd had enough by then. The ringing stops and her familiar voice hits me like an electric shock.

'It's me,' I say.

Loud breath travels down the line. At least she doesn't hang up.

'Molly, is that you?'

'Yes, it's me, Mum.'

'Let me sit down.' Shuffling sounds follow. 'It's been so long, Molly, are you alright?'

'I'm alright, better than when you last saw me, anyway.'

'Oh, Molly, you were a mess,' she says, her voice filled with pain.

'I know. I was upset, we both were… can I come and see you?'

'Are you still in Birmingham?'

'London.'

'Never settle, you. Seeing anyone?'

'Nothing serious.'

'A job?'

'Just finished one, I've been working in a pub. I've got some spare time, that's why I thought I'd visit.'

'Need money, do you?'

I can't help feeling hurt. Ashamed. 'No, Mum, I promise. I'd like to see you. How are you?'

'I'm still working at the doctor's surgery, I've got my own clinic now. The doctors are so busy, we nurses have to do more all the time. Five mornings a week. It gets me out of the house, and you know I like having people to chat to.'

I'm pleased she's keeping busy. Guilt gnaws at me for leaving her all alone.

'I spoke to Darren.'

'He rings me every week, he probably told you he's got himself a nice girlfriend, settling down. He always asks about you.'

'He said the same about you.'

Her breathing fills the silence and I close my eyes, scared she's going to reject me.

'I'm glad you rang, love.'

I let out the breath I've been holding. 'Will it be OK to come down?'

She doesn't answer immediately and my stomach plummets. She doesn't want me.

'Mum?'

'Of course, it'll be fine. The house isn't how you remember, though.'

Relief floods through me. 'That doesn't matter. It'll be in the next couple of weeks. I need to sort out a ticket. I'll let you know. Have you got a mobile?'

I write her number down and ring off. My hand still throbs a little. Speaking to my mum has stirred me up inside. She was hesitant about something. But why wouldn't she be? So much has happened. And all of it's my fault.

Ellis has cooked a lasagne and we eat in the kitchen, warmth spilling out of the oven, making me hungry.

'I was surprised to see you at Chez Elle last night. Especially after you told me about Steve.'

'Not as surprising as you rocking up with Grace Sutherland.'

'Not one of my best ideas. I thought it would be more discreet, but I got that wrong. Someone snapped her with me in the bar and posted it online.'

'I guess she's used to it. Is that why you were in a bad mood?'

'You noticed? It's difficult with her, so much to talk about. She's going to be pissed off about the photo. Another one of her smoking is all over the internet.'

She shrugs. 'It must happen to her all the time.'

'I guess.' Grace will be furious, but I don't want to think about that now. 'Have you been there before?'

'Every now and then. I like playing pool, that's all. It's less threatening than finding a partner in a mixed place. And that's if the men let you get a look-in.'

'I know what you mean.' I realise, then, that Ellis wasn't surprised about the photo. She must have seen it online already.

The chocolate mousse we eat for dessert is delicious.

'Do you want another?'

'I do, but…'

'It's sugar withdrawal, it's normal. And you could do with putting on a few pounds.'

'I guess so. Mum will enjoy feeding me up.'

'Have you lost weight since you last saw her?'

'No, she's used to me looking like this, but I was different before, healthier.'

'Before?'

'Before I started drinking.' But that isn't what I meant. 'You know what mums are like.'

'Mine's the same, every time I see her she "just happens" to have baked a batch of my favourite cakes.'

'Sounds like you get on well,' I say, feeling a pang of jealousy.

'Doing my amends cleared the air. Honestly, Molly, you can turn your life around too. Have you spoken to your mum yet?'

I tell her about our conversation. 'She was a bit hesitant about me staying at the house.'

'It's just nerves, don't take any notice. She'll be fine. I promise.'

'Maybe.' I'm not convinced. 'I need to sort out a date, get a cheap ticket. Jodie's been in touch again, mentioned a journalist. I should never have told her about Grace.'

'She's bad news,' Ellis scrapes the last of the chocolate out of her glass, a disapproving look on her face.

'I know, I haven't replied.'

'You and Grace were good friends, weren't you?'

I nod.

'So what is she worried about?'

'She's paranoid about her image, her brand, especially with the election coming up. I reckon she's scared of her husband. And that photograph of her smoking – well, it's her worst fear, isn't it?'

'Not so Queen of Clean.' Ellis laughs but I can't joke about it. 'Anyone who doesn't eat chocolate isn't normal in my book. Doesn't she trust you?'

'I don't know what she thinks. That's partly why I'm getting off to Dorset.'

'I'll miss you.'

'No, you won't. You've only just met me,' I say, smiling. But I can't ignore how nice it feels to have someone who cares.

'I feel as if I've known you for ages.'

'Me too.'

She grins as she clears the plates away.

After dinner we move to the sofa. Ellis brings over two mugs of hot chocolate. She folds a blanket around us and the flat is snug and warm. It's stupid of me to doubt her; I must just be paranoid, with everything going on.

She switches the television on. We watch a sitcom and I love the way she makes hilarious comments, copies voices. It's hard to feel jittery in her company.

The news follows and Grace's husband is on again. This time he's talking about road safety, standing in front of a busy junction where two cyclists have been killed this year. Ellis says I should get a bike helmet, but I'll need to get a job first.

I watch Richard. He's confident as he talks directly to the camera, wearing a relaxed smile. Even the hi-vis jacket looks stylish on him. Makes me sick. I wonder how he and Grace got together. In France, I think she said. I suppose that means she can speak French. Another skill for perfect Grace.

The reporter is interviewing members of the public now, canvassing their opinions of the crossing, and a woman with tears in her eyes talks about her best friend who was killed there last month. A line of words scrolls across the bottom and I read the breaking news that a body has been found near Ash Fenton. The scene switches to the village and Ellis turns the volume up. Everyone is interested in this, just like back then. Screaming black headlines.

The present will never go away unless I sort the past out. I hug the blanket around myself, suddenly cold as I listen to the report.

A body has been found in undergrowth in the village of Harping, five miles outside Ash Fenton, home to missing teenager Emily Shaw. The body was discovered by two schoolboys out looking for conkers. The body is of a young female, but at this stage no identification has yet been made. Anyone who has been in the area of Drake's Common this afternoon is asked to ring the number displayed on the screen below. Emily Shaw has been missing for four days since she was last seen with her school friends in a playground in Ash Fenton. We'll report more information as soon as it comes in.

Emily's picture flashes up on screen and once again I see Charlotte. Of course, Mum was leading the volunteers when it was reported she was missing. She rounded up everyone on the street and organised a search party. Charlotte was treated like a prom queen where we lived, the pretty girl who made the paper every week winning gold cups for gymnastics. Nobody knew what she was really like. I was sick with worry that someone would find out we had been fighting, but Grace said it was best not to tell anyone. She was the only one who knew what I had done. The only other person who knew what Charlotte was *really* like.

'Shall we go and see a film at the weekend? Keep your mind off you know what.' Once again Ellis says the right thing, stops my mood plummeting into darkness.

'I'd like that.' The chocolate at the bottom of my cup is extra sweet. 'It's alright, this non-drinking, sometimes.'

We laugh. Her smile is wide and her eyes flicker.

'Good, I'll see what's on and text you. Something funny – we deserve a good laugh. And Molly, you're doing great.'

The text arrives when I'm about to switch the light off for bed. Same anonymous sender.

Where are The Orchid Girls now??

Whoever is sending these messages has made the link with the name I chose for myself on that drunken night I contacted Grace. Somebody else is interested. *It must be Alex.* What have I done? I've started something I can't stop. Along with my reaction to the body on the news, and everything happening with Grace, the text makes up my mind. I'm right to do this. When I get to Dorset I have to dig up the camera. I buried it all those years ago, but it's time to unearth it. Maybe what's on it will help jog my memory. No matter what Grace says, now more than ever I have to know the truth.

16TH AUGUST 2002

CHARLOTTE BODY FOUND

The family of Charlotte Greene confirmed this morning that the body washed up on a beach near Lyme Regis, Dorset, was that of the fourteen-year-old, missing for two days.

The search ended around 6 p.m. on Tuesday, two days after the teenager went missing. Just before 5 p.m. on Tuesday afternoon a member of the public reported the discovery of a bag on Monmouth Beach while walking her dog. Police were dispatched to the area and the body was found soon after. Initial indications suggest she had drowned. A police spokesman, Detective Inspector Robert Sparks, said at least fifty people had been interviewed with regard to Charlotte's disappearance.

Hundreds of locals assisted with the search and Johnny Greene, Charlotte's uncle, thanked the community for participating, asking the public to respect the family at this tragic time.

The case of the bright young gymnastics star has captured the imagination of the nation. Charlotte attended Lyme Secondary School and was a successful gymnast, representing the county of Dorset in 2000, 2001 and 2002, when she held the title of Young Gymnast of the Year. She was believed to be heading for the next Olympics in 2004, due to start training next month. On Monday morning, British champion gymnast James Donovan appealed for witnesses to come forward on television.

On Sunday 4th August Charlotte spent the morning walking the cliff path with two friends who allegedly left her in the town centre at around 1 p.m. Her mother became anxious when she had not returned home by 6 p.m. and she was reported missing at 10 p.m., when an extensive search of the area began. A closed-circuit television camera located along the town's high street showed no images of Charlotte.

Grace Cavendish, fifteen, one of the friends Charlotte had been with on the day she went missing said, 'We spent the morning together, hanging out on the cliffs. Charlotte said she was going home for lunch and we walked back down towards town together. I can't believe this, we hadn't known each other long but she was the nicest person and I'm missing her so much already. Please come back, Charlotte, we love you so much.' Since Charlotte's body has been found, her two friends have been unable to comment.

CHAPTER TWENTY

GRACE

I force myself to work the next morning, editing the photos from my last few recipes and adding a flurry of posts to Instagram. That should keep everybody off my back. I eat a bowl of porridge for lunch. It's the first thing I've been able to keep down since Molly sent a text this morning saying she's received another anonymous message. She forwarded it to me and I retched in the sink, sweating, seeing the old Grace reflected there. But she can't come back. I won't allow it.

Where are The Orchid Girls now??

I look up Molly's OrchidGirl account, but no connection has been made to the old case yet. Her profile consists of the generic avatar, without any personal details. Nothing to link the photo of Molly with me in the bar to this account, thank God. My fear lessens. But it threatens to grow again when I fast-forward to Alex Foster's page. Today's unsolved case is a young girl whose body was found in the Scottish Highlands. Year 2000. Getting closer. I hate this Alex guy with his probing questions, prodding and poking and finding things out. Things I have tried so hard to bury. Could he be the anonymous texter? The idea seems ludicrous; he's a professional journalist. Is he in this with Molly? That ex she mentioned. How would I know?

My mobile rings and I pick up despite not recognising the number. A man introduces himself as a colleague of Lily, the journalist from *Eat Clean* who interviewed me the other day.

'I'd like to clarify a few points before we publish the story – could you spare a minute of your time?'

My throat feels dry. Why hasn't Lily contacted me herself? But he explains that she's been called away at the last minute, and he's friendly enough. I'm overreacting.

'OK,' I say, sitting at the kitchen island as if it's a formal interview.

'Lily feels the article lacks depth, and wants more of a human interest angle. She wants to follow your journey from childhood onwards. She said she raised this with you, but ran out of time during the interview. I'd like to go over those details with you now, if that's OK?'

My seat suddenly feels hard and I reach for a cushion. Should I trust him? 'I thought the article was more of a book review, going over the last twelve months of my career. As you know, the book follows the months through with my recipes, each of which has a new twist. The book also mentions my move to London from Paris, which is well-documented. The—'

'Yes, that's been covered. I know you studied nutrition in France. Lily's specifically asked me to find out more about your childhood in Dorset. This is what readers will want to know, to learn more about you.'

I push the chair back and it scrapes against the wood. I've never mentioned Dorset to Julia, let alone Lily. *How did she find out?* It struck me as strange that Lily didn't contact me herself, and now I hold myself rigid, convinced this man is not who he says he is.

'What did you say your name was again?'

'I didn't,' he says. I cut the call and drop to the floor, my legs like twigs, no longer able to support me. My movements are robotic as I call Molly, lurching backwards and forwards as I will her to answer. Only she will understand the terror that mentioning Dorset has unleashed in me. But she doesn't pick up.

I open my eyes. It's dark and my mobile is ringing. I must have fallen asleep – broken, sleepless nights catching up with me.

I let it go to voicemail. It's Richard, telling me he's working late tonight. Only a few weeks ago, an evening in would be the perfect opportunity to get on with my self-promotion on social media, upping my followers. I'm due to make vlogs to tie in with each chapter of my book, but the ambience isn't right and I'm not in the mood. I slice an avocado and some cherry tomatoes, placing some gluten-free bread in the toaster. Richard being out isn't unusual, but tonight I can't help wondering who he's with, trying not to fixate on the team of attractive young women who work in his office. Even more reason for me to up my game, to make sure the new Grace doesn't slip.

Seeing Molly has reminded me how few female friends I have in my life. Carrie is the only one, and now she's texted to say she's totally loved-up, which means she'll disappear for a few days, before deciding he isn't the one: her usual pattern. It's my choice to keep female friends at a distance, because I can't let anyone get too close. Women are more of a threat in that way. But when Carrie's not in a relationship, she's only ever got one thing on her mind – men. She's just like Charlotte was. You'd be in the middle of a conversation with her and she'd stop mid-sentence, a boy catching her attention. *Pathetic*. She was obsessed with Jason. I only got off with him to show her that I could. And she hated it. Women can't be trusted where men are concerned. But Molly was never like that. Meeting her again is like settling back into an old skin. I mustn't get drawn in; I need to remember why I'm doing this. There's too much at stake.

The balcony door is open and I step outside to cool down for a moment. Richard tried to prepare me for this: the long hours, the little time he would have for me, but it still hurts. I try not to think about what success would mean for us – if he were to be elected Mayor of London, would he have any time left for me at all? I shiver involuntarily. The feeling of being neglected reminds me too much of the time after the trial, when dark thoughts filled my head. I give myself a shake, reminding myself that this is what we both want. I breathe in the cool air and stare into the black night.

Late in the night I'm woken up by Richard crawling into bed. Afterwards I drift in and out of sleep and he's gone again when I wake at nine. At least he won't be able to go on at me to get my work done. No matter how successful I am, will he ever think I'm good enough? He forgets that I'm sacrificing having children, and the thought makes me well up with tears. Being with Molly was so easy compared to Richard. I didn't have to agonise over every decision, or worry about pissing her off. That special bond between women is such a different dynamic, so intense. She told me every thought that was in her head. Men don't do that. For the hundredth time I wonder what she put in the letters. To read them now would take me back to that time, remind me of the connection we once had. Dangerous, but… if I destroy them, the threat will be one less thing to worry about. After an hour in the kitchen, gazing at a blank work surface, I accept that until I ask Michael about the letters, I won't be able to settle down to anything.

I call Angela to let her know I'm on my way. She's surprised that I'm coming over again so soon, and I feel a pang of guilt at my loss of composure last time I visited. Now she's seen how strained my relationship with Michael is. But it's always been there, tension simmering under the surface. Ready to explode.

'I was going to ring you anyway, suggest you come over. Michael has been difficult the past couple of days – it's that missing girl on television. If he catches the news he gets into a right state. He keeps trying to tell me something, but I don't understand what he's getting at.' Her voice is laced with worry.

I inhale deeply, willing my voice not to shake.

'I'll be there as soon as I can.'

It's an easy journey once the rush hour is over, and I'm there in an hour. On the way I mull over Richard's comments from the other day. He has always accepted that I wasn't happy at home and would rather not talk about that part of my life. He understood my need to leave it all behind. So why his sudden outburst the other day? Pressure builds up in my head and I focus my thoughts on Michael, who long ago stopped being my father.

Angela lets me in, telling me Michael's in bed. She takes advantage of my presence to slip out to the shops. He's asleep when I enter his room and I pause in the doorway. Illness has taken away his strength, hurting his pride. The very same man who use to frighten us to death. His parishioners would listen to his sermons in awe, spellbound. They didn't see how hard he was to live with, his impossible expectations. Michael looks perplexed when I pat him on the arm, eyes blinking fast, his forehead furrowed like the pleats of a fan. He sits up in bed.

'What are you doing here?' His voice is wheezy, his chest sounds worse than usual.

'Visiting you, of course, Michael. Angela tells me you've not been well.'

The bungalow is quiet, reminding me we're alone.

'Michael!' He spits the word as if it burns his tongue. 'I'm your father, or have you forgotten that? Why can't you call me Dad like you used to?'

'You know why.'

'Going to France was the best thing that ever happened to you. My prayers were answered when you met a good man. You should be thanking me.'

'Successful man, you mean. That's all that matters to you. You don't care about my happiness.'

'Still difficult as ever. Why can't you let it drop?'

'Because,' I start, before stopping myself. 'Let's not argue.' I need to keep him on side if I want to find out where the letters are. What was I thinking of, going for a drink with Molly, allowing her to get close again? Richard used to be my confidant, but lately fear has crept in, making me question everything. Molly brought all this back. My head hurts and Michael stares at me with his intense eyes, blinking over and over.

'Angela says you've been getting confused. Is something upsetting you?'

'Charlotte came to visit me.'

For a moment the room spins, but then I understand.

'Molly, you mean. We've talked about that.'

'Not her. We had an argument. She told me what you two had been up to. Said she had a photograph.'

'What photograph?'

Not those photographs. A tremor starts up in my hand. Molly is lying. She's been stringing me along. Or is Michael genuinely confused?

'One of you and her when you were little. What photograph did you think it was, Grace? One of those other photographs? Of you and her, eh?' His eyes flash at me and I can't look at him. I don't want to see the disgust that he doesn't bother hiding on his face. Molly must have sent a photo with the letters. *How could she?* Those photos were meant for our eyes only. I thought she'd destroyed them. Sweat creeps over my scalp. I have to know what else she gave away.

'I don't know what you're talking about.' *But I do.* 'Where are the letters?'

I'm desperate to know. But he doesn't speak, twisting a handkerchief around in his hands, holding the ends tight, and I want to knock it away, horrified that he remembers so much. My heartbeat quickens and hot rage pulses inside me. Why is he doing this now, when it matters most? If he talks too much it's another threat to my anonymity. But it won't matter, I tell myself; everyone thinks he's losing his mind. No one will believe him.

His legs tremble as he pulls himself up in bed and stares at me with angry eyes. *What did she put in those letters?* My stomach lurches as if I'm on a fairground ride being thrown from side to side. Michael's face is white, he doesn't look well. But I have to know. I can't let it go.

'Where are the letters, Michael? Whatever Molly said in them was a lie.'

'Liar!' His voice is a shout which turns into a cough and his hands shake as he attempts to hold the cup of water, spilling it into his lap. The cough catches in his throat and he bends over double, his face almost touching the bed.

I'm frozen to the spot. His breath is bursting out in short gasps, but I'm unable to move. His fingers are white where they grip the sides of his cup.

'Hiding something, you were. Lying as usual. That's not how I brought you up.'

'You don't know what you're saying.' *But he does.*

'Say what you like, but I know the truth and I can prove it.'

'What do you mean?'

'Where's Angela? Get Angela. I need my inhaler.'

'She's not here. Forget her. Tell me—'

I'm on my feet now, leaning over him. My whole body shakes and I'm transfixed, looking down at his face. 'Tell me what you mean.'

'I—' The word comes out as a splutter. He's unable to speak, shaking all over as he drops his cup. It clatters down to the floor. He's struggling to breathe and his head flops back on the pillow.

'My—'

Hatred blazes from his eyes and I grab his shoulders. Gone is the father who thought nothing of striking me as punishment. His breath comes out in a horrible rasp and his arms flail above him. Time appears to stop as I look down on him, unable to believe what is happening. I'm not sure he's breathing. He moves his hands frantically around the top of the bed as if he's searching for something. I'm no longer afraid. The front door slams. Next thing I know I'm being shoved aside and Angela is there, scooping up the jug and pouring water into his mouth.

'How long has he been like this?' she taps Michael's face, picking up his wrist. I let out the breath I hadn't realised I was holding. Angela gets out her phone.

'Is he breathing?'

We both fall silent as we focus on the point where her fingers feel desperately for a sign of life.

'There's a pulse,' she says, and I sit down hard on the chair, collapsing into it. All I can hear is my own heartbeat thumping in my head as she punches the emergency code into her phone.

'He doesn't look good. What happened? Where's his inhaler?' She scans the room, a frown on her face. 'You know his breathing has been bad lately. Didn't you see him drop it?'

'No,' I say, my voice sounding sharp. 'It's my fault, I should have been more observant.'

'It's OK,' she says. 'The ambulance is on its way.'

'I have to go.' I leave the room as if she is chasing me, throwing the word 'appointment' into the air, making my excuses.

Angela stares in surprise, but I can't stay there any longer.

Back home, violent shaking takes over my body as I realise what almost happened. Michael knows about the photographs, and he knows what he is saying. But I'm the only person who knows. Aren't I? Has Molly realised too? She lied to me about her conversation with Michael, and to think I was beginning to trust her. How could I be so stupid? Finding the letters is crucial. I have to know what's in them. I sit on the floor and practise my yoga breathing, trying to block Michael from my thoughts, attempting to calm my mind and regain control of my life.

MOLLY'S DIARY

THURSDAY 8TH JUNE 2004

I'm writing this in the garden with my flask of vodka. Dad caught me in his drinks cupboard the other day – but he believed it was my first time. The actual first time was the day Dad told me the Charlotte business was going to trial. I hate lying to him of all people, but I hate everything about myself now. I'm hooked on the fags too. Have to sneak out of school at lunchtime.

Six months now and still no fucking letter from Grace. Want to die. I post them myself now because I don't trust Mum. She's different since the trial. She's stopped going on at me to tell her the truth. I've disappointed her, what can I do?

I'm thinking about running away. If I knew where Grace was I could go to her. She's sixteen now, and I will be next month. They can't stop us then. I can't stand living here any more. Everyone knows what happened, people give me evil looks in the street. I HATE whoever called us 'The Orchid Girls'. I hate it. Hate everything.

WEDNESDAY JUNE 30TH 2004

Another bust-up with Mum when she found out I was still writing to Grace. She said if Michael got hold of the letters he'd rip them up. Said I'd be making things worse for Grace's mum. But things can't be any worse for her than being married to him. No wonder she's depressed. I bet that's what's happened to my letters. Thank God Charlotte never told him about us like she was threatening to.

I've been kicked out of school for three days for drinking. So fucking what. It's a waste of time. Everything's a waste of time without her. I can't even take photos any more. The more I think about Michael, the madder I get. I remember one time we went to a party and came back an hour late and he went ape. Over a party! Imagine if he'd known about US!!! I'm still scared thinking about it now. Grace told me he hit her mum as well as her. How can I protect her when I don't know where she is?

WEDNESDAY 1ST SEPTEMBER 2004

It's been a year. Gracie isn't going to reply. I know that now. I'm off. Catching a train to Birmingham and getting away from here. Being kicked out of school was the last straw. Mum and Dad are fed up with my drinking. I don't want them to see I can't stop. Me and Mum used to talk, but she just seems angry with me all the time. In the beginning she said she believed I was innocent, but something's changed. And Dad – I can't bear how I've disappointed him.

I'm going to find her. I'll look and look and never stop until I do. Then we can be together again. Whatever it takes.

CHAPTER TWENTY-ONE

MOLLY

The text message is on my mind when I wake up. I have to work out who's behind it. One suspect looms in my head: Ellis. But I really don't want it to be her. Last night at her flat was fun, chatting, laughing, not drinking. But everything I do gets spoilt eventually. A shot of something would still my head and warm me up inside. Instead I run a hot bath and make some toast. When my phone rings I'm convinced it's the journalist, but I snatch it up when I see it's Grace.

'I've been to see Michael again. You lied to me, Molly. Why didn't you tell me you'd told him about our relationship?'

The liar. 'I didn't. What's he said?'

'He said he knew about us and you had a photo to prove it. You've been threatening me with this photo, so why not admit it?'

'I swear I didn't mention it to him. Are you sure he meant me?'

'Of course. Who else would he be talking about?'

'I don't know, but he's getting Charlotte and the missing girl Emily muddled.'

'They found her body. It's a murder investigation now.' I wish I could see her reaction to that word, wondering if it makes her insides cold like it does mine. But she's still speaking, skipping over that crucial detail.

'He was talking about the letters you sent. It's possible he still has them. Did you ever send a photo with them?'

I hate the thought of him reading the words I sent to Grace. They were only ever meant for her. *Bastard*. 'No, I swear. If you read them, Grace, you'll know what I went through. Why finding you was so important. It was hard for me.'

She ignores the hurt in my voice. 'Michael said he knows the truth. What does he mean?' Words spill out of Grace in panic.

'I think he means he knew about our relationship. He warned me off you, now that you're married.' I can't help stressing the last word.

'Really? Only because he thinks it will reflect badly on him.' She sighs. 'This sounds harsh, but maybe it won't matter. He was taken ill when I was there. He's in hospital now. And there's something else. A journalist contacted me, pretending to work with a woman who interviewed me recently. He asked me about my time in Dorset.' Grace's breath catches in her throat. The word 'Dorset' comes out in a whisper. 'I'm scared, Molly. You're the only person who understands.'

I hate hearing her upset like this. 'Let me come over.'

'How do I know I can trust you? You know people at that bar, you could have arranged for that photo to be taken. Isn't that what this is all about? You threatening to expose me, splash one of our photographs over the internet? How could you do that? It's not who I am any more, but what we had was special. It always has been.'

I sit down, winded. She's finally admitted it.

'I swear on your life it wasn't me. Someone else is involved and I don't know who it is. You can trust me, Grace, please believe me. I'd never do anything to hurt you. Let me come to your flat.'

'No. Richard's so stressed at the moment, especially after seeing the photo. He knows I was out with you. He'd go mad if he caught you here.'

'He doesn't have to know.'

She's silent for so long I wonder if she's still there.

'Grace?'

She's crying now. Quiet, steady sobs, and I can't bear it. I want to put my arms around her and make everything OK.

'When they announced on the news that Emily's body had been found – it was like I was back there all over again. Did you feel it too?'

Did I? 'It was like a punch in the gut.'

I keeled over when the policeman arrived at our door holding his hat and white as a ghost. Mum put her arm round me and Grace took my hand and squeezed it tight, pressing our scars together. She was reminding me to keep our promise. It didn't stop me throwing up though, over and over. That sick feeling, knowing what I'd done, has never left me.

She's still talking.

'I feel so alone. Richard… he's so hard on me. Wants me to be perfect. And he's never here, he's always working late. We rowed last night and he's out late again tonight.'

'Then let me come over.'

If we can just press our scars together again, maybe everything will be alright.

My nerves have been building, and by the time I'm due at Grace's, I'm a mess. I had to persuade her, promise I wouldn't come until it was dark. My bike's got a flat tyre and I can't be bothered to fix it so I walk there. I'm too hot in my parka and I wish I had something to drink. When I find myself going past the same pub twice, having circled around it, I go in to ask for a glass of water. The bar is empty and I sit on a stool, calling out 'Hello', but all I can hear is the sound of crates crashing about and glasses jingling. Familiar sounds, welcoming. Ellis would have told me not to come in here but it's too late now and I'm feasting my eyes on the rich colours of the bottles lined up behind the bar. The golden whisky right in my eyeline would take the edge off my nerves and help me say the right thing to Grace. It's not my usual drink, so one will do, I convince myself. When a barman appears in front of me, slightly breathless, hair dishevelled, surprised to see a customer, I ask him for a single shot. *A single can't hurt, just enough to stop the tremble in my hands.* I remember my conversation with Ellis last night. She'd be so disappointed if she could see me now. But who is she? Can I even trust her? I squash my thoughts, downing the shot in one, enjoying its burn.

The lift door closes behind me. My eyeliner is smudged and I touch it up in the mirror, making my eyes look more defined. I kind of look OK, as good as I can right now, so I press the button for Grace's floor, butterflies in my stomach.

Music is playing in the flat, upbeat but quiet, something sophisticated. It's not the kind of stuff we used to listen to, moody indie bands we used to blare out really loud.

Grace wears a loose silk skirt and a white vest, hair piled on top of her head. Papers are scattered over a leather couch. A half-empty glass of red wine sits on the coffee table. I curl my fists in my pocket to stop myself from reaching for it. But when she pours me a glass I don't stop her. I don't even think about it for a second. It tastes good and I long to lean back and close my eyes, savouring this moment: just the two of us, the rush to my head.

'How's Michael?'

'I've not heard any more since I spoke to you.'

'He was OK when I saw him.'

Grace runs her finger around the rim of her wine glass, concentrating.

'Michael knew about the photos we took. How did he find out? What did you put in the letters, Molly?'

Her pale blue eyes focus on mine and my insides flip. She always had that power over me, and it hasn't changed. She must feel it too. I top up my glass then go to fill hers, but she puts her hand in the way. The glasses are huge – big, round fancy ones – and the bottle is emptying rapidly, but I've already clocked the fully stocked wine rack in the corner of the kitchen.

'They were love letters, Grace, I loved you and I thought you loved me. I was devastated when you didn't reply.'

'So you didn't mention—'

'I don't remember the details. But he's lying. I definitely didn't tell him about the photographs. Do you really think he still has the letters? Burning them would be more his style.'

'I don't know, but we need to destroy anything to do with that time. Now that this journalist is poking about, it's urgent. Have you seen what he's published today? He's written about the 'Orchid Girls' case and at the end he asks what happened to them. I'm terrified, Molly. We have to find out whether Michael still has the letters. Now he's in hospital I can search his flat. Just promise me you've got rid of all the photos. If those came out it would end us.'

'I did, I'm telling you. I'm going to Lyme Regis tomorrow.'

'You're not? Why? Isn't that just asking for trouble?'

'I need to see my mum. Don't worry. I'll check for photographs. I'll destroy anything I find, I promise. This Emily case is a nightmare, isn't it? Does it freak you out? It does me. All that stuff about arguing in the playground, her running off – it's all so similar. It must be worse for you, what with him being involved.'

I hate saying his name; I was the same with Jason.

'It's the photograph of her in her school uniform.' Grace's voice is almost a whisper. 'The first time I noticed the likeness I almost jumped off my seat. It gives me goosebumps still. I know I've asked you this before, but did you really destroy the camera? I have to be sure.'

I look down at my fingernails, remembering scrabbling at the dirt with frantic fingers. How the mud wouldn't wash away, panic mounting, water splashing all over the floor.

'Yes, I got rid of it, like you said to.' I remember Grace's wild eyes as she dug her fingers into my wrist, making me promise. I'd do anything for her back then and she knew it. I make a point of staring into her eyes, so that she doesn't detect the lie. Besides, I doubt it has survived after all these years.

'Good girl,' she says, and smiles.

*

'Most importantly, Molly, you need to get rid of this.' Grace always knows what's best.

The camera bangs against my chest as I walk fast, desperate to get home and do what Grace wants. Desperate to please her. It's all my fault. I pushed Charlotte first but if she's really got one of our photos then she deserved it. How dare she? I can't stop looking behind me, convinced Charlotte is going to appear, wrench the camera away.

The house is quiet and I head straight for the back garden, going to the end of the long path behind the shed. Dad's shovel has been left out and it was raining last night so the earth isn't too dry. I choose a patch under the tree so I know where the camera is if I need it. I've put it in a metal box to protect it, can't bear the thought of harming it. I'll tell Grace the film is destroyed – my hands are too shaky to look at it now so the lie will have to do.

Sweat gathers on my back and I grit my teeth as I work. It doesn't take long to dig a hole deep enough. Once the camera has been buried I pile the earth back on top, brushing a few leaves and twigs over so that nobody will notice. As I lean on the shovel and catch my breath, I wonder about the photo Charlotte has. Did Grace get it from her? I forgot to ask.

*

'I've made some food. Are you hungry?'

My stomach feels like a rope twisted into knots. I shake my head. 'Not really.'

'A snack, then.' Grace fusses around in the kitchen, doors opening and shutting and packets rustling as she pours nuts into bowls. I take my wine out onto the balcony, listening to a gaggle of teenagers, arms around each other, tripping over heels not suited to the damp paths. One holds a bottle high, singing loudly, her friends cackling. Drinking was like that for me once. Fun and carefree. Not like now, when it's a necessity. An escape.

I look over at Grace, sitting back down on the couch. The wine doesn't seem to affect her much, just like when we were younger. Me throwing up at the school disco, Grace holding my hair back. My head is swimming nicely now, but I know I need to take it easy. I can't lose control.

'What time will your husband be home?' I avoid saying his name again.

She shrugs, adding a plate of cheese and crackers to the low table. These are no ordinary cream crackers, but fancy hexagonal shapes covered in poppy seeds and green strands of herbs. Delicate flavours. I don't do delicate. A chunk of cheddar would do me.

'Late. He works late most nights.'

She's not happy.

'Have some food,' Grace says, and I put a piece of strange-looking cheese on my plate to please her.

'You're so thin, Molly.'

My mouth is dry and I take a swig of wine, catching her eye. We both smile.

'I've been trying not to drink, but I couldn't not tonight, could I? Do you know how nervous I am?'

Grace puts her hand on my arm. It sends a shiver down my spine.

'Don't be. I didn't understand why you came back at first, obviously. I was terrified. But I get it now, I do. There aren't many people you can talk honestly to. It's the same for me. I don't care if Michael dies. There. I've said it.' She waves her hand like an actress on stage. The drink is affecting her, too. 'You're the only person I can say that to. The only person who knows what Michael was really like.'

We never spoke about the morning after the beach party, when Michael found out Grace had been mixing with older boys and drinking. I'd been up in the bathroom and when I came downstairs he was shaking her, his fingers white where they were digging into her skin. She let me rub cream into the bruises, and when I asked her if it had happened before she shook her head. But her eyes told a different story.

My arm tingles where she's placed her other hand. 'Doesn't your husband know anything about what happened?'

Grace shakes her head, causing strands of hair to fall forward over her face, shining gold as they catch the light from the lamp. Her plate of cheese lies untouched. She pours more wine and I slide down onto the floor, stretching my legs out and leaning back against the sofa. I light a cigarette and she doesn't complain, sitting on the floor beside me, our legs touching. Her silk skirt slides up her thigh. I blow out a cloud of smoke, trying to focus on the conversation. Images come and go and I remember what she said about putting them on buses and making them go away. But the wheels on my buses spin round and round, digging into the ground, refusing to budge.

'Are you ashamed of what we had?'

'No,' she turns her full attention to me, her leg pressing down harder on mine. 'But you have to understand Richard's position. You know what politics is like, how they try to dig up dirt on everyone. Richard has no secrets, I know that. We talked about it before we got married.'

'Shouldn't you have told him about Charlotte, about the trial?' I wonder how she could keep such a big secret from someone she loves.

'What's to tell? They acquitted us in court, didn't they?'

'The courtroom is a blur to me, I didn't know what was going on.' I was drinking even then, before I went into the courtroom.

It turned it into a dream, everything swirling around, long words hanging in the air, not making much sense. 'I thought they'd let me talk to you when it was all over.'

'But they didn't, and I moved on. Richard didn't need to know... I went abroad and started afresh, I made myself into another person. A better person. But now everything is at risk, with you coming back, the journalist. And the missing girl in Richard's constituency doesn't help. It brings it all back, doesn't it?'

'It never went away for me.'

'The last few weeks have been difficult, and I've disappointed Richard.' Grace drinks some wine, the red staining her lips, glossy in the dim light.

'How?'

'The photo in the press. You have to understand, image is everything to him. I can't afford to do anything wrong. Plus he senses that something's going on. Since you turned up, it's been hard for me to concentrate on my work. I should never have come back to England. If he knew about the journalist he'd go mad. It could be disastrous for us.'

Us. She means him. It stings.

'Do you love him?' I pour myself some more wine, not wanting Grace to see the flush on my cheeks, how much her answer matters to me. But when I look at her, her eyes glisten with tears.

'He never understood why Michael was so hard on me. But you do.' Her voice drops to a whisper. 'Seeing you, it's making me remember who I used to be. I've been fighting it, but...'

My lips part in surprise as Grace leans forward and puts her wine-stained lips on mine, breathing into my mouth as her hands circle my waist, pressing the length of her body against mine. The years fall away as we kiss fiercely.

It's only later that I realise she never answered my question.

CHAPTER TWENTY-TWO

GRACE

My hands are on the back of Molly's neck, her skin cool, my touch light. She tastes of red wine, top-quality, full-bodied expensive wine, and cigarettes. She slides her hand under the fabric of my shirt, her movements slow, teasing her way up my ribcage, counting her fingers up my back. A glorious tingle shoots down my legs. My shoulders tense and I pull away.

'Stop.'

Her hand rests, her fingers fluttering.

'What is it?'

'I can't do this.'

'Because of him?'

'Of course, and so many other things. It's not who I want to be. This isn't me any more.'

Molly runs her tongue over her top lip and my stomach lurches.

'You can't deny the feeling. The spark between us. Nobody could ever stop that.'

She untangles her legs from mine and sits back on the couch, reaching for her glass.

'Don't, Molly, you've had enough, you'd better go.' I stand up to make my point and she grabs the bottle, gulping some wine. My arms are folded against my chest, not trusting myself not to reach for her again as she makes for the door. She lurches, grabs at the wall and I try to steady her. It takes huge strength to stop myself from pulling her back into my arms.

'Don't push me away, Grace. You can't run away from this. I won't lose you again.'

I look away.

'You'll regret it if you do.'

She leaves me to the emptiness of the room.

Her empty glass isn't the only reminder of her presence. My skin still tingles from her touch, long-buried desire coiling inside me. Richard could have come home at any time – it was reckless, stupid. I knock back the wine that sits in my glass, pooled like blood. *Why did I let that happen?* But I know why. My emotions are in full flight and Richard and I aren't spending enough time together. Molly has wriggled her way in and outside forces are attacking our relationship. I need to get back to normality. Anyone who'd had a few drinks could have let the same thing happen to them, an emotional moment with a close friend. All that history. It doesn't mean anything, I almost convince myself as I clean up the kitchen, removing all traces of Molly's visit. I scrub at the table, determined to erase her memory from the flat, but no amount of scrubbing will lessen how good it felt to kiss her. I hate myself for that. The smell of bleach makes me want to gag. A missed call alert sits on my mobile. It's probably Richard. If he hadn't been out so late, this wouldn't have happened.

My mobile is ringing, a glow in the dark. It's Molly. I send the call to voicemail. Richard's sitting up in bed. I didn't hear him come in. I kissed her. I can't believe I kissed her. Guilt makes my heart thud.

'Who was that?'

'Nobody you know. What time did you get back?' I reach out to him, longing for his touch.

'Don't change the subject. It's not the first late-night call you've had recently. Are you seeing someone, is that what this is?'

He climbs out of bed and pulls on his dressing gown. It's dark outside and a fox screams into the night. I move myself up into a sitting position.

'I'm not seeing anyone. How can you think that?'

Although I've only just woken, my mind is racing. The street light outside catches the glint in his eyes and outlines his handsome profile and my stomach contracts. *I can't lose Richard. I can't.* I make a snap decision to tell him a half-truth, stop him from asking questions. 'But I have been worried about something. I didn't want to bother you with it, it seems so petty. It's that woman from school.'

'What's happened?'

'You were right about her stalking me. Once she saw you and realised who you were, she started threatening me.'

'What does she want?'

'Money.'

'You have to tell the police.'

'No.' My stomach clenches at the mention of the police.

'Why not?'

'Because that would make it real.'

'For fuck's sake, Grace! This is real. Phone calls at night, lying to me. How much more real do you want it to be?'

I hate how angry he is. 'Stop shouting. It's been horrible.'

He sits down on the bed, lowers his voice. 'Explain it to me. She must have some kind of hold over you, otherwise none of this makes sense.'

'I don't want you involved.'

'It's too late now. I am involved when you lie to me. Tell me. You can talk to me, Grace.'

For a moment the possibility of opening up hangs in the air, letting it all spill out. I'm being ridiculous.

'Honestly,' I look directly at his eyes, the way he's squinting in the half-light making him look vulnerable. I feel a rush of love; Richard only wants what's best for me. 'She's all talk. But I've got it under control. Promise me you won't worry.'

'How can I not?' He sighs. 'This is the worst possible time for this to happen.'

A rush of nausea hits the back of my throat and I swallow hard.

'I'll deal with her, I will. This mayor thing, Richard, you know I want it as much as you do. I won't let anything spoil it for you, I promise.'

'It's not just my career that's at stake.'

He doesn't need to remind me. Neither of us sleep much after that. I lie as still as I can, not wanting to give Richard any more reason to be annoyed with me. Every time I think about kissing Molly I want to scream, the snapshot blown up in my mind, only to be replaced with the photo Charlotte had in her possession, each image worse than the last. Will pushing Molly away make her angry? What if she's lying about the photos? My heart thuds so hard I'm scared it's going to wake Richard up.

I'm stirred awake by Richard throwing the covers off the bed. He switches the radio on; a drop in temperature is forecast, and I shiver at the thought of winter approaching. The topic switches to news from Ash Fenton and Richard stops knotting his tie as the newsreader announces that the body found in Drake's Common has been formally identified as Emily Shaw.

'Christ,' he says, 'I wonder how Mum is. I presume you heard they found a body yesterday?'

I nod. 'It's so sad. I was worried it was going to be her. Jean will be devastated. Are you OK?'

'Me?' He looks surprised.

'You knew her.'

'Barely, but yes, it hits you hard. She was so terribly young. Those poor parents, it's impossible to imagine how they're feeling.'

If only that were true.

Richard runs a comb through his hair, takes one last glance in the mirror. 'I'll make some coffee.'

Picturing Emily's body hotlines my thoughts to Molly. I remember last night and sit up, adrenaline pumping through me. How could I have let that happen? That isn't me any more. No matter what people say, it's unacceptable and it could damage my career. It could destroy everything I've built for myself.

Cold air tickles my bare legs and I heave the duvet back up to snuggle in bed. When Richard comes back I'll entice him in, take his mind off the news, make up for the bad feeling between us and erase the unwanted thoughts seeing Molly has stirred up in me. Today will be a fresh start. Richard clatters about in the kitchen but he doesn't appear with the coffee. An ominous silence follows and doubts creep in. Unable to wait any longer, I pull on a thick sweatshirt and some leggings and go to find him.

'I thought you were coming back up.'

He's standing by the recycling bin, an empty wine bottle in his hand.

He turns his face towards me and his eyes are cold.

'What's this?'

Shit. Molly must have left it there last night. How did I miss that, and why was Richard going through the bins? Is he that suspicious of me?

He paces up and down the kitchen. 'Trouble is, I don't believe you drank this. You never drink more than a glass. Someone was here, weren't they? Who was it, Grace?'

'Nobody, you've got it wrong.' I'm babbling, can't get the right words out. *What can I do? What can I say? He can't know Molly was here.* 'All that internet business really got to me. People can be so vicious. It's stupid of me to be shocked, but I am.'

'No wonder you didn't wake up when I came in. You drank a whole bottle?'

'Most of it went down the sink, once I realised it was a mistake.'

'Is that why you didn't answer the phone?'

'What?'

'There are unplayed messages on the answerphone. It's sloppy. The calls could be important. Why didn't you pick up?'

I don't remember hearing it ring. 'I was listening to music.'

'Right little party you were having. By yourself.' His jaw is clenched and my head throbs.

'It wasn't like that. I can't work all the time. It was only a couple of drinks.'

'That's exactly what you said about the other night. I can see a pattern developing here. Why would you sabotage everything we've been working towards?' An expression of hurt crosses his face and my gut clenches.

'Richard, please.'

'I need to get to work.' He heads back to the bedroom, and I check the message from the previous night. It's the hospital. A man with a soft voice is telling me Michael is critically ill and I should visit soon. I feel empty.

Richard reappears.

'Michael is ill in hospital. They want me to go straight away.'

'I told you it could be important.'

His mobile rings and he looks at the screen.

'Christ! What now? Hello.' His voice is loud and he paces round in a circle. When he cuts the call, a strange expression contorts his face.

'What is it?'

'It was the police.' He picks up his briefcase.

'What do they want?'

'It's about the missing girl, Emily. They want to ask me about the time I spent with her. They must be desperate. I hardly knew her. As if I haven't got enough to worry about.' Richard looks away from me when he says this, catching sight of the clock. 'Shit, I'm late now. I hope Michael is OK.' He slams the door without kissing me goodbye.

I sweep my arm across the kitchen counter, sending his mug crashing to the floor. It shatters and the floor is covered in milky coffee. I grind my slipper heel into a jagged piece of crockery until only shards remain. The front door rattles and I freeze, horrified. What if it's Richard coming back and he sees what a mess I've made? But the noise stops and I set about cleaning the floor, heart thumping. It must be the wind.

So Richard thinks I'm having an affair. Molly probably thinks we are too. What a mess. All my dreams of being married to the Mayor of London are blowing away like smoke. I tell myself I've been through worse, that I can get through this. But first, the hospital.

Angela is speaking to a nurse in a low voice when I arrive, but when she turns and I see her stricken face, I know I am too late. Michael's pleading eyes as he choked flash in my mind, and I put my hand on the wall to steady myself. *Michael is dead.*

Shock squeezes my chest, and all I can think about is how Richard doesn't need more hassle when his campaign is at such a crucial stage. I collapse onto a chair, barely able to breathe. I grip the armrests as my breath stutters in and out of me, and I will myself to be calm. This used to happen every time Michael hit me. Angela puts an arm around my shoulders, wiping away her tears with her free hand. She mistakes my shock for grief. But I can't feel sad for Michael. How can I, after everything? Now I have no parents; just Richard. *And no children of my own.*

'It was quick,' she says, 'he wouldn't have known anything about it.'

I hesitate to call Richard, but Angela insists. He doesn't pick up and I leave a message, relieved.

Before I leave, a nurse takes me into her office, handing me a sealed plastic bag with Michael's few possessions in it. A watch, a wallet and his wedding ring. A wooden cross he always carried makes my breath catch in my throat.

'He didn't have his inhaler. That's why he couldn't breathe. Did you notice him drop it?' Angela asks as we descend in the hospital lift. The mirror reflects my pale face and I turn my back, not wanting to look at the state I'm turning into.

'No, I was in such a panic. I'm so sorry.'

Angela bites her lip, looking as if she's about to cry. 'It's just that it was so sudden.'

Richard has calmed down when he comes in, and I tell him what happened at the hospital. Angela rings again later and Richard takes the call. He talks for a while.

'I've told Angela I'll take care of the funeral arrangements.'

'Thanks.' What he means is that his people will.

'She mentioned the missing girl in Ash Fenton, how much it was upsetting him. You never said anything about that.'

I shrug. 'He didn't know what he was saying, you know what his memory was like.'

'She said he was very insistent, kept calling her Charlotte, he—'

'Please, can we not do this now.'

My voice sounds loud and he registers surprise.

'I feel numb, and so guilty, because we didn't get on. You wouldn't understand, you're so lucky with your parents.'

'We have our moments, believe me.'

'It's not the same. They worship you. A star student, first-class degree, you've never disappointed them.'

'And they adore you too,' he says, rubbing my hand.

Richard's words don't encourage me; they add to the pressure. If I fail I'll let his parents down too.

'About this online mess—' I say, wanting to making things better.

'Forget it. You've spoken to Julia, haven't you?'

I nod.

'The argument this morning. I was disappointed in you. Staying out late, drinking. You never drink too much. Christ, you barely drink, your body is such a temple. And you've been smoking. Don't deny it, I smelt it on you the other night. If you're worrying about that woman, let me deal with it. We can't have it affecting your career. I thought you were stronger than this.'

'My dad has just died.' I'm shocked by how harsh his words are.

'I know, and I'll support you.' When I don't reply, Richard pushes his chair back with a scraping sound which makes me flinch. *What's making him so restless?*

'How did it go with the police?'

'Don't change the subject.'

My eyes fill with tears. 'Everything feels so difficult.'

'Are you sure there's nothing else? You've not been yourself for a while now.'

I know I'm playing with fire but my emotions get the better of me. 'I've been feeling broody again.'

Richard runs his hands through his hair, looking exasperated. 'Not this again. You know it's not possible right now. I thought we agreed. You can't afford to step back from your business, not when it's just taking off. Or it was.' He frowns. 'Is this what's making you lose focus? Because if it is, Grace, we've got a real problem.'

'I can't help the way I feel, it's hormonal. It's alright for men, they don't feel it in the same way. Men have everything easy.'

'So it's a gender thing now.' He paces about the kitchen, eyes glaring when he speaks. 'I'll say this once more, OK, just so you're clear. I'd love for us to have children at some stage, but not for at least five years. If you can't cope with that, then God help us, our marriage is in trouble.'

'Richard, no.' I rush over to him, putting my hand on his shaking arm. He doesn't push me away. 'Our marriage is strong, you have to believe me. I promise I won't mention having a baby again. I can wait, I can.' I compose my face so he doesn't see how my emotions are swirling inside. 'You know how I get when I don't sleep. That's all it is.'

His face is a mask of worry, but he takes my hands and I grip hard. I can't lose him. He strokes my hair and pulls me to him, and my pulse returns to normal. *This is where I belong*. I can't believe I've been jeopardising everything.

'You're right, you need a good sleep. I'll make you a peppermint tea. Have you remembered I'm going to the charity function tomorrow night? Will you be alright on your own? I could get Mum to come over if you want. Or you could go and stay with them.'

The thought of being alone terrifies me. 'You don't have to do that, I'll be OK. If I need company I'll sort something out. I might give Carrie a ring.'

'That's a good idea.'

'You're right, a good sleep is all I need to get back on top of things. A herbal tea sounds lovely.'

But nothing stills my thoughts. As soon as the light is off my mind turns to Molly. If she thinks we're having an affair, then I won't disillusion her. I could use this to my benefit. I'll sit it out for the next few days, until I know she's got rid of the photograph. Then I'll go through Michael's possessions to check there's nothing there. I have to get on top of all this.

Last night was a mistake, and Richard need never know anything about it.

As I fall asleep, I remember that Richard failed to tell me what happened at the police station. Maybe I'm not the only one with secrets.

GRACE'S DIARY

SUNDAY 3RD JULY 2005

I've been Grace Martin for a year now. I'm fluent in French and I have a wonderful new group of friends: Justine, Chloe and Natalie. Fabulous girls, who think I'm lovely and say my accent is cute. We don't wear school uniform over here and everything is more relaxed. Chloe is my best friend – special, if you get my drift – but I'm not going there again, I'm trying to keep my distance but it's hard. I'm different now. It's funny how easy it was to shed the old Grace, like a snake with unwanted skin. Kicked it under the bed – I'll always know it's there but no one else needs to. I've set my sights on Pierre in the *terminale* at school, just the right amount older than me. He's helping me with my maths – I don't need the help, but he doesn't need to know that. I so want a boyfriend.

Aunt Jenny's taught me how to cook and I'm really into baking. I've got an evening shift at a *boulangerie* and I'm working with the pastry chef. It's helped me decide what I want to do. I want to study the business side of catering and set up my own company. That way I'll never have to answer to anyone else.

Every now and then I think about it, of course I do. But it's easier to busy myself in the kitchen, bake a batch of croissants and let the buttery smell help me forget. And there are no newspapers here, no lurid tabloids with stupid made-up headlines. I catch sight of one, occasionally, an English-language *Sun* or a *Daily Express* at the kiosk on the corner, and it chills my blood. But then I look at the River Seine, hear flutters of French conversation and smell strong cigarette smoke in the air, and none of that matters. I'm Grace Martin now.

SATURDAY 5TH JULY 2010

Hello, diary! I'm back!! Because today is one special day. I've MET A GUY at last!! Boy, man, *homme*, *mec*, whatever. I won't think about girls any more, no more secrets, no more drama. I honestly thought it was never going to happen. But it has. His name's Richard and he's in France for a work placement. He's absolutely adorable. I met him in a cafe on the Boulevard St Mich and he was at the next table. He offered to buy me a coffee – he thought I was French!!! I've done a good job, Grace Cavendish is well and truly dead. He asked what I was smiling about and I told him I was flattered. I couldn't possibly tell him the real reason, could I?

Aunt Jen was pleased, but when I told her he was English she was dead against it. Warned me not to get serious. Said nothing good could come of being associated with England again. He's the first man I've liked in France. Why does he have to be English??

Being in Paris makes me a different person. There are women-only clubs in the Marais, but I've had enough of hiding away. Richard is my way out. He's going places. He makes me a better me. Grace Martin doesn't hide. She doesn't have those shameful feelings. That dirty past. My course in business nutrition ends this year and I've got plans to set up my own company, maybe an English bakery eventually. I never think about HER any more. Never.

Saturday 7th August 2010

Richard Sutherland. I've seen him every day since we first met. He graduated in political science from Durham last year and he wants to be a politician. He's here for six months before he goes back to work as an assistant to a Member of Parliament. He's ambitious, hard-working. He likes me a lot and we have fabulous sex. I knew all along I was straight underneath. I knew I didn't have to waste time with girls. You can't trust them. Molly taught me that.

But why does he have to be English??

WEDNESDAY 1ST SEPTEMBER 2010

Richard is going home next week. He said he loves me. He said he doesn't want to leave me, and we had our first row because he doesn't understand why I can't go back to England. I couldn't tell him the real reason, and he couldn't understand why. Aunt Jen is worried. So am I.

TUESDAY 2ND NOVEMBER 2010

Richard's gone. I've thrown myself into my apprenticeship at Patisserie Bleu and they love me. They let me do all the fancy sugar work. But I miss Richard like mad. He calls me as often as he can but he's so busy. He asked me loads of questions about my childhood before he left. I told him something bad happened but that I won't talk about it. Hinted at abuse, and that stopped the questions. For now.

SUNDAY 1ST JANUARY 2012

Over a year, and we're still together. I can't quite believe it but I've actually been thinking about it. Going back. There's less than a year left on my course and then I'll be free. I haven't told Jen because she'll try and talk me out of it.

It will be OK, though. Because SHE doesn't exist to me. Molly means nothing any more. I've changed my name, so much time has passed and we'll be in London, miles away from Dorset. Miles away from her and what happened.

MONDAY 3RD SEPTEMBER 2012

Richard lost it with me today. I've never seen him quite like that before. It scared me, seeing him so angry. Turns out he assumed I'd move to London when my course finished. I've run out of excuses for staying away. He shouted at me, said I was cold and that he hated my secrets. I'm not cold, though, just careful. I can't tell him. But I can't lose him. What do I do? He didn't call me for a day and by the end of it I'd made up my mind. Why shouldn't I be with him, whatever? Why shouldn't I lead a normal life? Why should I have to hide away? I love him, he helps me forget who I used to be. By the time he got back I was in a right state. I said I'll think about it. That'll put Aunt Jenny's head into an absolute spin.

WEDNESDAY 9TH JANUARY 2013

Richard's New Year's Resolution is to get me over the Channel. And I'm seriously thinking about it. My business is doing OK, but it's a tough market here. It's easier to visualise the range of healthy products I dream about working on over there. The French love their own culture and cuisine too much. They're so traditional, and they seem resistant to listening to an English girl. I want so much to be a success, to prove myself. I tell myself that I have to stop being so cautious. It was all such a long time ago. It's different now. I can start again. Can't I?

FRIDAY 7TH SEPTEMBER 2013

Richard has asked me to marry him!! He came over on the Eurostar and whisked me off to a posh hotel on the Champs-Élysées. He proposed on one knee. Just like in the movies. God, it was romantic. But then he said he's sick of us being long distance, and I had to choose. He meant it, too. I've seen that side of him when he wants something. Ruthless.

The restaurant he picked has a waiting list that lasts for months. The food was divine. Only the richest and most sophisticated people go there – I didn't realise he was that wealthy. Made me think about my lifestyle, about the life I want to lead. I belonged there. That's the crowd I want to be part of. Grace Sutherland deserves only the best.

Richard's career is taking off and he wants me to be part of it. He's worked everything out, now my business is online I can do it anywhere. He says it will fly in England. He believes in me, wants us both to build our careers together. The sky's the limit, he said. And he's found a gorgeous flat for us by a canal in London. There's nothing keeping me here except for the risk. Aunt Jen is resigned, and I've told her I won't contact Michael. That I'll keep the past in the past. When I change my name again there's nothing to connect me with Dorset. I can't wait to be Mrs Sutherland. Jen says what about HER, but what are the chances of our paths crossing? She won't find me in London. She must have forgotten about me by now, anyway. Richard hangs around with a crowd of people so different to how we used to be. Important people, who are going places. I've moved on and up. I couldn't be further from the silly girl she used to know. She wouldn't even recognise me.

Sometimes late at night fear creeps into bed with me but I'm getting better at learning to control it. I practise yoga now, meditate daily and eat only the best food. I do everything to better myself. Grace Sutherland will be the perfect wife.

I've booked my ticket.

Sunday 15th June 2014

This is my last entry in this diary as Grace Martin. I'm Grace Sutherland now. Once, twice, three times a lady. I love signing my name, saying it aloud. Mrs Grace Sutherland. New husband, new flat, new business. New me. A new, clean life.

I'm in London! Six months today, new city. I've done loads of research for my business, and clean eating is BIG here. It's made for me. Everything about me will be pure, holistic. Cleansed inside and out. This will suit my philosophy of a whole new Grace. A perfect Grace.

Introducing 'Clean Grace' – my new registered company. Richard's father gave me the money to set up my business. His parents love Grace Sutherland.

Richard's doing well in his career, and he's talking about standing for Mayor of London at some stage. I'm determined my own business will match his success. Together we'll be a power couple. I've got loads of Instagram followers already. Aunt Jenny was horrified I'd even consider a career that will put me in the public eye. But she doesn't understand that I'm a different person now.

I'll prove Jenny wrong. Hiding in plain sight. Except I'm not hiding. Grace Sutherland is out there, loud and proud.

CHAPTER TWENTY-THREE

MOLLY

Outside the street is quiet, with most houses in darkness. She must have been scared her husband would come back at any moment and didn't want him to catch us together. That's why she wanted me to go. But nothing can wipe out the look on her face with her hands on my neck and her lips on mine. Desire builds up in me and I blow air from my mouth, the wind sobering me as I walk fast towards home, wanting to be inside, alone with my thoughts.

Once I'm in the flat I collapse on the bed in my clothes. The blinds are open and the moon is round and full of life. There's so much Grace and I have to say and do, and it frustrates me that I have to wait, but I have no choice.

I grab my mobile, unable to resist calling her. The phone glows as it rings out and I picture her leaning out of bed, golden hair covering her delicate throat. But she doesn't answer. He must be back.

She kissed me. It's my first thought when I wake up. My head throbs when I sit up and I groan, retracing the path that led me to a drink. Nerves and excitement at seeing Grace drew me into the pub, the drinks glittering like jewels, enticing me, tricking me. I imagine Ellis's disappointed face and I'm full of remorse.

Grace was drinking too. *Why did she kiss me? Did she mean it?* I smoke three cigarettes one after another and stare hard at the wall as if the answers might appear amidst the faded pattern of the peeling wallpaper. My phone is dead so I plug it in to charge, raking my hands through my greasy hair. I try to eat a slice of toast but as soon as it hits my stomach I throw it back up. My cigarette pack is empty and I hunt around the flat, searching all the places where there might be another stashed away. But all it results in is a pile of papers on the floor and a lump in my throat that won't shift.

On my way to the station to get my ticket my phone rings. It's not a number I recognise. I'm in the mood for winding up a PPI salesman so I pick up.

'May I speak to Molly please?' The voice is male, plummy.

'This is Molly.'

'My name is Alex Foster. I'm a journalist.'

There's a bench outside the station and I sit down on it, taking a breath.

'What do you want?'

'Are you a friend of Grace Sutherland?'

Blood rushes to my head and I grip the side of the bench, pressing my feet hard to the floor to ground myself. I'd hoped the online photos would be forgotten by now.

'Who?'

'Grace Sutherland. The food blogger, wife of Richard Sutherland. You know her, don't you? You were seen with her the other night.'

'I don't know what you're on about.' Thoughts fight for space in my mind. This must be Jodie's doing, the journalist she mentioned, some bloke from the pub, sending me those texts. But he doesn't sound like one of Jodie's mates – his accent is way too posh.

'My sources tell me you're the woman in the photo taken with Grace Sutherland.'

'What photo?' It's best to play dumb, but I'm shaking. I hope my voice doesn't give me away.

'Are you telling me you haven't seen it? You were photographed with Grace at Chez Elle. Are you saying it wasn't you?'

'So what if it was?'

'Can you tell me a bit about your relationship with her?'

'I'm not telling you anything. How did you get this number?'

'A friend of yours who told me you'd be willing to talk. I can pay you good money, Molly.'

'Fuck off.'

I switch my phone off, light a cigarette, will my hands to stop trembling. *Fucking Jodie.* The best thing I can do is buy my train ticket and get as far as I can away from here.

I go straight home after I've booked my tickets, google the journalist and have another look at the photos online. It's so wrong. The way they've captured her makes her look drunk. The shot of her outside smoking bothers me. Did she get the cigarette from that woman who was eyeing her up? Thinking about that bitch makes me squeeze my fingernails into my palms.

The call from this journalist bloke gives me a good reason to ring Grace. She answers straight away this time and my pulse flutters.

'What do you want?' Her tone sends my mood plummeting back to zero.

'That journalist called me. Alex Foster.'

She goes quiet and I reckon she's having the same panic I had.

'Grace?'

Grace's voice is low. 'This is awful. This is why we should never have met. What did you tell him?'

Her words have got me shaking again. I can see her slipping away from me. I don't like it one bit.

'Nothing, Grace. I told him to get lost. Hung up. I won't speak to him. Please don't push me away. This is nothing to do with me.'

'But Molly, have you seen his blog? It's only a matter of time. He's planning to write about The Orchid Girls. If he's digging into your background, what's he going to find out? You haven't changed your name.'

'No, but it's a common name. Have you ever googled me?'

'No.' *That hurts.*

'There are hundreds of us.'

'You've still got the tattoo, for Christ's sake!'

'I'll keep my watch on and I'll deny everything. Mum won't have anything to do with the press. There isn't anyone else.'

'What about that woman, Jodie?'

'She doesn't know anything about it.' Thank God I didn't tell Ellis.

'Not even where you come from?'

'Shit. Yeah, she does know that.'

'You need to get away as soon as possible.'

'I've booked my ticket for Monday.'

'For Dorset? I still think it's a bad idea.' Grace sighs. 'Don't talk to that journalist, OK? Or anyone else. I mean it, Molly.' She hangs up.

She still doesn't trust me. My head thumps and I need a drink. I call Ellis instead and we arrange to go to the cinema later.

'You sound a bit down, Molly. Are you OK?' Ellis sounds concerned and I can't help feeling guilty.

'I'm great. Just need to get out.' I can't tell her about last night, she'd be so disappointed. I need to get back on track.

That evening Ellis and I go to see a film on the South Bank. It's a thriller, with lots of car chases and action, nothing arty, no foreign subtitles, which is what I imagine Grace would like. She insists on treating us to a box of popcorn and I eat it robotically throughout the film. I can't remember the last time I went to the cinema, and I try not to let my guilty hangover spoil it. Afterwards we sit in the cafe, outside, overlooking the Thames. There isn't much to see in this light, but the distinctive smell of the river sends a rush to my head. I ignore the sounds of clinking glasses nearby. We drink hot chocolate and I wonder whether I should confide in her. Probably not, but the silence gets to me and I end up telling her about the phone call earlier.

'Gosh, you're involved in a celebrity scandal.'

'I suppose I am.'

'Are you going to talk to the journalist?'

'No, Grace would kill me.' I fiddle with my cup.

She misinterprets my discomfort. 'You like her, don't you?'

'I don't know what you mean.' I make a joke of it, but Ellis is watching me carefully. I wonder why she's so interested in how I feel about Grace. Must be because she's a celebrity. Or is it something else? Am I right to trust her? I look at her open face, and she smiles. It warms me. All she's done is be nice. I can't believe I'm doubting her – she's done nothing to deserve it. It's not as if I'm fighting off friends.

'Do you want to come back to mine for a coffee?' I find myself wanting to spend more time with her.

'Sure,' she says, her eyes lighting up.

As I'm letting us into the flat, I remember my photo board, but it's too late, Ellis is already inside, pulling her hat off which makes her hair stick up, looking around.

The noise of the kettle fills the room. She goes straight over to the noticeboard and I have to stop myself from grabbing her shoulders and spinning her round so she doesn't look.

'What's this?' She looks concerned and I bite my tongue, not knowing what to say. It was a mistake inviting her back here.

'They're great photos, but…' She sits cross-legged on the sofa. 'You do like her, don't you?'

I open the window wide, light a cigarette and suck in the smoke, watching the street below me. The cut on my hand itches and scratching it releases tension. Blood bubbles out.

A fox stands under the lamp post opposite, eyes glinting.

'Something bad happened when we were young and we were separated. I've been looking for her ever since. Taking photos, it's how I work things out.' I realise how pathetic I sound and I hate myself for it.

'What happened to you?'

I'm tempted to talk, but Grace's warning stops me. Plus, I can't ignore my niggling doubts about Ellis. I don't really know her. It's way too soon for her to know the truth.

'I can't talk about it.' I stub my cigarette out on the window ledge and slam the window shut, which sends the fox scuttling down the street.

'That's OK,' she says. 'The photos of Grace I sort of get, but why have you got photos of her husband too?'

'You'll laugh if I tell you.'

'Try me.'

'He's good-looking and he's powerful, isn't he? He's bound to get loads of female attention. If I catch him playing away, Grace needs to know. Also he's on the news all the time, talking about the missing girl. It's weird. What if he was involved?'

'That's a bit far-fetched.' I can see she's trying not to smile. 'Don't take this the wrong way, but it's what we addicts do, give up one addiction for another.'

'You think this is an addiction?'

'Well, it is a bit obsessive, you have to admit. And, dare I say, unlikely. It sounds like it could be a case of wishful thinking…'

'Just a bit,' I say, realising how right Ellis is. We both burst out laughing. It's weird how well she gets me. I feel lighter already.

After that we chat about the film until she decides it's time to go. I pass her jacket over and she spots dried blood on my hand.

'That looks nasty.'

'It's nothing,' I say, hiding it behind my back. 'I'll see you out.'

Concern crosses her face. I walk to the end of the path, surprised that Mrs Bird's light is still on. I watch Ellis until she gets to the street corner, where she turns and waves twice. At the same time a figure emerges from the opposite direction. For a split second I think it's Jodie, but this person is taller and bulkier. After a moment, I realise it's a man.

'Molly? Molly Conway?'

He walks towards me, heels like shots in the quiet street. 'We spoke on the phone,' he says. 'I want to ask you a few questions.'

Oh God, it's him. 'I've got nothing to say.'

'I recognise you, Molly, you're the girl in the photograph.'

'So what if I am? Get off my property. What are you doing here?'

'It's not your property, though, is it? Mrs Bird is the homeowner, very friendly she is too, told me lots about you and your friends. Chatty lady, Mrs Bird.' He looks proud of himself, like he's got one up on me.

'You've got no right to hassle me. Get out of my way or I'm calling the police.'

'Oh, I don't think you want to be doing that, Molly, do you? Might bring back nasty memories.'

His words send a chill right through me. 'You're not making sense.'

'All I'm asking for is a few comments about Grace Sutherland. How you know her, that kind of thing.'

'I just met her, OK? For the last time, get out of my way.' I hold my arm out in front of me, trying to put some distance between us.

'Threatening me, are you?'

He holds his phone up and the shutter sound goes off. I squeeze my hands around my keys, willing myself not to lose my temper. I can't make a scene.

'If you let me get past I'll think about it, OK? That's the best you'll get from me.'

'Fine.' He shoves his phone into his pocket. 'Your mate Jodie said you'd be willing to talk. And quite a story it might be, I reckon.'

'There is no story.' My shoulders slump as exhaustion washes over me. I just want to get into bed, shut the world out.

'Oh, I dunno,' he says. 'Maybe you might want to think about that little comment you left for your friend Grace, who you hardly know.'

'What comment?'

'The one where you called yourself "OrchidGirl".'

Gracie, it's me...

The keys slip out of my hand and clatter to the floor, echoing in the night.

'I've left my card with Mrs Bird,' he calls out as he disappears into the darkness.

DAILY TRIBUNE

22ND AUGUST 2002

TEENAGE GIRLS QUESTIONED IN CHARLOTTE CASE

Two teenage girls are being questioned in connection with the murder of Charlotte Greene in Dorset. The two girls reported leaving their friend in town, but no images of Charlotte have been detected on CCTV camera and witnesses have failed to come forward.

DAILY TRIBUNE

28TH AUGUST 2002

MYSTERY OF THE ORCHID GIRLS

Police have revealed that parents of recently murdered teenager Charlotte Greene failed to recognise the tiny tattoo of an orchid found on the inside of the girl's left wrist. The two friends last seen with her also sported identical tattoos, initially unnoticed as they were hidden under jewellery. The girls allegedly got the tattoos at a summer fair and insist the orchid has no significance.

CHAPTER TWENTY-FOUR

GRACE

The best thing I can do today is work. Keep busy. Stay distracted. Take back control of my life. Maybe look at flight prices. But it's impossible. The Orchid Girl story is scheduled to appear online any moment now. I'm determined not to look until I've done everything I need to do. Molly's promised to destroy the photos, and that eases some of my worries. I briefly allow myself to remember the feel of her lips on mine, and I know that she will. I believe that I can trust her.

I choose a seeded nut bread I often bake, but it's hard to keep my mind in one place. Nuts jump around noisily in the food processor, chips bouncing around, hitting the glass. Kneading the dough, I press down hard, pummelling the sensations Molly has awakened in me. I won't be that girl again, I have too much to lose. Nothing could make me live a clandestine lifestyle again, having to hide who I am, being ashamed of my feelings. I want to be able to show off my business, show off my husband. Live in the limelight. The dough isn't perfect but it's the best I can do under the circumstances. As long as the photographs turn out well, that's what counts. Adding a filter and editing the photo should do the trick.

Angela calls just after I've left the loaf to rise.

'How are you?' She sounds tearful.

'Oh, you know, it's always been difficult between us…'

Angela protests, but I hold my hand in the air to stop her as if she's in front of me.

'It's true, there's no point pretending otherwise. We were never close. As awful as that sounds.'

'You know I never understood that, Grace. You're such a lovely woman, so inspiring.'

'Thanks Angela, that means a lot. Richard has been great, he's organising the funeral arrangements so I don't have to worry about all that. And I'm coming over soon to clear the house.'

'Why don't you let me take care of it?'

'No,' I say quickly, needing to shut her down. 'There are things that belong to Mum over there, sentimental stuff. You understand. Thank you for the offer, though.'

'I guess you can come any time now that the police have been.'

'The police? What did they want?' I lean my weight against the wall, pressing my spine into the hard, cold surface. Any mention of the police takes me back in time, making my pulse race.

'Just following up from last night. It's routine. It's hard to believe it was such a short time ago. So much has happened since then. They asked me about when he choked, but I told them I wasn't there.'

I lower my voice. 'I feel awful now, but at the time I froze on the spot, I went into a complete panic. I just didn't know what to do.'

'I'm glad you've explained that, I thought something like that must have happened. You looked like you weren't responding to him. You must have been in shock. His inhaler was under the bed. Did he have it when you were there?'

'I think so. It's a bit of a blur, to be honest.'

'Are you sure that you didn't notice him drop it?'

'No, I would have said. What did you tell the police?'

She hesitates. 'I told them what I saw, that's all.'

'Of course.'

The oven bell rings. The dough looks ready to go in, and I spend the rest of the day working on recipes for the book. The smell of freshly baked bread fills the kitchen, and for what seems like the first time in ages I'm satisfied with my work. But once I've stopped baking, the thoughts I've held at bay flood back in, overwhelming me, and the evening ahead feels interminable. The dark sky outside brings an oppressive atmosphere to the flat, a mood that's hung around ever since Angela mentioned the police. And what did the police want with Richard? My thoughts claw at me, leaving me feeling claustrophobic. I have to get out.

Michael's house is in complete darkness when I arrive; the nearest street light is further along the road. My hand shakes as I turn the key in the lock, feeling as if I'm intruding. I haven't been here alone before.

It takes longer than I thought to search through his things, although Michael doesn't have much. His wardrobe contains a row of pressed shirts and trousers, neatly folded jumpers on shelves and polished shoes lined up in a row at the bottom. He's organised; it's where I get it from. I hope that's the only quality I've inherited from him. On one shelf is a large box which contains all his paperwork. I take it downstairs and flick the kettle on. The cupboard contains a jar of instant coffee and regular tea bags. I make do with a black tea to warm myself up.

Most of the paperwork comprises bills which he has kept for the last five years, all neatly labelled in a box file. One compartment contains birth and marriage certificates, along with Mum's death certificate. My hands are unsteady as I hold the yellowing piece of paper. Cause of death: pneumonia. I didn't know that, another thing Michael kept from me. Tears spring into my eyes. I see Mum, so weak from throwing up, it must have been the chemo that did that. Me, the selfish teenager, just wishing she was my old mum whose strong arms held me so tight when I was hurt.

Wiping my eyes, I go back into the bedroom. I'd expected to find something here. The wardrobe is tall and I stand on a stool to check the shelf where the jumpers are. The smell of mothballs welcomes me as I pull the clothes down and reveal an old suitcase. I knew I was missing something. Michael refused to throw this battered old case away when he moved. I'd have got rid of it years ago, it's disgusting. Bits of cracked leather fall away in my hands, crumbling into dust. I take it down to the kitchen.

A quick flick through the contents and a cardboard folder catches my eye. *This is it, the letters must be inside.* The folder contains a stack of newspaper cuttings, faded with age. Dread overwhelms me as I recognise long-forgotten headlines, the photograph of Charlotte, the street where she was last seen, the beach where her body was found. Looking at that photo – the old school photo they always used – takes me back to the jagged cliff, wind roaring in my ears, making the wild orchids dance, Molly sobbing. The frantic activity that evening after Mrs Greene rang to say that Charlotte hadn't arrived home, the realisation that there was no going back. Michael refused to have newspapers in the house, didn't want them poisoning our home, but I used to go and read them in the library, desperate to know what was going on. Why would he go to the trouble of cutting them out and keeping them? Unable to stop myself I leaf through the articles, time disappearing through my fingers as I become a frightened teenager again. There's nothing new here until I find an article from the local paper: the front-page news in July 2002.

LOCAL VICAR QUESTIONED IN CHARLOTTE DISAPPEARANCE
Michael Cavendish, vicar at St Mary's Church, was taken in for questioning regarding his whereabouts on the afternoon of Charlotte's disappearance.

Police confirmed that a 45-year-old man has been helping them with their enquiries.

My knees have gone to sleep underneath me while I've been crouched on the floor reading, and I'm suddenly aware how cold it is. It comes rushing back, Michael's fury at being questioned by the police. His closed face when he arrived back home, lips pinched in anger. The way he always looked before he lashed out at one of us. My body shakes now, like it used to then, scared that he could see into my mind, know that I had been wondering what he was up to that afternoon, where he went on one of his drives.

There is no central heating, and the windows rattle as the wind picks up outside. A large crash makes me jump and my heart bangs furiously at the thought of someone breaking into the house. I see dark shapes in the dimly lit back garden, but nothing moves. There's no trace of any letters or Molly's photos amongst the documents I search through. Eventually my fingers are too cold to move and I'm forced to stop. I've seen everything I need to. Reading the cuttings was a mistake. I feel like a frightened fifteen-year-old all over again. I wander around the flat, unable to settle. I stuff the jumpers back into the wardrobe, leaving the documents on the side, but I take the suitcase with me. I stash it in the boot of my car. No need for Angela to see what's inside.

Once I'm back home, I can't face checking Alex Foster's website, not with everything else swimming around in my head. It can wait. I take a sleeping tablet but it has no effect. I'm fully awake, body rigid, tired eyes staring at the ceiling. The phone rings but I let it go to voicemail. Late in the night Richard climbs into bed behind me and pulls me close, but I don't want him to feel how tense I am so I roll away as soon as he falls asleep. Outside, a car alarm wails into the blackness.

An insistent ringing wakes me in the middle of the night. It can only be Molly. Snatching the phone, I tiptoe down the mezzanine stairs to the living room, cursing her for calling at this hour.

'Why are you ringing so late?'

'I couldn't decide whether to or not, but I thought you'd want to know.'

'Know what?'

'That journalist was here, Alex Foster.'

'What happened?'

'He was waiting outside my house when I got back home this evening. The thing is…' Molly hesitates. Ice crawls through my veins.

'He asked me about The Orchid Girls.'

The flat is quiet when I wake. Richard is gone again. Despite the silence my mind is anything but still. Before I go downstairs I stash the cigarettes I bought on my way home last night in my bedside drawer. Richard never looks in there. I put Richard's breakfast plate in the dishwasher and switch it on. I clean the kitchen until the breakfast bar is so shiny my tired-looking face is mirrored back at me. In the glossy reflection I see the fear in my eyes that I thought I'd left in Paris. I decide I won't let myself look online until the flat is perfect. As I scrub and polish and shine I think about Molly's phone call last night. The journalist looms in my mind and I rub at the counter, harder and harder, wishing I had a giant eraser that I could rub him out with. Now that he's made the OrchidGirl connection to Molly, he's not going to leave her alone. Can I really trust her? She's been threatening me with the photograph but I don't know if she's telling the truth about the camera. But cutting myself off from her is too risky – I'm doing the right thing keeping her onside.

I click on to the internet and open Alex's website. A headline from that time goes round in my head like breaking-news subtitles that won't stop. ORCHID GIRLS ARRESTED

If we're going to beat this man, I need all the facts. But my prayers for him to change his mind have gone unanswered. The headline leaps out at me.

CASE NO. 5: THE ORCHID GIRLS

On 14th August 2002, a fourteen-year-old schoolgirl, Charlotte Greene, was reported missing by her parents after failing to return to her home in Lyme Regis, Dorset. Following an extensive search, her body was discovered two days later on Monmouth Beach along the coast from Lyme Regis. Cause of death was given as drowning, her injuries indicating she had fallen and hit her head on the rocks.

On the day of her disappearance, Charlotte had allegedly spent the morning with two friends, who reported leaving her in town at around 1 p.m. However, a witness reported seeing three girls on the cliffs at around 2.30 p.m. but was too far away for any positive identification. Under questioning one of the girls admitted to an argument, suggesting they had parted on bad terms. Despite inconsistencies in the girls' stories, the girls decided against changing their statements, and after initial questioning, they refused to speak further. The girls were arrested and taken to trial.

National press dubbed them 'The Orchid Girls' on account of the identical tattoos of a purple orchid that the three girls had on the inside of their left wrists. The girls refused to comment on the significance of the inking and eventually the case collapsed in court due to insufficient evidence.

The Greene family moved to Scotland after the trial collapsed. Greene's parents divorced and Greene's mother founded a charity to help find missing young people, YOUNG MISSING.

A documentary of the case was broadcast on ITV in 2005,
but no new information was discovered.

My eyes are glued to the screen and I read fast, hands clenched,
telling myself it's nothing new, it's as removed from my life today
as any of the other random cases that he has reported on. But
when I see the last line, I freeze.

Whatever happened to The Orchid Girls? Coming soon on this
blog…

CHAPTER TWENTY-FIVE
MOLLY

Grace is all I can think about as I pack my overnight bag, stuffing in a couple of T-shirts and something to wear in bed. A few toiletries, my charger and headphones and I'm done. I decide not to tell Mrs Bird I'm going away; that way, if the journalist comes back she won't know where I am.

I hesitate for a moment outside the shop, but *no*. I stop myself. I got through yesterday and I can't let myself drink today – the other day was a blip, that's all. Being around Grace made me weak, just like it did all those years ago. I close my eyes and give in to a wave of nausea. A cold beer would feel so good, refreshing and bubbly, slipping down my throat, but then I think of Ellis and I'm glad that I haven't got enough money to buy one. When I get to Dorset I'll ring her and she'll help me fight it. The constant battle in my head between drinking versus not drinking makes it throb even harder.

On the train I call Mum to let her know I'm on my way. She sounds pleased, I think. But maybe she's just being polite? I give in to my urge and call Grace, but she doesn't pick up, and disappointment crushes me. Is she with her husband? I scratch at the scab on my hand, trying not to feel jealous. For the rest of the journey that night at Grace's plays over and over in my head. A newspaper has been left on the seat opposite and I kick my feet at it when I see a photograph of Richard Sutherland. No doubt it's a piece on how well he is doing in the polls. But when I pick it up, I see it's not about that. The first line reveals that his father-in-law has died and I sit back in shock. Grace said Michael was ill, but… why didn't she tell me when I rang? My pulse quickens, questions racing through my head.

Michael being out of the way must make things easier for Grace – no more comments about the past, bringing up what she's trying to forget. Ellis sends me a text and an urge to talk to her overcomes me. She'll know what to do. Should I tell her I've had a drink? It niggles at me, not telling her stuff. The train jolts to a standstill and I jump to my feet. We've arrived at Axminster and the guard is blowing his whistle.

My favourite front seat on the top deck of the bus is empty. Most of the passengers are elderly and seated downstairs, apart from a Japanese couple who exclaim at the scenery and jump up and down to take lots of photos. The constant movement winds me up. The bus twists around the Jurassic coast, its wild beauty still so familiar despite all my years away. As the scenery flashes past I wonder what it will be like seeing Mum. I watch the sea, thinking about how long it's been since I've swum amongst the waves. It's windy today, and the waves are choppy as they move forwards and backwards relentlessly; the tide is on its way out, leaving a trail of debris behind. Imagining what it may leave makes me shudder and I turn away. I used to love swimming, but that was before. I haven't been in the sea since. I can barely bring myself to look at it.

Arriving in Lyme, the bus station is achingly familiar. I used to loiter there with my school friends, drinking cider while they attempted to talk to boys. It was where I'd once watched Grace leaning against Jason, not understanding the pain that had jabbed at my ribs as I watched his hand tentatively stroking her hair. The lights of the bus switch off and the engine judders to a halt – I'm the last person to get off, reluctant to arrive now I'm here. My insides feel icy at the thought that someone might recognise me.

*

Our home is at the end of a tree-lined street, cut off from other houses. I take a step back when Mum answers the door. The woman who stands in front of me has little colour, and she's heavier than she used to be. Mum was always full of energy, but the lady standing before me looks tired and drawn. She's wearing slippers that were once pink and fluffy, but are now dull grey and ratty, and she shuffles her feet along the floor, dragging them behind her, as if she's cleaning as she goes – except for the fact that the place is filthy. I put my hand on the wall to steady myself. Dust clings to my fingertips. This place used to be spotless. Her pride and joy. Darren was right. *What's happened?*

'I'll fetch some tea.'

She nods to the front room, but the door is stiff and I push hard against it. I climb over a book which is lying abandoned on the floor, stooping to pick it up before realising that there's no point. Piles of newspapers are stacked like an extra layer of wallpaper against the back wall, so high they obscure the window. The rest of the floor is a jumble of shoeboxes and carrier bags.

'Mum?'

The sofa is an island in the middle of the room, and I clamber over to it. A multi-coloured blanket is slung over the seats. Gran crocheted it when I was little – she tried to teach me but I wouldn't sit still. The sofa is hard and uncomfortable, and I perch on the edge of it, shrugging my jacket off. A cat yowls and leaps off the other end, straining my already stretched nerves. The windows are closed and the autumn sun is beating down on them, the room stifling with the radiators blasting out on full. Mum enters holding two mugs of tea.

She pushes a pile of papers aside to make space on the table.

'You look thin, Molly,' she says, worry etched in her expression. 'Why has it taken you so long to get in touch?'

'I'm sorry, Mum. I wasn't sure you'd want to see me.'

'You're my daughter, whatever you do. How are you?'

I consider lying to her for a second before changing my mind. There are too many secrets in my life. 'I'm not doing great. Working in a bar until recently, same old stuff. I miss you, Mum, I wanted to see you.' As I finish my sentence, I realise how hard it's been without her.

'I've missed you too, love. Where are you living?'

'I rent a flat in a house, just me and an old lady downstairs.'

'Don't you get lonely? You always used to like company.'

'We look out for each other.'

'That's not what I've heard about London.'

'Yeah, I'm lucky I guess.'

'You're always welcome here, you know that.'

'Really? Last time—'

She waves her hand. 'It was an emotional time, we were both upset.'

'How have you coped, without Dad?' *But I know the answer. Obviously not great.* She's like a deflated balloon and the place is full of crap. Once he'd gone she'd lost both of us, and it looks like she's fallen apart. Remorse hits me. I should have been there for her, thought less about myself.

'It was hard at first, but it's getting easier. Work keeps me busy.'

'I won't let you down again, Mum. I wanted to be sure of that before I came.'

Her pale blue eyes look watery and I know she's remembering how drunk I was at Dad's funeral, what an idiot I made of myself. But it was the only way I could cope with coming back.

'What do you want, Molly? Why have you come back, why now?'

I crack my knuckles, not knowing what to do with my hands. 'Don't suppose I can smoke in here?'

She shrugs and points to the balcony, a tiny space behind a stack of cardboard boxes, where there's just about room to stand.

I lean against the wall so I can talk to Mum across the clutter of the room.

'I want to make a fresh start. Thought it might help to be back here.'

'You've stayed away long enough.'

'You know why that is.'

She picks up a spoon and stirs her tea, staring into the mug. I blow smoke back over my shoulder, catching a glimpse of the cliffs in the distance, which makes me feel cold. The sky is dark purple like the wild, violet orchids which peeped out at the cliff path if you knew where to look. The sky was broody on the day I showed Grace the wild orchids, and she picked me one to put in my hair. We carved our initials into a chestnut tree, and she held my hand as we charged home, thick drops of rain pelting on our heads, laughing; nothing mattered once we had each other. I stub out the butt and go back in, shutting the door against the threat that lurks outside. Maybe it was wrong to come back. The memories are too much.

I move a pile of magazines so I can sit back down again. 'Mum, why is all this stuff piled up in here? How can you live in this mess?'

Her cheeks go crimson and she hangs her head. 'You're right, maybe it's got a bit out of hand.'

'A bit. What have you done with my stuff?'

'I haven't thrown anything away.'

I look at the dusty ornaments on the shelves, the piles of newspapers in the corner.

'Your room is as you left it, I shoved your stuff into that old wardrobe. I shouldn't think there's anything much you'd want now, though. I know everyone's into decluttering these days, getting rid of everything. But I can't understand it. I like to have my things around me. Comforts me. That's all I've got since your dad died and…' Mum's voice trails off, her eyes glazing, as if she's left the room.

A lump fills my throat.

She wheezes and the clock ticks. 'I suppose you'll want to be staying the night?'

So much stuff everywhere makes the walls crowd in. I can't imagine sleeping here. I can barely move my feet for all the stuff around them.

'It might be better if you stay in Uncle Bill's cottage.'

'Won't he mind?'

'He died, love, six months ago. Cancer.'

'Oh, no.' Uncle Bill was my mentor. He taught me everything I know about photography. Sadness weighs down on me. 'Why didn't you tell me?'

'I tried, but I didn't know where you were. To be honest, I feared the worst, after last time.'

'I'm trying hard not to drink, Mum.'

'Good girl. He left you his camera in his will, it's up in your room. The cottage is as he left it. I haven't got round to doing anything about it. It needs a bit of looking after.' She breathes heavily after each word, as if speaking takes up too much energy.

'I'll stay at the cottage,' I say. It'll be good to have my own space. I just hope it isn't crammed full of stuff too.

'You always were at home there. But you're alright here for a couple of nights. I'll make us something to eat.'

Mum sticks the telly on after lunch while I wash up, but when I go back into the living room her eyes are closed and gentle snores rumble out of her. Time to go and have a rummage around upstairs. I'm pretty sure I destroyed all those risky photos of us, but I promised Grace I'd make sure.

My old room is miraculously free of junk. It looks more or less as I left it, the faded wallpaper bearing marks where my posters used to be. Morrissey, Dad's hero and mine, huge in black and white, dominated the room, his angst-filled eyes looking up to my ceiling as if all the answers were to be found up there.

The wardrobe door creaks when I yank it open, stiff after not being opened for so many years. Mum has left it untouched, and memories hit me with the smell of old clothes and dust. Long-forgotten sweatshirts still hang from the coat hangers, along with my favourite old jeans and my denim jacket. I remember packing in the dark to leave home, sneaking out when Mum and Dad were asleep in their separate rooms, exhausted by arguing once again about the same old thing. Mum was losing her energy even then. The night bus I escaped on had been empty except for a middle-aged man, and I'd sat as far away from him as possible.

Mum has left Bill's camera on the bed, still in its original packaging. I stroke the box, remembering Uncle Bill – flat cap on, whistling a tune as he pottered around his studio, making us hot mugs of tea that we'd drink outside on the doorstep while he explained to me what he was doing. My old sports bag is at the bottom of the wardrobe, the leather split into cracks, but the photographs are still there. I sit cross-legged on the floor and pull the bag into my lap, taking out the shoebox which hasn't been opened for years. The elastic band that held the box together falls apart in yellow clumps. My hands are trembling but they're at least shaking less since I've stopped drinking. Then I wish I hadn't had that thought because instantly I crave something to take away the cramping in my stomach that these photographs bring. Dust rises as I lift the first packet of photographs from the tissue paper which pads the box, crackling as I pull it. Dates are written on the envelopes, and I start with the oldest; the first photos I ever took. I'm only interested in the pictures Grace is in, and I flick carelessly through the ones where she doesn't feature. The first ones are from when we were about ten, sharing bunk beds in my room. I'd forgotten those; she always bagsied the top one but I didn't mind where I slept, I was just so excited she was there. I shuffle through the rest of the packets, but just as I thought, there are none of *those* photos here. There wouldn't be; I got rid of them before the police searched my room. But I promised Grace I'd check and I've checked. Had Mum been through my stuff too? Unlikely, given the state of shock she was in as our family were dragged into a public enquiry. Mostly I sat in my room with my music, Morrissey misery at full blast, and she sat downstairs staring at the television, eyes glazed over. Dad meanwhile was in the shed, hiding away. I went looking for him once and he was sat smoking a roll-up, gazing at the wall. He didn't smoke before that summer, I'm sure he didn't.

The final photos are of our last family holiday. Me, Darren, Mum and Dad together for a week by the seaside in Weston-super-Mare. I remember that holiday. Mum and Dad in deckchairs facing in opposite directions, me sneaking off for a fag behind the rocks. Grace ever-present, despite her absence, Charlotte's ghost hovering over the cliff.

I place the photographs back in the box. It's four in the afternoon but I can't have a drink and I'm not sure what else to do. Before I leave the room I peel the carpet back, checking the photo is where I left it. I let out a deep breath when I see it. The most important photo of all. The one that Charlotte must have swiped from my bag at the summer disco, wanting to get even with Grace for stealing Jason. The only one I didn't destroy. No need for Grace to know about it.

Mum's bedroom door is ajar and I can't resist a look to see what state it's in. There's resistance behind the door and I know it isn't good. Jigsaw boxes are stacked on shelves and spill out onto the floor; one has split open and coloured pieces are sticking out of the thick carpet, which once upon a time was orange. Now it's the colour of pale salmon. The wardrobe doors stand open and dresses hang over a huge ball of knitwear. A musty smell lingers in the air. I can't open the windows or she'll know I've been up here.

I take some tea into Mum, who is just waking up. My phone, which I'd left on the coffee table, takes us both by surprise. The name *GRACIE* flashes along with a recent photograph of her, one I'd found on the internet where she looked exactly how I remember her. Hair swept back from her face with strands deliberately stroking her cheeks, those full lips in a pout. Mum stares, her hand stopping mid-air where she's reaching for my mug. The pretty face pouts from the screen and Mum drops back onto the sofa as the call goes to answerphone.

'Oh, Molly,' she says, 'what's going on?'

CHAPTER TWENTY-SIX

GRACE

The kitchen is calm, conducive to work. *Where I need to be.* Despite Molly's call and the journalist's words ringing in my ears, I'm determined to immerse myself in work. I slot a coffee pod into the machine and sort through my emails. For once I'm able to concentrate and I get a lot done, fuelled by caffeine. I'm about to break for lunch when the ping of a new email gets my attention. It's from Lily at *Eat Clean*, informing me that the article she's written is online. A pang of fear paralyses me when I recall the journalist pretending to be her colleague. What if he is somehow connected to her and she's been delving into my past? My fingers hover over the keys, scared to open the link. But then I tell myself I'm being ridiculous and I open the attachment, holding my breath.

The article covers two pages. There's a thumbnail shot of me and a photo of the cover of my book. A quick scan of the text and I let go of the breath I'm holding, relieved that I can't see the word 'Dorset' anywhere.

It's a good article, and I breathe easier. I copy the link and add a reference to it on all my social media pages, emailing it to Julia. That should keep her happy. For the first time in ages, I'm hungry for some lunch.

While my soup is heating my phone starts to ping. Over and over. I smile to myself, enjoying the thrill of the article being shared, commented on, liked. A lift after the bad press is just what I need.

But when I open my Instagram, the hashtags are not what I'm expecting: 'Queen of Clean', 'smoking', 'power couple in decline' – words swim in front of my eyes. The source is a trashy blog piece focusing on Richard, regurgitating some anti-smoking comments he once made. Somebody else has pointed out that Richard has his own problems, and posted a link to a recent update on the Ash Fenton case, where it says Richard is 'helping police with their enquiries'. The words pulse in big lights and tears prevent me from carrying on. I've seen enough. My chest tightens and I'm full of fear. He fobbed off my questions about the police; there's something he's not telling me. We need to have a conversation.

The tremor in my hands has transformed into a full-blown shake, which ricochets throughout my body. I sit on my hands to stop the juddering, my mind racing. Why hasn't Richard said anything to me? I'm his wife, aren't I? Have I really been so distant and unapproachable lately, letting Molly get to me? I swore I wouldn't let that happen. I search the Emily case online and soon find the information referred to. Richard apparently gave the girl a lift. I sit back, stunned. *Why don't I know about this?* It hits me like a punch in the stomach that I'm doubting him. I'm desperate to talk to him, and I have no idea when he's going to be home. He might not have had time to tell me, is that it? We've barely seen each other over these past few days and I've been preoccupied. I try to convince myself it's not as bad as it looks. Part of me is relieved that it's not just me who's affecting 'the brand', and guilt swoops in at such a thought. But it's true, and if he criticises me, at least I'll have something to come back at him with. I hate that our marriage has been reduced to this.

Richard might not be home for hours, so I go back to reading the online news, unable to resist looking at Alex Foster's page. Since Molly's call he's never far from my mind. The fridge makes a loud cracking noise. It's not unusual but it makes me jump. The article he wrote about The Orchid Girls has been picked up by the *Daily Tribune*. I pick up the phone without thinking and call Molly.

As it rings out I wonder whether she really has gone to Dorset. I can't stand it if I can't talk this through. But she doesn't pick up.

I can't settle after she doesn't answer. Why wasn't I more careful? It doesn't take much to set Molly off, and now she's angry with me. It's the last thing I need. I throw open the balcony doors and drop onto a chair, lighting a cigarette and inhaling hard, wishing I could blow the past few weeks away into the starry sky. I haven't posted on my blog for days now, not since the photograph episode, and I need to take control. But Michael's death is a factor, distracting me on top of everything else. That gives me an idea and I email Julia, letting her know about Michael and telling her that I need to take a week off to deal with everything. A week should be enough to sort this mess out, get myself back on track.

Decision made, I can't stay cooped up in the house, so I grab my keys and purse and walk down to the local shop, heading over to the paper rack. When I see the headline on the *Daily Tribune* I stop and stare: NEW EVIDENCE IN EMILY MURDER CASE. I take a copy of the paper, pick up a carton of soya milk and pay for my purchases. I stop at a cafe on the way home and take my coffee to a table at the back of the room, where I can read the newspaper privately.

I read through everything that's written about Emily, partly to put off reading Alex Foster's crime series, partly because the case is like a magnet, drawing me to it. The similarities are uncanny – the news headlines; communities uniting; a missing girl of a similar age, last seen arguing with her friends. But no, that's the difference – we weren't *seen* arguing. Emily is once again allocated the front page, as Graham Atkins, forty-two, father of Emily's school friend, has been taken in for questioning. I read how Emily Shaw and her two school friends had spent the afternoon in their local park. I know the park well – Richard took me there before I met his parents for the first time and I was so nervous, shivering by the duck pond. I remember the overwhelming relief that he came from such a normal family and that they accepted me so readily. Jean so free with her affection, filling me with sadness about my own mother. Des welcoming me with a handshake, less emotional but friendly, so like his son. Carefree times that seem so long ago. I continue reading. The girls argued and Emily ran off. One of the girls rang her father and he came to pick them up in his car. This is the man who is helping police with their enquiries. All the while I'm reading, the thought niggles that Richard also gave this girl a lift. Why hasn't he talked to me? I need to hear about it from him.

Afterwards, I can't resist another look at Alex's latest article.

My attention goes straight to the photograph of Alex. I study his features; his cocky smile, oozing confidence. There's a résumé of the cases he's been looking at, but what worries me is the last paragraph.

All these cases are unsolved, each of them has ends that need following up. I will do as much as I can to help bring resolutions to end the suffering of the many friends and families involved. A number is listed for anyone with information to call. Our names aren't mentioned, but we already know that Alex is on our case.

A chill envelops me and I need to get outside. On my way out I drop the newspaper in the bin, where it slides into a pool of cold coffee and soiled tissues. My phone rings and I pick it up without thinking, my mind still rooted in the past.

'Grace Sutherland?'

'Yes.'

'My name's Alex Foster, I'm a journalist. I'd like to talk to you about—'

'I have nothing to say to you.' I'm shaking as I press hard on the screen and swipe the call away. But I can't swipe him away so easily. He's on to us, and it's only a matter of time.

Something in me snaps and I know what I have to do.

I'm going to find Molly in Lyme Regis.

DAILY TRIBUNE

30TH SEPTEMBER 2002

ORCHID GIRLS ARRESTED

A police spokesman has revealed the cause of death in the Charlotte Greene case. The autopsy has determined the fourteen-year-old did not drown as originally thought, but that death was caused by a blow to the head prior to immersion in the sea. Two schoolgirls are being held in connection with the murder. Dubbed 'The Orchid Girls' by the local paper on account of matching tattoos the three girls have, the teenage girls were arrested after the discovery of one of the girls' diaries. Comments in the journal hinted at a rivalry over a local boy, along with suggestions that two of the girls were more than close friends. While being questioned, conflicting accounts of what happened that afternoon were given, and the girls vehemently denied any romantic involvement with each other. Inaccuracies in their statements led to the girls' arrest, but police have refused to comment on whether they hold any evidence.

CHAPTER TWENTY-SEVEN

MOLLY

Mum stares at the phone even though Grace's picture has long stopped flashing. She didn't leave a message.

'It's her, isn't it? Why are you in touch with her?' Her voice is filled with dread.

'I saw her on television. Don't you know who she is?'

'What do you mean? I know who she is alright.'

'I wasn't trying to find her. She was on the London news. Her name is Grace Sutherland now. She's well known in London, she does food stuff on the internet. Her husband is standing to be Mayor of London.'

'I don't watch the news much. I've heard about the Mayor but I don't know who any of the people are. Why are you in touch with her? I thought you'd stopped all that, Molly.' Mum looks older, her skin more lined, her eyes more sunken, but her words take me back to that time, when she said the same thing. It was all over by then, and I wondered whether she had guessed. Prayed that she hadn't.

'I wanted to know why she never answered my letters. After she moved away I wrote to her. I know I wasn't supposed to but I couldn't help myself. We were best friends, Mum. I sent loads of letters and she never replied.'

'I know you did, love.'

'What?'

She nods, but looks sorry. 'Deborah phoned me, told me to stop you sending them. She said if Michael found out – well, you know what he was like. I tried to explain you would carry on whatever, I hadn't got the heart to tell you to stop. But I was glad, I can't deny it, that Grace didn't reply. After everything that went on that summer I didn't want her in your life.'

'Why did you let her come and stay here, then? If you hated her so much?'

'I didn't hate her, Molly. And it was only after the trial I began to have doubts. That summer I had to take her in, for Deborah's sake. When she was having treatment she couldn't cope with Grace, and I didn't like to leave her alone with Michael. I tried to tell him he should spend less time at church and more time with his family but he wouldn't listen.' Mum collapses into the chair, the cushions wheezing behind her in sympathy.

I wonder what Dad made of all this. He and I were always close – he would have told me, surely? And he usually got things right.

'Promise me you'll forget Grace, Molly. Don't get involved with her again. She was a bad influence on you.'

'No she wasn't. Tell me what you mean.'

Mum sighs. 'You're defending her even now.' She picks up the mugs, which clatter against one another. 'I'm not wasting any more breath on her. We've got enough to sort out. Spaghetti bolognese alright with you, is it?'

We eat in front of the television, Mum engrossed in a quiz show, her hand dipping into a box of chocolates at her side. Every now and then her glance flickers at me when she thinks I'm not looking. Her earlier words are going round in my head. So it was Deborah who intercepted my letters, not Michael. Why did Mum turn on Grace? Was she suspicious about our relationship even then? Questions taunt me.

I'm knackered from the journey and not drinking makes me narky so I take myself off to bed at nine. I should call Ellis, but since I had that drink I know I have to tell her and I can't face it now. I text her that I've arrived and leave it at that. I haven't drunk today, that's what counts. As soon as I'm settled in bed my mind keeps replaying everything, struggling to make sense of it all.

I don't drop off until long after I've heard Mum's steps coming upstairs.

The next morning the front door bangs as Mum heads off for work. In her nurse's uniform I'm relieved to see she's more like the capable mum I remember, always taking charge. Downstairs everything is still apart from the old clock which thuds mechanically as it ticks off the minutes. It feels weird, being here alone, memories crammed into this house. I need to find something to do or else I'll go mad.

Boxes are piled high on the windowsill and washing-up is stacked around the sink. I decide I'll go out and get some cleaning stuff, start with the kitchen and walk down to the cottage later. As the clock counts out long seconds, I grab my jacket from the hook by the front door and set off in search of fresh air.

Outside, the shock of the wind forces my mouth open into a surprise and salt tickles my lips. The taste takes me back years, trailing along behind Grace when she had a crush on Danny Jones. He was the one before Jason. I hated Danny, with his sticking-out ears and floppy hair that covered his eyes. Even now I feel the stab of jealousy, like no time has passed. The road winds down towards the seafront and there are more tiny shops than ever before, full of jewellery and knick-knacks for tourists, and clothes boutiques with prices in the windows that stop me from stepping inside. What do I need turquoise rings and seashells for? And I never did get the point of fossils. On a school trip to the fossil museum one time, Grace got us kicked out of the store for knocking over a display of books which landed on the teacher's foot. We couldn't stop laughing. Grace can't have forgotten how we used to laugh together – a side-splitting, rolling-on-the-floor kind of laughter which made us fear we'd lose our breath. I haven't laughed like that in years. And I can't imagine the uptight Grace of today letting herself loose like that.

When I walk around Lyme I keep my gaze low, pretending to be fascinated with the cobbled roads and the street kerbs. I'm convinced someone will recognise me, point a finger, set it all off again. I'm also trying my hardest not to look over towards the cliffs, which swell wildly above the sea. But it's impossible, and when I turn into the main street and the full force of the cliff side slams into view, I stop short and someone collides into me. My hair bounces as I turn around and glare, as if the man with the sad comb-over who's almost lost his balance is somehow to blame for the presence of the brooding cliff face, sheltering a beach with sharp rocks, treacherous dips and swirls. *And blood.*

Once I've taken it in, filled my lungs with sea air and salt and stared hard at the crag which I can even pick out on picture post-cards, I can't tear my eyes away. My feet follow the familiar path they haven't trodden in years. It doesn't matter that the shops have changed, it's as if nothing ever happened in Lyme Regis. There are cars honking and drivers cursing and a steady flow of pedestrians who lick at ice-cream cornets as they stroll along. Like nothing tragic happened here. *The place of my nightmares.*

A vibration against my leg tells me I've had a text. Only a few weeks ago the only person it could have been was Jodie; today it's more likely to be Ellis or even Grace. I want it to be Grace, but dread that it will be the journalist. Fear scratches my skin when I remember him turning up on my doorstep.

It's Ellis. She wants to know how I'm getting on. Seeing her name gives me a lift. I change direction and walk to the end of Broad Street, heading up the winding streets towards the grassy bank that looks out over the sea. Up here I'm at a safe distance from the water. Couples laze on the grass, half-naked in the sunshine despite the wind that blows across from the sea. An old man unfolds himself from a bench and leans on his stick, gaining his balance before taking a hesitant step on his way. I sit down with my feet up, light a cigarette and call Ellis.

'I made it here.'

'Good for you,' she says, sounding genuinely happy for me. 'How's your mum?'

I feel the familiar pricking of guilt again. 'She's… had a rough time. Lost her way since Dad died. She's like a different person. She's got so much stuff, Ellis. It's all over the place. So bad you can't get into the rooms without climbing over things. I've never seen anything like it. She's not right. I should have been there for her. I can't stay in the house the whole time because there's so much crap, but we own a cottage nearby and I'm going to stay there.'

'Oh Molly, I'm so sorry to hear that. I hope she's OK. Will you be alright on your own?'

'I'm used to it. The cottage belonged to my uncle, the photographer I told you about. I used to spend a lot of time there. He's died, and I didn't even know.'

'I'm sorry. But don't beat yourself up. You can help sort her house out. And each day that you don't drink she'll see what you're like now. It's good to have something to occupy yourself with. Have you heard from the journalist?'

'Not since I arrived.'

'That's good.'

I don't mean for her to hear my loud sigh, but the guilt of drinking again sits like a weight on my chest, suffocating me.

'What's up?'

'Mum is hard work, that's all. The hoarding is bad.' A little boy pats at a sandcastle he's made down on the beach. He looks so innocent. So different to the scenes playing out in my head. 'But it's so calm here. London is too hectic.'

'Would you like to live there again?'

I look across to the right, the cliff above the beach drawing my gaze to it. I throw my cigarette butt down, stamp it out as I stand up.

'No way. Too many memories.'

On the way home I stop at the small supermarket for some cleaning stuff, then at the bakery where the smell of bread makes me feel faint with hunger. I pull my cap down over my eyes, imagining pointing fingers everywhere I go. I pick out two Cornish pasties for lunch. I wish I could afford a cake as well, but I've got to make my money last – I can't bear to ask Mum for handouts. Back home I'm making tea for us when I hear her key in the door. I stand out in the hallway, happy to see her, which surprises me.

'I've got us some lunch, Mum.'

She smiles for the first time and I see a glimpse of the old Mum, the boss of the family. For a second I think she'll give me a hug, but she pats my arm as she passes, going into the kitchen before stopping dead.

'What have you done?' She looks horrified. 'Where's my stuff that was on the windowsill?'

'I wanted to help.'

'You should have asked. Nobody is allowed to touch my things.' She narrows her eyes and looks around. 'It's a mess, but that's up to me. It's not easy for me…' To my alarm, a tear squeezes out from her eye.

'Don't, Mum. You can't live like this. Let me help you. We can take it slowly, bit by bit. You can choose what you want to keep. That way you won't get upset. I've got time, it's the least I can do. I want to help.'

She touches my arm. 'That means a lot, Molly.'

I clear a space on the sofa and she switches the TV on while we eat our pasties. After she makes tea, she stirs her three spoonfuls of sugar round and round.

'How involved with her are you?'

'Grace?'

The spoon clatters against the mug.

'Of course, Grace. I know about you carrying on with her.'

My face burns red. I always thought we'd got away with it. I shouldn't have underestimated her.

'Deborah told me. She read your letters, made sure Michael didn't know what was in them. She was frightened of what he might do. He was talking about sending Grace away.'

'He did, though, Mum. You know I went to see him the other day.'

'Why?'

'To ask him about the letters. Whether it was true he'd stopped Grace from seeing them. All that time, I thought she'd forgotten me. I thought she was ignoring me. I had to know.'

'Michael was angry, Molly, you have to understand that. He was out that afternoon and had no alibi for his whereabouts. It incensed him that anyone would question his word. He took it out on Grace, came down very hard on her, sending her away like that. But in hindsight it was a good thing, giving her a fresh start. I hated the way everyone inferred you girls were guilty.'

If only you knew. My insides lurch.

'My gut said you weren't. They had no evidence. I believed in you, Molly, but I knew you were hiding something. I wish you'd tell me what happened. You were both keeping secrets, I could tell. Sneaking around, acting suspicious. Was it just about the two of you?'

'Do we have to go over this again?' I wish I could talk to her, put it right. But I can't do that, I've promised Grace.

'I still think you're keeping something from me. You never told me exactly what went on. And you always confided in me, until she came along and got a hold on you. I never trusted her.'

'We were best friends.'

Mum swills her coffee around, staring into the cup.

'Come on, Molly. It's not the fact that you had a relationship with a woman that bothers me, but the way she influenced you.'

If my face was red before, it's on fire now. I don't know where to look.

'You were children, don't forget. I was worried about you, I could see something was weighing you down.'

'It's not surprising, is it? Charlotte died.'

'It was more than that. I know my own daughter. You didn't like Charlotte, I knew that. She was spoilt, all that attention from her gymnastics, her mum pushing her into the limelight. But kill her? There was something you weren't telling me, something you were afraid to tell me.'

'You can think what you like but you're wrong.'

She means well but I can't tell her. I can't tell anybody. I'll never be able to.

'Is there anyone special in your life now?' I'm relieved that she's changing the subject. Ellis flashes into my head – it's her I'll be telling about this conversation, not Grace. But she's just a friend. Nothing more. It's Grace who I want more with.

'No.' I can't bring myself to say any more.

As we talk it gets darker outside, the black sky pressing down on the house like Mum's words press down on me. She switches the lamp on and it shines on a pile of carrier bags, full of plastic bottles for recycling.

'I'm tired, Mum, think I'll get off to bed.'

Mum shrugs and stuffs a chocolate in her mouth.

I send Grace a text telling her I'm doing what she wants with the photograph, but by the time I go to bed she still hasn't been in touch and I can't relax. Before I go to sleep I try her number. The phone rings for so long I don't think she is going to answer. When she does I can tell by her voice that she's been asleep.

'What do you want?'

She's whispering, and there's a dig in my heart at the way she doesn't sound pleased to hear from me. I picture her face the other night, tender in the dim light of her living room.

Her voice is so low I strain to hear, picking up a muffled sound in the background.

I'm not imagining the husband's voice. It hurts me that she's with him. That I'm not there instead. I remember how she pushed me away the other night, left me wondering, wanting more. I think about how I'm still unable to confide in Mum. How I'm willing to come down here, after years of staying away, and check for photographs. *All for her.*

I hang up.

CHAPTER TWENTY-EIGHT

GRACE

The *Evening Standard* has a recap of the Emily case. Before I read it I make myself a camomile tea, in the hope that it will calm my nerves. Clutching my cold hands around the hot mug, I read through the article. When I turn a page and see Richard's photo staring at me, I grip the mug so hard I burn my fingertips, but I don't care; it stops the pain that doubting him causes me. He's climbing down steps outside a police station, flanked by two of his staff. He's not wearing his tie and his hair is sticking up, his face grim. He'll hate this picture. There's a short piece written underneath.

> Richard Sutherland, MP for Fenton North, was seen leaving Camden police station earlier this week. A spokesman for the mayoral candidate said that he had been 'helping police with their enquiries'. Emily, thirteen, who had been missing since last week, was known to Sutherland as she had interviewed him for work experience, and he allegedly gave her a lift in his car which he failed to reveal to police. Emily was no longer working for Mr Sutherland when she accepted a lift in his car.

The buzzer sounds three times and I jump. It's Richard, and I close the newspaper, composing myself. He mustn't know I'm going to Dorset. He won't like it, not one bit. Not with his campaign kicking off and my slip-ups recently. But he's being cagey about the police questioning him; I'm sure he's been keeping stuff from me too. I busy myself with the dishwasher, taking everything out and putting the glistening crockery and shiny cutlery away to restore order to the kitchen. As I work my way through methodically, I plan to confront him as soon as he comes in. Richard bursts into the room, throwing his briefcase onto the sofa.

'Fuck!'

He takes his jacket off and pulls at his tie, breathing deeply. I tell myself to stay calm, keep my breathing steady, not to mind that he doesn't even say hello.

'What's the matter?'

He opens the cupboard and takes out a bottle of whisky, pouring himself a glass.

'Richard. Isn't it a bit early?'

'Have you seen the news?'

'Yes. I had to read online that you gave Emily a lift. Why didn't you tell me?'

'Don't. I've just spent all morning being questioned by the police. Again. Complete waste of time.'

He's breathing deeply and I wish he'd sit down. One mention of the police and I'm back in that sickly green room with the flickering light, sat in front of two police officers, refusing to answer questions, Dad curling and uncurling his fingers at my side.

'I can't believe they're making such a fuss.'

'What happened?'

'Shortly after Emily interviewed me I saw her walking home from school and I stopped to offer her a lift. No big deal. I didn't think it was important, otherwise I would have said something. But this is exactly what I wanted to avoid. I haven't got time for all this questioning.' He looks furious. His cheeks are red, his breathing is laboured.

'How did they find out?'

'One of her friends saw her getting into my car. They've assured me they're just doing their job, but it's hard not to worry.'

He knocks back the rest of the whisky and pours himself another.

'I wish you'd told me, Richard. I hated having to learn about it from the news. We're husband and wife. We're meant to be able to tell each other everything.' As I finish my sentence I realise what a hypocrite I am.

'Stop interfering, Grace. You've got enough to worry about. The internet is full of all that smoking nonsense. I still can't believe you'd be so stupid. You need to do something big to counteract this.'

'I know. I'm planning to, but it will have to wait a few days.'

'Why?'

'I'm taking a week off work.' I grip the back of the chair, determined to stick to my decision.

'Really? Are you sure you can afford to?'

'Richard, my father has just died, have some compassion.'

'But you hated each other. I'm surprised you're that bothered. I've never known you to take time off before.'

He's right. 'Maybe that's why I need a break now, what with all the fuss in the press and everything. Julia thinks it's a good idea. I'll come back stronger, fighting.' I only need a couple of days to sort things out, get back to normal.

Should I tell him about the journalist? I can't decide. Richard scrutinises everything I do; it's only a matter of time before he makes the connection. But no, he'd only worry more.

'I need to finish sorting through Michael's things. I'm going over there again tomorrow.'

Richard looks concerned.

'It won't take long, I promise. I'm excited about my new range – the sooner I get this sorted, the sooner I can get back to what's important. Like you and me.' I pull him in for a lingering kiss.

When Richard goes to shower, I step onto the balcony and call Molly. She doesn't pick up, so I leave her a message, whispering.

'Molly, it's Grace. Look, I'm sorry I lost it with you. The same journalist has been in touch with me and I'm terrified. We need to work out how to deal with this.'

Sometime during the night Richard shakes me awake.

'Your phone,' he says, his voice thick with sleep. 'Make it stop. That's the third time it's rung.'

'Hello?' I pull myself up onto my elbow, facing away from Richard. A long silence is followed by Molly's voice.

'It's me. I got your message.'

I hunch over my phone. 'I'm convinced it's only a matter of time before they track us down,' I say, my voice laced with fear.

'I'm not making it easy for him, I'm in Dorset. I'm shit-scared someone local's going to recognise me, never mind him.'

Molly's words transport me back to the beach, a late-night barbecue, Charlotte's eyes glittering with envy when Jason put his arm around me, Molly kicking sand into the air.

'If Alex Foster finds out you're in Dorset, he's bound to suss you out.'

'He won't find out. Nobody else knows where I am. I read about Michael. Bit sudden, wasn't it? You OK?'

'It was a shock, but you know how I felt about him.'

'I can't say I'm sorry. You've got bigger things to worry about anyway.'

Something about her tone gets to me.

'What do you mean?'

'I've been reading about your husband and that Emily girl. Sounds like he's in trouble.'

'That's ridiculous. You don't believe everything you read, you must know that. But I could do without it. What's it like being back there?' I can't believe she has the guts to go back, if I'm honest.

'Weird. I'm going to be staying at Uncle Bill's old cottage, remember it?'

Memories that I've tried for so long to suppress surface. Molly developing photos in that darkroom, me guarding the door in case her uncle came back. Which reminds me. 'Have you got rid of those photos?'

'There's only one, the one Charlotte had. I told you. I burnt the rest. Don't worry, it's precious to me, not for anyone else to see. What we could have – I'm not going to risk that.'

The phone slides out of my hand and I manage to catch it, grip it so hard my knuckles go white.

'You have to get rid of it, Molly, otherwise you are risking everything. Promise me.'

'OK.'

'Thank God you got rid of the camera.'

She hesitates.

'You didn't. For fuck's sake, Molly!' Her betrayal stings.

'It was precious to me. Don't worry. I put it somewhere nobody will ever find it.'

'You mean it still exists? You idiot.' I'm so angry I could scream.

'What? I was in a panic. I started the fight with Charlotte, remember? Which you so cleverly caught on camera. And then you swanned off into town, leaving me feeling like shit. Then when Charlotte didn't come home… I didn't know what to do. And I did get rid of it – kind of, I hid it where nobody would ever find it. Of course I did, it's me that looks bad on it.'

'You have to destroy it.' My tone is sharp.

'Why? It's probably rotted away by now, and if it has survived, it might not be so bad. Maybe it could help me come to terms with what happened.'

I exhale slowly, willing myself to stay calm. 'Do I have to spell it out? It might have photos of us on it. You promised me, Molly, this can't come out. It would damage your reputation too. You've already had the journalist hassling you. Just to be safe, it's best to get rid of it.'

'There's something you don't want me to see, isn't there?'

'No, there isn't.'

'I knew it. Something happened that day, didn't it? Between you and Charlotte.'

'I don't understand why you're being like this.'

'Oh, you don't? It might be something to do with spending the last fifteen years thinking I'm responsible for someone's death. Tell me what happened, Grace.'

'This is a mistake. I should never have rung you.'

'Stop lying. You're making me have second thoughts about everything. Bet Alex would love to find out about the camera.' Richard calls out to me from the bathroom, making me panic, but I can't leave it like this.

'Who is it?'

Sweat prickles my skin.

'One of my friends. Go back to sleep. I'll get rid of her.'

Silence at the end of the phone. When Molly speaks there's a chill to her voice which causes my skin to explode in goosebumps.

'Get rid of me, will you?' She hangs up.

Richard is working in the kitchen the following morning. I should say something. I don't want today to get off to a bad start. I press my cheek against his.

'Sorry about the call last night.'

'It seems to be happening a lot lately. It's her, isn't it?'

I nod, biting into my lip.

'I knew it. I think she's been following me too. You know when you sense somebody is there. That red hair is pretty distinctive,

I'm sure it was her. Twice now it's happened. Do you know where she lives? I could look into it.'

'No, I don't. But you don't need to get involved. I'm dealing with it. Please, Richard, you'll make it worse. I know what she's like.'

He looks at me suspiciously. 'Make up your mind. You said you barely knew her at school.'

'I'm getting to know how her mind works. Look, I'm thinking about changing my number. That way she won't be able to contact me.'

He frowns, nodding. 'OK, but if that doesn't work I'm going to get this sorted. I won't have you being harassed like this. You're still jumpy.' He turns his attention back to his laptop.

My fingers cradle my mobile in my pocket, itching to ring Molly. Richard doesn't look like he's going anywhere, but I can't face going out, convinced the whole world will have been online, made a judgement on me. I need to get myself together first.

'What are you doing today?'

'Going into the office. I've got calls to make.' He closes the laptop. My mind turns to Emily – is he telling me the truth?

I grip the edge of the table, plucking up the courage. 'Richard. I need to be clear about what's going on with you and the Emily case.' He raises his hand to stop me but I carry on, words falling out. 'If I'm asked about it, we need to be on the same page. Otherwise it will look terrible. It goes without saying that I trust you, but I need to be clear about the details.'

'You're right. She was in the car for about ten minutes. She'd argued with her friends, she was upset. I tried to say the right thing, but what do I know about teenage fallings-out? She seemed brighter when I dropped her off close to the river.'

His reference to the river is unexpected and I feel a trickle of fear. *What if the police don't believe him?* An image of the detective leading the Charlotte case flashes into my mind. A tall man with a sandy moustache barking questions at me, me squeezing Mum's hand. The memory is like a hand twisting my insides. It was so rare for us to spend time together, and it had to be in front of a policeman. My heart clenches. I can't bear the thought of him going through that.

'You believe me, don't you?'

'No need to ask.' I jump up, hugging him, and we stay like that for a few moments.

'Time I should be gone. Sort that mobile out, OK? Let me know your new number.'

I don't remind him I'm going back to Michael's – I can't face another lecture on taking time out from work. And now I've told him I'll change my number. As if I don't have enough to do.

As soon as Richard's gone I sit out on the balcony and call Molly, inhaling deep breaths of fresh air into my lungs, wishing my stomach would stop churning. She was pissed off last night; she might not pick up now. But I picture her face last time I saw her, the way she looked at me. Back then, the way her eyes danced when she looked at me used to light me up inside. She's still in love with me, always has been. Which is why she's so dangerous. It won't hurt to let her think I want to see her again. Finally she picks up and my shoulders relax.

'I wasn't sure you'd answer. I'm sorry about last night, Molly. You must know I didn't mean it. Richard was right there with me. I'm confused, that's all. You've had a glimpse of what my life is like. You have to understand this is huge for me. And I do love him, in answer to your question. But I didn't expect to see you again. It's difficult.' I'm speaking quickly, wanting to get the words out so she understands.

'You said you wanted to get rid of me.'

'You don't want him to get suspicious, do you? Have you been following him? He thinks you have.'

Molly doesn't reply. I hear the wind in the background, muffled traffic. I wonder where exactly in Lyme she is, how it feels to be there. Can she see the cliffs frowning down on the town? Do they make her tremble like I imagine they would me? I have so many questions.

'Promise me you'll stop.'

'I can hardly follow him from here, can I?' She sounds reconciliatory.

'We need to decide what to do about the journalist. We have to assume he knows, and we have to work out what to do. I can't have him exposing me to Richard, let alone anyone else. It'll be the end of my career. I've worked so hard to create a new identity, Molly. There's only one solution I can think of.'

'What's that?'

'Paying him off. We talk to him, make him realise there's nothing to find out, so he understands that digging around is futile and stops nosing around. It helps no one to discover what really happened to Charlotte.'

'Her family might disagree.'

'I searched Michael's things, looked for your letters. I couldn't find them. They must have been destroyed. But he kept all the newspaper cuttings from that time. I'd forgotten he was questioned about his whereabouts. Maybe he had something to hide.'

'Me and Mum were talking about that. Apparently he didn't have an alibi for that afternoon. He even refused to be interviewed at first, couldn't believe anyone dared to doubt his word. That only made him look more suspicious. And there's something else. When I went to see him he said, "I warned her what would happen if she wouldn't keep quiet". That's why I accused you of telling him about us. But I think I know what he meant. He must have thought I was Charlotte. Maybe they had some kind of row? I knew you wouldn't have told him, that's what confused me. I'm sorry, Gracie, doubting you like that.

But it makes sense, doesn't it? Charlotte had found out about us, she made that clear.'

Grace gasps down the phone. 'What?'

'What if she showed him the photo?'

'That doesn't make sense. Why threaten she was going to if she'd already done it? No, the photo was her trump card. The proof.'

'Imagine how angry he would have been. Did he never say anything to you?'

'He barely spoke to me, couldn't wait to get rid of me. Do you think…?'

Grace knows what I mean. And it's true he had such a temper. He put the meaning into the word rage.

'That he did it? Oh, God. Could that mean I didn't kill her? Maybe we should tell the journalist – he could help us find out for sure.'

'No. You can't be sure you're right, and what if you're not? Blame will fall on you. We can't let this get out, Molly, please listen to me. Nobody else knows about our relationship. Don't hang onto that last photo and get rid of the camera, and then we're safe. That's assuming the letters have been destroyed.'

Molly hesitates. 'Mum knows about our relationship.'

'What? How? Have you told her you've found me?' I feel a burst of anger that someone else knows.

'She saw your photo. My phone was on the table when you called me. She's always known, she told me. Deborah asked her to stop me sending the letters and she read one. This is huge, Grace. If Michael did it… how can I find out for sure?'

'You can't, Molly. Why would you want to do that? Let's just leave it behind us. Please.'

'Haven't you been listening? I killed her, that's what I've always thought. You know how hard I hit her. I was protecting you. I'd do the same now. But there's a chance I might not be guilty, Grace. This could change everything.'

'Then promise me you'll destroy the camera. Today. Do it for me, please.'

'OK. But I need to see you. My old bedroom, it brings back so many memories.'

Vivid images assault me. Molly curled on the floor, the room lit by candlelight. Secrets shared, warm hands on my skin.

My arm feels wet and I see it's raining. I've been so engrossed in the conversation I hadn't noticed the sky getting darker, umbrellas opening up down below.

'Call me back when you've got rid of the camera. We'll arrange something, I promise.' I ring off, close my eyes and give in to the thought fermenting at the back of my mind. *I want to see her too.*

MOLLY'S DIARY

I can't even tell Grace about this. No need to anyway, because I'm not going to let it happen.

Fucking pencil keeps breaking cos I'm pressing down so hard on the paper, imagining it's Charlotte's eye I'm sticking it into. No, she deserves worse than that. And I've made a plan.

Charlotte came to talk to me. I was listening to loud music in my bedroom through my headphones to stop myself from thinking about Grace being out with Jason. I can't stand the thought of them together. Makes my skin crawl. Charlotte stood in the doorway and asked me if I was feeling lonely without my friend. She said the word *friend* extra loud in case I didn't get her meaning. Made some snide remark about us being close.

I hated her being in my room, the way she stood there looking down at me. That's when she said it. That she always knew there was something different about me, and Belinda was going to love it. Charlotte stood there with a sneer on her face, asking if I was dreaming about Grace. Said she knew all about us and what we got up to. Her words made me feel cold inside and I jumped off the bed, knocking my radio onto the floor, telling her to get out. But she kept talking poisonous words, said she'd followed us to the cottage and seen us in there and I knew what she was saying was true from the nasty look on her face. She said Grace was leading Jason on and she was going to tell him, put him straight. Shame I couldn't tell her the truth – that Grace is using him so nobody will find out about us. But I hated her reminding me about Grace with him and I lost it with her. I grabbed her arm and twisted it, her puny arm no match against my strong one.

Her face was screwed up in pain and she threatened to tell Grace's dad about us. But she wouldn't dare, would she? I was so shocked I let go of her and she left me standing in the middle of the room, staring after her. I locked the door so she couldn't come back in and my whole body was shaking. If she tells Grace's dad I can't imagine what he'll do to us. Worst of all would be separating us, and I can't let that happen. Never. I'd die without her.

I have to stop Charlotte before she speaks to him. Find a way to silence her.

CHAPTER TWENTY-NINE

MOLLY

The low ceiling is cracked and needs painting. For a second I'm not sure where I am. Then it hits me. *Dorset*. I remember talking to Grace, talking about Michael. Was it him? Did he kill Charlotte? If it was, it's too late, he's dead. If we're right and he was guilty all along, then I need proof. I have to know for sure I'm innocent. Never telling the police about the fight between me and Charlotte is lodged like a stone in my chest which gets harder every time I think of it. Grace didn't share my guilt; that's how she could put it all behind her. I wish I was the same. Then I wouldn't have been haunted all these years. I drag myself out of bed. The room spins but I didn't drink yesterday. That's good. And I can stay at the cottage tonight – I need my own space.

After pacing around the kitchen, going over the conversation with Grace, I get to work in the living room. The tower of newspapers in the corner is a good place to start, and I'm sorting out magazines when Mum opens the door, knocking it against my knee. Pain ricochets up my leg and tears spring to my eyes. I imagine a cold vodka, crunchy with ice.

'Ouch.'

'I'm not throwing these away,' she says, grabbing a handful of *Nursing Today* magazines. 'I haven't read them yet.'

'Fine. I won't bother then.'

I kick at the pile of newspapers and they slide over the floor. She leaves the room. Moments later, I hear a crash. Mum's voice calls out and I run into the kitchen. She's on the floor surrounded by a pile of plastic Tupperware.

I pull her to her feet and she sits at the table while I make her a cup of tea, her eyes shiny with tears.

'What is it, Mum?' I hate seeing her like this. So different to the strong lady that brought me up.

'The landlord's given me a month to clear up, otherwise I'm being evicted.'

'Why didn't you say?'

'You've only just got here. I didn't want to burden you with it.'

'It's going to be OK, Mum. I've already told you I'll help. We can do this.' I reach over and grab her hand.

'You're a good girl, Molly. Although you'll have enough to do sorting out the cottage.'

'It's good for me to have lots to keep busy with.'

'If you're sure.' She looks so grateful, and I hate myself for not being here to help earlier.

Up in my room, I log on to my phone. Alex Foster has sent me a link. The title alone makes my stomach clench in dread.

INTERESTING STORY FROM THE *DAILY TRIBUNE*
ORCHID GIRLS – LATEST
Two fifteen-year-old girls have been found not guilty of the murder of schoolgirl Charlotte Greene. The jury at Yeovil Magistrates' Court also acquitted the girls of manslaughter. The accused schoolgirls had been the last people to have spoken to Charlotte, whose body was found on a beach in Dorset seaside town Lyme Regis. The two girls shot to fame when they were dubbed by the

media as 'The Orchid Girls', growing to notoriety for refusing to
elucidate on the case of their missing friend.

I don't need to read any more, remembering how they still thought we were guilty, no matter what the judge ruled. How could I forget? I go to Alex's comment instead: *The* Daily Tribune *went mad for this story, didn't they, Molly? I thought you were a liar. I'm right, aren't I? Are you sure you have nothing you want to say to me?*

I just make it to the bathroom in time for my breakfast to slop down into the toilet bowl. At least Jodie doesn't know where I am; she can't tell him that. Even if I'm right about Michael, who will believe me without evidence? Michael can't defend himself, plus everyone thinks he's a good man. Terror overwhelms me as I realise this is never going to go away. Going back to the cliff seems like the only solution. As much as it frightens me, I need to exorcise some demons.

The wind blows my hair out when I leave the house, glad of the thick jumper I'm wearing. Time to face the cliff side. Fear prickles my skin. The sea is choppy today, but blue compared to the dingy green of the London canal where rubbish is dumped and bodies are hidden. I walk fast to try and warm up, but it's the sight of the water stretching out that's making me cold. The path continues down towards the beach and I stop at a point where I can look out over the bay, see the town in the distance, the dark wet sand as yet unmarked. The salty air makes me feel alive, my whole body on alert. I feel the tug of memories pulling at me.

The breeze gets stronger closer to the shore and I make myself head to the beach where the sand lies undisturbed. I pick up some stones and hurl them across the waves, putting off the inevitable. The wind stings my eyes when I peer across to the beach where the rocks become more treacherous, under the highest point of the cliff. It looks exactly the same as last time I was there. I can't help shuddering.

The steady climb up the beach makes my heart bang, but it's more than just the exercise. I'm getting close. *I want to be at the exact spot.* I stop when I run out of breath, chest heaving, calves killing me. I sit down to take a drink of water. But it won't quench this thirst that never goes away.

When I see the place for the first time, I almost lose my balance. My head feels like candyfloss and my legs collapse under me. Here is where it happened, the place where everything ended and nothing began.

The path is quiet apart from the screech of a seagull overhead. The memories are like a dam coming loose, bursting through and flooding my mind. No matter how sorry I am, how much I regret it, nothing can take away my guilt. And Alex Foster is on the trail. He has to be stopped. Before the truth comes out and destroys us.

*

Rage propels me forward and she stumbles back, not expecting me to push her. I've wanted to do that forever. Push and push until she's gone. She loses her balance, reaches out but there's nothing there. She presses her lips hard together as she rights herself. She's so close I hear her draw in breath and the sea crashes below, sending a burst of spray into the air.

'Oh, but it isn't made up, is it, Molly?' She spins around as if she's in her gym class and then shoves her face into mine. My chest flutters like a trapped bird, my fists clenched, ready for her. Her hair lashes against her face as she talks. Words spill from her lipsticked mouth and when she tells me what's in her bag, rage rockets around me. She slides her bag off her shoulder and there's no going back.

*

My body shakes violently and I stumble as I run, desperate to get away from this place. What was I thinking? It was a mistake to come back. I can't undo what I did. Along the coastal path, memories I don't want to be haunted by mix with thoughts of Michael. The sea lurks to my right, churning, waiting.

At home, the shower runs as hot as I can bear but it doesn't take away the chill of the cliff. Tears mingle with the stream of the shower on my face. Water pounds onto my head, as do Alex's threats, my longing for Grace and my fears about Michael. A memory flashes: Charlotte's twisted face as a fist collided with her cheekbone.

When Mum comes back after work I'm itching to get to the cottage. I wrap my arms around my body so that she won't touch me, won't see my fear. Mum gives me the key and I promise to return in the morning. I stop off on the way back for bread, milk and orange juice, pushing the other crowding thoughts away. *Won't drink, I won't.*

The cottage sits along a track veering off one of the roads behind the beach. Tall poplar trees stand like a row of servants awaiting my arrival and the cottage is exactly as I remember it. The key squeaks in the lock, the door stiff from lack of use. Unlike Mum's house, the cottage lacks furniture, there's just a basic kitchen with a large wooden table, and a sofa and chair in the living room. The windows rattle when the wind blows and it's too cold to take my coat off.

Without thinking I head straight for the cellar which Uncle Bill made into his darkroom. A flick of the switch bathes the cold space in a yellow glow. It's as if Uncle Bill has just gone out for a cup of tea – everything's left exactly as it always was. The old white sink, the photographic equipment, various solutions in bottles. I examine a couple, sniffing at what's inside – memories flood in. Uncle Bill at work, developing photos in the dark, always in his old flat cap. I'm surprised to see that the equipment looks good to go. My fingers itch to get back into working here again. And I've got an idea.

Ellis doesn't sound surprised when I ring, and I picture her amidst a basket of wools, a rainbow of colours, brightening her room. I try to feel her calm, focusing on the soft click of needles as she talks.

'How comes you won't give up on me?' I imagine her wide smile that lights up her eyes. But then my doubts about her creep in, spoiling the picture. *What if she knew the truth?* I hope I'm wrong. And I haven't told her about the drinking, either. We don't really know each other at all, do we?

'You'll get there in the end.' Maybe she's right. 'And I'm so pleased your mum trusts you enough to let you stay.'

She sounds so happy for me, I can't ignore the guilt any longer. 'There's something I haven't told you. I had a drink the night before I came up here.' Shame burns my cheeks.

'OK.' She stretches the word out. 'Do you know what made you do it?'

I lie back with my head resting against Uncle Bill's favourite armchair; I want to trust Ellis. 'Grace invited me over. She was upset because her dad died. I got so nervous, I denied it before but we were together when we were young. She was my first love.'

'I guessed as much.'

'I stopped off at a pub to get some water.'

'Not one of your best ideas.'

'Tell me about it. I had one to calm me down, and when I got there she was drinking wine, and—'

'You don't need to explain. You stopped again the next day, didn't you?'

I'm relieved that she doesn't sound too disappointed.

'Yes. But that's not everything. Grace has been getting hassle from a journalist – he's been after me, too. He was waiting on my doorstep the other night.'

'Molly, that's harassment. He's trying to dish dirt on Grace's reputation, that's all. You don't want to be part of that. That's the last thing you need. Getting away was definitely the right thing to do. Is that everything?'

I pause, before deciding to tell her. 'Grace kissed me.'

The line hums into the silence.

'You don't approve.'

'It's not that, but you've got enough going on as it is. Grace is married, she belongs in the past. Why not try and forget her?'

'It's more complicated than that. I think she still likes me too. Years back, things happened that I don't want to talk about. Plus there's something I need to do.'

'Are you sure you can't talk about it? You know you can trust me.'

Can I?

I wish I could tell her, I wish I could unburden myself, but I daren't, just in case. 'I'm sure. Thank you, though.'

'I'm here if you change your mind. This change of scenery could be good for you. Use the time to work out what you want to do. And if you can talk to me it will help. Think about it. I won't judge you, Molly. Otherwise it could be dangerous, being on your own, stuck in that cottage with bad thoughts. Try not to drink tonight?'

'I'll try.'

Cold air hovers inside the cottage and my jacket is too thin. A tatty overcoat hangs by the door and I wear it to go outside, gathering up some of the logs scattered in the forest area at the back of the garden. A battered wicker basket is perfect for holding the twigs and branches. The wind blows my hair into my eyes, and by the time I've finished stocking up I can no longer make out my surroundings, other than the light from the kitchen, which creates a warm glow in the garden.

When I've lit the fire, the blackness outside presses against the windows and the wind lashes at the walls. Trees are rocked back and forth in the wind, and thoughts batter my head. The desire for something to drink chews at my stomach and I can't help looking in all the cupboards but there are no bottles stashed anywhere. The orange juice has bits in which catch in my throat. Beats from the large clock on the wall remind me that a solitary evening stretches ahead of me. There's still an hour to go until the shop closes. In my mind I make the journey, walking fast back into town, the sea a black mass to my right, picking up a large bottle of vodka to take away the shakes. Ellis doesn't sound surprised when I call again.

'I'm desperate for a drink.' A whisper.

Her voice is calm.

'Have you got anything in the house?'

'No.'

'That's good. The first days are the worst, you know that. I've got an idea. Say no if you want, I won't be offended, but would it help if I came down for few days, to be with you while you get over the worst? You'd be doing me a favour, too, as there's a fellow craft blogger I've been meaning to catch up with. She lives in Dorset.'

Wind rattles against the windows. I huddle closer to the fire.

'I'd like that.'

'I've got a few things to sort out in London, but I'll be down in the next couple of days. Until then, we'll stay in touch, OK? You can do it Molly.'

I'm not so sure.

CHAPTER THIRTY

GRACE

Richard rings this afternoon with good news. New evidence has come to light in the Emily Shaw case and he's been exonerated. A news bulletin on the radio broadcasts a clip of him insisting that the police are only doing their job and that he is doing all he can to assist them with the search. The euphoria I feel is short-lived. All day long I've been alone in the flat. I feel safer in here; I don't want to go outside, and the thought of going online makes my stomach cramp. I'd been counting the hours until he arrives home – I completely forgot he was out until he reminded me.

It seems a bit sudden. He's out so often; what if he's not where he says he is? Now I know he's not involved in anything shady, an affair crosses my mind. Would I want to know if he was seeing someone else? Could I object, given that Molly was here, given what happened? And, more importantly, the way I can't stop thinking about her since she mentioned the cottage? There's only this evening to get through before I begin the journey I swore I'd never make again.

I pour myself a large glass of red wine. Watching the ruby-red liquid spill into the glass reminds me of Molly – she's clearly got issues with alcohol. She said she was drinking during the trial, but I didn't notice. Michael had forbidden me to look at her, said it could affect me, make me emotional. I was scared to even glance at her after that. Michael hates emotion. *Hated*. I feel a little skip of glee that he's dead, followed instantly by guilt. But he won't be able to control me any more. He always made me feel so ashamed. I drink more wine.

The first night Molly and I drank alcohol was the first night we kissed. I'd wanted to for ages, keeping up the stupid pretence of fancying Jason. I only did it to get on Charlotte's nerves. I wonder if she knew that Molly had told me exactly what she and Belinda did to her at school. Fluttering her over-mascara'ed eyes at him, flicking that annoyingly high ponytail over her shoulder like a restless horse. I didn't expect him to fancy me or for it to go so far. But seeing Charlotte flounce about, permanently pissed off, was so worth it. Served her right for locking Molly in the school toilet. Jealousy making her as green as her too-thick eyeshadow. But Molly getting jealous, that was unexpected, interesting. It made me sad. I wanted to take that feeling away from her, to kiss the pout from her lips. I started to notice how she watched me all the time when she thought I wasn't looking. How she could make me laugh like nobody else in the world; make me forget my sick mum and my dad's rages and religion, which he rammed down my throat at every opportunity. I'd have disappointed him whatever I'd done, I know that now. If he'd known I'd lost my virginity to Jason only a week before, would that have made him less angry? I don't think so. Sex before marriage was a major crime to him, for Christ's sake, never mind if it was with a man or not. Molly never found out, but that was another thing Charlotte was threatening to tell.

That night, we were allowed to stay in the cottage. When Molly's Uncle Bill was out at the pub and we knew he'd be back late, singing and stumbling into things, and we thought we'd see why he liked to drink so much. Molly stole a bottle of wine from her mother's cupboard and we took it with us. The first taste was vile and I spat it out, but Molly ran her tongue around her lips stained red by the wine and that's when I realised I wanted to kiss it off. After the third glass, the room glowed and being together in the cosy cottage seemed like the perfect place. She was lying on the carpet, stretched out like a cat, and I lay down beside her and told her I wasn't interested in Jason, never had been. Happiness danced in her eyes and she pressed her lips against mine and I tasted raspberries and wine and she pushed my mouth open with hers. It felt so right.

With my head swimming with wine and memories, I quickly put a stopper in the bottle.

As I pull onto the motorway, all I can think about is the fact that Molly is back in Bill's cottage and all the memories we have there.

This is the furthest I've driven in a while; an endless stream of traffic crawls along, every lane of the motorway full. The air conditioning surrounds me with cold air, but inside adrenaline pumps around me. Now I have decided on this path I want to be there, back where this all began, but cars clog the motorway and the smell of petrol fills my lungs as I wait in a line of slow-moving vehicles.

By the time I arrive the town is shutting down for the night, shopkeepers pulling at shutters, lamp posts lit, people scurrying home from work. The tide is in and the wind is whipping up the waves, sending them thrashing against the shore. My eyes are drawn to the cliffs as I wait at the traffic lights in town, and a hoot from an impatient driver behind alerts me to the fact that they have changed to green.

The hotel is off the main road – it's new, anonymous and exactly what I need. I've deliberately chosen a nondescript place away from the centre of town and anyone who might recognise me. I wrap a scarf around my head and put my dark glasses on. Check-in is fast, I transform into 'Maria Browning' as I sign in and accept a room at the back of the hotel. There's a kettle and a coffee machine, plus a small television fixed to the wall. I leave my overnight bag in the tiny wardrobe.

Richard's voice sounds strained when I call him.

'Where are you?'

'I'm still at Michael's, it's taking longer than I thought. I'd rather get it all done without Angela being in the way.'

'But there's hardly anything in that house. He didn't own much.'

I let out a long sigh. 'There are a lot of papers to go through. I don't think he's thrown away a bill in years. I want to be thorough. I think I'll spend the night here. It's something I need to do. It will help me come to terms with his death.'

'We'll need to register the death, and Angela said something about a police report.'

Just hearing the word 'police' makes my throat seize up, picturing that small, stifling room, so many visits there I'd lost count, the policewoman being nice, the policeman not so much. I tune into what Richard's saying.

'My solicitor is dealing with it. That should be the end of it.'

'I hope you're right. Let's talk about it when I'm back.'

He grunts, not sounding convinced. 'Have you heard from that woman today?'

The way he says 'that woman' sends a chill through me. 'No, I think she's got the message. I threatened to set your lawyer on her.'

'OK. Oh, before I forget, you didn't text me your new mobile number.'

'I didn't get time. I'll get one tomorrow, I promise.' I try to make light of it. 'I need a PA, don't I?'

'Well, that could be an option if you keep the business going the right way. But it will mean lots of hard work. If you still want it to work out, of course.'

'How can you say that? I want it as much as ever. Nothing's changed, Richard.'

Everything's changed.

'Let's hope not. I hope staying there helps. I'll see you tomorrow.'

He hangs up. I switch off the light and attempt to get to sleep. The wind crashes around outside, battering a sign back and forth against the wall of the building. After what feels like hours, I finally drop off.

In the morning I hear voices from the greengrocer's below, so I go down and buy enough fruit to make a salad for breakfast. The coffee machine chugs a decent smell into the room and I check the map to remind myself of the route to Caroline's.

Sitting down in the driver's seat, I switch the car radio on in the hope that the chatter will still my thoughts.

I park in the shade of some trees away from Molly's old house, watching a postman working his way down the street towards me, whistling. He glances in at me and I adjust the large sunglasses I'm wearing. The door of the house opens and Aunt Caroline emerges carrying two bin liners full of rubbish. She's mostly unchanged, just a bit older, maybe a bit heavier. The postman stops at her front gate, they talk for a moment and she goes inside. It's been so long I doubt she'd recognise me, but I don't want her to see me anyway. I'll sit it out in the car for a bit, waiting for her to go out. I turn the air conditioning off and make myself comfortable.

As I sit down, settling in, the terrible night I had catches up with me. After what seems like just a flicker of a second after closing my eyes, I wake to darkness outside. I've slept for hours, and lights are now on in the house. My phone is flashing with a voicemail. It's Richard.

'Grace, what's going on? The police are about to call you. They went round to Michael's and you weren't there. Where the hell are you?' The message continues. 'Call me.'

I have to get out of the car. I make for the end of the street, waiting until I'm round the corner and lean over at the waist, gasping. What do the police want? Have they found out? Has Alex Foster been interfering? Or has Molly lost it? Inhaling deep, deep breaths clears my head. It will be to do with Michael, just routine. I did nothing wrong. But I'm panicked to my core.

Back in the car it's hard to stay still, my legs cramped from sitting in the same spot for so long. But suddenly I see Molly coming along the street. The street light catches the red sheen of her hair and a burst of desire hits me. I hunch down in the seat, not ready for her to see me yet, but she's hurrying, as if she's running away from something. She disappears inside the house.

I drum my fingers on the steering wheel, thinking about what to do next. I don't want to see Caroline. Molly's threats return and I groan aloud at the way she's making me feel. She mentioned she was staying at her uncle's cottage. Best to talk to her there. Or will her uncle be around? I decide that some alcohol will help sweet-talk Molly. But there's no need to hurry. I'm not ready to be cooped up in my hotel room yet. The lure of the sea is too strong. It's so long since I've been back here and I never get to be by the ocean any more. The sea was blue and beautiful on our honeymoon, the sand golden and soft, but it wasn't the same as the rugged English coast, the blistering sound of the waves a permanent backdrop. Decided, I park the car and set off towards the beach. There are traces left from holidaymakers who've spent the day here, juice cartons and crisp packets spilling out of the bins. I take my shoes off and roll up my black chinos, wandering across the sand away from the cliffs, which tower menacingly above me. Pebbles stick between my toes and I slide on a clump of seaweed. As the waves lap at the shore, I inhale the salty air and I'm transported back. A memory hits me, sitting with Molly on the beach one night as darkness folded around us. My arm around her shoulders, her breath on my cheek. A feeling of belonging. But that was before.

*

It's early evening when I get back to the hotel and I order a salad from room service. While I'm waiting for the food to arrive, I go online to check my emails. As I wait for them to load, I'm filled with nervous energy. My eyes are drawn to one from Alex Foster. I thought I was safe here but he's everywhere I turn. I put the tray of food on the table, my appetite draining away, and open the email.

> *Dear Grace,*
>
> *I'm a journalist specialising in crime. If you've been following my blog then you'll know I've been looking at a series of cases that interest me, stories which throw up unanswered questions. My enquiries suggest to me that you're one of the so-called Orchid Girls, involved in the final hours of Charlotte Greene.*
>
> *I've spoken to Molly Conway and she's agreed to a financial deal in return for everything she knows. I'm in Dorset and planning to interview her. If you want to put forward your side of the story, then get in touch before Saturday, when I'm planning to meet her.*
>
> *Cheers!*
>
> *Alex*

I can't believe it. I stand in front of the window, petrified, gazing out at the dark street below. A lone seagull cries into the night, a loud, gut-wrenching wail. I clutch my arms around my body, digging my fingernails into my arms until it hurts. This journalist isn't going to give up. Is he telling the truth? Has Molly agreed to talk to him? She could do with the money. A flash of anger makes me gasp aloud. It's her fault for drawing out these feelings again after I've managed to suppress them for years. For years, I managed to forget this part of me. How can I gain control of it again? I think about the lust Molly has in her eyes, and I make a split-second decision. I have to get it out of my system. It's the only way.

CHAPTER THIRTY-ONE

MOLLY

It's dark and cold and I don't know where I am. I stare at the wall in front of me where the wooden blind blows backwards and forwards as the window doesn't close properly. The cottage. Fixing that blind is another job to add to my list. At least I haven't drunk, despite the way talking to Grace has stirred me up inside. *When will I see her again?* There's a craving in my stomach but coffee will have to squash it and I'll try a slice of bread, see if it will stay down. While the ancient kettle is boiling on the stove and bread heats up in the rusty toaster, I make a list of stuff I want to do today. A bit more work on Mum's living room. If I can get rid of all those newspapers, that will be a start. It's a relief Ellis is coming. Hope it's soon. Otherwise I'll crack, have a drink. If she's staying with me I'll be able to keep an eye on her; that way I'll know if she's really on my side. Then I'll try and speak to Grace again.

Mum has already left for work when I arrive. The space I created on the floor is still there and after half an hour hauling newspapers back and forth from the garage, a whole wall is clear. I'm admiring my work when a text pings through. It's Grace.

Don't forget what we talked about. Get rid of it.

All she's interested in is the photo and the camera. That hurts. Then it gets me thinking. I'm not getting rid of the photo, no way.

It's too precious to me. And I have to know what's on the film in the camera – if it survived. Aside from our photograph, it's the only link left to that time and I'd be stupid not to look. Grace's insistence that we don't talk to the journalist is bugging me. Why wouldn't she want my name cleared?

I don't bother to reply. Instead I stomp out into the garden, desperate for fresh air. I find it hard to breathe as anger builds inside me. Is she really into me? Or is she only interested in the camera? Why, though? Why does it matter to her whether it still exists? An image of her soft mouth pops into my head and my lips tingle. I hate myself for thinking bad thoughts about Grace. I know what Ellis would say, but what does she know about any of this? That's the trouble. I can't talk to anyone. But there is something I have to do.

The shed door is stiff and I hurt my shoulder pushing against it. When it opens a fraction I see there's something blocking it. The door suddenly falls open and bashes against a pile of boxes which teeter and threaten to crash down on my head. I throw my arm up to stop them and inhale the damp, earthy smell. The shovel is in the corner, covered in thick cobwebs which make me sneeze as I pull it out. My heart is already pumping from the effort and it beats harder as I walk over to the tree in front of the shed. I slow my pace as I realise what I have to do.

The garden shovel is rusty and heavy. The faint noise of traffic can be heard, but otherwise there's no sign of anyone around. The gardens on either side of the house are still, unoccupied, the houses dark and silent. A black T-shirt on the washing line next door whips about in the wind, flapping like a crow. I hesitate, gathering courage to face what lies under the earth. Memories of burying the camera are vivid; I was frantic to do as Grace said and keep myself safe. I bend down over the earth, see worms wriggling in the dark soil. I hesitate again and then push down so hard on the shovel that pain rips through my shoulder. It takes me a while to find it and sweat pools under my arms; my breathing is fast. At last the shovel clangs as it strikes something metal and I get down on my hands and knees, clawing the soil away from the box. The plastic bag I stored it in has rotted away, pieces visible amidst the mud, and the box is rusty but intact.

For a while I hold it in my lap and stare at it. I sit for so long my knees get sore. The box makes a scraping noise when I open it. The dark brown case of the camera has a leathery smell which reminds me of Uncle Bill. I hang it around my neck, like Grace wore it that last time. A rustling from a nearby bush makes me scramble to my feet.

Another text comes through. I'm frantic to know what's on the camera, but I'll have to be patient.

I dump the camera on the kitchen table and clean up before I check my phone. It isn't Grace, but a message from the journalist. Just what I need.

Enjoying your holiday in Dorset, are you, Molly? If you're not coming back to London, I could come to you. Let's negotiate fees.

Pacing around the kitchen doesn't get rid of the anger that's raging inside of me. I need a drink for that. Should I stop Ellis from coming, give in to the urge? But I want to see her; talking to her calms me down, and having her here would make it easier to work out what to do. Maybe I should tell her the truth?

Whatever I decide to do about Ellis, I'll head down to the cottage and see if I can develop the film from the camera. That's my plan. Before I leave the house I slide the photo out from under the carpet where I'd hidden it. The photo that Charlotte had, the one that started all this.

*

We're both naked, the angle slanted.

'Hold the camera up high, aim the shutter at us.'

We giggle. With my left arm I pull Grace towards me, and my right arm stretches up with the camera. Grace's hand is on my breast.

'Look sexy,' she says, and we're both still as the flash goes off, then burst into giggles.

*

I kiss the image, putting it in my rucksack. I want to keep it close to me, a memory of how we were. How we will be again.

I take a shower to wash the soil from my hands and body in the hope it will make me feel better, but the water is freezing and I can't work out how to make it hotter. My mood darkens as daylight slips away. I try my hardest to stop the descent. I remind myself that I didn't drink last night, despite everything. Speaking to Ellis helped. As if she can read my mind, my phone starts ringing, and I run downstairs to where I left it, making it just in time.

'Ellis?'

'How's it going? Did you get through yesterday evening OK?'

'Yes, sorry, I should've let you know. Part of me wants to hibernate, shut you out, but I'm trying to fight it.'

'You mustn't give in to it. That's the voice telling you to drink, whispering away in the background.'

'All the time.' My voice is a whisper too.

'Molly, the journalist you told me about, Alex Foster, I looked him up.'

Her words are like a thump to the stomach.

'I've read all his case files, did some digging… Molly, is the Orchid Girls case something to do with you? One of the girls has the same name as you. And there's that tattoo on your wrist. I couldn't help noticing.'

It's a relief to hear her say it. I sink into the sofa, clenching my hand around the phone so hard that my veins stick out, ugly and blue.

'If it's so easy for you to work out, what chance do we have against him? He left me a message saying he knows I'm in Dorset, that he might come down here.'

'No wonder you're having such a hard time. Going through this can't be easy.' Ellis pauses, as if she's working out what to say next. 'Is Grace the other Orchid Girl?'

There's no point denying it. This secret is like a volcano, with tremors underground, threatening to erupt. 'Yes, she is.'

We're both silent while she works out what this means.

'Christ, Molly, this is huge.'

'And you wonder why I drink?'

'How is Grace taking it? She must be terrified it's all going to come out. Does her husband know?'

I laugh out loud. 'Hardly. She's furious I've intruded into her perfect life. That photo of us in Chez Elle caused a right stir. And now the journalist is digging, I don't know what she's going to do. But we were so close when we were younger. I know she still has feelings for me. And the other night, when I went round there and she kissed me. For a moment I thought—'

'No way, Molly. You have to stay away from her. This situation could explode. Besides, it's not a good idea to start a relationship so early in recovery. Not for the first year is what's suggested. You need to be careful, she might just be using you.'

I hate her talking about Grace like that. 'You don't know anything about it.'

'No, you're right. It must have been a terrible time for you, with what happened to your friend. Do you want to talk about it?'

Friend? If only you knew.

'I can't.' I wish I could.

'Well, I'm here for you when you want to talk. And you've made my mind up for me. I'm coming down earlier, the day after next. If you'd still like me to?'

'Yes, I would.' *I'm not sure I can do this alone.*

That evening I cook some pasta and heat up a tomato sauce from a jar, eating at the table and wondering what to do now that Ellis knows who I am. Can I trust her to keep it to herself? I'm being paranoid – all she's done is help me, but I don't really know her. Grace hasn't been in touch. We need to unite, fight this journalist together. All I want is the truth. And Grace is the only other person who was there. Grace holds the answer to everything.

I wash up my plate and make some coffee, settling down with my laptop. I'll develop the film in the morning. One more day can't hurt. I want to read Alex Foster's page as if I'm Ellis, try and see the story from her point of view. But as soon as I start to read cramps seize my stomach, feeding my anxiety. I close the page and google Ellis instead, see what I can find out about her. Most of the pages that come up are links to her craft business. Her Instagram page, where she has thousands of followers, is full of how-to videos on crochet and knitting techniques. I wonder who takes her photos and videos, or whether she does everything herself. Her Facebook page isn't private, and I look through her profile photos. In the most recent image she's with a woman, arm slung effortlessly around her shoulders. She looks happy and I wonder who the lady is. I zoom in on Ellis. Her hair is bleached whiter and her eyes are alive, she's laughing. Looking at her, so carefree and happy, I realise she's an attractive woman.

As I'm preparing for bed I pick up my phone. When I see a new message, it reawakens the tension that had eased and my throat feels dry. Another text from Alex Foster lights up the screen.

I'm in Dorset now, Molly. Wouldn't you rather tell me your side of the story before I speak to Grace? There's big cash involved.

I throw my phone down.

I've already done a full check of the cottage but I go around again, pulling at the handle of every door, testing each window to make sure it is locked. I draw all the curtains so no light escapes. Despite the lamp that illuminates the darkroom, I feel the cold air sucking me in as I go down the stairs to the basement, placing my feet carefully on the uneven steps.

A scratching sound makes me freeze. I tell myself it's most likely a mouse and that it's stupid to be so on edge. Back in the kitchen I pick up the camera, turn the lights off and the moon casts a pale yellow glow into the room. I switch my phone to silent but leave it with the camera close by the bed, so the torch is within reach in case I need it in the night. Alex Foster and his story are closing in on me, and I'm not sure how much longer I can hold it all together. Time is running out.

CHAPTER THIRTY-TWO

GRACE

The hotel bar looks inviting, and I'm in no hurry to get back to my room. A solitary drinker sits on a high stool and a couple dressed in walking gear are reading books, pints on the table. A scarf covers my hair and I'm casually dressed in skinny jeans and sweatshirt.

'A dry white wine, please,' I say to the barman, and take my drink over to a table in the corner. Despite promising myself not to look at social media, I can't resist checking my phone.

'Excuse me.' Oh God, it's not a fan, is it? The man has walked over from the bar. He's in his thirties, with cropped hair, dark like Richard. He looks familiar. His eyes flicker as he takes me in. I suddenly realise where I've seen him before, but it's too late to get away. It's Alex Foster.

My feet are rooted to the floor.

'Alex Foster,' he holds out his hand. 'We haven't met before.'

I ignore his hand. *Thank God I had that tattoo removed.* 'I know who you are. Please leave me alone.'

Alex pulls out the chair opposite me and blocks the barman from view. I feel trapped in the corner and my throat is dry. I sip my drink, wishing I'd ordered my usual sparkling water, trying to look at ease. He's good-looking and his shirt and chinos look well cut. No wedding ring, expensive gold watch. Clearly successful.

'Have you been following me?'

He shrugs. 'I'm just doing my job.'

'This is harassment.'

'You've gone very quiet since that photo appeared in the papers.'

'I've had a family bereavement. It's a difficult time and I want to be alone. Please respect that.'

'As I said, I'm working. But it's interesting that you and your friend Molly are both here in Dorset.'

Her name hangs between us and his brown eyes meet mine. I hold his gaze, determined not to let him see my fear.

'I wouldn't call her a friend. She comes to most of my events. I had no idea she was here.'

'That's not where you first met her, though, is it?'

I pick up my wine glass, twisting it around in my hands.

'I know who you are, Grace.'

'So do lots of people.' I pick up my phone. 'Excuse me, I have things to do.' I'm not going to be fooled. He's trying to catch me out, but I won't let him.

He doesn't move.

'I know who you really are.'

My legs begin to shake. 'I have no idea what you're talking about.'

He still doesn't move. I get to my feet, stumbling and grabbing the back of the chair to steady myself.

'I want to talk about The Orchid Girls.'

Heat rushes to my cheeks and my collar is strangling me. 'Leave me alone. This is harassment.'

'Why are you really here in Dorset, Grace? You must have known your friend Molly's down here too. She's agreed to speak to me.' He stresses the word 'friend' and my pulse quickens.

I hold myself still, composing my face.

'If you've got nothing to hide, there's no need to worry. It could work to your advantage. It's happened before. Remember that Australian case, woman turned out to be Juliet Hulme, imprisoned for murder. She's a writer, a different person now. It's what she does with her life today that counts. The same could apply to you. It wouldn't necessarily mean the end for you.'

I pick up my bag, clutching it to me. 'I have no idea what you're talking about. I'm tired, it's been a long day. I wish I could help you, but I can't. Please leave me alone.'

I walk fast across the room, hearing him calling as I go.

'I'll soon find out when I speak to Molly. I think you'll find the money I'm offering makes a huge difference.'

The lift is waiting and I will it to speed up, terrified Alex will follow me. Scared eyes look back at me from the mirror. The same look I had when Aunt Caroline told us that Charlotte hadn't come home. My hands shake and I drop my door keys, taking ages to open my room. I have to get to Molly before he does. Has she agreed to talk to him? Is she lying to me? Has this all been a game just to get me back? I know how strong Molly is underneath that damaged exterior. Rain slides down the windows as I feel my successful life slipping away from me. The Grace I have tried so hard to carve out is crumbling to pieces.

In bed I sling the duvet off, unable to sleep. It's too late to do anything now.

I dream of Molly, trapping me in her arms, me fighting my desire. I wake, angry with my unconscious mind. I've allowed Molly to distract me and I'm forgetting what I stand to lose. Grace Cavendish and everything she stood for has to stay dead.

*

I tell Molly to act normal when we get home, but she is so pale Aunt Caroline tells me to take her up to bed.

'What's the matter with you?'

'I keep expecting the police to ring. Come and arrest us. I shouldn't have hit her, it's all my fault.'

'I told you, she won't remember anything.'

'You can't know that.'

'Shush...' I settle her and go back downstairs.

About thirty minutes later the phone rings. Aunt Caroline comes back into the living room.

'It's Pauline. She was supposed to meet Charlotte in town three hours ago. It's getting dark and she's worried. Come and speak to her.'

Pauline sounds breathless on the phone and speaks so fast I can barely keep up with her. I tell her how we'd met up with Charlotte.

'We left her in town. She said she had some shopping to do.'

'What time was this?'

'Maybe one o'clock.' They'll never know it was much later.

'Do you know where your father is, Grace?' Caroline sounded stern after I got off the phone to Pauline.

'No, should I?'

She sweeps her hair from her face. 'He's borrowed my car, that's all. His is in the garage for repair. He didn't say where he was going. I suppose it's better if I stay here, but Pauline sounded in a bit of a state. Are you sure you don't know anything about where Charlotte is?'

'No, I told you.'

I go up to see Molly, who is waiting in the doorway. I close the door behind us.

'Who was that?'

'Charlotte's mum. She's in town. Charlotte hasn't turned up yet.'

'But we left her hours ago. Did you tell her to go to the hospital?'

'No.'

'Why not?' Her voice squeaks. 'I'm going to tell Mum.'

'No you won't.' I grab her wrist. 'I told Pauline we left Charlotte in town at one o'clock. Just in case she was more hurt than we realised. I'm sure she wasn't, but this is for you, Molly. You don't want anyone to know you hit her. You could get in big trouble.'

'But she'll come back, of course she will. And I'll deny it.'

'Just in case, Molly. You have to say the same as me, we agreed, remember? We made a promise. I won't tell them either. Two against one.'

'But—'

'This is really important.'

The harsh ring of the front door bell jangles downstairs and Molly jumps.

'Pull yourself together. If you don't stick to our story I'll never speak to you again.' I grab her hand, push my palm down onto hers. 'We're blood sisters, remember?'

I hear Aunt Caroline's voice along with the static blurt of a police radio.

'Girls,' she calls. 'Will you come down here?'

*

The next morning the only trip I make is a dash to the hotel shop to buy newspapers, hood pulled up, not wanting to bump into Alex. I spend the rest of the day holed up in my room, phone switched off.

A development in the Emily case makes the headlines today. A forty-two-year-old man has been arrested. My heart races and I sink down onto the bed and burst into tears. Relieved that Richard has nothing to do with this, the pent-up stress erupts out of me. Thoughts crowd into my exhausted mind. All this time I've been terrified of him finding out about my past, when... The realisation that I had suspected him, even for a short while, is overpowering and I try to stop crying, but the tears continue to spill. I read the rest of the article, words swimming through the tears. The news from yesterday is repeated, how Emily's neighbour was taken in for questioning. I'll feel better once I've spoken to Richard, reassured him of my faith in him. I need to know he's OK – he must be feeling terrible. I chastise myself for ever doubting him, for being so wrapped up in myself. Knowing the huge secret I've kept from him, how well can I ever really expect to know him? I fetch a glass of water, sip it slowly. I try his mobile, pacing up and down as it rings and rings, but he doesn't pick up. While I wait to speak to him my own problems need action. It's imperative I get to Molly before the journalist does, stop her talking about The Orchid Girls. I'm terrified it's only a matter of time before it all comes out. Or is it? There is still a way.

The photo in the paper shows an earlier shot of Emily's friend's father, Graham Atkins, outside the police station. He has a defiant look on his face and it triggers a memory. I take the envelope of cuttings I found at Michael's house which are packed in the pocket inside my suitcase, flicking through them for the picture I'm looking for. There it is: the same furious expression on Michael's face, with the caption *Vicar questioned in Emily drama.* Michael wouldn't talk about it, he never told me anything. I spent years resenting the mystery illness that took Mum away from me for weeks at a time, leaving me alone with Michael, or being packed off to stay with Grandma, and later Aunt Caroline. It was Caroline who finally told me what was wrong, going against Michael's wishes. No wonder Molly was like a sister to me. She was the only family I had left. Especially as Caroline was different that summer, slightly distant. At the time I wasn't sure why, but now I realise she was suspicious about my relationship with Molly.

Richard doesn't pick up his phone. I call repeatedly, getting more and more frustrated. My room feels hot and I open the window, hearing slow footsteps passing, locals going about their business at a less frantic pace than in London. I don't belong here. The sky darkens, and when Richard answers his phone I'm so surprised I gasp out loud.

'Grace, what's wrong? I thought you'd be home by now.'

Tears prick at my eyes again and I sniff them away. Richard hates me crying. At least my father's death is a good excuse.

'Where are you?'

'I was at Michael's much longer than I anticipated – you know how it is, looking at photos, old documents. I needed to distract myself. I've been so worried. After that I went out for something to eat. I'm going back again later. I read in the paper a man has been arrested for Emily's murder. I'm just so relieved…' I hadn't meant to blurt the words out.

He doesn't speak at first, and a huge lump builds in my throat.

'You mean you doubted me? I told you it was all sorted this morning.' His heels clip as he paces. I wish I could see his eyes, get a sense of his thoughts. Would I see exhaustion from stress, or a glint of fury that I could doubt him like this? Does he still love me? I couldn't bear it if he doesn't.

'Is that the real reason you're staying at Michael's?'

'Of course I didn't think it was you. I just hate myself for doubting you.'

'Why won't you come home? There's no way you'd want to spend another night there. I know you, Grace, you'll be missing your home comforts too much. Have you spoken to the police?'

'What on earth did they want?'

'It was just routine, to do with Michael. They've spoken to Angela now.'

Richard's breathing is heavier now. He's pacing about as he always does when he's working something out. 'You should be here. We need to talk. Have you been online recently?'

I'm about to say there's no wi-fi but I stop myself in time. My pulse is racing.

'Joanne brought it to my attention to me this afternoon. People posting on your social media.'

I curse his PA, who is sickeningly efficient, like everyone around him. Like I used to be. But all thoughts of Joanne are blasted out of my mind when I hear his next words.

'Who the fuck are The Orchid Girls?'

CHARLOTTE'S DIARY

The opportunity came today. I hung around in the cafe until I saw them come out of the house. The girls got into the car, Grace in front and Molly in the back and I spoke to Mrs Conway before she got in, telling her I'd left my bag at their house the day before. She told me Michael was still in there as his train wasn't due until later. The house was so quiet, spooky. On the way up I snuck into Molly's room. Grace's side of the room was tidy, but Molly's bed was a mess, her jacket and bag tossed on top of it, stuff spilling out onto the flowery duvet. I rummaged around in Molly's bag and pulled out various items, her camera, pens, sweets and a magazine. At the bottom was an envelope and I took it out, hands shaking, all the time listening in case Michael came out. The stairs had no carpet so I'd hear if anyone came up. The envelope contained a pile of photographs: Grace, more Grace, pouting and posing. Does she think she's a model, or what? My breath stopped when I got to the last few photographs. There's no way her uncle developed these. This is what they've been doing at the cottage. They've taken a photo of themselves – Molly's behind Grace, her arms wrapped around her chest. And they're both topless. Dynamite. I slid one into my pocket. A creak outside made my stomach lurch and I held myself still, waited. Nothing. I stuffed Molly's crap back in the bag and went to see her dad.

He was surprised to see me and my legs were shaking, but I had to go through with it. I needed to get revenge. I told him I wanted to talk about Grace. He looked at his watch and asked if it couldn't wait as he had to get the train at two but I said it was important and he'd want to know. I was so embarrassed I had to rub my hands over my jeans, they were so sweaty. I can't remember exactly what I said – something about Grace and Molly messing about with each other and taking photos and it was wrong. He made me spell it out and I think I said something like 'what girlfriends and boyfriends do'. Then he stood up and a vein was pulsing in his neck. He stared at me for ages and my legs got all wobbly. His hard eyes drilled into me and he spoke in a harsh voice, told me to stop saying such filthy things or he'd make me stop. Mum would go mad if she knew, but I can't tell her. Way too embarrassing. His eyes were black and scary and I turned and ran and ran. I thought my heart was going to burst out of my chest but I didn't stop until I got to the end of the lane, as far away from him as I could.

CHAPTER THIRTY-THREE

MOLLY

The banging blind wakes me. I've managed a few hours' sleep and I run the shower as cold as I dare to feel more alive. I need to be alert. After breakfast I'll look at the film in the camera, leave it to develop while I go to Mum's and carry on with clearing out her rooms. I must keep busy. Ellis will be here soon and I'm longing to see her, to stop feeling so alone.

A loud noise makes me jump and I pull a sweatshirt over my head, stepping into my jeans as I go outside to investigate. Another bang and I realise it's a knock on the door. It won't be Mum. Could it be Alex Foster? There's a large umbrella resting by the door and I pick it up, just in case. I tell myself I'm being stupid and open the door.

Ellis stands on the doorstep.

'What are you doing here?' I drop the umbrella to one side, but she's already seen it and frowns.

'I was worried about you, decided I might as well come earlier. And Nikki, the craft blogger I told you about, has invited me over this evening after I got in contact with her.'

'But—'

'Are you going to let me in? Or were you going to bash me around the head with that umbrella?'

I hover awkwardly for a moment, then laugh nervously. I'm not sure why I feel uncomfortable. She follows me into the kitchen.

'Have you had breakfast?'

'Not yet.'

'Good, I've brought croissants. Put the kettle on, will you? I'm starving.'

Over breakfast I tell Ellis about Mum's hoarding and the progress I've made. I push the journalist from my mind. Plenty of time to think about that later.

'I'm going round there again this morning. I've cleared a space in the living room, so Mum has somewhere to sit down at least. It means I'll be out this morning though.'

'No worries, it's good for you to keep occupied. I'll have a look round town, do some shopping. I'll get something for lunch.'

I show Ellis the room she's going to be sleeping in, washing up after us while she sorts herself out. We walk down to town together and I leave her to do some window shopping while I go off to Mum's.

'The spare key is under the flowerpot outside.'

'Original,' she says, smiling. 'See you later.'

When I get back at lunchtime, the first thing I see is a vase of bright yellow roses on the table. I rub my finger over the orchid on my wrist – these purple flowers are still my favourite, despite everything. A pot simmers on the stove and Ellis is chopping vegetables at the table. The air no longer feels chilly and stale, and I relax.

We eat vegetable chilli with fresh crusty bread and strong cheese from the local market. It's the best meal I've eaten in ages.

After lunch she makes some coffee and we take our cups outside, sitting on a blanket on the grass.

'Are you OK, Molly, really? Who were you expecting earlier? I'd like to have seen you try and knock me round the head with that umbrella! Did I tell you I'm a blue belt in judo?'

'I thought you looked pretty fit.'

She blushes, pulling up some blades of grass. 'The umbrella?'

'I had an email from the journalist I was telling you about. He's threatening to come to Dorset, and I thought it might be him. Got myself into a bit of a state last night.'

'It's a good job I came then.'

'Yeah,' I say, smiling.

'What are you most frightened of?'

My back rests against a tree and I try to make myself comfortable, stop the bark from digging into my spine.

'Is it coming back here, does that bring it all back, what happened to you?'

I nod. 'Back then, it was all a bit of a blur, I didn't understand what was happening to me.'

'Why don't you tell me? It can only help, and you know you can trust me.'

I pull my knees up to my chest, squeezing back against the tree.

'Can I? We've only just met.'

She takes my hand and my fingers tingle. 'What do you think this is? We're talking, getting to know each other. That's how it works. I like you, Molly.'

Our eyes meet and I realise what she means. Feeling a spark, I drop her hand. She obviously doesn't get how serious I am about Grace. And she'll only lose interest as soon as I've spilled my guts.

'After Charlotte died, Grace and I were separated. We never got to talk about it. Everything that's gone on recently is because of me. Since I've found her again the urge to go over it won't go away. I've always felt responsible, and she's the only person who knows what we went through. And because I was in love with her, I couldn't believe she wanted to leave me. I never got closure.'

Ellis stiffens.

'I thought if she could forgive me then I could forgive myself, stop leading such a self-destructive life, punishing myself for what I did. But she won't talk about it.'

'Forgive you for what, exactly?'

I pause, trying to find the right words. 'You've read about what happened with Charlotte. It was such a difficult time. I started it, Ellis, it was all my fault.'

'Started what?'

'We had a fight. I hit her so hard I fell over, knocked myself out, but I thought she was OK, I really did. Then her body was found. That's when I discovered Dad's drinks cabinet. And Grace and I made a promise not to talk about the fight but I feel so guilty.' I'm scratching at the old scars on my arm as I'm talking and Ellis takes hold of my hand.

'You were kids, Molly. Sometimes promises need to be broken. It seems to me you weren't responsible, it was all in your head. What happened after you blacked out? I read that Charlotte drowned.'

'I don't know. I was only out for a second. Grace rushed me away, said we had to pretend it didn't happen. She said Charlotte was going to be OK. Then she turned up dead. I hit her so hard, Ellis, I killed her.' I've never said the words aloud before and my head feels light. I feel tears rolling down my face.

'Weren't there any witnesses? Is there anything you can think of that would help?'

I close my eyes. 'The camera.'

'What camera?'

'I told you I used to take photos of everything. On that day Grace had my camera. I was going to show her how to develop them here, in Uncle Bill's darkroom. She was taking photos when we started fighting. Charlotte and her mates at school had bullied me for years, and Grace wanted to get a shot of me getting my own back, standing up for myself. Show Charlotte for what she really was. She never expected me to hit her. When Charlotte didn't come back, Grace told me to get rid of the camera because she was taking pictures when I lunged at her. I had to promise to destroy it.'

'And did you?'

'Kind of. I buried it. My uncle gave me that camera. It was my favourite thing in the world. I couldn't bring myself to throw it away. Burying it meant I always knew where it was, could get it back when all the fuss died down. I thought Charlotte would be OK, you see.'

'But I don't really get it. Why would Grace want to destroy it?'

My cheeks burn. 'We used to take pictures of ourselves, you know, together. Charlotte caught us once and that's what we were arguing about. She threatened to tell Michael. Threatened to expose us. He was a homophobic bigot, we would have been in so much trouble. Everyone was terrified about him back then. The photos were the only evidence of our relationship. Yesterday I dug up the camera.'

'And?'

'That's as far as I've got. I was planning on developing it this morning. I buried it in a metal box to protect it. The film might be OK, but I've not had a chance to look at it.'

'Does Grace know you've got it?'

'No.'

'Don't tell her.'

'Why not?'

'Just a feeling. You don't know what happened when you were knocked out. Look at it on your own first. Decide what to do after that. This journalist, it seems to me he wants the same thing as you.'

'What do you mean?'

'To find out what really happened.'

She's right.

'You think I should talk to him?'

'Maybe. Think about it. Can your life get any worse? Bringing everything out into the open can only be a good thing. He might be able to uncover things you can't. It could be a fresh start for you.'

'And if I am guilty?'

'You wouldn't have to live with the guilt any more. I'm sure that's what makes you drink.'

'But we promised back then never to talk about it.'

'This is about what you need today. Obviously it's in Grace's interests not to talk. Look at the life she has – she's not going to want to give that up readily.'

'But we love each other, you don't know her.' I grip the handle of my cup, annoyed once again that Ellis is doubting Grace.

'It was a long time ago.' Ellis squeezes my hand. 'I don't want you to get hurt. I really like you, Molly.' This time she looks into my eyes and there's no mistaking her meaning.

I shrug her hand off, feeling stung by her comments about Grace. I don't mean to hurt her, but she has to understand it's always been me and Grace. It always will be. The sun has gone in now and Ellis looks at her watch.

'I need to go back into town, I'm meeting Nikki at six. She's picking me up and driving me out to her place. She lives out in the sticks so I'm staying over.' She isn't looking at me any more, and I feel guilty for pushing her away.

'I'm sorry, Ellis, but I have to see where this thing with Grace leads. But I feel better for talking, thank you. I'm glad you came early.'

'It's OK, I understand.'

But how can she?

She looks away as she shrugs her jacket on.

I walk to the bottom of the lane with Ellis, watching her until she's out of sight, hating myself for hurting her feelings but knowing in my heart that I had to say it. My phone rings and my pulse gallops in case it's the journalist, but it's Grace. I swipe to answer and sit down at the side of the road.

Rage explodes down the phone.

'How dare you, Molly? I knew I was wrong to trust you.'

'What?'

'How could you?'

'I haven't done anything.'

'Stop lying.'

'I'm not. For fuck's sake, Grace, tell me what I'm supposed to have done.'

'Alex Foster told me you've agreed to talk. He's offered you a load of cash and you can't resist, can you? This will ruin my life. Don't I mean anything to you?'

'Grace.' I cut her short, hearing her breathe out hard as if she's smoking. 'He's lying. I swear. He texted me too. He's in Dorset, wants to see me, but I haven't replied. You have to believe me.' Ellis's advice flashes in the background and I remember her hunched shoulders as she walked away. But I shut her words out. *Grace is all that matters.* She was sent back to me for a reason. 'It's true he's offered me money, but I'm not interested.'

'How do I know you're telling the truth? He's offering a lot, you must be tempted. If it's money you want, Richard—'

'Shut up, Grace. I don't want your money. I can't believe you would even say that. It's you I want, surely you must have realised that, the other night?'

She doesn't reply and I grip the handset, terrified she'll hang up. I have to keep her on the line. 'Maybe we should talk to him together.'

'No!' The panic in her voice is undeniable. 'He could get you arrested, locked up. It's better keeping it to ourselves. We've managed so far, haven't we?'

'You have. You're not the one responsible. At least I'd know for sure what happened to her.'

'There's nothing to find out. If the police couldn't solve it, how do you think some journalist can? Even if we're right about Michael, we'll never know. You can't do this, Molly. We've talked about it, it could destroy everything.'

'OK, fine. But I have to know, why did you kiss me the other night?'

Silence.

'Will you leave Richard?'

Silence.

'Talk to me, Grace.'

But she's gone.

The supermarket's still open and I buy one of those strong bags and fill it with booze. Grace won't pick up her phone. I'll keep trying until she does – I can't bear to leave it like that. And Ellis isn't coming back tonight. She need never know. So much has been said today that I'm drained of energy, can't fight myself any more. Bottles clink as I stomp back through town, determined to get home before the black clouds loitering in the sky burst over my head.

As I walk back, thoughts are raging around my head. There's Ellis. She knows the truth and she hasn't rejected me, but I can't give her what she wants. There's Michael. *Is he behind Charlotte's death?* There's Grace. *Does she want me like I want her?* Mum's right about one thing – I was besotted; she had this grip over me. Still does. And then there's Charlotte, the way Grace taunted her with Jason. Her two puppets on a string. Everything revolved around her. Nothing much has changed. Thinking so much makes my head pound.

Back at the cottage, it takes around half an hour to check everything I need is here. Getting the film out of the camera is easy and miraculously it doesn't look damaged. The metal box kept it safe and dry. It might be too old to develop, but it's worth a try. It will definitely be worth it if the old photographs of me and Grace come out. Not that I need photos to remember. It feels good to be doing something with my hands, despite the shakes that won't stop. Working in the dark feels familiar. The air is so icy in the cellar that my skin feels damp. One drink would stop my hands shaking, warm me up. I think of the vodka upstairs – as soon as I get this done my reward is waiting. I imagine the cold liquid sliding down my throat as I peg the photos out to dry.

The sky explodes and rain clatters down. I want to be with Grace. But would she leave Richard? Give up the chance of being the Mayor's wife? I've seen how much she wants it, the way she speaks, the fancy clothes she wears. She won't give that up for me. Or would she? What if I can make her see?

I empty the shopping bag onto the living room floor and take out a bottle of vodka. I think about Ellis, hoping she won't give up on me just because I've had a drink. But it isn't fair on her, and I feel guilty for being so weak. Once the vodka is inside me, settling my fears, all I can think about is the feel of Grace's mouth on mine. I look at our photograph in the firelight. If the photos from the camera come out, there should be lots more of us; memories coming back to life. I have to make her want me. I'm happy to be Grace's puppet, and nobody can change my feelings. She's worth it. I know she is.

Feeling resolved, I text Ellis, telling her I'm drinking and to leave me alone. Then I switch my phone off.

The fire flickers and I warm my hands. Flames cast shadows across the scuffed wooden floor and the only other glow in the room is from a dim lamp. Outside, the storm rages alongside the clouds of thought puffing around in my head. The warmth of the fire and the alcohol stoke the flames swirling inside me, and I let them burn.

MOLLY'S DIARY

She's never coming back, I know that now. It means I can't ask her to fill in the gaps. I'll have to write it down. Just once, for me, before I leave this place, get it out of my system. Because we promised never to tell. And it's killing me.

I didn't want to see Charlotte after she threatened me, but I had to go with them that day, to stop her telling Grace. If Grace knows someone's found out about us, she'll dump me. She's paranoid about anyone finding out. Says it isn't right, what we're doing. It's her dad who made her like that.

The bloody wind was terrible that day. I had an idea, a way of stopping her. I thought it was gonna rain cos the sky was so dark grey. The weather meant no boats, no one on the beach except mad tourists in those hideous plastic ponchos they wear. Better for my plan.

Charlotte wasn't happy when she saw me. Good. She made us follow her up to a high cliff shelf out of the wind.

Grace borrowed my camera, said she had an idea. I hung it around her neck and we climbed up after Charlotte. Straight away Charlotte had a go at Grace for going out with Jason when she knew she liked him. Then she said it. In that stupid high-pitched Minnie Mouse voice of hers, she said to me, 'And you can't be very happy, following her around like a stupid sheep. You just want her to yourself. I know what you two are.' She was pointing with her painted false fingernails and I was tempted to rip them off. I told her to stop making things up, because I was scared of how Grace might react.

Grace is watching us, taking photos. Said she wanted to goad Charlotte. Capture her looking a right state, expose how mean and horrible she was to me, show me getting my own back. But Charlotte wouldn't shut her mouth, stepped right up close to me and called me a 'dirty lezzie'. She said she'd got proof, she'd got one of the photos from my bedroom. Said she was going to show it to Jason. Grace started yelling at her and I was breathing hard, rage bursting inside me like a Catherine wheel. I grabbed the bag, she pulled it back and I couldn't stop myself, I had to get that photo off her. There was too much to lose. I lost my temper and punched her. Hard, really hard, in the face. She fell backward, opened her mouth like a stupid goldfish. It was only at that point that Grace stopped clicking the camera and went for the bag. Charlotte kicked out at me, knocked me over. Then I hit my head and everything went black.

When I came round, they were both gone. I was shaking, afraid. I'd hit Charlotte so hard, I couldn't believe it. Then Grace appeared over the edge, said we had to go. She said Charlotte was OK and had gone home. Grace said it was important we didn't tell anyone, otherwise I'd get into trouble. My head was fuzzy, it was all a bit of a blur. She gave me my camera back and told me to get rid of it. I was scared Charlotte would tell, but Grace said if we stick to the same story, there's two of us, so they wouldn't believe her. She made me promise to get rid of the camera cos she'd taken photos of us fighting and she was scared it made me look worse than it was. It frightened me, her saying that. She said it was the most important thing, that it would protect us. Otherwise they would separate us, and I burst into tears. That's when we made our promise. She made me kneel in front of her and she got my penknife and sliced across my hand, then across hers. The pain felt good, stopped me feeling so bad. Then we pressed our hands together to mix the warm blood between our cold hands.

OUR PROMISE

'Now we are bound together, I will never tell anyone what you did, I swear. This is between you and me. Now you swear too.'

Molly and Grace 2002 – until forever.

Mum keeps asking me what happened. Every time she asks me I repeat our promise in my head. Keep my mouth shut.

CHAPTER THIRTY-FOUR

GRACE

Somehow I managed to convince Richard I had no idea what he was talking about. I promised we'd discuss it over dinner tomorrow. The thought terrifies me, but I'll deal with that later. First it's imperative I make Molly see sense. Once that's done, I'll suggest the weekend in Rome to Richard – it's exactly what we need. I didn't tell Molly I was down here for a reason – I want to surprise her. The temperature has dropped and I've chosen what to wear carefully – black skinny jeans, a roll-neck jumper and boots, with no bag to weigh me down. I pat the bulge in my pocket – everything I need is in there.

When Molly opens the door to the cottage her eyes are wide with surprise and she throws her arms around me. *This has to go the right way.* Her movements are loose as she pivots around and moves into the main room of the cottage, a small sitting area leading on to a dark kitchen. An open fire lights up the room. An empty bottle stands by the bin, reminding me of Richard finding the wine bottle from the night she came over. I push the thought away – I won't be able to do this if he is lurking in my thoughts.

'I can't believe you're here.'

We sit and she passes me a bottle. 'Have a drink with me.'

I pour a glass of wine, which I have no intention of drinking. My mind needs to be razor-sharp.

'I wanted to see you. I've taken some time off work, what with the funeral and everything.'

'This is where I'm supposed to say I'm sorry,' Molly says, looking hopeful. Firelight flickers, casting shadows on her face. 'But I can't. Charlotte told him about us, you know. She threatened to – I never told you, because I knew how much you'd be hurt, but we argued about it. I didn't think she'd dare go through with it. But I worked it out – that's what he was trying to tell me the other day when I visited him. You know how angry he would have been. Mum says he didn't read your letters, Deborah did, but she was scared of what he might do. It's likely she got rid of them. But I think he might have been involved with Charlotte's death. Lost his temper and lashed out. You told me he hit your mum, and I saw him hurt you too.'

I shiver. 'That's what I thought when I found the letter suspending him from the church. Can you imagine what that would have done to his pride? Plus he kept all the cuttings about the case. Why would he do that?'

'Mum says he didn't have an alibi. You could be right.'

'You've been talking to Caroline, then.'

Molly's eyes light up, orange from the fire and sparked by the conversation. How she used to be. Her face glowing, she looks more attractive in this moment than ever before, but I hate her, too, for making me have these feelings. I've spent years suppressing them, finding Richard, building a new life. I'd just begun to believe they were gone for good, and she comes back.

She speaks quietly. 'It's early days but we're talking, yeah. It feels good. Do you realise what this means? That I'm not guilty. All my life…' Molly takes a long drink from her glass, the red of the wine staining her lips.

A memory catapults into my mind: her lips stained with strawberries; one of the first times we kissed.

'And to find out while I'm here, with you.'

Our eyes meet, making my stomach surge and her thin arms pull me down on top of her, her mouth finding mine. 'Gracie,' she whispers. This time I don't stop her. I let her hands move over my skin and I give into the pull, remembering us, me and Molly, how good we are together, how good we always were. Her mouth tastes of thick red wine and I can't get enough of the taste. I don't resist when she removes my clothes. The heat from the fire warms me from the outside, while Molly's touch sends my temperature roaring from the inside, her breath on my breasts, light hands on my thighs. Her body arches as a guttural sound wrenches out of her and she gasps my name into my neck.

Afterwards, Molly lights a cigarette, looking into my eyes as she places it in my mouth. Our smoke mingles together in the air. We could be sixteen again, gawky shoulders and undeveloped bodies. But even then we always knew what we were doing; we fitted together. The urge to capture the moment, to take a photo, that came from Molly.

'We were ahead of our time, weren't we?' I look into the fire as I speak.

'Dykes have been around since forever, didn't you know?' she says, finishing her sentence with a laugh.

The word makes me shiver despite the heat from the fire, and I pull my sweatshirt back on, shaking Molly's hand from my thigh.

'That's not what I meant. Taking photos of ourselves. Everyone does it today. Selfies, sexting.'

She twirls my hair in her fingers and I shift my head to make her stop. Revulsion for what I've allowed to happen is blurring my vision. I must stay focused. 'The photo you mentioned, do you have it here?'

'I might have.'

So that's how it is.

'Why didn't you get rid of it like I asked?'

She flinches and I put my hand over hers briefly.

'It's OK, Molly, I'm glad you kept one.'

'You are?'

I nod. 'It captured us together. I get that. But why risk it?'

'I wouldn't lie to you, Grace. I burnt all the personal photos we took, you know, the other naked ones.'

I blush as she speaks.

'But it's not those photographs I'm talking about,' she continues. 'Before Charlotte's parents moved away, I went to see them.'

'Why?'

'Mum made me. It was excruciating. I spent most of the time in the toilet pretending I had bellyache. Pauline didn't want us there, it was obvious. While they were talking downstairs, I went into Charlotte's bedroom, found the photo.'

'I don't believe you. The police would have found it.'

'They didn't know where to look. She'd hidden it under another photo. It's how she hid photos of her crush. She showed me one time. So it was in her room all the time, the one of us. She never did have it in her bag.'

The implication of Molly's words hits me and I take in a long breath. Trying to grab her bag was what started the fight, and...

'Let me see it.'

Her eyes narrow. 'Later. I want to stay like this forever.' She reaches to pull me towards her and I shift away.

'What's up?'

'Let me see the photograph, Molly.'

'Is that what all this is about?'

The fire hisses and a spark hits Molly's leg but she doesn't react.

'You know if you sold it to the press you wouldn't destroy me? It would be embarrassing, sure, but we'd survive. Richard knows about it, I told him.'

Molly fiddles with the frayed edge of her jeans. 'You still love him, don't you?'

'It's complicated.' I take a cigarette from the packet on the table, pulling smoke into my lungs to ease the tension. 'That's why contacting me was never a good idea, surely you can understand that now?'

Molly drinks half a large glass of wine in one go.

'But this would never have happened if I hadn't.'

'This?'

'Us.'

She doesn't get it.

'Sometimes you can't always have what you want.'

Molly finishes her drink, reaches for the bottle and her brown eyes flash. She swipes at her leg as another spark jumps from the fire, her mouth tight. As she pours more wine, she misses the glass. She wipes the drops from the table into a smear and licks her fingers, making her lips a deeper shade of red. I sip the wine; a little will be OK. The taste surprises me, a cherry burst to match Molly's cherry mouth. When she runs her tongue around her lips, my stomach surges, and not with fear. I place the glass down, tempted to squeeze it until it shatters.

'How did Michael die, exactly?'

'He had a heart attack. It was very sudden.'

'It must have been.'

I take a long drag on my cigarette. 'Michael blamed me for Mum's death. The trial was too much for her. He and I never got on, you know that. I stayed away from him for years. I only visited him because it was my duty, but it's probably for the best.'

'I bet it suits you to have him out of the way.'

'What do you mean by that?'

'He was getting confused about that Emily kid.'

'That didn't mean anything.'

'Whatever. He can't stop us now.'

'What do you mean, *us*?' I ask.

Molly looks confused, then runs her tongue over her lips. That feeling down there. I hate her.

'This.' She puts her hand on my leg and my stomach muscles clench into a tight knot.

'There is no *us*, Molly.'

DAILY TRIBUNE

1st September 2003

ORCHID GIRLS SENSATIONALLY RELEASED

Grace Cavendish and Molly Conway, otherwise known as 'The Orchid Girls', were today acquitted at Yeovil Crown Court as the case collapsed due to lack of evidence. The girls were charged with murder and conspiracy to commit murder. Judge Justice Robinson issued a statement saying there was 'no evidence to support either charge'.

Police believed the teens lured the gymnast Charlotte Greene to the cliffs on Sunday morning in order to kill her. An autopsy concluded that she had died from blunt force trauma and there was no evidence of sexual assault. Her body was swept up by the tide, which is why she was initially undiscovered.

Judge Justice Robinson ruled accidental death, stating that 'although there were signs that the girls had some kind of altercation, evidence suggested that Charlotte had sustained the head injury after falling and striking her face and head on the rocks'.

CHAPTER THIRTY-FIVE

MOLLY

Warmth from the fire encloses us. Grace is covered up now but I want to undress her again so that we can lie naked in front of the fire forever.

'There is no *us*, Molly.'

'What do you mean?'

She stares into her glass, which is still full, her mouth pulled tight into a grimace. Doesn't she realise I'll do anything for her? Some things never change. But I don't want to share her and I will fight.

The wine misses my glass and slops onto the table. Ellis's face flashes into my mind and I push the image away. I can't remember why she warned me to stay away from Grace. Grace touches her mouth to her glass, licks her lips. *Why doesn't she drink?*

'Show me the photograph.'

It's not the first time she's asked. Firelight flickers on her beautiful face.

'Why do you want to see it?'

'What?'

'The photo.'

She touches my face, traces her finger along my lips. 'To remember how we were. Please?'

'It's in my case. I'll go and get it. I'm nipping to the loo as well, won't be long.' I lean and kiss her neck and she flinches, I'm sure of it.

'Just a bit cold,' she says.
Liar.

Getting the photograph is an excuse for me to look in the cellar. My hand's shaking as I reach for it. We look so vulnerable with our thin, bare shoulders and shy smiles. I hate what happened after it was taken – the terrible outcome that this photo caused. *Is it really too late for us?* My bare feet make no sound as I creep down the stairs. The chill of the cellar wraps itself around me and I dim the flashlight on my phone while I check whether the photos from the camera are ready. My breath catches in my throat as I unclip the pictures one by one. I mustn't take too long; I don't want Grace coming down here. The images show the three of us together, then grass, a rock, shots of the ground at different angles. That must be when Grace had the camera. Then something else.

I stumble back against the wall when I realise what I'm looking at. My arm on Charlotte's head. Grace captured the fight. I knew she had, but I'm unprepared for the effect seeing it has on me. But it's the last photo that makes the contents of my stomach rise up. At first I'm not sure what I'm looking at, and my mind rewinds the scene. It must have been after the fight, when I was unconscious and Grace went to look for Charlotte. For a moment I'm back there, lying on the hard ground, wind whipping my hair around my face, wondering where Grace and Charlotte have gone.

*

I open my eyes to the grey Dorset sky, the loud rush of the sea. Tree branches rustle and the bushes whisper words to me, 'Charlotte, Charlotte'. What's happened? Blood beads on my skin where thorny bushes snagged at my legs on the long climb up from the beach. There's no sign of either of them. Images tumble into my head, a fight, the camera clicking, a girl broken on the rocks. Sweat pools on my back, clammy fingers knead at my chest. I clutch at the grass, grab a fistful and hoist myself up, the sound of the sea crashing onto the rocks below. The wind flings my hair into my eyes, my mouth. I move one strand away and another takes its place. I spit it away, eyes smarting. I won't cry, despite the lump at the back of my throat that makes it hard to swallow, the ball of fear that gets bigger as I remember what I've done. I didn't mean to push her so hard – it just burst out of me, the anger, electrified my arms, and I flew at her before I knew what I was about to do. Did panic make me pass out, or did I hit my head?

'Get back.'

She's clambering up towards me, hair blowing out in the wind like sea spray against the grey sky. All I can see is her dark T-shirt; her body blocks me from seeing what's down below.

'Come on,' she says, 'we have to go.'

'Have you called an ambulance?'

'No need, she's OK. She's gone home. She had a nasty knock on the head, that's all. She'll be confused, she won't remember.'

*

I just about make it to the sink. Charlotte's face in the photos flashes in my mind, her expression changing from defiance to terror in a sequence of snapshots. She did that, Grace. Taunting her. Charlotte lies broken on the rocks. Glassy eyes and blood. Tears run down my face as I stare down into the red vomit because I know the truth. I know what Grace is capable of. And she's waiting for me upstairs.

The photos hang like damp clothes on a line and are still wet to the touch. Forcing myself to look at them I select one, suppressing the urge to vomit again as I choose the photo showing Charlotte's smashed head. I unclip it from the line, my hands jittery, out of control. I need a drink to calm me down. On the way back I grab another bottle from the kitchen. It's the last one. Will it be enough? Panic overcomes me and I grab hold of the counter to steady myself, just about keeping hold of the wine. My stomach swoops. I put the photo I've retrieved from the darkroom into an empty kitchen cupboard, face up to keep it dry. Just in case.

Grace doesn't see; she's typing a text on her phone, blonde hair tickling her fingers. I stand in the doorway, watching her.

'Who are you texting?'

She's fully dressed now.

'Richard.' Her fingers move fast. 'Have you spoken to the journalist?'

Why won't she believe me?

I sit on the sofa this time, looking down at her. I pour myself a glass of wine, drinking greedily.

'I'm tempted. It would be easy money. Unlike you, I could do with it.'

Anger flickers in Grace's eyes like the flames in the fire. 'It's taken me years to drag myself from that shithole I was born into. And you think I'm just going to let you destroy that? Have you told the journalist anything? We need to know what we're dealing with.' She means her and her husband when she says 'we'. Not *us*. She's been playing me all along. But I won't let her know I've sussed out what an evil bitch she is.

'I haven't told him anything.'

'Good, because I have. He's here in Dorset. He tracked me to my hotel. I've denied being one of The Orchid Girls, and you have to do the same. But just in case you're thinking of talking, I've put him straight about you following me around, making up stories.'

'But—'

'I know what you were going to do with the photograph. It was your plan all along, to get me into bed and then expose me, blackmail me and ruin me.'

How could she think that? 'Grace, no. I love you. The photo's precious to me, can't you understand? It's the only reminder I have of that time.'

She has a strange expression on her face.

'Show me.'

I pull the photo out of my back right pocket, holding the corners tight as she looks over my shoulder. I look at Grace's pale arms slung around my neck, our young, naked bodies, remembering how it felt to have her long blonde hair tickling my shoulder, the perpetual high I was on: the high I've been searching for ever since. I remember looking into her marble eyes for clues of what she would do. The glint of steel I'd never had cause to fear before. I swallow hard to keep the nausea at bay; mustn't let her suspect what I now know.

'This is all I had to show how close we were, all I've ever had, until now. It was the only one remaining of both of us.'

'Let me have it.' She goes to snatch it.

I shove it back into my pocket. 'It doesn't matter now. I know what you did.'

Her eyes narrow. 'What are you talking about?'

'Why did you dislike her so much, Charlotte?'

'Where do I start? She was trying to turn Jason against me.'

'But you weren't interested in him.'

'I didn't want him to know that, did I? She guessed about us, I saw her watching us with those Bambi eyes, a sneer on her face. She'd have done anything to get Jason. And she was a bully. You told me what she and Belinda did to you at school. I wasn't going to let her get away with that.'

'So you did it for me? You must have loved me then?' Despite everything, I have to know. I drain my glass, but my throat still burns with fear.

She shrugs. 'It wasn't just that. She was threatening to tell Michael.'

'You knew that? How could you not tell me? That's not possible unless she told you when you—' I clap my shaking hand to my mouth.

'You've found the camera. So you know.' Grace stands up, the realisation hitting her. Now she's looking down at me.

'You killed her.' My voice is tiny. 'Why?'

'You know why. She knew about us. She was in the way, a threat to everything, just like Michael.'

'Did you kill him too?'

She shrugs. 'I kicked his inhaler under the bed, let them think it was an accident. He was becoming inconvenient. I'd put up with him long enough.'

My throat is so tight I can barely swallow. 'Christ, I need another drink.' I reach for the bottle and Grace snatches it away. The room sways. My heart is thumping at the news that she killed Michael; how cold she is, how matter-of-fact. *Is this really the Grace I've been searching for all my life? My Gracie?*

'Look at you. You can't stop. What if I pour this down the sink?' She grabs the bottle and holds it out of reach.

'Give it here.'

'There. I've proved my point.' She moves away from the fire, her back to the kitchen. 'Here's the deal. You give me the photos from the camera and you can have the wine back.'

My mouth is dry with fear. My churning need for alcohol can't be stopped, and she knows it. My feet trip as I pull myself to my feet, stumbling against the wall. There has to be something I can do. A drink will help me think.

'Give it to me, Grace. I need it, you don't understand.'

She thinks I've got them on me. I'll keep her guessing.

'Look at you! You're pathetic. Hand them over.'

I put my hand over my back pocket. Her eyes are narrow as she watches me and I shout as I lurch forward, but she's too quick, she lifts the bottle high. Before I know it, it smashes into the side of my head, hurting me more than Charlotte ever did.

*

Grace is lying on top of me, hands groping around behind me. But this time there is no desire, and despite the sickness in my stomach, my thumping head, the loud noise that rings in my ears, what hits me the most is that she doesn't want me. She never has. All she wants is the photographs. She doesn't want anyone to know what she did; how she murdered a teenage girl. She doesn't care that I spent my whole life thinking I killed her, plagued with guilt. All she cares about is not wanting her perfect world to be torn apart. That was her plan all along. She wants to carry on with her charmed life as Lady Mayoress. I have to stop her.

'Without this, you'll have nothing. No proof I was even here. Who do you think people will believe, a media star whose husband is the Mayor of London, or a drunken waste of space?'

My mouth is open as I struggle for breath. She's holding me down with one hand as she tries to slide her hand behind my back. I squeeze down hard on the floor, trying to stop her. I have to get her to speak – this is the only way she'll ever tell me the truth.

'How did Charlotte die? What did you do to her? You told me she was alright.' My voice is loud, hysterical. 'I saw the photo, Grace. Her head, what did you do to her? I didn't do that. How could you let me think it was my fault? I thought you loved me.'

Her eyes blaze. 'You should never have made me feel like that. It's not who I am. Being with a man, it's natural for me. Not this.'

'Liar. Why can't you accept what we have together? You weren't faking that. This is Michael's doing, isn't it? He's made you ashamed to be who you are. He's gone now. Thanks to you. And it's the twenty-first century, Grace. Society isn't how it was back then. Gay people even get married now.'

Her face screws up in repulsion. 'Never. It's not the life I want.'

'Tell me you don't love me.'

'I love Richard.'

'That's not what I asked. Say it.'

Her lips are pressed firmly together. I pull the photograph of us from my pocket. 'Look at this, don't you remember?'

Grace snatches it out of my hand, rips it in half, dropping it into the fire. I watch it blacken and curl, disintegrating as what I thought we had is falling into bits around me.

'You bitch.' Sparks spit out onto the carpet.

She slaps me hard across the face. My eye stings. 'Have you forgotten what happened to the last girl who threatened me with a photograph?'

Her fist comes towards me, blackness swirls. Have I lost consciousness? It can only have been for a second because Grace is still talking.

'Stupid bitch brought it on herself. Threatening to tell people about us! Hand them over.'

She hits me again and I curl up in pain. She grabs my rucksack and I kick out at her. For a second she stares down at me, breath ragged, then reaches into her jeans pocket.

The knife glints in the glow from the fire. Silence fills the cottage, followed by the sound of a crash. She raises her arm.

GRACE'S DIARY

Molly's on the ground, passed out. Charlotte stumbled and I pushed her away, hard, so that she fell over the edge. I checked Molly was OK, then went after Charlotte. I scraped my legs against the rocks as I slid down after her.

Blood trickled from a wound in Charlotte's head and her leg was sticking out at an angle. I leant down over her, so close I could feel her breath.

She spat words at me, threatened to show the photo to my dad. Saliva landed on my cheek. Big mistake. I put my hand to the wet patch, rage throbbing. I moved to stand over her, Molly's camera bouncing against my chest. My foot on hers, keeping her down, where she belongs.

'So you're going to tell my dad, are you? Why would he believe a little tart like you? He hates girls like you. It's pathetic the way you follow Jason around with your tongue hanging out. He's not interested in you. You're just a stupid little virgin.'

'So are you.'

She tries to drag herself up onto her elbow and I shove her back down with my foot. She gasps, but she's still got that defiant look in her eyes.

'That's what you think.'

Her eyes narrow, her chest heaves up and down against my foot. 'You're lying, you're just a dirty lezzer. He'll drop you when I show him the photo.'

'You won't get the chance. Not unless you beg.' I hold the camera up. 'Beg for the camera.'

I lean my weight down on her and she gasps, her face turning red. The camera clicks over and over. Serves her right for threatening us. Who's the one in control now?

She tried again to push herself up and I kicked her shoulder, forcing her back down. She whimpered and the camera captured the fear in her eyes. That made me feel good. I dangled my foot over her face. That made a good shot. She doesn't realise what my dad is capable of, how hard he hits Mum, how clever he is at hiding it, what he would do to me.

I leant across her body and picked up a rock.

She pleaded for help, but didn't make a sound when I smashed it over her head. I can't resist one more click. Maybe I'll show Molly what I'm prepared to do for her. The camera fell back against my ribs. She won't be telling my dad anything.

Not now.

Not ever.

CHAPTER THIRTY-SIX

GRACE

For a moment I think it's the crash of the wine bottle, but that's already smashed and Molly lies in a pool of dark red. Cold air rushes into the room making the fire flicker. A tall woman pushes through the back door, where the noise has come from.

'What the…'

She lets out a cry when she sees Molly, and I hold the knife up to make sure she can see it. She's not the journalist, but this woman has seen what I'm doing. *Is she alone?* My eyes dart across the room but there's no sign of anyone else. She's tall and strong-looking but her eyes are fixed on the knife, which gleams in the firelight, and fear makes her face glow white in the dark. The sound of heavy rain seeps in through the open back door. Wind pushes the door back and forth.

'Don't move.'

She hasn't stirred since she first saw the blade.

'Is he with you?'

She looks confused.

'Who?'

'Your accomplice, the journalist. Think you can dish the dirt on me? Nobody's going to believe your words against mine. People know who I am, they trust me.'

'I don't know what you're talking about.' She looks down at Molly, fast, then back at the knife. 'Please, we should help her. Is she…' Her last word is swallowed in a gulp.

'Stop lying. Your girlfriend's told me everything.'

'She isn't my girlfriend.'

'Shame she thinks she's mine. Pathetic, really. She's obsessed with me. She'll never be interested in you, you know that? It's only ever been me for Molly. Nothing you do can change that.'

Molly groans and I dig my foot into her ribs.

'No!' The woman sounds hysterical. She starts to shake. 'Please, we've got to help her.' She pulls a phone from her pocket.

'Stop.' My voice is calm but rage pulses inside me. *Grace never loses control.* I lunge forward to grab the phone, knife outstretched. But her hand grabs my leg and I crash to the floor, knife catapulting from my hand.

Molly is on her knees.

'Grab it, Ellis,' she says.

Something crashes down on top of me.

CHAPTER THIRTY-SEVEN

MOLLY

'Ellis?'

'Don't move. It looks like you were lying in a pool of blood.'

'It's wine.'

'Ironic.'

My face hurts, I can't smile. 'Is she dead?' My voice is hoarse.

'I'm not taking any chances.' Her voice is shaky but clear as she speaks into her mobile. 'Police, please. As fast as you can.'

Grace is handcuffed and taken away. Ellis comes in the ambulance with me. She won't let go of my hand.

'What are you doing here? You said you were staying out. I told you not to come back.'

'Something didn't feel right. When I got your text I tried to call you, then when you didn't reply—'

'My phone was off.'

'I decided you needed my help sooner rather than later. I didn't like the idea of you being alone in that cottage. A gut feeling. I called a taxi.'

'I've been drinking again.' My head feels strangely clear. The fear must have sobered me right up.

'Shhh,' she says. 'The hospital will look after you.'

*

Next time I see Ellis I'm in a hospital bed. It's a private room with my own policeman outside. Mum has gone downstairs for a break. She's been here all night. I feel so grateful to have her when I need her most.

'Where are you staying?'

'At an Airbnb in town. But I've been talking to your mum. She says I can stay in the cottage as soon as the police have finished with it. Get it cleaned up for you.'

'I'd like that.'

'It turns out your mum had a feeling about Grace all along, suspected that she was somehow involved in Charlotte's death.'

'Why didn't she tell me?'

'She didn't want to believe that Grace was capable of it, so she didn't see the point in telling you. She said Grace was like a daughter to her, but after what happened with Charlotte she had her doubts. She saw a different side to Grace during the trial, how cold she became.'

'I thought Grace told me everything back then.' I feel so betrayed.

'It turns out you didn't know her that well at all, did you? But she fooled everyone. And would you have even believed Caroline? She could see you were devoted to Grace, but she thought it was just an intense teenage friendship. She didn't realise the truth about the relationship until it was playing out in front of her. Caroline went to see Grace shortly after the trial, asked her outright. Grace denied the relationship.'

I can't believe what I'm hearing. 'Sounds like you and Mum have talked a lot.'

'We have. She said you coming to stay helped her see what a mess she'd got herself into. Your dad dying was such a shock to her, and she took it out on the house. She'll be fine, she's a strong woman under all that. Like her daughter. Tough, underneath it all.' As Ellis finishes her sentence, she reaches out to me.

'Thank fuck you came back.'

She squeezes my hand and grins. 'You really thought you'd killed her, didn't you?'

I nod, tears welling up. 'Grace told me Charlotte was OK and I believed her. It was only when she didn't come home that I began to wonder. I started it all when I pushed her – I thought it was all my fault. Then she tried to make me believe it was Michael. If Grace hadn't taken the photos, I'd never have known. How sick can you be? To photograph that?' The image makes me feel ill. I wish I could erase it from my memory. I push myself up in bed, heart thumping. 'The photos from the darkroom, what happened to them?'

'The police took them. The policewoman who helped you into the ambulance. Do you remember?'

'The last thing I remember is a knife in my face, then you.' My body starts to shake. 'Where's Grace?'

'It's OK, she's in police custody. She's been charged with the assault on you and they're questioning her about what happened to Charlotte. The photos prove that Grace was the last person to see her alive. She'll get herself an expensive lawyer, but whatever happens she'll be punished for attacking you. If you press charges, that is. You are going to, aren't you?'

'I thought she loved me, Ellis.' Tears fall down my face, and my sobs are so violent my ribs ache. *I've wasted years on her; how stupid could I be?* The future looks black, empty. I'm exhausted.

'You're not stupid, don't say that. And she did love you, in her own way. But it sounds like she couldn't cope with it, didn't understand it. I feel sorry for her, in a way. Even though she did some terrible things.'

'How can you? She killed Charlotte. And she attacked you.' The truth is finally sinking in. 'You're too good for me.'

'I wish you'd stop talking crap. I believe in forgiving people. This will ruin her, Molly.'

'Like she ruined me.'

'Yes, past tense. But you've got the rest of your life to live. The doctors have told your mum they'll help you – go through a proper detox, get professional help.'

'And I've got you.'

'I'm not going anywhere.'

Ellis leaves when Mum comes back in. She puts her arms gently around me and I let myself cry. Once I'm done I feel different. Lighter.

'You did good, Molly. I always knew you were innocent. No wonder you've been so messed up.'

Relief floods through me, hearing my mum's belief in me. 'I like Ellis,' she says.

'Me too, Mum. My first proper friend. Since—'

'She was never your friend. Forget about her. Please.'

I hope I can.

'Why don't you stay down here for a while? I could help you rent a place.'

'Could I move into the cottage?'

'With everything that happened there? Would you want to?'

'It was Uncle Bill's home. Grace is done spoiling my life. I won't let her take that away from me, too. Besides, it's where I found out the truth. That freed me. And I'm going to take up photography.'

She smiles. 'Uncle Bill would be proud.'

I go to pour myself some water but the jug is empty and Mum goes off to fill it. Alone, I realise that the weight that was pressing down on my chest has lifted. The dark shape of the future is lightening, and I sit up straight in bed, squaring my shoulders. Rehab, photography, Ellis. Anything is possible now that I know I'm not guilty. I run my fingers over the scar on my hand, faint now, but a reminder; trace my finger over my orchid tattoo. It's a link to Dad, that's what it means to me now. I don't need to punish myself any more. I've got a smile on my face when Mum comes in.

'What are you thinking about?'

'I'm gonna be alright, that's what. And we'll sort out your house, Mum.'

'We'll sort you out first.'

When Mum leaves, I close my eyes, feeling different, calm. A slight sound makes me flicker my eyelids open again. Darren is standing there. Same boyish face, jeans hanging down off his skinny bum, sensible jumper. He grins and I want to smile back but my mouth is wobbly, my cheeks feel wet.

'Don't go all soft on me, sis.'

I reach out for his hand.

'This is getting to be a habit,' he says, pulling up a chair, scratching the stubble on his jaw. It doesn't make him look any older. 'Visiting you in hospital.'

'Crap sister, aren't I?'

'No, you're alright. I've been talking to Ellis, she seems to think you're pretty cool.'

I open my mouth to speak but a yawn overtakes me. He squeezes my hand.

'Sleep,' he says. 'You know I'm here for you, yeah?'

I squeeze it back.

CHAPTER THIRTY-EIGHT

GRACE

Richard is allowed to visit me in custody.

The policewoman points to the seat. 'Sit down.'

I glare at the officer who guards me and sit back down. Richard's in a new suit. I can't believe he's had the cheek to go out shopping while I'm stuck in this dump. He looks tired, his eyes full of pain.

'What's going on Grace? What are you doing in Dorset? This is like a mad nightmare. But it isn't, is it?'

I go to talk, but he carries on. 'You're not the person I married.'

'It's all lies, Richard. The girl who went missing at school, that's what all this is about. I had a teenage fling with Molly, the woman who's been stalking me. Big mistake. Turns out she's borne a grudge for years, has come up with a ludicrous story about me being responsible. It's all nonsense.'

'Your solicitor tells me there's photographic evidence.'

'About that solicitor. He won't do. Why haven't you appointed Douglas? This is some idiot the police appointed, and apart from anything else he's got bad breath.'

'Christ, Grace. You don't realise how serious this is. Even if you're right and there's no case to prove you killed that girl, you attacked Molly. With a knife? Really? I don't know you any more.'

'It was self-defence.'

'That's not what the witness says.'

'Her? She's one of Molly's mates, she's got a string of mad girlfriends. And that reporter had an intern snooping around for him, sending texts, following us, did you know that? That must be a criminal offence, surely? Everything I did was to protect you and your reputation. I know what scandal can do to you. I've done this all for you, Richard.'

He looks appalled. Disgusted. 'Have you seen the papers? The damage has been done. Marianne's party are thrilled, although they won't come out and say it.'

'You didn't answer me. What about Douglas?'

'I don't think it's appropriate to appoint him to you. It's over, Grace. I'm filing for divorce.'

'No, Richard. Don't do this. Don't let her win.'

'This has nothing to do with her.'

My fingertips are white where I'm gripping the edge of the table. I lean towards him.

'Richard, please. What about us? What we have? Everything we've built together?' I hate how desperate, how needy I sound, but I can't help it.

Richard pushes his chair back with a scraping sound that rips through me. He leaves the room without looking back.

GRACE'S DIARY

The one blemish on my new clean life is Michael. I'm his only relative, so inevitably I end up being responsible for him. He's a sick man, but then he always was sick in the head, I was just too young to understand. Stupid to think I could leave him behind.

Richard loves me, he understands about my difficult childhood and he's paying for Michael to have a full-time carer. Understanding I couldn't talk about it, he insisted on a therapist on Harley Street. Only the best for Grace Sutherland. The stories I tell him are the best, too. I'm good at telling stories. Playing the game.

In return I'll do my duty, play the good daughter, attend to Michael's needs.

When the time is right I'll get my own back. Get him for killing my love for Molly. Get him for making me hate my sexuality, making me hate myself.

He'll pay.

All in good time.

A LETTER FROM LESLEY

Thank you so much for reading *The Orchid Girls*. I hope you enjoyed reading it as much as I loved writing it.

To keep up to date with the latest news on my new releases, just click on the link below to sign up for a newsletter. I promise never to share your email with anyone else.

www.bookouture.com/lesley-sanderson

The germ of an idea for the story has been with me for a long while, and it has grown and changed over time. It is a very different story from the one I originally began writing, but the secret, obsessive heart remains the same. I wanted to explore a female friendship which develops from the intensity of the teenage years and continues into adulthood, enhanced by the suppression of a terrible secret. The story also enabled me to look at different attitudes towards sexuality twenty years ago and today. With *The Orchid Girls*, I hoped to create an evocative novel about obsession, secrets and the blurred lines between love and lies.

If you enjoyed *The Orchid Girls*, I would love it if you could write a short review. Getting reviews from readers who have enjoyed my writing is my favourite way to persuade other readers to pick up one of my books for the first time.

I'd also love to hear from you via social media: see the links below.

@LSandersonbooks

lesleysandersonauthor

www.lesleysanderson.com

ACKNOWLEDGEMENTS

So many people have helped me along the way with *The Orchid Girls*.

This book started out as one chapter which got me accepted on to the Curtis Brown six-month novel writing course, and I'd like to thank everyone at Curtis Brown Creative for helping me develop my novel. To all of my fellow students of the 2015 cohort, your feedback and support have been invaluable. Neil McLennan, Tamsin Hopkins, Abby Rae Delbianco, Moya Poulton, thanks for reading earlier versions.

Particular thanks go to Erin Kelly, whose summer school of 2017 showed me how to be the writer I hope one day to become – you're a true inspiration.

Thanks to the judges of the Lucy Cavendish Fiction Prize for shortlisting me for the 2017 prize, and for the kindness of everyone involved with the event.

I can't say a big enough thank you to my lovely agent Hayley Steed for seeing the potential in my shortlisted piece and asking me to submit to the fabulous Madeleine Milburn agency. Meeting Hayley and Anna Hogarty for the first time, and seeing how much they loved my book, will always remain a special memory. Thanks to you both for your editorial input and to everyone else at the agency for the constant support and championing of your authors. Hayley, I'm so proud to be your first 'official client'.

To the Next Chapter Girls – Louise Beere, Cler Lewis and Katie Godman – you know how much you and this writing group mean to me – I couldn't have done it without your belief in me and my writing.

To my lovely editor, Christina Demosthenous – working with you is a joy and from the very first email 'Best News Ever…' I knew it was going to be a dream partnership. To everyone at Bookouture – you all work tirelessly and with infectious enthusiasm for your authors and I'm so proud to be one of them.

And to everyone else – all the other writers I've met along the way, too many to name but nonetheless important. I'm so happy to be one of such a friendly group of people.

To my family, to my friends old and new for believing in me, I daren't name you in case I miss anyone out, but thank you.

And most of all to Paul. I couldn't do it without you.

Lightning Source UK Ltd.
Milton Keynes UK
UKHW021957300419
341862UK00013B/1457/P